USA TODAY bestselling author **Heidi Rice** lives in London, England. She is married with two teenage sons—which gives her rather too much of an insight into the male psyche—and also works as a film journalist. She adores being an author, which involves getting swept up in a world of high emotion, sensual excitement, funny and feisty women, sexy and tortured men and glamorous locations where laundry doesn't exist. Once she turns off her computer she often does chores—usually involving laundry!

USA TODAY bestselling, RITA®-nominated and critically acclaimed author **Caitlin Crews** has written more than one hundred books and counting. She has a Master's and a PhD in English Literature, thinks everyone should read more category romance, and is always available to discuss her beloved alpha heroes. Just ask! She lives in the Pacific Northwest with her comic book artist husband, she is always planning her next trip, and she will never, ever, read all the books in her 'to-be-read' pile. Thank goodness.

T0337237

BRIDES OF SCANDAL

HEIDI RICE

CAITLIN CREWS

MILLS & BOON

First published in Great Britain 2024
by Mills & Boon, an imprint of HarperCollins*Publishers* Ltd,
1 London Bridge Street, London, SE1 9GF

www.harpercollins.co.uk

HarperCollins*Publishers*, Macken House, 39/40 Mayor Street Upper, Dublin 1, D01 C9W8, Ireland

Brides of Scandal © 2024 Harlequin Enterprises ULC

Queen's Winter Wedding Charade © 2024 Heidi Rice

Greek's Enemy Bride © 2024 Caitlin Crews

ISBN: 978-0-263-32036-7

12/24

MIX
Paper | Supporting
responsible forestry
FSC
www.fsc.org
FSC™ C007454

This book contains FSC™ certified paper and other controlled sources to ensure responsible forest management.

For more information visit www.harpercollins.co.uk/green.

Printed and Bound in the UK using 100% Renewable Electricity at CPI Group (UK) Ltd, Croydon, CR0 4YY

QUEEN'S WINTER WEDDING CHARADE

HEIDI RICE

MILLS & BOON

To my sister-in-law Isabel,
whose wonderful hospitality I enjoyed while writing
this book and who is a queen in her own right. xx

CHAPTER ONE

'HER ROYAL MAJESTY, Queen Isabelle of Androvia is ready to see you now, Mr Lord.'

Travis Lord turned from the spectacular view of spruce and pine forests and virgin snow through the mullioned window, to find an old guy in fancy velvet knickerbockers and enough braid to sink a gunship standing behind him.

About damn time.

'Cool,' he said, hiding his mounting irritation behind a relaxed smile, because he guessed it *was* cool, in a weird way.

When was the last time a guy from a trailer park in Snowton Colorado got an audience with a queen? Even if he did have more money now than the oldest of Alpine monarchies.

'Let's go,' he murmured.

The guy bowed then directed him out of the antechamber he'd been waiting in for a solid twenty minutes and into a large salon, which, according to Travis's research, was just one of the White Palace's ten staterooms.

Luckily Travis had spent his whole life not being impressed by unearned wealth—and the sort of people his mom had once cooked and cleaned for—so he managed to contain his awe. But it was more of an effort than usual. Because the collection of antique furnishings, the vintage oil paintings adorning every wall, and the fanciful gold-plated plasterwork—not to mention the even more stunning view of the Alpine gorge the palace perched on the edge of through six enormous floor-to-ceiling stained-glass windows—made one hell of a statement. In fact, the impressive décor looked like something out of a Disney princess's palace. Probably because this bastion of old-world elegance— a six-hundred-room, three-centuries-old ice-cream castle, which towered over Androvia's pristine slopes—was the real-world equivalent.

After walking the length of the gleaming parquet flooring, the courtier led Travis up a wide marble staircase. 'You have been briefed on the etiquette when greeting Her Majesty, sir?' the man asked as they stopped in front of a carved mahogany door.

'Sure,' Travis replied, humouring the guy.

No way was he executing the bow he'd been advised to do—he was an American, and his ancestors had fought a war so they didn't have to bow to anyone—but he wasn't about to get booted out before he'd met the woman he'd flown eight thousand miles to see.

He wanted to buy a piece of her kingdom for Lord Culture's first European resort and from their research Queen Isabelle might be in the mood to make a deal. She had wealth, and lots of it, but it was all tied up in historic properties like this one, fancy bits of jewellery and the other antique collectables that came with a legacy dating back to the sixteenth century—all of which cost a fortune to maintain and operate. What she didn't have was disposable income. Plus, his intel suggested she was also having a spat with her Ruling Council over the future of the monarchy itself. They wanted her to 'merge' with the heir to a neighbouring kingdom— one of those Eurotrash princes who played hard and didn't seem to work at all—while she was holding out. Travis Lord could take the pressure off by bringing jobs and investment to her country.

This was a business proposition between equals—so no

bowing was required. But he kept that to himself as the courtier nodded, then tapped on the ornate door. A muffled voice told them to come in.

Travis stepped into a large library, which smelled of old paper and lemon polish, the walls covered in bookcases, with an antique desk at the far end.

The young woman sitting behind it, her blonde hair pinned up in a ruthless updo, was a surprise—especially when she stood and walked towards him. Instead of velvet and ermine and the crown he had been expecting, she wore a tailored pantsuit which was probably supposed to look businesslike but hugged her figure as she moved. She was also tiny. Or he guessed the word was petite. She barely reached his collarbone. She looked a lot taller in her press pictures. Her heart-shaped face, wide, slightly sloping green eyes and porcelain skin also made her look younger than her twenty-two years. Her make-up was subdued, conservative even, but instead of making her appear regal and reserved it made her seem oddly innocent—like a teenager who wasn't yet ready to advertise her charms, instead of a woman in her early twenties, who had to be well aware of the effect she had on men. His gaze tracked to her mouth—the pale pink lip gloss couldn't disguise how lush her lips were... A bolt of lust shot straight into his groin. And he tensed.

What the hell?

'Your Majesty, Mr Lord to see you as requested,' the courtier—who Travis had forgotten was there—announced while executing another deep bow.

'Mr Lord, we meet at last,' the Queen said in perfectly accented English, her voice a soft purr of privilege and purpose.

She didn't offer him her hand in greeting.

Travis yanked himself out of the fugue state he had lapsed into unintentionally, and managed to stop fixating on her lips long enough to figure out she was probably waiting for him to bow, too.

Yeah, not gonna happen.

The courtier cleared his throat, obviously thinking Travis had been struck dumb by his first encounter with royalty—which, annoyingly, wasn't far from the truth.

Travis ignored the prompt. 'Your Majesty, you're a hard woman to get an audience with,' he said, then offered her his hand. 'But it's good to meet you at last.'

The courtier gasped. Travis ignored the guy some more.

The Queen glanced at his open palm. If she was surprised, or even annoyed, by his refusal to follow protocol though, she managed to contain it and hesitated for less than a second before accepting the handshake.

Her palm was cool, and her fingers long and elegant, but her small hand disappeared in his much bigger one. Her tiny jolt of surprise, the little frisson of electricity, echoed in his groin.

Was he getting turned on? Weird, but kind of intriguing, too.

He released her hand, but then caught a lungful of her scent—and wondered how something so subtle could be so intoxicating.

The courtier had stiffened up like a poker, his outrage at the break in protocol emanating off him like a force field.

The Queen sent the guy a polite smile and he melted like a snowman on a Florida beach. 'Arne, could you leave us now?' she said. 'And tell Mel we'll be ready for the tea tray in twenty minutes,' she added.

She turned to Travis, the polite smile becoming politely inquisitive. 'Unless of course you would prefer coffee, being an American?'

'Coffee works,' he said, trying not to get dazzled by the

smile—which managed to brighten her whole face despite her reserve.

'We can dispense with the titles now,' she said, as soon as the courtier had disappeared. 'I'm afraid Arne worked for my father and he's a terrible stickler when it comes to protocol.'

Travis nodded, relieved. Being unexpectedly turned on by this woman was one thing, having to treat her with fake deference was another. Maybe she didn't consider him to be an equal, but she was well bred enough not to show it—which was good, because he didn't really give a damn what she thought of him. He'd never let anyone's opinion of him—high or low—stop him getting what he wanted.

She directed him to a leather armchair in front of her desk. 'Please take a seat, Mr Lord, we have a lot to discuss.'

He detected the tight tone and noticed the polite smile had left the room with Arne the Stickler. *Interesting.*

He took the seat she suggested and watched her walk back around her desk and sit down. Her movements weren't quite as fluid as they had been when she'd walked towards him, nor as precise. Seemed Her Majesty was a little tense. *More interesting.*

'So, I take it you know why I wanted this meeting?' he said, deciding to cut to the chase.

Fast and direct was how he rolled. It was the way he'd ridden a snowboard to a gold medal in the world championships as a teenager and made his first billion while creating his own brand sportswear in his twenties. He'd also told his negotiators to give the Queen's advisors a heads up while they'd been angling for this meeting. As interesting as it had been meeting the woman in the flesh—and getting a glimpse of how European royalty lived—he hadn't come here to sightsee. Or genuflect.

She gave a stiff nod. 'You wish to acquire a three-thousand-acre portion of Androvia's White Ridge to build a ski resort. Land which has belonged to the royal household for ten generations and has remained untouched.'

'That's about the size of it, yeah.' He leant forward, surprised she was being equally direct, but also impressed by the shrewd intelligence in her gaze. He hadn't expected her to be a pushover, but he also hadn't expected her to handle the negotiations herself. *Even more interesting.*

'Although it's going to be primarily a snowboarding resort—not a ski venue,' he said. 'And while we want to develop the land, it's the untouched quality of the wilderness which makes it attractive to us. Lord Culture is all about exclusive bespoke resorts which blend with the natural environment. Any construction we do will be ecologically sustainable and supremely sensitive. The idea is to enhance the White Ridge, not destroy it. We give our clients unique wilderness experiences. Our two resorts in the States are award-winning and speak for themselves.' He took a breath, then went in for the kill, because straight talking was one of his superpowers. 'Plus, we both know you're between a rock and a hard place at the moment, Your Majesty,' he added, enjoying the way she stiffened even more.

'How so?' she asked, the prim tone not matched by the flash of fire in her eyes. So, the Queen had a temper, good to know.

'A deal of this size with Lord Culture will bring thousands of much-needed jobs to your subjects and substantial investment in your infrastructure and will also give you, personally, increased financial clout. Enough so you won't have to contemplate hooking up with the playboy prince next door if you don't want to.'

Isabelle jolted with shock at the audacious—and far too personal—observation.

She'd met Americans before, she knew they didn't tend

to stand on ceremony, but she'd never met anyone as forthright as Travis Lord.

She'd thought she'd been prepared for this meeting. She'd done her research after all, as what she had to suggest to this man had to be managed *very* carefully.

But the minute the former snowboarding champion and billionaire entrepreneur had strolled into her study, she had begun to wonder if she had bitten off a lot more than she would ever be able to chew. For starters, Travis Lord was enormous. Lean and muscular—as befitted a man who had once reached the pinnacle of a dangerous and demanding sport—but also incredibly tall. He had to be at least six four when she was only five three in bare feet. And while she'd known he wasn't a small man, and had worn her highest heels to compensate, even so, he made her feel exceptionally short.

The feel of his callused palm, closing over hers—the scrape of roughened skin, the warm dry flesh—had been supremely disconcerting too. Even that brief contact had made sensation sprint around her entire body. And that was before she had factored in the question of why exactly she had given in to the impulse to shake his hand in the first place. The whole concept was completely alien. But when he'd offered his palm, something untoward had come over her and she'd had the unprecedented desire to take up the dare. Because that was exactly what she had seen in his eyes—the warm hazel flaring with provocation, challenging her to allow him to demolish centuries of protocol less than a minute after meeting her.

She'd also been prepared for his striking appearance. She'd seen the many photos of him over the years. First as a teenager, taking every title and breaking numerous records with a reckless natural talent that had dared fate at every turn, until he'd fallen to earth in a brutal accident that had almost cost him his life at the age of only nineteen. But he had risen from the ashes of his athletic career in his twenties, modelling his own skiwear, which had become North America's most sought-after brand within a decade.

Now he was in his early thirties, his looks had matured from the sun-kissed athletic beauty of his youth to a supremely masculine handsomeness. His features, once so finely drawn, were now weathered by a scar on his cheek and another that slashed across one brow, not to mention the break on the bridge of his nose. His dark wavy hair was glossy but needed a trim, being long enough to curl against the collar of his shirt. And while the designer suit he wore was perfectly tailored to all those muscles—the man obviously kept in shape even if he was no longer a professional sportsman—the expensive fabric still only barely contained his rugged physique.

What she hadn't expected though were for his looks to have such a profound effect on her. She'd met good-looking men before, but she'd never had the urge to stare at one… Or, indeed, allow him to shake her hand.

And then there was his scent, which she had got far too intimate an acquaintance with as he had loomed over her. Not expensive cologne, but clean cedar soap underlaid with something musky and even more compelling.

She had been taught from a young age to keep a ruthless leash on all her emotions, and never to let her reactions show. But something had overwhelmed those years of training from the moment he had walked into the library.

As she stared back at him now, trying to compose herself after his shockingly inappropriate comment, she realised the brilliant scheme she had come up with late at night, over many months, after stressing about the prospect of having to consider marriage to Rene Gaultiere, the neighbouring Prince of Saltzaland, might not be so brilliant after all.

She'd assumed she would be able to make this man an offer he couldn't refuse and then control the outcome. She wasn't anywhere near as confident about the second part of that equation now. But as his audacious comment echoed into silence and his dark eyes narrowed, the masculine challenge—and dominance—in his gaze reawakened the strange compulsion which had prompted that ill-advised handshake.

Struggling to channel it rather than succumb to it this time, she delivered the line she had been rehearsing for weeks. 'That being the case, I have a counter offer.'

He didn't look surprised, but then she hadn't really expected him to, as she had already gathered he was even better at controlling his reactions than she was. Either that or he'd had all semblance of sensitivity ironed out of him long ago. A distinct possibility, given his difficult upbringing—as the child of a single mother who had cleaned lodges in an expensive ski resort in Colorado while living miles away in a trailer park. She'd found no reference to his father in the press clippings.

'You haven't heard what I'm willing to offer you for the land yet,' he said, not taking the bait. *Yet.*

'I cannot sell you the land, Mr Lord,' she said. On that much she had to be clear. No Androlov had ever sold off any of the kingdom, it was the royal family's heritage and, as the last of her line, she did not intend to be the first to break that tradition. It was why she was being forced to think outside the box—*way* outside the box.

'Then why did you agree to this meeting?' he said, his scepticism searing.

'Because I have another proposition.'

'Uh-huh. Let's hear it,' he said. Taking the bait. *Finally.*

'I will lease you the land you require for your resort.'

'A lease is no good to—'

'For one hundred years with all requisite permissions to

develop it which you may require, as long as you stick to Androvia's strict rules on sustainability,' she countered before he could sidetrack her again. 'But on one condition.'

His frown levelled off. 'Go on.'

She took a steadying breath, let it out slowly, and—feeling oddly exhilarated—forced herself to let go of twenty-two years of caution and control, so she could finally take charge of her own—and her country's—destiny.

'You agree to marry me, Mr Lord.'

CHAPTER TWO

'I BEG YOUR PARDON, ma'am?' Travis growled, finally managing to contain his astonishment—and the uncomfortable jolt of lust—long enough to form a coherent sentence.

Had the Queen of Androvia just proposed to him? Because that was what it had sounded like. But maybe the twelve-hour flight here from Colorado was messing with his hearing—he sure as heck hoped so.

'You are absolutely correct to suggest Androvia needs investment, Mr Lord,' the Queen replied in a calm, measured voice, as if they were still discussing a land deal, and not something totally nuts. 'And my people desperately need the employment opportunities a resort such as yours would offer. But the only way to allow a construction of this nature on the White Ridge is for you to marry me because the ridge, like all Androvia's royal real estate, is held in a trust, which stipulates any development can only be authorised by a man of royal birth, in other words a king, or by a queen if she is married.'

Not hallucinating, then. Damn.

'I am assuming, of course, you have no royal heritage of your own,' she added, her tone clipped and condescending.

'Funnily enough, no,' he said, his own tone caustic.

He wasn't ashamed of his heritage, or rather the lack of it. His old man had been a rich guy, but he'd been married to someone else when Travis's mom had fallen for the bastard as a teenager and then fallen pregnant. But so what? Travis had never wanted the guy's wealth, or his acknowledgement. He hadn't needed it. Because he'd done just fine on his own.

The Queen didn't seem aware she had insulted him though—because her expression barely changed as she started to outline her nutty scheme.

'Then marriage to me is the only way you would be allowed to build on the land. Or I would be allowed to let you,' she said, still in that matter-of-fact tone. But then he noticed her gaze wasn't meeting his and her posture had stiffened.

Maybe the controlled indifference was a bluff? Why that gave him a rush he had no idea, but he'd take it, if it meant he could regain the upper hand.

'Hold on,' he said. 'Who the hell has the power to stop you doing what you want if you're the Queen?' he asked, because he was beginning to smell a rat. 'Androvia is similar to a constitutional principality, like Monaco, right? You're the head of state and the Ruling Council run the government, but you still own all the land.'

She would have to be desperate to offer a nobody like him marriage—and that was before they considered the fact he was a stranger, unlike the prince next door.

'I see you've done your homework,' she said, clearly surprised he'd bothered. He bristled, but he let it go. He was used to people underestimating him. And it usually worked in his favour.

'In answer to your question, as I am the monarch I am the beneficial owner of the land, but I cannot break this trust, as it was set up by my father, to protect me, when I was still a child,' she said.

His frown deepened. How the heck did stopping her from having authority over her own financial affairs just because she wasn't a guy, or married to one, protect her, exactly?

'I believe my father felt an alliance between myself and

Prince Rene would be good for both our kingdoms and he wished to facilitate that. But I'm sure if he had lived long enough to know me as an adult, he would have realised I am capable of making intelligent decisions about the land on my own.'

Despite the telling lack of emotion in her voice as she spoke, something flashed in her gaze, when it met his then flicked away again. He wasn't sure what that something was—disappointment maybe, confusion perhaps, even unresolved grief.

The pulse of sympathy pushed against his chest. Hadn't both her folks died in a helicopter crash when she was still just a kid?

But the something was gone again so fast, his sympathy evaporated.

Whatever issues she had with her old man's refusal to trust her just because she was a girl weren't his business. Being orphaned as a kid was tough, but he'd lost his mom too when he was still a teenager, and he'd survived. And prospered. Plus, it wasn't as if Queen Isabelle had ever wanted for anything. If you were going to get orphaned, better to have it happen in the lap of luxury.

'Okay, so you can't control your own land without getting married,' he said, determined to establish the facts here. 'But if you need a husband so bad, why not just hook up with the guy he wanted you to marry...then lease the land to me?'

While the playboy prince sounded like a loser, she had to at least know the guy.

'Because the Prince and myself are not compatible in any way,' she said swiftly, her gaze direct now and impenetrable, but the colour on her cheeks blossomed.

'And you think *we* are?' he countered, ruthlessly controlling another inconvenient shot of lust.

Seriously? She might be beautiful and one hell of a challenge to a guy like him, which was weirdly hot, and, sure, the White Ridge had been his first choice by quite a wide margin to locate Lord Culture's first European resort… But marriage was way too drastic a solution to close this deal.

Maybe European royalty didn't have an issue with using sex to sweeten business deals but he sure as heck did.

Marriage had never been part of his game plan. He enjoyed good hard sweaty sex, and lots of it, when the chemistry and the timing were right. And companionship, up to a point, as long as it didn't get in the way of his work commitments. But he had never believed in hitching your future to someone else's star—thanks to all the losers he'd watched his mom hook up with over the years, starting with the bastard who had got her pregnant at seventeen then hightailed it back to his wife…

But even if Travis *had* been the marrying kind and hadn't been deeply cynical about any relationship that required more than supplying his dates with an orgasm—or two—her proposal would still be nuts, because they'd only just met. Literally.

'Our compatibility is completely immaterial,' the Queen replied tightly, throwing him even more. How exactly was a marriage between them supposed to fly when they knew not one thing about each other?

'Uh-huh,' he said. Was she really going to make him state the obvious?

Seemed she was when she only stared back at him, clearly waiting for him to make the next move.

He took his time, checking her out—man to woman. Her eyes narrowed, and her chin lifted, her expression one of pride and no small amount of indignation. He smiled at her reaction, appreciating the way her full breasts pressed against the tailored blouse she wore as her breathing accelerated.

Tough luck, Belle baby, you started this.

He refused to relinquish eye contact, rewarded when the blush spread up her neck. He relaxed back into his seat, starting to enjoy himself—the shift in power from her back to him almost palpable.

Yeah, Her Majesty might be an accomplished diplomat, and stateswoman, used to getting her own way despite her current fix. But he'd hazard a guess she was a lot less used to propositioning guys, especially guys like him, who weren't at her beck and call.

'It may be immaterial to you,' he said, eventually. 'But it isn't to me.'

Her blush intensified. Yup, this was definitely her first rodeo, marriage-proposals-to-American-roughnecks-wise.

She opened her mouth to reply, but he beat her to it.

'Correct me if I'm wrong, but you've just asked me to hook up with you on a permanent basis. Which makes our compatibility important. Because no way am I gonna agree to marry someone before I know if we're good in bed. And so far, all we've done is share a handshake.'

Isabelle sucked in a breath. So shocked by the forward comment, she was momentarily speechless.

She had never, in her entire life, been spoken to so disrespectfully. She forced herself to school her features and breathed through the forceful reaction. She must not respond to Travis Lord's attempts to provoke her. Although maintaining her usual composure was not helped by the hot blush currently incinerating her face. Or the rush of blood making the indignation sink into her abdomen—and throb, disconcertingly.

She contemplated her response—and tried to find a positive in the most excruciating conversation she had ever had with a man. Or anyone for that matter.

After several pregnant seconds, she finally managed to control her outrage while attempting to view his candour with as little emotion as possible. Perhaps, his directness was…well, refreshing. At least it meant she could speak plainly, too.

While the man clearly had no respect whatsoever for her position, could she find a way to make that work in her favour? After all, what she had asked of him was the opposite of conventional… Harder to put a positive spin on, though, was the hot brick that seemed to have got wedged between her thighs when he had studied her as if he couldn't see her position, her title, her legacy, all he could see was her. Which was not good. Because the only way to make this proposal work was for her to remain calm and dispassionate with him at all times.

She cleared her throat. 'I think you misunderstand me, Mr Lord. I'm not suggesting a marriage in which…' She paused, aware her blush was probably radioactive by now. 'In which conjugal rights are involved.'

'Conjugal?' He spat out the word on an astonished breath. But then his dark brows launched up his forehead, and he laughed. The deep, husky sound made the throbbing worse, even though his amusement was clearly aimed *at* her. 'Are you for real?'

'Of course,' she said, and he laughed again.

What exactly was so funny?

'Is a marriage without conjugal rights not the correct term for a marriage without intimacy involved?' she pointed out. Then realised she'd made another error when he chuckled again—the amusement in his dark eyes turning the hazel to a rich chocolate… Annoyingly.

'Yeah, sure, maybe back in the eighteenth century,' he said, still amusing himself at her expense.

Before she could point out how rude he was being—because, *really*?—he carried on talking. 'So let me get this straight, you want me to marry you, but you don't want me to sleep with you?'

She dismissed the strange pang in her belly—which made no sense whatsoever, because it almost felt like disappointment. 'Of course not, we have only just met.'

And she had never had sex with anyone. She cut off the errant thought before she could give him any inkling of that inconvenient truth.

Her sexual history was hardly relevant. And something about the way he sat in the leather armchair—unfazed by the direction of the conversation, one ankle hooked over his opposing knee as if he were the master of all he surveyed, the smile on his face both knowing and relaxed and far too confident—made her suspect letting him know she was a virgin would only make him more arrogant, and give him more power, when he already had enough. It was more than clear that Mr Lord had a *lot* of experience in the bedroom— something he seemed to be not so subtly advertising to her, quite deliberately—making her sure she was at enough of a tactical disadvantage in this negotiation already.

Unfortunately, it was also a message her body was getting loud and clear—hence the insistent throbbing.

He released his ankle, to lean forward. 'You want to marry me…' he said. 'But you don't want to enjoy it? How is that gonna work…for either one of us?'

She frowned. Was he being deliberately obtuse, or was he just trying to antagonise her? Maybe it was a bit of both. Either way, she tried not to rise to the bait, or get derailed by the over-confident smile and the mocking twinkle.

Maybe this idea had been doomed from the start. She certainly hadn't factored in the extent of Travis Lord's insouciance, his irreverence, his arrogance, his strange sense of humour or his industrial-strength disregard for the strictures by which she had lived her entire life... His very masculine Americanness, basically. But she had become desperate to find a solution to her situation—when it had become apparent that to get her country the development and investment it so desperately needed—i.e. to drag it into the twenty-first century—she would have to either marry Rene or find someone else.

And as far as she was concerned, Travis Lord—for all his faults—was still the better option.

Yes, he was an unknown quantity, but Rene—and a marriage with him—certainly was not. It would be a disaster—Rene was, and had always been, a man much more interested in the reckless pursuit of debauchery than the needs of his kingdom and his monarchy. Plus, Rene would *insist* on a sexual relationship. And expect a real marriage if they were to wed. For the simple reason that, as the last of his line too, he required an heir. And providing one, given his many sexual conquests, seemed to be the only thing he had any aptitude for.

She shuddered at the thought. One day, she would need to think about the continuation of her line, too. But not for a while. And when she did, she intended to take the necessary time to find a suitable match—a man she could admire, who would respect her and her duty. Perhaps she could even find love, the way her parents had once loved each other, but it would not be a dealbreaker. Because her duty to her throne, and her subjects, would always be her paramount concern. So, finding a man she could enjoy a settled, productive life with, who could share the burden of responsibility with her, rule by her side, enrich her kingdom with his wisdom, and be a good father to guide their children to maturity, was a distant goal at this point.

Obviously neither Travis Lord nor Rene Gaultiere would ever be that man. But all she required at present was a husband, in name only, to help her secure her country's future, while also honouring the conditions of her father's will.

'It's fairly simple, really,' she said, determined to take his question at face value and ignore his attitude problem.

'Enlighten me,' he said.

She took another deep breath. Then proceeded to do just that. 'I need a husband to be able to lease you the land. I do not wish to marry Rene, which was my father's preferred choice when he set up the trust. But he did not stipulate who my husband had to be...' *Thank goodness.* 'Or that it was necessary he be of royal blood.'

He was still listening, and he hadn't interrupted. Hope sparked. Maybe this didn't have to be complicated after all. A simple transaction that would give them both what they wanted.

'I can marry anyone. The man does not need to be a prince. Nor does it even need to be a real marriage. But I think, in view of the fact the Ruling Council are likely to be surprised by you as my choice...' because the traditionalists on the council had already dropped enough hints that they considered Rene to be the best option '...it would make sense for us to pretend this *is* a real marriage.' She was starting to babble, but she couldn't seem to stop herself, his silence somehow triggering the nerves that had once made her talk too much as a child on those rare occasions when she'd had her parents' full attention. 'Which would mean us pretending to be in love. For appearances' sake... But given that you are such a successful businessman and you would be bringing a large portion of the infrastructure investment we all want for Androvia with this project, I'm sure the council will come around quickly.'

He nodded. 'I get it. So, you think we can fool the council guys that we're madly in love, while not touching each other?'

She blinked, taken aback by another direct question and the rueful amusement still sparkling in his eyes. Why was he so hung up on the sex bit? When she'd already explained it wasn't relevant?

She forced herself to take a breath, and control her irritation… And her dismay. And give him a straight answer… After all, it was utterly impossible to tell what the man was thinking, so it was probably best not to overthink his question.

'Displays of affection would be necessary in public, to sell the relationship as real. Obviously,' she said, laying her cards on the table—while trying not to imagine those firm lips on hers. 'But it's generally not expected, in royal circles, for a couple to be too…' Her face heated again. *Wonderful!* 'Too demonstrative. So, it really won't be necessary for us to do anything too overt in public. And obviously in private, we would do nothing at all.'

He nodded, slowly. But then his gaze narrowed.

'How long would this marriage have to last?'

The hope blossomed under her breastbone. This could work. He was considering it. The relief alongside that strange surge of sensation was almost palpable.

'I think a year would suffice. After which we could get a divorce. We would of course agree to the terms of the separation in a legally binding confidential contract to protect both our interests before we marry. I believe Americans refer to it as a prenup.' She'd already hired a respected divorce attorney in the US who had agreed to do all the necessary paperwork in absolute secrecy. Because Lord hadn't said anything, though, Isabelle's nerves demanded she fill the silence.

'Fortunately, there is also no stipulation in the conditions of the trust that the marriage needs to last. Just that it needs to be in place for me to make commercial decisions about the land. And a year would give me sufficient time to develop and sign off on a number of other projects, as well as the lease agreement for your resort.'

Her heart thudded heavily in her chest, the sadness—that her father had been robbed of the chance to know her as an adult—springing from nowhere as she conjured up the precious image of his face. He had been so handsome and strong whenever Isabelle had been called into his and her mother's presence as a little girl. She had idolised both her parents, always mindful that their time together was precious, their duties all-consuming. She would never blame him for putting conditions on her accession, which had become increasingly onerous in recent years. She knew he had had her best interests at heart. But she also refused to feel guilty about finding a way around them that would allow her to do her best for Androvia—without having to marry Rene.

'Okay,' Lord said, the amusement in his eyes turning to approval—and making the jolt of adrenaline worse. Which was preposterous. She did not require this man's approval, simply his co-operation. 'That's super sneaky, but I like it,' he said. 'Your old man sounds like a sexist jerk, so it makes sense to game the guy...'

What?

Isabelle bit her tongue to prevent her horrified reaction to his thoughtless accusation from slipping out of her mouth.

Travis Lord did not know the first thing about her relationship with her parents, nor did he need to.

'I'm not gaming him,' she said, as calmly as she could. 'I'm simply finding an effective way to fulfil the trust's conditions.'

'Like I said, sneaky.'

She huffed out a breath. And drew it back in sharply.

Do not let him provoke you, Issy.

'You're pretty smart, aren't you, Belle?'

Belle? She startled at the nickname. And the strange warmth at the thought of anyone using such familiarity. She steeled herself against reacting, though. Even if it was becoming a titanic effort.

'Yes, I am,' she concurred, pointedly, to make it clear his opinions did not interest her in the slightest. Although, to be fair, it occurred to her he looked intrigued now, and impressed, rather than amused, so perhaps that was a good thing.

'So, what do you say, Mr Lord? You pose as my loving husband for a single year, and I will lease you the land on the White Ridge at a very reasonable price, so you can build your resort?'

He leaned back in the chair, crossed his ankle back over his knee, which made the fabric of his trousers tighten across his thigh muscles in disconcerting ways. His searing gaze roamed over her again, making awareness prickle across her skin.

And the throbbing got worse.

She crossed her own legs and tried to squeeze the distracting sensation into submission.

'It's an intriguing offer,' he said at last. 'And I've got to admit, a tempting one. But the answer's no.'

'I beg your pardon?' she said, sure she could not have heard him correctly.

'The answer's no, Your Majesty,' he said, with a finality that shocked her more, and a mock deference that had the spark of temper igniting.

'But… *Why?* This is the only way to give us both what we want,' she demanded, hating the hitch in her voice.

If he refused, she would surely be forced to seriously consider proposing to Rene? Not only did she shudder at the humiliating thought of having to go to him, cap in hand, and beg him to marry her. After she had already turned him down once. But she knew he would absolutely insist on a real marriage. And would probably make her jump through several hoops beforehand, just to pay her back for her previous rejection.

Travis Lord was her only hope of avoiding that humiliation. Because she simply did not know any other eligible men whom she could bribe into a marriage in name only.

'I want the land on the White Ridge, sure,' Lord said with maddening insouciance as her frantic thoughts began to spiral into the abyss. 'But I don't want it *that* much.'

'Would a marriage to me really be so onerous?' she asked, then winced at the note of desperation. She must not let him see how much she wanted this to work, or she suspected he would take advantage and become even more arrogant... And contrary.

'Yeah. Because I'm guessing you'd want me to live here, with you, for the duration of our fake marriage.'

The tension—and panic—in her gut eased.

Perhaps this was a problem with a practical solution, not an outright rejection. A solution she was more than willing to negotiate.

'I'm afraid you would have to reside in the White Palace for the majority of the year, yes,' she said, because that much was non-negotiable. Not only did she need to sell this marriage to the Ruling Council, she wanted to sell it to her subjects too, so they would get behind the construction of the new resort—and the other changes she hoped to bring to the country's infrastructure to help drive economic growth. 'But you would be able to keep up your business commitments. I would endeavour to keep your official engagements to a minimum. And I could certainly make your commitment to me personally worth your while.'

'How?' he asked, bluntly.

So, he wanted to play hardball. She could handle that.

'We could discuss the terms of the lease—negotiate a very favourable rate for your business,' she said, a backup position she'd planned for. The truth was, she'd be happy to lease the land for a lot less than it was worth, if she had to. The investment in the country's infrastructure and the chance to circumvent the trust that had hamstrung her monarchy for so long would be worth it. The preliminary plans his company had already submitted included a heliport and an upgrade to the country's aging rail system as well as over a thousand skilled jobs during the construction alone. But she wasn't about to let him know that yet.

Then he derailed her, again.

'I'm not talking about the money. Or the land.'

'You're... You're not?' she asked, hopelessly confused.

'You really don't see the massive problem here?' he countered. But it sounded like a rhetorical question, which only confused her more.

'No, I do not.' She stared, waiting for him to elaborate, knowing she had exposed herself enough—and also suspecting if she started talking again, her nerves might not allow her to stop.

'If I'm going to live here, for an entire year,' he drawled, as if he were talking to someone who was not all that bright, 'as your loved-up husband, I'm guessing I won't be able to date anyone else, because that isn't gonna sell the "we're madly in love" vibe if the media find out.'

The skin on her cheeks burned, the wildfire spreading across her collarbone, as what he was implying finally dawned on her.

'Being celibate for a year is a problem for you?' she murmured.

'Hell, yeah, isn't it for you?' he shot back.

The blush intensified as she tried to cover her dismay—and the now insistent throbbing at her core.

'Well, obviously, it's not ideal,' she managed, attempting to sound as if she knew what she was talking about, when sexual frustration had never, *ever* been an issue for her. 'But I'm sure I could make the sacrifice worth your while...'

'Oh, yeah? How?' he demanded, the heated purpose in his gaze suddenly making her palms start to sweat. And the throbbing in her core become turbo-charged.

We could dump the no-sex rule.

She swallowed down the utterly inappropriate thought that popped into her head—and made her sex clench and release.

What was happening to her? She did not wish to be in an intimate relationship with any man, *yet*. And certainly not with a man like Travis Lord, *ever*. He was far too arrogant and overpowering... Plus, the American billionaire might as well have had 'sex god' tattooed on his forehead, while she was a complete novice. He would almost certainly laugh at her inexperience and could use it against her—when he got bored with her, which of course he would.

She was a queen, not a courtesan. And while she needed this marriage, she had no intention of risking emotional intimacy with any man—least of all a man like him who had already proved to be wholly unpredictable and not anywhere near as easily controlled as she had hoped. So, she blurted out the only thing she could think of to keep the negotiation on track.

'What if I offered to lease Lord Culture the land you want on the White Ridge for a single dollar?'

CHAPTER THREE

TRAVIS STARED AT the woman in front of him, struggling to contain his surprise, and that vague feeling of insult that he remembered from when he was a kid—and he'd had to help out his mom on her jobs, while the rich kids they were cleaning up after looked at him like dirt. This wasn't personal, that much was obvious, so why the hell was he insulted she'd rather sell a tract of her precious kingdom to him for a dollar than consider sharing a bed with him? It wasn't as if he had been suggesting they hook up. But her desperation to get this deal, without going there, still got his goat. And he wasn't even sure why.

The truth was, he'd decided as soon as she'd made the offer not to accept it. Sure, he was intrigued and kind of flattered—at first—that she would ask him. But at the same time, he wasn't about to relocate his whole operation, and sign some secret agreement, or pretend to love someone he didn't know just for a piece of land. He had his pride and, now he was a billionaire, he could afford to keep it.

The White Ridge might be perfect for what he wanted, but it felt as if he would be selling his integrity—along with his time—and, while he'd always been ruthless, even he had balked at the thought of posing as a loving husband when he was about as far from ever being that as it was possible to get. Hell, how would he even pull off the charade she was suggesting, given he wasn't a professional actor? But weirdly, as he had glimpsed emotions that she had been try-ing to hide flit across her face—shock, confusion, panic—pretending that he wanted her, a lot, hadn't seemed like such a stretch. Because the truth was, for reasons he could not begin to figure out, the whole 'ice princess' act she had going on was a challenge that he found surprisingly hot.

Maybe that explained why he was so mad right now. When he shouldn't be...

'A dollar?' he said. 'Are you serious?'

He'd already decided not to go for this deal... But now he was forced to reconsider. Because more than anything else, he had always been a shrewd businessman. His business had saved him after the accident, when he'd had to give up the sport he loved, and eventually become his life's work. And while he had resigned himself to start scoping out the other places his team had shortlisted before they'd settled on this one, there was nowhere better for the resort than the White Ridge. He had been ready to offer her up to a half a billion dollars for the land. His turnover was enough at the moment he could afford to pay top dollar, but it would still have been a risk—because Lord Culture's brand wasn't yet established in Europe. Getting the land for nothing would take that risk away. And give him the opportunity to invest even more in the construction. And the marketing.

In fact, while he hated to admit it, marrying the Queen would be a huge PR boost, not just for the resort itself, but also for him personally. It would give him class, and an ex-clusivity he would never have been able to achieve on his own, not just in the States, but globally. And the kind of or-ganic, viral, wall-to-wall publicity that couldn't be bought. It annoyed him he needed to care about that stuff, because he'd never aspired to be anyone other than who he was... But from a business standpoint, he'd be dumb to ignore the opportunity to turn Lord Culture into something more than just the fastest-growing winter sports brand in the market. This deal could send his business over the top. Give him global reach. And seal his legacy for a generation. And for that, he had to consider his integrity—and his hurt feelings—an acceptable price to pay.

'Yes,' she said, staunchly. 'One dollar.'

He stood up. To hell with it, he'd be nuts not to take a deal like this, no matter the pitfalls. And when it came to business he always went with his gut. And his gut was screaming at him right now to take the deal. 'Okay.'

She blinked, several times, her cheeks reddening again. His heart rate sped up. And the heat in his groin pulsed, hard.

'Really?' she asked, momentarily nonplussed. 'You'll agree to the marriage?'

For some reason, he found himself smiling. When he'd walked in here, he'd got the definite impression this was a woman who was well versed in ruthlessly controlling her emotions, and her reactions. That he unsettled her, and seemed to have knocked her off kilter, felt like an important win.

If they were going to spend the next year bonded at the hip, he was going to need something to entertain him—and pushing her boundaries seemed like a great place to start. Especially if he wasn't going to be having any sex—the one recreational activity he really enjoyed, other than boarding.

'Yeah. Have your attorney send the paperwork direct to my EA, Claire Ainsley. She'll handle everything from my end.'

'Excellent.' Her breath gushed out as she came around her desk. Her face brightened, and her expression became unguarded for the first time.

The heat surged.

Great, he was going to have to get a handle on that reaction if he was going to deal with her for a whole year. But even as the thought occurred to him, he couldn't resist the urge to poke at her composure again.

'I guess we'll have to figure out a dating itinerary for the next couple weeks. So we can be seen getting up close and personal before you tell everyone how you've fallen madly in love with me.'

'Oh, yes, of course, absolutely,' she said, even though he suspected she hadn't considered doing any such thing—which only made the urge to push more irresistible.

He lifted his hand and traced his thumb down the side of her face. Her brows rose and he felt her vicious jolt of reaction. But she didn't pull away.

His grin widened. 'Perhaps we should practise before I go,' he teased, unable to resist.

'I beg your pardon, Mr Lord.'

'Call me Travis, Belle,' he said, using the nickname he knew had horrified her earlier. He'd used it then to unsettle her deliberately. It had a similar effect now.

'Belle is not my name. It's Isabelle, or Issy,' she whispered. 'That's what my mother called me.' Sadness shadowed her eyes before she could mask it.

'I prefer Belle. It's better if my pet name for you is unique.' He brushed his thumb across her lips. Her eyes widened, and he had the weirdest suspicion she'd never been touched by a man before... But then he got a clue.

She was just skittish with him because she didn't know him.

This situation was super screwed up, whatever way you looked at it, but the sooner she got used to his touch, the better.

'Okay, if you insist,' she said, the intelligence in her eyes dispelling the shock. 'And what should my pet name for you be?' she challenged. 'Trav, maybe. Or Vis?'

He chuckled. Was she making a joke? Because as outlandish as it seemed, it was also kind of cute.

'They used to call me Killer on the slopes,' he said, trailing his thumb down the elegant line of her neck and pressing the pad against the rampant pulse in her collarbone. Still she didn't draw away.

'Killer doesn't seem very romantic,' she managed, although her breathing had become ragged. Her throat contracted as she swallowed, the heat rising like a wall. Tall and infallible.

He was playing with fire. He'd agreed to no sex. But hey, they had to be convincing for this to work, and anyway, when had he ever been the type of guy who denied himself something he wanted…? And right now, he wanted to find out how soft her lips really were.

'Brace yourself, Your Majesty,' he murmured, giving her one last chance to tell him no.

But she didn't, so he lowered his head slowly and pressed his mouth to hers.

She sucked in a breath, the giddy pulse beating double time against his thumb. He eased her into the kiss, slicking his tongue across the seam, gently, then more insistently, until she got the message. And opened for him. He pressed his advantage, tasting sweetness and spice… And all things nice. But as he probed, ready to go deeper, she jerked back.

He lifted his head, just as a knock sounded at the door.

She stared up at him—dazed.

Damn, but he could drown in those eyes, the mossy green sheened with heat and yearning, but also the panic he had sensed earlier.

Then she blinked and the shutters slammed down again. She took a step back.

He jammed his fists into his pockets to contain the urge to cup her cheeks, feel the heat against his palms—and take a heck of a lot more than just a kiss.

'Was that sufficient?' she asked.

Not nearly.

He eased a tight breath out of his lungs, and tried to remember this was all for show... And for his own amusement. Although his little joke had backfired, the heat now pulsing painfully in his gut.

'To be convincing?' she added, having regained her composure a lot faster than he had. Except... Her gaze wasn't meeting his again.

'I guess so,' he said.

She walked back around the desk, sat behind it, and steepled her fingers in front of her, but he could see her hands trembling and guessed she wasn't quite as composed as she was making out.

Well, good. Because neither was he. Somehow, though, she'd turned the tables on him and he didn't know how the hell she'd done it.

'Come in, Mel,' she called out when the knock sounded again. A young woman in a dark suit walked in pushing a silver carriage loaded with fancy china and set it up on the bureau at the back of the room.

'I hope you'll stay for coffee, Mr Lord,' the Queen said, polite as you please, which annoyed him more.

So, they were back to the formal. And that reserved shield of polite indifference. They were definitely going to have to work on that, once they were doing their loved-up act for the cameras. The thought of more kissing practice had adrenaline surging through his veins.

He thrust his fists further into his pockets as he watched Mel smile and leave the room. 'I need to head to the airport. But I'll be back in a couple of weeks with my surveyors,' he said. 'And the construction boss to do the initial surveys. If we can get the paperwork handled by then, let's arrange a time and place to make goo-goo eyes at each other and practise our lip action for the cameras.'

'Of… Of course,' she said, looking a little less sure of herself.

He smiled.

My work here is done.

'See you around, Belle,' he said, then strode out.

But as he headed back through the stateroom towards his waiting car, the feel of her mouth under his, and the vivid memory of that sweet sob of shocked arousal before her lips had softened and accepted his kiss, echoed uncomfortably in his groin.

And he couldn't help wondering what the hell he'd gotten himself into…

CHAPTER FOUR

Back in Androvia TMW, checking out Ridge. Meet me @ 2 @ top & tip off press 4 pix.
T

ISABELLE REREAD THE message she had received on her private mobile phone yesterday, for about the ten thousandth time. She'd had to get Mel to translate it for her—because she had never received a text written in code before in her entire life. Luckily, her assistant was also her best friend and confidante, and knew about Isabelle's cunning plan to arrange a marriage with Travis Lord—and therefore release her from the strictures of her father's trust.

'How am I supposed to tip off the press?' Isabelle murmured. 'The only conversations I've ever had with them have been in press conferences. It's not as if I have the paparazzi on speed dial.'

Mel walked out of the dressing room with Isabelle's ski suit. 'Don't worry about that. I'll have a word with Hans in PR. He knows some local photographers. If he tells them you'll be skiing on the ridge this afternoon, they'll stake out Sariyelva,' she said, mentioning the picturesque town nestled at the bottom of the White Ridge gorge. 'Once they have photos of you with Lord, they'll be able to sell them to the highest bidder worldwide,' Mel added as she laid out the suit. 'It'll be a great boost to the local economy. Just make sure you end up there after your meet-up,' she finished with a quick grin.

Isabelle scowled. 'Easier said than done. I suspect directing Travis Lord to do anything is going to be like trying to herd a cat. A very big cat,' she added, barely able to contain a shudder at the thought of all those muscles.

She already knew he was going to look annoyingly magnificent in his skiwear. Because she'd seen photos of him modelling the Lord Culture brand. She tugged on her thermal undergarments. The silk felt like sandpaper against her oversensitive skin.

When exactly was her bizarre reaction to him going to end? She pursed her lips, aware of the tingling sensations that had tormented her for two weeks. She'd even had dreams about his kiss. His *stunt* kiss.

'Just remember, you're a queen, he's a commoner,' Mel said, giving her a confident smile. 'Dazzle him with your authority.'

'Believe me, Travis Lord is not a man who can be dazzled by anyone's authority but his own,' she said. And certainly not by someone with as little experience as she had of men. 'I got the definite impression he was more disdainful of my position than dazzled by it.'

'Then kiss him—and dazzle him with that instead.'

'What?' Isabelle swallowed heavily, the buzz on her lips joined by the hum at her core, which had plagued her at night, too.

'Do I need to kiss him?' *Again.* 'Won't being seen with him be enough?' She didn't want another fortnight of disturbed sleep, thank you very much. It was just over two months until Christmas—which meant her schedule was packed with official engagements already, because Androvia, with its array of Christmas markets and winter activities, was a luxury tourist destination for the festive season.

One of her responsibilities as Androvia's sovereign was to promote that to the best of her ability.

Mel laughed, counting the reasons on her fingers. 'Firstly, you want to give the photographers an exclusive they can sell, and, believe me, a clandestine kiss will fit that brief perfectly, especially as you've never been caught kissing a man on camera.'

'Perhaps because I've never kissed any man on or off camera before I met Mr Lord,' Isabelle protested, then winced, realising how gauche that sounded.

No wonder her one stunt kiss with Travis Lord had had a far greater impact on her than it should. She was a complete novice. And how sad was that for a woman in her early twenties? But after acceding to the throne as an eight-year-old, she had not been afforded the romantic opportunities other girls took for granted.

Home-schooled in the palace until she was eighteen, she had then been enrolled in a private all-female college in Switzerland. But while the other students had been able to enjoy the nightlife in Zurich, Isabelle had concentrated on her studies—and been accompanied at all times by her security personnel.

'My point exactly,' Mel said, unfazed by the revelation, because Mel knew exactly how inexperienced Isabelle was when it came to men. And kissing.

Despite their differences, she and Mel had become firm friends as ten-year-olds when Mel's mother had become the palace's head chef. But while Mel had learned how to flirt with boys at the local community college as a teenager, Isabelle had been busy learning the protocols of how to host a dinner party for two hundred VIPs, or address the UN assembly. In many ways, Isabelle had lived vicariously through Mel, because she'd had no romantic adventures of her own—which would be sad, if it weren't so pathetic.

'Secondly, you're meant to be in love with the guy, that means making out like you can't keep your hands—or your lips—off him,' Mel continued.

'It does?' Isabelle said, her throat tightening. And the hum in her abdomen becoming a definite throb.

'Of course.' Mel smiled. 'Don't look so worried, Issy. You said you liked kissing him.'

'Well, he's very accomplished at it.'

'Then, kissing him again shouldn't be a problem. He's agreed to go through with this farce,' Mel added, because she had never been one hundred per cent on board with Isabelle's plan, believing a fake marriage was going above and beyond the call of duty. But then Mel had never really understood Isabelle's devotion to her role as Androvia's queen. 'Let him take the lead,' she said easily. 'It sounds like he's more than capable. And given that he's such a good kisser...' Mel's blue eyes twinkled with mischief '...you should enjoy it. Plus, you *definitely* need more practice, if you're going to have any hope of pulling this off.'

Isabelle nodded. 'All exceptionally good points,' she said—but her panic did not downgrade much. She sighed and breathed through the anxiety.

She needed to view her relationship with Travis Lord as a transaction—pure and simple. Lord was getting the land he wanted for nothing and she would finally be able to grow Androvia's economy with a string of infrastructure projects.

But just because this would not be a real romance, or a real marriage, there was no reason not to use this opportunity to explore being a woman as well as a queen.

She had never even flirted with a man before now. And when would she get the chance to develop those skills on a man as accomplished as Lord? He'd been mocking her when he'd initiated their library kiss. She'd understood that—while she'd been analysing the kiss in minute detail at two in the morning. However embarrassing that was on one level, it also gave her an opportunity. Because if he was going to use her—and their fake marriage—for his own amusement, she need not feel guilty making the most of his kissing skills.

He had not been indifferent to the kiss, any more than she had. Even with her total lack of experience she'd seen the dark shadow of awareness, maybe even arousal, in his gaze.

And the thrill had been… Not insubstantial.

They had already agreed that physical intimacy would not be a part of their relationship, but public displays of affection were required. So, really, more practice would not go amiss.

As Mel helped her pull on the ski suit, Isabelle decided she would not worry about her physical response to Lord— when it was a basic biological urge—especially as she would be able to control the outcome, thanks to their deal.

As the cavalcade of security vehicles drove to the end of the mountain track, Isabelle spotted a single black SUV stopped on the ridge, the engine still running. Lord stood alone a few feet from the vehicle with a large snowboard under his arm. He looked suitably striking and intimidating in a bright red ski jacket and black ski pants fitted perfectly to his athletic build.

Figures.

He signalled to his driver, and the SUV reversed and drove past them as Lord himself kept his eye on her entourage approaching.

After her security team had checked the perimeter, she stepped into the pristine snow, the lightweight ski boots she preferred sinking into the icy blanket with a crisp crunch. She dragged in a heady lungful of the clean cold air. They were a good three and a half thousand metres above sea level here, which had to explain why she felt light-headed, while the throb of anticipation could only be the rare chance to spend an afternoon skiing.

One of her staff placed her skis in front of her. She dug her feet into the bindings and thanked the young man, before putting on her goggles and gloves while she waited for her guards to equip themselves.

Once the whole party was ready, she skied smoothly across the ridge towards Lord, who hadn't budged. Why was she not surprised he was making her come to him?

She reached his position, with two of her security team flanking her and two more trailing behind.

'Hello, Mr Lord,' she said, his expression unreadable behind a pair of designer sunglasses. He wore no hat, or goggles, his dark unruly hair ruffled by the slight breeze. She kept her gaze fixed on his face, and not on his physique in the striking outfit.

'Call me Travis, Belle,' he said, using the ridiculous nickname again. Before she had a chance to comment though, he directed his gaze over her shoulder. 'What's with the circus?'

'Excuse me?' she managed, before she realised he was referring to her security team. She had become so used to taking the guards with her wherever she went, she didn't really notice them any more, but she could see from his scowl he was not pleased.

'Your babysitters,' he clarified, with typical bluntness. 'Why do you need them in the middle of nowhere?'

'It's procedure,' she said stiffly, determined not to let him aggravate her straight away. 'And we won't be in the middle of nowhere once we arrive in Sariyelva,' she added, pointedly. 'Which is where we are supposed to end up so the local press can photograph us together.'

'Then tell them we'll meet them there,' he replied coolly.

At least he hadn't objected to their destination, she thought ruefully. 'I also need them on hand to protect me.'

'From what?'

'Threats against my safety,' she said, firmly.

Why was he being so difficult? Having the security detail with her had felt hideously restrictive when she was younger. For years, the constant shadow had made her feel both suffocated and self-conscious, her every move monitored and measured, but she had come to accept the intrusion as a requirement of her position over time. And he would have to do so now, as well.

'Are we talking assassins and kidnappers or bears and broken bones?' he asked.

She bristled. What exactly was he implying, that Androvia was the Wild West? Or that she couldn't ski as well as he could snowboard?

'We do not have any intelligence about bad actors in the region. The bears are hibernating at this time of year, and I'm not going to fall. I happen to have been skiing almost as long as I've been able to walk,' she announced, her irritation getting the better of her, despite her best intentions.

'Terrific,' he said, dropping the snowboard onto the ground. 'Then tell your minders to scram and we'll see them in Sariyelva.'

'I can't ski without them,' she said, her patience starting to fray. 'They need to know I'm safe at all times.'

'You *can*, you're their boss,' he said, giving her instructions as if *he* were *her* boss—the self-righteous bastard. 'I'll make sure you're safe on the ride down. And they can track your phone if they need to.'

'I'm not going to ask them to...' she began, but he cut off the protest, by placing his chilled hand on her cheek, his familiarity shocking her into silence.

'Belle, listen up. This is non-negotiable. The deal's off if you can't get rid of the audience for an afternoon. I'm not comfortable with them trailing us everywhere we go. And no way are we going to persuade anyone we're an item if we're never alone.'

She started, shocked not just by the demand, and the ultimatum, but the familiar touch. And the way it made her feel—as if she wanted to jump out of her skin and lean into his callused palm at one and the same time.

'I just... I'm not used to doing anything alone,' she said, then wished she hadn't, because it made her sound pathetic.

But instead of mocking her, he brushed her cheek with his thumb. The caress was slight, but had a predictably shocking effect, before he let her go to lift his sunglasses.

What she saw in his expression wasn't the disdain she had expected.

'You're not alone, you're with me. We're gonna need privacy to figure stuff out. And the downhill will be a lot more fun without the guard dogs.'

She cleared her throat. *Fun.*

Her temper deflated.

Hadn't she once longed for the freedom to do exactly what he was suggesting?

She took a steadying breath to consider his request—without letting her annoyance at his high-handedness get in the way.

It was a glorious day, the afternoon sunlight making the snow glisten and sparkle, and the forested gorge was the perfect gradient for a fast and challenging descent. The aloneness, the stillness, the silence—only broken by the cry of a raptor hunting in the blue above them—were spellbinding, vibrating with the possibility of adventures she had been denied for so long.

Would it really be so wrong to indulge yourself, just this once?

She swung round to address the head of her security detail before she could overthink the impulse. 'Jensen. Could you and the team meet us at the trailhead near Sariyelva?'

'Are you sure, Your Majesty?' the man said, frowning.

'Yes, myself and Mr Lord are going to ski alone,' she added with an authority she didn't entirely feel—but which only made the thought of playing hooky for the afternoon more exhilarating. 'We should be there in two hours at the most. Give me the satellite phone,' she said, holding out her hand to take the device. 'If there's a problem, we'll contact you.'

The man looked past her towards Lord, not at all happy about the instruction. Lord simply raised an eyebrow, and she could almost hear him saying, in that deep, husky American accent: *Yeah, so what you gonna do about it, buddy?*

The silence stretched, the stand-off between the two men vibrating with tension… And annoying her. Why was Jensen confronting Lord when this was her decision to make?

But then her security chief nodded and handed her the phone. Capitulating to her or Lord she wasn't quite sure—but she would take it.

'We will be waiting to escort you into Sariyelva,' he said. 'If we don't hear from you in two hours, we will send out a search party.'

'Of course, and thank you, Jensen,' she said, the spurt of adrenaline becoming intoxicating at the thought of having the whole afternoon to herself.

Jensen and his men returned to their vehicles and drove away, leaving the two of them alone on the ridge.

Lord fixed his feet into the snowboard's bindings, then bent to tighten the straps, apparently so confident he would win this round, he wasn't even going to gloat over his victory.

Isabelle's irritation spiked. She dug her sticks into the snow, determined to take back control of their afternoon excursion.

'Race you to the bottom, Mr Lord. The last one there is

a rotten egg,' she shouted over her shoulder as she launched herself off the crest, flying into the undriven snow like a missile fired from a starting pistol.

The adrenaline was like a drug as she slalomed down the slope at breakneck speed, her muscles singing, and heard him shout from behind her: 'You're on.'

Who knew? Her Majesty has some serious moves—and a killer instinct to match.

Travis grinned as his fake date for the afternoon shot down the steep slope, switching through the turns to carve tracks in the untouched snow ahead of him...

The old exhilaration pounded through his veins as he gained ground by taking the more direct route. Her lithe figure bent over her skis as she ramped up her stick action to increase her speed—aware of him catching her.

Strictly speaking, skis were a faster way to travel on snow than a board—because two long thin sticks of fibreglass were aerodynamically a more efficient form of transportation than the shorter board he was using. Plus, the rider could distribute their weight more efficiently.

But he had a few key advantages. He was bigger, more badass, and, however good she was, she was still an amateur who had never risked her neck to win a race...

His bad leg jarred as the board hit a rock under the snow. He rebalanced himself, then gritted his teeth and crouched lower to push harder.

She glanced over her shoulder—her face a picture of shock, then grim determination.

His grin widened, despite the pain in his kneecap, as he swept past her. He could ice the knee later. Much later.

The slope reached the tree line, the conifers too tightly packed for even him to risk racing any further, so he looped round and slammed into a stop.

'I win!' he shouted.

She skidded, spraying him with snow as she was forced to brake hard a couple of feet above him.

He tugged off his sunglasses and flicked off the film of ice. 'Guess you're the rotten egg, Belle.'

She yanked off her goggles. Then threw them into the air and laughed, her delighted expression making his heart pound.

'I don't care, that was glorious!' she announced. 'It's been so long since I've been permitted to ski that fast.'

'Yeah, who was stopping you?' he asked, intrigued, not just by the joy in her eyes, but also the sense of fellowship. He knew what it was like to get back something you'd figured might be lost for ever. While he'd never be able to board at the level he had before the accident, being able to ride at all felt precious now, even with the price he was usually forced to pay afterwards if he pushed too hard... As he had today.

'No one...specifically.' She brushed her hair back from her face, releasing the long blonde locks from the updo— which hadn't survived the ride. 'I just have certain responsibilities, ever since my parents died.' She glanced away, her complexion reddening in the chilly air. When she met his gaze again, the unguarded look had been replaced by something pensive. And wary. Was she thinking about her folks? Or just embarrassed she had revealed so much to a stranger? Because, although he hardly knew her, he had already figured out Queen Isabelle was not an over-sharer.

'That must be a royal pain in the butt,' he said, thinking it was a damn shame she never got to cut loose. 'Always having to do what you're told.'

'Not at all,' she said, the swift denial and the stiff tone contradicted by the colour still making her cheeks glow. 'I welcome the responsibility.'

'Uh-huh,' he said, letting his scepticism show. She'd enjoyed the race, why not admit it? After all, there was no one here to punish her for not being queenly enough.

'I didn't know you could race like that... After your accident,' she said.

'The accident wasn't that bad.' He lied smoothly, not liking the flicker of sympathy in her eyes, or the abrupt change of subject. 'And I'd have had to be dead to stop boarding. Or to let an amateur beat me on the downhill,' he added. 'Although you gave me a decent run there for about a nanosecond.'

A frown formed on her forehead—and he congratulated himself on locating the killer competitor again, behind the responsible rule-follower.

'A nanosecond?' she scoffed. 'You only beat me by a whisker, you...you...'

'Spit it out, it'll do you good...' he coaxed, enjoying her indignation almost as much as the sight of all that gold hair, flowing around her heart-shaped face. She really was a looker, especially with her hair loose.

'Your attempts to provoke me won't work, Mr Lord,' she said, trying to regain the decorum she'd lost so comprehensively during their downhill.

But he'd glimpsed the reckless girl, and he wasn't about to let her shut that girl down again so easily.

'Oh, yeah?' he said, then scooped up a handful of snow, pressed it into a ball and lobbed it straight at her.

She ducked just before it hit her, but the shock on her face was worth the miss.

He laughed, while arming himself with another handful of snow.

'What are you doing, Mr Lord?' she declared, while working her boots out of her skis.

Clever girl.

He snapped his own boots free, then tossed the ball from hand to hand. 'Declaring a snowball war,' he said as he stalked towards her. 'Fair warning, Belle, you call me Mr Lord again and you're gonna be in big trouble.'

Her brows launched up her forehead as she retreated.

'You wouldn't dare…' she gasped, but he could see exhilaration—alongside her astonishment.

'Wanna bet?'

'But I'm a queen,' she said, falling backwards as she scrambled to get away. 'I could have you arrested.'

'I'll take my chances…' He fired the snowball, just as she turned and ducked again.

It sailed over her head. She jumped up and let out a triumphant hoot. 'You missed me…'

The second ball hit her square in the neck, filling her mouth with snow.

She let out a shocked gasp.

He grinned as she raced to arm herself.

He continued to advance on her—scooping up snow as he went—his adrenaline pumping.

He didn't care how much she loved the responsibilities of being a queen, everyone deserved a chance to cut loose occasionally. And seeing the mask of perfection slip was almost as much fun as beating her on the downhill.

They followed each other around the snowy clearing, snowballs exploding off the trees as they ducked and dived and shouted trying to gain an advantage. She was quicker than him in the cumbersome boots and had one hell of a throwing arm. But he was persistent and more willing to take the hits—which kept coming.

She landed pretty much every shot—but he kept advancing, ignoring the ice sliding down his neck, his frozen fingers or the snow coating his hair.

Finally, he had her cornered. Realising she was trapped, and all out of ammunition, she turned to make her getaway—a second too late.

'Oh, no, you don't…' He charged, throwing himself at her. Wrapping his arms around her hips, he swung in mid-air to take the brunt of the fall. They crashed together into a drift, her shrieking and him laughing so hard he was surprised he didn't bust a rib.

He lifted over her, pinned her wrists above her head, then shook his hair, until the snow landed in her face.

'I win again,' he declared, but he was still chuckling, while she was huffing and puffing and wiggling furiously under him.

'You bastard!' she announced—finally getting out the insult she'd wanted to call him earlier… Good to know a snow-ball fight could demolish all those years of stellar breeding in five minutes flat.

'Belle, sweetheart, you're only just figuring this out now…' He laughed some more, enjoying the flush of outrage and the sheen of exhilaration in her eyes. Until she wriggled some more, and a surge of heat hit him.

She went still, they both did. Then her gaze dropped to his mouth, her lips opening. The soft sob she made was like a siren call to his senses.

The urge to capture those full lips again streaked through him—as intoxicating as it was ill-advised. But he'd never been a guy to ignore his instincts, or the clear invitation in a woman's eyes. So, he lowered his head, ready to feast on her this time—until she tensed and murmured, 'Mr Lord?'

He stopped, registering the shocked tone, and the panic in her eyes, alongside the awareness.

He let go of her wrists, rolled off her—and flopped onto his back.

Dumb move, Lord.

He stared at the snow-covered pines—and took several long deep breaths of the frigid air, while willing the heat to take a hike.

What the hell had he been thinking? Or rather not thinking.

'I'm sorry,' she murmured. 'I should not have let you provoke me into the snowball fight,' she added. 'It was totally inappropriate given our circumstances.'

Annoyance—mostly with himself—kicked him in the gut.

Why was she taking the blame when he was the one who had started the snowball fight...and initiated their almost kiss?

He let out a gruff chuckle—although he wasn't at all amused—to release the knot of tension, and the weird regret.

Playing rough and tumble with her had been a schoolboy error. But seeing her lose her usual reserve had also been fascinating—so he refused to beat himself up about it too much, even though the ache in his groin was even more pronounced than the one in his cruciate ligament now.

He turned his head, to find her lying beside him staring back, a confused, questioning look on her face.

'No apology required. The snowball fight was my idea, Belle,' he said gruffly, to get that straight at least.

He rolled away from her to stand, then leant down to offer her his hand.

'Come on. Let's head to Sariyelva,' he said.

She clasped his hand. Even through her glove, he could imagine her skin so soft against his own as he tugged her onto her feet. *Terrific.*

She really was a petite little thing, he realised as he waited for her to brush the snow off her suit. When exactly had that become a major turn-on, too?

She lifted her hair, tied it into a knot, her expression closed, her movements cautious.

Shame, he thought. But he held back the urge to tell her how much he liked her hair down.

She's not yours, Lord.

'How long to the end of the trail from here?' he asked, to get his mind back on business.

'Sariyelva is nestled in the valley below. It shouldn't take us more than an hour to ski down to it through the forest.' She began to talk in that clipped rushed tone, which he had figured out from their first meeting was a sign of her nerves. He relaxed a bit. At least he wasn't the only one affected by their horseplay.

'The PR team have let some local reporters know I'll be there this afternoon with you—incognito.' She continued to talk too much.

'Cool, so I guess we better make sure we put on a convincing show. To clue your subjects in to our torrid love affair.'

Her gaze snapped to his, the blush firing across her cheeks.

Damn, but teasing her was irresistible—however dumb.

'Um…well, yes…' she murmured, her expression an engaging mix of panic and awareness.

She couldn't possibly be *that* sheltered—she'd been the monarch of a major Alpine country for most of her life. But even if the strange innocence that clung to her wasn't real, it wasn't helping him get the heat under control either…

He headed to the board, fitted his feet back into the bindings. 'It's your call, Belle,' he said, and tried to mean it.

Giving in to the temptation to kiss her would not be smart. But as they headed through the forest trails towards their rendezvous with her security team and the local paparazzi the urge to get his mouth on hers again resolutely refused to take a hike, along with the desire to tempt the reckless girl back out of hiding.

CHAPTER FIVE

'BY THE WAY, Mr Lord, I'd like to thank you for signing all the paperwork so promptly,' Isabelle announced as she stood beside Travis Lord, staring at the huddle of historic buildings below them that made up Sariyelva—the town's fairy lights already twinkling in the gathering dusk.

The journey here had taken them over an hour and during that time they'd barely exchanged a word. Perhaps because they were both mindful of the barriers that had been lowered far too readily with their race and the snowball fight. Barriers that she had been determined to rebuild.

But as much as she did not wish to test those barriers, Isabelle knew she couldn't remain silent any longer. There was too much they needed to discuss… Especially concerning the wedding ceremony itself. And its immediate aftermath.

Unfortunately, she had been unable to address these important details as they'd skied, and snowboarded down the trail, because she had been tongue-tied by the memory of him wrestling her to the ground. And the intent expression on his face as his gaze had shifted to her mouth. In that moment, while he'd held her down in the snow, she'd seen something intoxicating in his eyes—not just approval, but need. And for a second—a pregnant, endless, disturbing second—her heart had slowed from a giddy two-step to a heavy, one-two punch—and all her hopes and dreams had centred on the fierce desire to have him kiss her again.

Utter madness, obviously.

What had she been thinking? Cavorting with him like a teenager? Because, even after an hour, the memory of his big body pressing hers into the snow, his heavy breathing from their exertions visible in the frosty air, his gaze dark and serious, still felt like too much—and also not nearly enough.

He glanced at her, his lips quirking in the half-smile she found aggravating and captivating all at once.

'I thought I told you there would be trouble if you called me Mr Lord.'

'Sorry, I meant Travis, of course,' she said, flustered—again.

Her gaze strayed to his mouth, then jerked to his face, to find him watching her. Her cheeks burned.

For goodness' sake, Issy, stop thinking about the kiss that never happened.

'We have a lot to discuss,' she blurted out. 'Especially concerning the wedding ceremony. I think it best we marry as soon as possible—to facilitate the lease agreement.' She began to talk too fast, the words tumbling out of dry lips as she struggled to regain her composure. And keep her focus firmly on logistics and not the memory of his mouth lowering to hers.

'Obviously neither of us wants to have a full-blown royal wedding, especially as this is not a real marriage, and time is of the essence, but once I tell the Ruling Council about our engagement there will be expectations that we—'

'What expectations?' He interrupted her.

The scowl had returned. The one he'd worn on the ridge while asking—or rather demanding—she dismiss her bodyguards. It had occurred to her several times in the past hour—as she had tried to understand her subsequent behaviour—that giving into that request had been the rock on which her common sense had perished. Or rather, very nearly perished.

'As I'm Androvia's monarch,' she began, attempting to gather what was left of her wits, again, 'my wedding will have to be in the public eye.'

The scowl deepened. 'How public?'

'Public enough to convince the world ours is a real marriage.'

'Give me specifics,' he said. 'A ballpark figure for guest numbers, media imprints, time frames, et cetera.'

'I can't possibly give you those figures until I've spoken to my Privy Council and employed a team to do the planning.' She scowled back. 'I just wanted to make you aware a royal wedding—however low-key—is a public event. We will also have to arrange a short honeymoon. But I've already cleared my schedule to accommodate a wedding date on the twenty-first of December, if that is amenable. So, a few days off over the Christmas break during which we would remain in the palace should suffice to fulfil the honeymoon commitment.' She stopped abruptly, aware she was babbling again.

'That's a lot of extra stuff you're asking me to commit to,' he growled.

Really? Was it that much to ask? When he was getting land worth millions for a single dollar? 'As I said,' she began *again*, 'I will endeavour to ensure the time requirements are not onerous for you.'

He stared at her for the longest time. 'Okay.'

Relief coursed through her—even though she wasn't sure why. If getting the most basic of commitments out of him was this hard, how would she ever make this work for an entire year?

But before she could point this out to him, he added, 'I

can make the twenty-first work, just about, to relocate my base to Androvia for the resort project.'

'Fabulous,' she said, unable to keep the edge out of her voice.

'But I have a couple of conditions.'

'What conditions?'

'We make the honeymoon trip two weeks instead of a couple of days and we stay at my cabin in Colorado.'

'But… *What?*' she asked, or rather croaked. 'But that really isn't necessary,' she said. 'A working holiday in the palace on Christmas and Boxing Day will be more than sufficient. Plus, we will be expected to make some public appearances in the days immediately after the nuptials. And between Christmas and New Year.'

'No way. The wedding is public enough. Plus I always take a couple of weeks off over Christmas to recharge. And if I'm going to have to play nice for the wedding, not to mention spend a year in Androvia, I'm gonna need the break even more than usual.'

She could hear the surly tone, but also the steely determination.

Panic made her throat close. 'But I can't commit to that… It's…' *Too intimate? Too dangerous? Too exposing?* 'I can't possibly take two weeks away from my official duties in December, and at such short notice,' she said hastily, trying to come up with a viable excuse not to spend a fortnight with him—especially at Christmas.

She hated Christmas. It had always been a difficult time of year for her, even before her parents had died, and one she had never enjoyed. The thought of being forced to celebrate it with a man like him, who she suspected already had the ability to see too much, was untenable. 'And it makes no sense to leave the palace,' she continued, 'when it will create a security nightmare—'

'Stop panicking,' he cut in, making her brutally aware she had revealed too much already. 'I'll agree to ten days in total, to accommodate your schedule,' he said. 'And I'll get my people to liaise with Jensen about the security once we go public with the engagement,' he continued, as if it were already a done deal. 'But it shouldn't be a problem. My place is secluded and private with only one access road. And if we keep the location under wraps, it'll take at least ten days for anyone to find us there.'

Secluded? Private?

The thought only horrified her more. Keeping busy was the way she got through the season, the way she rode out the storm of memories—and the hollow ache of loneliness—that had dogged her at this time of year ever since she was a child.

'But I...' she began, desperately trying to come up with reasons not to agree to his request. 'That's really not—'

But he interrupted her again. 'Quit freaking out, Belle,' he said, sounding reasonable. Far *too* reasonable. But the determination—which she remembered from their stand-off over her security detail—told a very different story. 'Consider those ten days a chance to let off steam and figure out the logistics of this arrangement. We're not gonna have any time together before the marriage, so we're gonna need time after to get to know each other.'

'But I never take more than a few days off at Christmas...' she tried again, feeling her panic rising. 'I have too many commitments. And I—'

'Then you'll have to cancel them. Like I said, Christmas is the only chance I get to go boarding and chill. Plus, I'm gonna need some guaranteed downtime away from the media after the wedding circus you're insisting on.'

Christmas? Downtime? The idea horrified her.

'But there's going to be so much to do...' She trailed off as his expression remained implacable and unmoved.

'There's always so much to do. What are you so scared of?'

'I'm not scared,' she said, desperate to convince herself now, as well as him.

She made herself breathe. Letting Travis Lord know of her fears, of how vulnerable she felt at that time of year, would just expose her more... Especially as the prospect of spending ten days alone with him was already catapulting her so far outside her comfort zone she was practically on Mars.

'Then what's the big deal?' he said, still being Mr Far-Too-Reasonable. 'My place has enough space we won't bump into each other if we don't want to, and you're probably gonna need some downtime, too.'

But I never take downtime.

She swallowed the revealing remark.

How had he managed to box her into a corner again? As he had during their snowball fight? With no ammunition left.

Blast the man, he's outmanoeuvred me again. This is getting to be a really annoying habit.

'Okay, fine.' She sighed, knowing it was not at all fine. But continuing to freak out, as he had so indelicately put it, would just put her at more of a disadvantage.

You are a queen, you can handle anything, including a ten-day Christmas break with Travis Lord.

Perhaps it wouldn't be that bad? She would simply have to keep her wits about her while she was in his home. And, strictly speaking, this would still be a working Christmas. He certainly did not seem the sentimental sort, so surely he would not insist on any of the trappings of Christmas that she had always avoided. And she did *need* to get to know him better, if only to figure out how to stop him outmanoeuvring her so easily. Plus, if she was going to spend a year pretending to be intimate with him, she needed to become comfortable with spending time with him. She would consider this a baptism of fire. And anyway, they would not be alone—because she very much doubted he cooked and cleaned for himself.

'Cool,' he said. 'You won't regret it.'

Unlikely, seeing as I already am.

He glanced at the sun, which was about to dip below the horizon. 'Come on, we have a date with the paparazzi.' He stamped his feet back into the bindings of his snowboard. 'FYI, don't forget to look like you adore me as soon as we hit town, Belle.'

Her heart pounded against her ribcage—and pulsed between her thighs.

Precisely!

CHAPTER SIX

'PERHAPS WE SHOULD be holding hands, Travis?'

Travis felt the inconvenient shot of lust at the tentative question from the woman beside him as they strolled through the sleepy Alpine town together and he tried to ignore the five guys flanking them and scanning the chocolate-box houses of Sariyelva like Rottweilers.

The heat sparked in his gut at the artless expression on her face.

He'd been edgy ever since their almost kiss earlier. But as the hot flush spread up her neck he couldn't resist a smile.

This deal was already a lot more complicated than he'd imagined it would be. He hadn't counted on their chemistry—which was looking more problematic by the second. But even so, he'd pushed for a Christmas break when she'd insisted on a public wedding.

Their 'honeymoon' would be his last chance for at least a year to visit the hideaway he'd built in the Colorado Rockies—and where he always headed over Christmas and New Year to de-stress.

He'd be damned if he was going to break that tradition to accommodate his fake wife, when he was already accommodating her enough.

'Holding hands is kind of lame, don't you think?' he said.

'What exactly do you suggest, then?' she asked, frowning.

'How about we try this,' he said, and slung his arm over her shoulder.

She let out a huff of surprise against his neck. And the heat spiked.

Yeah, their chemistry was definitely going to be a problem... But he only hugged her closer when her security chief gave him the stink eye again.

'Your Majesty?' Jensen asked, clearly not at all happy seeing Travis manhandle his queen.

Tough.

'Tell your guard dog to back off, Belle.' He nuzzled her ear, deciding to go for broke as he spotted the flicker of a camera lens in the distance. 'We're on candid camera already.'

She shuddered—which he felt all the way to his toes—but announced crisply, 'It's okay, Jensen. Mr Lord has my permission to hold me.'

'Now put your arm around my waist,' he instructed, because she was as stiff as a board beside him. Seriously, if he didn't know better, he'd think she'd never snuggled with a guy before.

She reached around his waist, her fingers curling into the fabric of his ski jacket—the gesture so awkward, it was almost sweet.

Go figure.

He tried to stroll with her under his arm, but her body was so rigid beside his she couldn't get into step with him.

'Relax, Belle,' he murmured. 'You adore me, remember.'

She huffed out a scoffing breath, but the teasing had the desired effect and she finally began to soften enough not to fall on her face.

They headed into the main town square followed by their entourage, including the still scowling Jensen.

Dusk had fallen and fairy lights hung from the rafters of the wood-framed buildings, sparkling in the evening light.

The place looked magical, like the set of a romantic movie, or a winter fairy tale. The locals stopped to stare and smile at them but kept a respectful distance. Spotting a coffee house in the corner of the square, he released her from the shoulder hug and grasped her hand to tug her towards it.

'Let's get a hot chocolate,' he said as inspiration struck. 'I'm parched.'

Isabelle's eyes widened. She was clearly taken aback by the suggestion.

He knew the plan had been to get photographed together and then split before they could cause too much commotion. But he wasn't ready to let her go just yet.

'I… Okay. But I'll need to check with Jensen,' she said.

He forced himself not to object. 'Go ahead.'

The presence of her security team had annoyed the hell out of him up on the ridge—and was one of the reasons why he'd nixed any official engagements straight after the wedding and pushed for the Colorado trip. Putting up with the constant scrutiny was going to be a major pain in the butt during his year in Androvia, which he hadn't really considered until now.

It took a good five minutes of negotiation for Jensen to agree to the detour on the condition they remained in sight.

'Of course,' Isabelle said. 'But could you find somewhere discreet to observe us?'

Jensen gave a curt nod and the team fanned out ahead of them. Once they'd checked out the café, and alerted the proprietor, two of the team sat at a table on the far side of the porch while the others took up positions at vantage points around the square.

Isabelle turned to him. 'Okay?' she asked.

Not really.

He swallowed his frustration and squeezed her fingers. 'I

guess.' Leading her up the porch steps, he asked the proprietor—who had rushed out to greet them—for a table for two.

'Yes, of course, *monsieur*,' he said, then bowed so low to Isabelle, Travis was surprised he didn't topple over. 'It is a great honour and privilege to have you frequenting our establishment, Your Majesty.'

Travis bristled some more. Isabelle might be their queen but she wasn't a supreme being—and the way people treated her like one was getting old fast.

The guy directed them to a table on the porch beneath the eaves, with enough bowing and profuse thanks to get on Travis's last nerve.

He was used to some media scrutiny, and occasionally to being spotted and asked for his autograph—especially back when he'd been a champion sportsman—but this was next level. He was going to need the ten days after the wedding just to figure out how to handle this kind of attention for a year. How the heck had she managed to deal with it for a lifetime?

Isabelle, though, seemed unfazed, the polite shield firmly back in place as she thanked the man graciously.

Travis ordered a couple of hot chocolates, fully loaded—even though he was jonesing for a beer.

Once the proprietor had left them alone, he lifted her hand to tug off one of her gloves, then threaded his fingers through hers. The photographers were still shooting from across the square—but he knew the move wasn't entirely selfless when she shivered deliciously.

'That's gotta suck,' he said, keeping his voice low, so only she could hear.

'What has?' she asked.

He gauged her reaction, and realised she had no clue what he was talking about.

He had a vision of her as she had been as a young girl—

taking on the responsibilities of a monarch when she was still grieving, still just a little kid. The weird pang of sympathy—and anger—on her behalf stabbed under his breastbone.

Not your business, Lord. Not your problem.

As far as he was concerned, monarchy was a load of hooey, a clever way to push tourist numbers and maintain the status quo. But he'd never given any thought to what it might be like for the people born into those roles. Was it a privilege or a curse?

A perplexed expression furrowed her brow and he had the sudden desire to make her forget they were on show.

He traced his thumb down the side of her face. Her vicious shudder had the heat curling in his groin—and the desire to distract and unsettle her became even more compelling.

Who cared if this was a business proposition? Didn't mean they couldn't give those parasites a show they'd remember.

He lowered his hand to rub his thumb across her knuckles.

'Don't you hate people treating you like a queen, instead of a woman?' he asked, attempting to focus on the conversation, while also focussing on that plump bottom lip—which had captivated him in the forest.

'Oh, that…' She released a breath, her relief obvious. 'You get used to it. I suppose.' The wistful sigh made him wonder if she was lying to him now, or to herself.

Their drinks arrived, and an unguarded smile brightened her features. 'I've never seen so much cream. Thank you, this looks delicious,' she said to the young server, who beamed then left them alone again.

She lifted the long-handled spoon beside the tall glass, scooped a marshmallow off the top and popped it in her mouth.

'You're doing it all wrong,' he murmured.

'I… I am?' she asked. The concerned furrow made him

smile, her artlessness almost as appealing as how easy she was to tease.

'Yeah.' He lifted his own glass and took a sip, aware of the cream hitting his upper lip.

She gave a surprised chuckle when he lowered his glass. Then pulled a paper napkin from the dispenser.

'Here,' she said, reaching across to hand him the napkin, the stiff self-consciousness finally fading.

He snagged her wrist—and felt her stiffen right up again as awareness flared in her eyes.

'Not so fast, Belle,' he said, the devil in him ramping up as her pulse punched his thumb. 'Why don't you kiss it off?'

Her delicate brows shot up her forehead. And he saw her throat contract as she swallowed. 'I... *Really?*'

'Uh-huh. It'll make the perfect picture,' he said, as if this were still just for show... And had nothing to do with the heat that had been building all afternoon.

She turned, but he grasped her chin to prevent her from searching out the photographers.

'Pretend they're not there,' he said. 'And it's just the two of us, on a hot date. We want this to look convincing,' he said, smoothly, even though he felt the opposite of smooth right now—the desire in his gut already convincing enough.

She gave a slight nod. But uncertainty and self-consciousness still shadowed her expression—as if she really had no clue how to approach this.

'Take a sip of your own drink,' he directed, realising he was going to have to talk her through the process... Why did that only make the need more vicious? The desire more intense?

Surprise flickered in her eyes, but the awareness remained—rich and vivid—as she did what he told her. The lust in his gut twisted and pulsed.

What would it feel like to have this woman following his instructions in bed?

She placed the glass back on its saucer, her fingers trembling but her gaze direct. The white moustache on her top lip made him grin, even as the heat plunged deeper.

'Good girl,' he said, then tugged on her wrist to draw her closer. 'Come here.'

Again, she followed his instructions without question.

But as she leant across the table, that telltale sob issued from her lips. It was like a bullet to his gut, triggering a chain reaction.

And suddenly not one damn thing—certainly not the security team standing guard, not the photographers busy taking intrusive pictures, not even that uneasy feeling in his gut that was screaming at him this felt way too good to be fake—was going to stop him taking what she offered this time…

He slanted his mouth across hers, letting go of her wrist to cradle her cheeks, angle her head for better access, and capture that sob at last.

He licked and sucked and nipped—coaxing, encouraging, exploiting—until she opened for him on a heady breath, and let him in.

Her taste was even more intoxicating than the first time—warm rich chocolate, thick luxurious cream, and heady elemental desire.

He devoured her, exploring the recesses of her mouth. Until he had forgotten about everything but the hot sultry taste of her… And what he planned to feast on next.

Desire and longing barrelled through Isabelle's body, her mind dazed, her pulse thundering, as Travis Lord's lips claimed hers in a kiss that went from coaxing to carnal in a heartbeat.

She shivered, only vaguely aware of the table edge digging into her ribs, or his fingers caressing her scalp while he held her head. And took more.

Sensation vibrated from her breasts to the sweet spot between her thighs, and every pulse point in between. Her mind drifted into a sensual fog, dominated by the thrust of his tongue—and the desperate ache in her sex. The yearning to feel him there too, conquering her most intimate place in the same way as he was conquering her mouth, shot through her consciousness—wild, reckless, exciting, and absolutely terrifying.

She wrenched her mouth free, shocked by the direction of her thoughts, and how quickly they had roared out of control.

'Damn.' He groaned, then grinned at her—the smile knowing and arrogant.

Panic sprinted up her spine, doing nothing to obliterate the gush of need still making her sex ache.

He dropped his forehead to hers, his breathing as strained as hers, his strong hand massaging the tight muscles in her neck.

Sensation feathered her cheek, the scent of chocolate on his breath so rich and evocative she couldn't seem to make her mind engage.

'That should convince them,' he murmured, his thumb brushing the hammering pulse in her collarbone. She stiffened, the words throwing ice water over her flushed skin.

Of course, this kiss wasn't real for him, any more than the first one had been. It was all for the benefit of the photographers. She lifted her head, dislodging his hand, and blinked furiously, trying to control the brutal yearning and the cruel twist of humiliation.

His pupils had dilated to black, but other than that he was totally unmoved—as assured as always—while the heat he had incited still raced through her bloodstream, threatening to incinerate what was left of her common sense.

'Yes, I think that will be more than sufficient,' she managed around the boulder lodged in her throat.

Did he know? What his kiss had triggered? That the minute he had taken her mouth with that sense of entitlement and demand, she had been lost to the passion?

He captured her chin and turned her face to his, then wiped away what was left of the cream on her top lip with a napkin.

'You good?' he asked.

'Yes, thank you,' she said, although nothing could have been further from the truth.

Especially when his lips quirked. 'What are you thanking me for, Your Majesty?'

For kissing me as if you meant it.

The pathetic thought humiliated her even more.

'For making that so convincing,' she said, still trying to wrestle her wayward emotions back under control. 'I appreciate it,' she added, desperate to persuade herself this was still just a transaction.

But then he tilted his head to one side, his gaze roaming over her with the same fierce entitlement that had made his kiss feel so overwhelming.

'It wasn't exactly a hardship, Belle,' he said. His gaze dipped to her mouth, which began to tingle alarmingly—the memory of his conquest still playing havoc with her senses. 'That mouth is kind of irresistible.'

It is?

She sank her teeth into her bottom lip to stop herself from acknowledging the foolish feeling of validation at the compliment.

'I'm glad you think so,' she said. 'You happen to be a very accomplished kisser, so I guess that makes us even,' she added, trying to sound sophisticated and not devastated.

She had the awful suspicion she hadn't fooled him though, when he let out a gruff chuckle.

But the intense heat in his gaze didn't seem to have the cynical edge she had come to expect when he replied, 'Yeah, I guess it does.'

He was humouring her. They weren't even at all. Because sex was a game to him, while it could never be one to her. But still her pulse slowed when he stood and offered her his hand.

'Show's over,' he said, grasping her fingers. Sensation shot up her arm—because of course it did. 'We've given those vultures enough to run with for now.'

'Yes, of course.' She gulped down the spurt of regret—knowing that giving in to the impulse to spend more time with him would be even more dangerous than that ferocious, all-consuming kiss.

He dumped some of the local currency on the table.

'I can get my security to pay,' she offered.

His gaze flattened, the amusement gone.

'No, thanks, Your Majesty,' he said, the cynical edge back. 'When I take someone on a date, I pay.'

Except this isn't a real date, she wanted to protest.

But how could she, when it had felt far too real to her?

CHAPTER SEVEN

Two months later

ISABELLE BREATHED OUT SLOWLY—but the constriction under her ribs from the corset she wore under antique ivory silk was nothing compared to the constriction in her throat as she observed the seven hundred carefully selected guests from her vantage point in the vestry.

Androvia's famous White Chapel was looking suitably stunning, its five-hundred-year-old eaves decorated with a thousand ivory and red Alpine roses, accented with edelweiss and local greenery, and artistically arranged by a team of fifty florists. The tall candles tied with velvet bows—which lit her route down the aisle—shimmered in the wintry light that shone through arched stained-glass windows and made the whole scene glow with a timeless beauty.

She stepped back to allow the hairdresser's assistants to finish fussing with her hair, while the stylist and her team made the final adjustments to her gown and the wedding planner briefed the six pageboys and bridesmaids who had been selected from local schools to carry her train and throw rose petals.

'You look beautiful, Your Majesty,' the stylist said in hushed tones. 'Mr Lord is a lucky man.'

I'm not sure he would agree with you.

Isabelle cut off the errant thought. 'Thank you, Maria.'

She took another constricted breath as she imagined seeing Travis Lord again, for the first time since their kiss in Sariyelva.

The correspondence between her government officials, the Ruling Council, the wedding planner and Travis's coterie of assistants and advisers and Lord Culture's management and PR teams had been fast and furious and at times exceedingly fraught ever since the pictures of their kiss had broken in the press, the morning after their fake date.

The media attention—when the engagement had been officially announced two days later—had been intense and intrusive ever since. Even though Travis had returned to the US that night and she had spent the past two months fulfilling as many of her official duties as was practicable, the whole world had continued to speculate feverishly about every aspect of the 'fairy-tale romance' between the 'bad-boy billionaire and the alpine queen'.

Given the media scrutiny, it had been decided they wouldn't release official engagement photos as any more meetings in person could only add to the furore. Not to mention distract from the intense planning necessary to arrange a major state occasion—however low-key—in a scant eight weeks.

The Ruling Council had been aghast at her haste, and her privy council had gone into a complete meltdown over the logistics, but they hadn't objected when she had insisted on a very short engagement. Each time she had repeated the lie though—that she was madly in love with Lord and could not wait to marry him—it had become harder and harder not to panic at the prospect of seeing him again.

Their marriage was a fraud, so why had her nerves only increased as their wedding day drew near?

Ironically, the only things that had alleviated the stress were the texts she had received on her private phone from

Travis, himself, which had started when their engagement had been announced and continued every time he had an issue with the wedding protocols—which had turned out to be rather a lot.

Her heart bounced against her ribs as she recalled those unconventional texts—the man's demands and her increasingly forthright responses...

The truth was, she had begun to anticipate his messages—reaching for her phone first thing each morning to see if another had arrived—almost as often as she had panicked about her wayward response to his kiss, which was also far too frequent an occurrence.

She pulled her phone out from the gown's secret pocket—as the stylist continued to fuss—and scrolled through their latest exchange from four days ago, while struggling to even her breathing.

Travis: Tell Arne no way am I wearing a uniform when I'm not in the military. A monkey suit is bad enough.

Isabelle: I will tell Arne not to insist, as long as your monkey suit passes muster.

Travis: Don't u worry about my monkey suit.

The winking and laughing emojis that had accompanied the text had confused her when she had first read the message. Was monkey suit a euphemism of some sort that she was unaware of? She had puzzled for two agonising hours over how to respond appropriately, as she had done with so many of his texts. This time though, with her nerves already on edge, she had become so annoyed with herself she had opened the emoji keyboard for the first time in her life and dashed off one of a hand with a middle finger lifted.

Of course, the second after she had pressed send, she had realised how utterly inappropriate her reply was—despite the increasing familiarity that had seeped into their conversations over the past weeks. But while she had still been frantically trying to figure out how to delete her reply, his response had appeared.

Travis: Expect payback for that on our honeymoon.

The thrill that had shot through her had been even more inappropriate—and disturbing—than the impulse to use a profane emoji in the first place.

And after four days, during which her anxiety had continued to build, she still hadn't been able to figure out where that urge had come from, or how to repress the thrill at the thought of seeing him again, which had only become more pronounced.

'Shall I take that, Your Majesty?'

Isabelle glanced up to find the wedding planner smiling at her politely.

'We don't want it going off while you're walking down the aisle,' the woman added.

'Of course.' Isabelle switched off the phone and handed it over, but the stab of loss and regret—as the planner tucked the phone into her pocket—only increased her anxiety.

Why had she become so excited by those silly communications over the past weeks? Checking incessantly every morning to find out if he'd sent another? Being secretly thrilled when she opened the app to find one of his disgruntled complaints waiting for her, no matter how contrary? Then procrastinating endlessly over her response.

In the last week, she'd even taken to scrolling through their past conversations, late at night, like a schoolgirl with a silly crush, instead of a queen negotiating with a business partner—albeit a somewhat unconventional one. She'd found his irreverent sense of humour and his dogged determination to ridicule Androvia's centuries-old traditions amusing, when she should have been appalled. She was Androvia's monarch, surely it was her job to respect and uphold those traditions, not joke about them?

With those thoughtless exchanges she had blurred the boundaries between them, exactly as she had during their snowball fight and while obsessing about their stunt kiss?

'Hey, Issy, are you okay? You look kind of spooked.'

Isabelle lifted her head to find Mel standing in front of her. Her best friend handed her the bridal bouquet, while looking beautifully poised and relaxed in her cream silk maid-of-honour gown. But Issy could see the concern in her eyes.

'Yes, yes, of course,' she managed, pasting on what she hoped was a competent smile. After all, she could hardly confide in Mel the reason for her latest panic attack—because she hadn't told anyone about her clandestine text conversations with Travis.

She could see she hadn't fooled Mel though when her friend frowned. 'It's not too late to call this whole thing off, you know, Issy,' she whispered gently.

Of course it was, but even if it weren't, Isabelle knew she didn't want to call it off… She refused to examine the reasons why too closely.

'Really, I'm just tired,' she tried to reassure Mel, as well as herself. 'The stylist and the beauticians have been fussing for hours already, and I'm keen to get this over with now.'

The itinerary that had finally been agreed upon for the wedding day included events right up until midnight. But the thought of what would happen after that—when she and Travis were supposed to repair to her private apartments for their wedding night—had her anxiety, and the pulse of yearning that had refused to die for two solid months, spiking.

She ignored it.

Not a real wedding, not a real wedding night. End of.

Thank goodness her apartment in the palace had several bedrooms. And Travis had already agreed to the terms of their marriage. She might have blurred the lines a little over the past weeks—thanks to the wedding stress, and his innate ability to make her do stupid things, not to mention stunt-kiss her senseless—but she would never put her end goal in jeopardy.

Never.

'Okay, well, if you're sure,' Mel said, not looking convinced. 'By the way, Rene has just arrived. Late. And hungover,' she added, her voice edged with contempt.

Mel had never liked Androvia's neighbouring playboy prince. When they had been ten-year-old girls together in the palace, Issy's friend had often called out the teenage Rene for teasing both her and Isabelle whenever he came on an official visit accompanied by his father. But in recent years, her friend's contempt for the neighbouring monarch seemed to have intensified.

Isabelle felt a pang of sympathy for the man. 'I really wish Arne hadn't asked him to stand up for me,' she said. 'I hope he's not hurt.'

She'd been horrified when her chief courtier and the head of her household had informed her that, as a third cousin twice removed on her mother's side, Prince Rene was her nearest male relative—and therefore would be expected to walk her down the aisle.

Unfortunately, she'd been unable to come up with a viable excuse not to ask him.

'Hurt? How can he be hurt, when he doesn't have any

emotions, other than narcissism, arrogance and lust?' Mel shot back.

'Because he asked for my hand himself, once,' Isabelle offered, her guilt mounting. Luckily no one but she and Rene and Mel knew about the proposal, but even so, this situation could not be more awkward.

'You were eighteen at the time, Issy. And you know as well as I do, he only asked for your hand because he was looking for a royal virgin to be his brood mare. Given the number of women he's dated since you turned him down, I think he got over your rejection pretty fast.'

'Then why does he seem upset now?' Isabelle asked, the guilt still weighing on her. Mel might dislike Rene, but Isabelle had started to believe he had been trapped by his circumstances and might never have been happy with the role assigned to him by fate—unlike her... From what she could remember of Rene's father, Sven Gaultiere, the previous Prince of Saltzaland, the man had been a cold, cynical and ruthless autocrat. Was it any surprise his son had become a reckless libertine as soon as he had acceded to the throne at eighteen? That said, after ten years, it probably was about time Rene settled into his duties.

'He's not upset, he's hungover,' Mel hissed.

The delicate strains of the violin solo shimmered on the air, introducing Pachelbel's 'Canon in D', played by the chapel's famous string quartet, and lifted the hairs on Isabelle's neck. And thoughts of Rene were superseded by a shocking rush of yearning.

Isabelle tensed as everyone took their places—and the knot of anticipation threatened to cut off her air supply.

But as she stepped into the chapel's nave with Mel and her pageboys and bridesmaids arranged behind her the knot tightened. And throbbed.

Rene appeared from the shadows, resplendent in a dress

uniform, and gave a curt bow before offering her his arm. 'Your Majesty,' he said, with barely a hint of his usual sarcasm.

He was a strikingly handsome man—if you could ignore the brittle cynicism that never left his eyes—but as Isabelle placed her fingers on his arm, she noticed his complexion did look a little pale, his expression pained.

'Hello, brat,' he murmured to her maid of honour.

'Go to hell, Gaultiere,' Mel snapped under her breath, because she had never stood on ceremony with Rene.

'Could you two behave?' Isabelle whispered, but the familiar animosity had some of the tension in her gut easing. At least a little.

You can do this, Issy. It was your idea and now all you have to do is see it through.

The strings swelled accompanied by the chapel's antique organ as the canon built to a crescendo—along with Isabelle's rabbiting heartbeat.

'Ready?' Rene asked, with surprising thoughtfulness.

Isabelle nodded, unable to speak.

They headed down the aisle together, her heartbeat going into overdrive as she spotted the tall man standing alone at the altar, his broad shoulders, lean hips and long legs perfectly displayed in the expertly tailored morning suit.

The eyes of the congregation—made up of everyone from European royalty and heads of government to tech billionaires, supermodels and Hollywood stars—followed the bridal procession, the hush somehow pregnant with purpose, but Isabelle couldn't detach her gaze from the back of her groom's head, even as she struggled to keep the wave of panic and yearning under strict control.

Then he glanced over his shoulder—and their gazes collided.

Her breath became trapped in her lungs as she found

herself marking each minute difference in his appearance since Sariyelva.

He'd had a haircut, she thought inanely, recalling those silky locks against her skin while they'd devoured each other in the café.

His gaze glided down her body, searing and intense—and with a sense of entitlement that made her panicked heartbeat plunge between her thighs.

Did he like what he saw? Why should it matter? When this whole circus was simply for the benefit of their onlookers?

His gaze landed back on her face as she reached him, potent and provocative. Her lips buzzed—almost as if she could feel his mouth branding hers again.

Rene presented her arm to Travis and murmured, 'Here you go, Lord, you lucky bastard.'

The Prince stepped back. And she forgot all about him as Travis folded her fingers over his arm and brought her to his side. Her constricted lungs filled with the clean, spicy scent of cedarwood and man. And suddenly she couldn't breathe. Had he got taller? How could he seem even more overwhelming now than he had that afternoon?

He adjusted the collar of his shirt, loosening the grey silk cravat at his neck.

'I hope to hell that dress is more comfortable than my monkey suit,' he murmured.

She smiled at his mocking tone—which reminded her of those irreverent texts—not easy given her breathing difficulties and the nerves that were now threatening to strangle her.

'You lose,' she whispered back. 'I'm wearing a corset.'

His gaze raked over her cleavage, which pressed against her décolletage. His eyes darkened and she wanted to bite off her tongue. Why had she said something so provocative? So flirtatious?

He lifted her hand to his lips—watching her as if she were the only person there—and pressed a kiss to her knuckles.

She jolted, the firm pressure like a lightning bolt to her already overwrought senses.

'You win this round, Belle,' he said.

But as the surge of awareness rioted through her body on a wave of need and panic she suspected she was not the winner of this round.

Because she suddenly felt like that reckless girl again, the girl she had glimpsed again in the forest clearing with him... The one who had once yearned to be loved and cherished, but who had ended up unable to control anything in her life, at all.

CHAPTER EIGHT

Eight hours later

IF I HAVE to listen to another damn speech, I'm gonna lose what's left of my ever-loving mind.

Travis Lord tapped his foot under the banqueting table, in the four-centuries-old hall the size of a football field filled with hundreds of people, the vast majority of whom he didn't know from Adam, and tried to control the frustration, and the energy overload, that had been driving him nuts for hours.

He'd never been good at sitting still for long periods—even in high school he'd been thrown out of class more times than he could count because of the adrenaline that hurtled through his veins when he had to focus on any task for more than thirty minutes straight.

He'd trained himself to stay focussed for longer than that over the past decade—because being the CEO of a multinational brand meant attending a ton of really tedious meetings. Plus, he'd known getting through today's schedule was going to suck from the outset, but he'd thought he'd prepared—by working out for three hours in the palace's gym this morning before getting trussed up in this monkey suit.

What he hadn't factored in, though, and he should have, was being close enough to touch his new bride for eight solid hours without a break. Having to breathe in that tantalising aroma of flowers and female musk, feeling her delicate shivers—every time he pressed his palm to the small of her back, or held her hand for the benefit of their audience—had been bad enough. But for the past two hours, he'd been less than five inches away from her—during ten never-ending courses of cordon bleu cuisine—forced to watch as she took delicate bites of the fancy food or judicious sips of the vintage bubbles, unable to forget exactly what it felt like to have those lips on him.

He stole another glance and took a swift hit to the gut, ramping up his frustration even more... But he couldn't seem to look away, even for his own sanity.

The embroidered silk gown emphasised every one of her subtle curves, while her blonde hair was piled on top of her head in an artful array of jewelled clips and combs that he'd been itching to pull out for hours. He stared again at the single curl that dangled down and caressed the graceful curve of her neck every time she moved. He imagined placing his lips, right there, to lick the spot where her delicate skin pulsed, then sucking it until she moaned. His gaze glided back to her cleavage, her full breasts plumped up against the neckline of her gown, and imagined the corset she'd mentioned at the altar, eight long hours ago, which he'd been obsessing about ever since.

He tore his gaze away and stared at the crowd of guests.

Lifting the spoon from the dessert he hadn't touched—because the last damn thing he needed right now was a sugar rush—he rapped it against the gold rim of his plate in a vain attempt to distract from the heat in his gut.

One thing was for sure, he should have made more of an effort to control this reaction before today.

Why hadn't he taken the edge off in the past two months as he'd planned?

He'd known their chemistry was going to be a major issue, ever since that kiss in Sariyelva.

The memory of her livewire reaction had consumed him ever since. Enough that he hadn't been able to face the thought of hooking up with any of his old dates since having his mouth on Isabelle—even though he was now staring down the barrel of twelve months of enforced celibacy.

And how exactly had he gotten suckered into their weird semi-sexting conversation in the past eight weeks too, which had somehow upped the ante even more?

He still didn't know what had possessed him to send that first text to her private number. But she'd replied. And he'd begun to prise open the box of polite reserve she wore like a shield to uncover the smart, witty, forthright girl beneath... He hadn't been able to resist pushing and poking at her for a whole lot more. Until she'd shot the bolt and sent him a middle-finger emoji.

The desire he'd been struggling to control ever since he'd turned to see her walking towards him this morning kicked him in the gut again.

He placed a hand on his own knee to stop the incessant foot tapping as the Androvian prime minister continued to drone on about 'the wonderful new union between our two countries'.

But then the words Isabelle had whispered to him at the altar shimmered across his consciousness.

'You lose. I'm wearing a corset.'

And the insistent foot tapping began again.

Damn it, Lord. Time to make a break for it.

He needed to get out of here. Before he got any more fixated on all the ways he wanted to seduce his fake wife on their non-wedding night.

Reaching under the table, he placed his hand on Isabelle's knee and squeezed. She jolted, and her head swung towards him. The shudder of awareness did nothing to control the pain in his groin... But the delicious blush sprinting across her features—which had only become more vivid as the endless day wore on—was some consolation.

At least he wasn't the only one suffering.

He leant close to whisper in her ear. 'I need to leave now, or I'm going to throttle your PM and ruin the wonderful new union between our two countries.'

'But the schedule is not finished...' she began—but he could feel her jolt of shock as he rode his hand up her thigh. 'There is still dancing.'

'No buts, Belle. And definitely no dancing,' he added.

'Why not?' she asked, her thigh trembling, even as her eyes widened.

Was she really that clueless about what her nearness was doing to him? Surely she couldn't be? But when she continued to stare at him, her full attention on him for the first time since they'd been at the altar, he decided there was no harm in being straight with her.

They were both adults after all. And while he'd made a deal and intended to stick to it, ever since *that* kiss, the thought of suggesting a compromise—so they could both work this chemistry out of their systems—was starting to make a lot more sense. They were due to be spending ten nights alone together in Colorado. If he'd been frustrated sitting next to her for eight hours, how the hell was he going to handle a week and a half?

'I can't dance, Belle,' he said, pressing his lips to her ear. Her delicate shudder fuelled his resolve to stop avoiding the obvious. 'Because I've been hard on and off ever since that damn corset comment.'

A hot blush scalded her cheeks, but he could also see the flash of panic in her eyes.

Okay, what now?

Why did she look so shocked? She'd kissed him back that

day, and hadn't they been flirting—after a fashion—for eight weeks via text message?

'I see,' she said, biting into her bottom lip—the thought of which had been driving him wild for months, too. 'I'm sorry... I don't know why I mentioned that.'

'Hey.' He squeezed her thigh then let her go. 'Don't apologise.'

He'd thought they'd been on the same page. But maybe they hadn't been, because she still had that surprised look on her face.

'It's not that big a deal,' he said, even though it was getting bigger by the second. 'But I want to split now, before I explode.'

She signalled instantly to Arne, the stick-in-the-mud courtier who had been directing the schedule all evening.

The man hastened to her side and bent low. 'Your Majesty? How can I assist you?'

'Arne, myself and Mr Lord would like to repair to our private quarters now,' she said.

Hang on a minute... They were *both* leaving?

Her face had gone the same shade as the beets his mom had once badgered him to eat. He'd hated them then, but he was liking them a lot more now.

'I'm afraid that's not possible, Your Majesty, the event schedule does not conclude until—' the guy began stiffly.

Travis's temper spiked. 'Forget it, Arne,' he interrupted. 'We're out of here.'

Arne went scarlet, but then bowed. 'Yes, certainly, Your Highness. I will make the necessary arrangements immediately.'

Your Highness?

He cringed, uncomfortable with the form of address all the staff had been using since the wedding.

Arne the stickler backed off—then began directing traffic to facilitate a speedy exit. It took less than ten to get the go-ahead, because Arne was nothing if not efficient.

Travis escorted Isabelle from the banqueting hall—through the throng of people giving them a standing ovation and sending them looks that suggested they knew exactly why they weren't hanging around.

But as they left the hall, Travis could feel her trembling under his guiding hand. Leaving him wondering again, what was going on?

Had the corset comment been a come-on or not?

Did she want him to strip it off her, as he'd been dreaming of doing all evening? Or did she want to stick to the original deal? She'd kissed him as though her life depended on it in Sariyelva, and their flirty text convo over the last couple of months had exposed more of that girl who intrigued the hell out of him. But she'd barely looked at him since they'd met again at the altar.

The staff finally left them as they reached the door to her private apartments in the palace's east wing.

'Alone at last,' he murmured as he shoved open the door, and she walked into the ornate salon ahead of him.

She didn't respond, didn't even look over her shoulder as she walked into the elaborately furnished space. She banded her arms around her waist, her stance rigid, then flinched as he shut the door.

Why did she look like a lamb being led to the slaughter…? Because it was making him feel like an overbearing jerk or, worse, the kind of guy he had always despised. Men like his old man, who seduced women for the hell of it.

He dumped his jacket on one of the overstuffed antique chairs, loosened his cravat—and decided to address the elephant in the room, which was now sitting on his chest.

'We need to talk, Belle.'

She swung round. 'About… About what?' she asked as

their gazes locked for the first time since they'd declared their vows. Their *fake* vows—which didn't feel quite as fake as they should as she stood there in her wedding dress, trembling like a leaf, her expression a captivating mix of awareness and anxiety.

'About whether you want to change the terms of this agreement? Or not?' he asked.

The pulse in her neck beat double time. 'Which terms are you referring to?'

He yanked off the cravat, undid the top buttons of his dress shirt and frowned, not sure if she was playing games now, or if she was actually serious, because her expression had gone carefully blank.

He wanted her, and he was fairly sure she wanted him. But she was sending him a ton of mixed messages. Messages he needed to decipher before they went any further.

Because, unlike any other woman he'd ever dated, they were going to be stuck together for a year, so he didn't want to screw this up right off the bat.

He sighed. Plain speaking it was, then.

'The no-sex terms,' he said bluntly. 'What else?'

'You... You wish to have sex with me?' Isabelle said, so shocked—and, God help her, excited—by the blunt statement, she didn't realise how gauche she sounded until his lips quirked.

Her grandmother's antique Louis XVI armoire creaked as he leant against it, then crossed his arms over that magnificent chest and let out a chuckle—which was so husky it scraped against all her most sensitive spots.

He didn't answer her for the longest time—making her wonder if he was trying to unnerve her.

'Yeah,' he finally replied. 'Correct me if I'm wrong, but

I kind of thought we got that straight downstairs. Isn't that why you left with me?'

'No... I...' The denial choked off in her throat as he crossed his legs at the ankle—making the fabric of his trousers stretch over impressive thigh muscles—and drew her attention to the ridge in his pants.

I've been hard on and off ever since that damn corset comment.

She swallowed around the rock in her throat, which had also become wedged between her thighs. She forced her gaze back to his face. He was still watching her. Her nipples drew into tight peaks. Thank goodness, he couldn't see that reaction thanks to her corset, although...

Stop thinking about the corset.

'I just... I had to... I couldn't.' Her explanation got stuck behind the rock.

For goodness' sake, Issy, spit it out.

'I couldn't *not* leave with you. This is supposed to be our wedding night. We had to leave together, for appearances' sake...' she finished, which was mostly true, except—leaving with him had not been a hardship.

'Right.' His lips curved into a wry smile, as if he knew just how much she was lying to herself. 'Which brings us back to my original question...'

'I'm sorry, what was that?' she asked, because her grasp of the conversation had become tenuous at best.

'Do you want to go for a real wedding night to kick off this fake marriage in style?'

Ah yes... *That* question.

The rock wedged between her thighs grew to impossible proportions.

'Because I'm thinking we deserve some light relief,' he continued in that matter-of-fact tone, which made the rock pulse and glow. 'After the eight-hour show we've just had to put on—not to mention the two months of crap we had to deal with to get to this point—don't you?'

His gaze raked over her and the hot rock pounded.

She should say no. Encouraging a sexual relationship between them would be fraught with all sorts of problems. Problems she had considered insurmountable when they'd agreed to this marriage.

But even though she knew she should reject his suggestion, her tongue refused to cooperate. She was still struggling to give him an answer when Elsa, her lady's maid, burst into the salon.

'Your Majesty, would you like me to undress you now?' the woman asked as she crossed the room, having failed to spot Travis leaning against the armoire.

'Um…' Isabelle began, tongue-tied all over again.

'I don't think so.' Travis stepped in front of the maid, blocking her path. 'Undressing Belle is my job now.'

Isabelle felt a burst of excitement at the commanding tone, but right behind it was embarrassment. Especially when Elsa's mouth dropped open and she blushed.

'I'm so sorry, Your Highness,' Elsa said, addressing Travis, her tone horribly chastened.

Travis frowned at the maid. 'Yeah, don't call me that. Mr Lord will do just fine.'

She heard the impatient tone, and his contempt for the title bestowed on him by their marriage, and shame washed over her. Why was she allowing him to speak to her staff like that? She should never have allowed her duty to her throne and her subjects to be obscured by her foolish obsession with this man, who didn't respect either.

'It's okay, Elsa,' she began, determined to smooth over the awkwardness even though she needed Elsa's help to get out of this dress. But when the woman began backing out of the room, Isabelle had no choice but to let her leave. 'I'm sure His Highness and I can manage tonight,' she added, before Elsa darted out of the door.

Suddenly, they were alone again. The visceral yearning was still there, but the sensual fog that had built up over the past hours had lifted.

'Now where were we?' he said, thrusting his fingers through his hair.

At the exact same moment she said, 'That was uncalled for, frankly—'

'Frankly, I don't think so,' he shot back, interrupting her. 'You're entitled to some alone time.'

'That's not your call to make...' she began, annoyed the statement had made her anger soften.

He doesn't care about you, Issy. He's just throwing his weight around.

But before she could say more, he rolled up his sleeves—to reveal tanned forearms, covered in a supremely masculine dusting of dark hair that matched the hair peeking out from his open collar.

Isabelle blinked, her indignation momentarily derailed by the realisation she had never seen this much of him before. Him or any man for that matter.

'Stop changing the subject. You still haven't given me a straight answer,' he announced. 'Are we hooking up tonight or not?'

This time it was a lot easier to find a reply. 'You actually expect me to sleep with you now? After you were so rude to my staff and—'

'I guess that's a no, then,' he interrupted her tirade. Then he strode across the room and grabbed his jacket. 'Where am I sleeping? I need to crash.'

Temper sparked and tore at her self-control—its force as unfamiliar as the hot rock still pulsing between her thighs.

'The main guest bedroom is through there.' She threw out

an arm to point. 'I believe your luggage is already there. We share a bathroom, so I would appreciate it if you could be prompt,' she added, wondering how on earth she was going to get out of her dress.

'I'm gonna need a while in the bathroom,' he said. 'So *you* be prompt. And let me know when you're done.' He slung the jacket over his shoulder. 'I'll see you tomorrow morning, for ten fun-filled days in Colorado. Not.'

He strolled out without another word.

She stared at the space he had vacated. Furious with herself now as well as him. Why had she behaved like such a ninny all day? Good grief, she'd even considered taking him up on his insulting offer. The last thing she needed was to allow him to demolish what was left of her self-control— simply because he had an itch he wanted to scratch.

She was still fuming when it occurred to her she had a far greater problem than her fake husband's temper tantrum as she began trying to dismantle the elaborate chignon. Within minutes it had become a tangled mass that would put a bird's nest to shame.

She wrestled with it, becoming increasingly frustrated and frantic—and only making the mess worse—when three sharp raps made her jump.

'Time's up, Your Majesty,' came the low voice through the door to his bedroom.

'I'm not finished,' she said with as much authority as she could muster, while feeling flustered and upset. This was his fault. He'd dismissed her maid and now he was trying to bully her out of her bathroom time.

'Tough. You've been in there over thirty minutes. It's my turn now.'

What? How could she possibly have been in here half an hour? Surely, he was exaggerating.

But as she stared at her hair in the mirror, the blonde bird's nest starting to list to one side, she was forced to admit defeat. She hadn't been able to locate any pins for a while and her scalp was starting to ache. But how was she going to sleep with it like this? Because she needed her sleep, to deal with this infuriating man in the morning.

'But I haven't even bathed yet,' she said, miserable now. Why had she let Elsa leave? When she needed her? It would be humiliating to call her back.

And how had he brought her so low, after only one night?

'Why not?' he asked through the door, the tone of arrogant superiority almost as unjust as the snap of self-righteousness and impatience. 'What the hell have you been doing in there?'

Temper rose up to choke her, obliterating the misery until all she could see was her ruined hair through a red mist of fury.

She marched to the door, flicked the lock, and swung it open.

'You arrogant bastard,' she declared, not caring any more about the use of profanity. 'This!' She threw her hand up to indicate the mess on her head. 'This is what I've been doing.'

But then the red mist cleared, and shock followed, as she realised he was leaning against the door frame practically naked.

Where were his trousers, and his shoes?

And why did his bare chest, visible through his unbuttoned dress shirt, have to look so magnificent? Was that a tattoo on his left pectoral muscle? Whose name was that scrawled across his heart under a dusting of chest hair? Her gaze trailed down, tracking the tantalising line of hair bisecting ripped abdominal muscles, and hip flexors that made her mouth water, only to land on a pair of stretchy black boxer briefs. The waistband hung low on his lean waist, the legs stretched tight over roped thigh muscles while leaving virtually nothing to the imagination at his crotch.

She swallowed heavily, before she choked. If she had thought that thick ridge was impressive before, it was making her abdomen turn into a lava flow now. Was he erect? Or just extremely well endowed?

'What the hell happened to your hair?'

The gruff question had her gaze shooting back to his face so fast she almost got whiplash. Horrified heat seared her collarbone.

'Y-y-you…' She cleared her throat as the lava flow rose up to incinerate her cheeks—and dry her throat to dust. 'You happened to it,' she managed, beyond grateful to discover he had been focussed on her hair and was unaware of her checking out the contents of his boxers.

His gaze dropped to her flaming face. 'Uh-huh? How exactly is the Leaning Tower of Hair my fault?'

The asinine comment had her anger surging back to cover her mortification. Especially when his gaze roamed over her cleavage again—with that arrogant entitlement that had derailed her common sense earlier in the evening.

Well, he wasn't going to derail it again, she told herself staunchly. Despite the continuing lava flow from stretchy-boxer-briefs-gate.

She was now fully focussed on her main priority—which involved making this marriage work for the duration of the year they had agreed upon, and not risking torpedoing it for the reckless pursuit of temporary pleasure, which was clearly his priority.

She would have to be the adult here, because it was becoming increasingly obvious Travis Lord had never had to think about anything but himself and the pursuit of his own gratification.

Her spine stiffened with self-righteousness. Unfortunately,

even standing tall, it didn't do much to decrease his massive height advantage, especially when he levered himself off the door, and stared down at her from his full height.

She lifted her chin, so she could glare at him—and not his left pec.

'It's your fault because you were so rude and obnoxious to Elsa earlier, she was scared to stay in the same room with you,' she said, upset all over again at the way he had spoken to her maid. 'And I've never had to do this without her.'

To her utter astonishment though, instead of mocking her for being unable to handle dismantling her own chignon, flags of colour appeared on his tanned cheeks. 'Yeah, you're right, I screwed up,' he murmured. 'So I called her and apologised.'

'You… You *did*?' she asked, so surprised by the admission she wasn't sure she could believe him.

But when he began to speak, his contrition was unmistakable, and disarmed her temper completely.

'I lost my cool. I'm not great at being on show for eight hours straight,' he said, the weary tone forcing her to admit she might have misjudged him. After all, she was used to official events, and today had been extremely taxing even for her.

'But I behaved like a dick and there's no excuse for that,' he continued. 'Plus my mom would have given me hell if she'd ever heard me talk to the help like that…' He trailed off. The dark sincerity in his gaze—and the mention of his mother, who Isabelle recalled had been a cleaner—made her heart slow and guilt prickle at the back of her throat.

She *had* misjudged him.

She had assumed he was one of those rich, entitled men who treated the people who worked for them with contempt, and she had disliked him intensely for it—on very little evidence. Which forced her to question her own motivations.

She could see now, she had *wanted* to judge him because over the last two months—during all those silly texts—she had found his blunt sense of humour so enjoyable, his irreverence so exhilarating and the way he saw her—as a woman and not a queen—impossibly exciting. And it had scared her. Because wanting him to kiss her again, to make love to her even, wasn't nearly as terrifying as acknowledging how much she had enjoyed his attention and approval.

It would be pathetic if it weren't so cowardly.

'I apologised to Arne the Stickler as well,' he said. 'Cos I was kind of a dick to him, too.'

'Thank you, I appreciate that,' she said, humbled by his honesty, and his willingness to admit his mistake not just to her staff but also to her.

He shrugged. 'You're welcome, Your Majesty,' he said with the wry humour that she found incredibly beguiling. As well as annoying.

He stared at the bird's nest on her head again. 'How about I take a crack at it?'

The sharp tug under her breastbone at the bold request was complicated by the heat sinking deep into her abdomen.

'Seems the least I can do after scaring off your maid.'

'I'm not sure that's a good idea,' she managed, far too aware of his state of undress and the slow thunder of her heartbeat.

Admitting how much she had come to enjoy certain aspects of his character only made him more dangerous to her peace of mind... And her flagging boundaries.

'You got a better idea?' he said. 'Cos it's close to midnight now, so hauling Elsa out of bed to do it is only going to make us both look like dicks.'

She huffed out a laugh, despite the rising tension. Why did she find the familiar way he spoke to her so appealing?

She dismissed the sentimental thought. Or tried to. And

pressed her palm against the mass of hair, hopelessly aware of his focussed stare as he awaited her answer…

'It's okay, I should probably just sleep on it and let Elsa deal with it in the morning. It's a fairly major job and you're probably tired too,' she tried to reason.

'I'm not *that* tired,' he said, the sensual smile having a disturbing effect on her already erratic heartbeat. He captured her wrist—his touch as bold as it was sure—and drew her hand down. 'Seems like a job I ought to learn, just in case,' he added, his thumb rubbing casually against the pulse throbbing wildly in her wrist. 'Even as your fake husband you never know when I might need the experience.' The slow sensual smile spread. 'Plus, I've been wanting to demolish that hairdo for hours.'

'I… *Really?*' she said as her sex clenched alarmingly.

'Yeah. I should probably tell you,' he said, lifting her hand and opening her fist as he continued to speak in that lazy, husky tone. 'I've acquired a major hair fetish in the last couple months.'

'You… You have?' she said, inanely, but unable to think clearly.

'Uh-huh.' He pressed a kiss into the centre of her palm.

She jolted as sensation arrowed into her sex. She should object, should tug her hand free, but she appeared to be unable to do anything but inhale the enticing cedarwood scent that clung to him.

'Kind of perverted, I know, but I think we should work with it.' Letting go of her hand, he placed his palm on her waist and directed her back into the bathroom.

Stopping in front of the large marble vanity, he placed his hands on her shoulders and turned her towards the mirror. He stood behind her, his broad shoulders somehow filling the large bathroom.

'So where do I start?' he asked, his tone casual, but the

fierce purpose in his gaze as it met hers in the glass staggering her.

She directed her gaze to the rigid tangle of curls and clips and pins—trying to focus on the question, and the task at hand... And not the sight of him—so large and overwhelming behind her.

'If you could get the rest of the pins out, that would be a big help,' she murmured, feeling both hopelessly self-conscious, but also strangely exhilarated.

'Right, here goes. Tell me if it hurts, okay?'

She nodded, watching as he spent some time assessing the damage, then located a pin at her crown. He wiggled it then dragged it free, with infinite patience. Sensation sparked across her scalp, waking up nerve-endings that had been deadened hours ago.

His gaze met hers as he threw the pin on the vanity. 'One down,' he said. 'Only ten thousand to go.'

She chuckled, releasing a little of the tension in her stomach.

'Hey, don't laugh, I take my work seriously.'

She smiled, trying not to fall for his charm... Or get too fixated on the muscular torso so close to her back.

True to his word he worked diligently, watching her reaction intently as he located and pulled out each pin, each clip and comb. She stood as still as she could under his care, but it became increasingly difficult with each slow brush of his fingertips, each gentle tug, the silence as he concentrated on freeing her hair only making the task seem more intimate—and arousing.

By the time he had wriggled the final clip loose, her entire scalp had become a riot of sensation, her heartbeat thundering in her chest and echoing in her sex.

How had he made her head an erogenous zone?

He thrust strong fingers into her hair and the heavy mass

cascaded onto her shoulders. A moan escaped her as he kneaded her scalp, massaging away the soreness.

'Better?' he asked as he dropped his hands to her shoulders.

Their gazes collided in the mirror.

'Yes, thank you,' she murmured, aware of his nearness, knowing how much she had enjoyed his ministrations. 'I should probably go to bed now.'

She went to step away from him, but he held her in place.

'Hold up,' he said. His hands skimmed down her bare arms to land on her waist. 'How about I help you with the dress?' he murmured, resting his chin on the top of her head.

The question sounded innocent, but the wicked light in his eyes as he awaited her answer was anything but.

The throbbing in her sex became unbearable.

'And the corset?' he added, with no pretence at all of innocence now. 'Because I've been dreaming of getting you out of that all day.'

The husky comment reverberated through her torso.

Would it be so wrong? To admit how much she wanted to feel those strong hands on her again? A part of her knew this was leading somewhere she had already decided they could not go.

But her previous cowardice came back to taunt her now. The hot weight in her sex impossible to ignore. And all she could do was nod.

CHAPTER NINE

HUNGER TORE THROUGH Travis as Isabelle lowered her chin in the barest hint of a nod.

She was beyond beautiful, the cascade of curls like a golden cloud, her eyes dark with the desire she'd denied earlier.

Progress.

She'd never looked more like a queen in that moment—regal and proud. But also somehow fragile and untouched, the wary light in her eyes making her seem vulnerable.

The realisation he was going to have to work to earn her trust only captivated him more.

He inhaled her intoxicating fragrance—wild flowers and sin—then gathered the heavy locks, feeling her delicious shiver in response, and swept them over her shoulder.

He studied the fastenings of her gown. The tiny hooks were a problem, his hands weren't exactly made for delicate work, but he'd managed to deal with her hair without hurting her. He just needed to take it slow.

Locating the hook at her nape, he released it—the hunger surging as she shuddered. He worked his way down her back, freeing her from the garment, as each delicious quiver ricocheted through her body and into his.

Did she know how responsive she was to him?

By the time he reached her waist, the gown was gaping open to reveal the corset. He eased the ornate silk off her shoulders and she released a deep breath as the fabric pooled at her feet.

Damn, but her cleavage was like a work of art, her slender curves displayed in nothing but the cream silk corset, and some lacy panties.

'Thank you,' she said again, in that studiously polite tone, which only made her livewire responses to him more of a turn-on.

'Corset next?' he murmured, shifting back so she didn't become aware of the growing bulge in his shorts.

Again, she nodded. Triggering another surge of desire.

He needed to pace himself again so he took a moment to stare out of the bathroom window and slow his breathing. Snow drifted down in thick flakes from the canopy of stars in the night sky, blanketing the gorge below.

Mostly in control again, he assessed the corset's intricate tapes, rubbing his thumb across the reddened skin where the panels had dug into her back.

She bucked against the slight touch.

'Why did you need this thing anyway?' he asked.

'The stylist and the designer felt it would enhance my figure,' she said.

'Like it needs enhancing,' he scoffed.

The flush on her face flared, and he wondered again if she knew how gorgeous she was.

He went to work on the corset. But her vicious shivers as he released each tape only turbo-charged the heat that had been building between them for hours, days, months even...

Peeling off the stiff silk contraption at last, he placed his mouth between her shoulder blades and kissed the dewy skin. A soft moan broke from her lips.

Desire flared as the corset landed on the floor and he took in the sight of all that flushed deliciously pink flesh in nothing but a pair of minuscule lace panties and silk stockings held up by a suspender belt. She had clasped her arms over her bare breasts. But her shyness was as captivating as the arousal darkening her green eyes to black.

'Don't cover yourself, Belle,' he groaned. 'You're beautiful.'

He could see her surprise and pleasure at the compliment—which made no sense. Surely he couldn't be the first guy to tell her that?

The streak of jealousy—and possessiveness—at the thought of all those other guys made even less sense. They might be married, but she wasn't his.

Even so, he skimmed his thumb across her nape, delighted when her eyes flared with need.

Her arms remained folded over her breasts, but they weren't hiding much.

He stroked her bare shoulders, causing more of those delicious shivers. Circling her waist, he flattened his palms against her belly, just above the lace of her panties, to draw her against him.

'I want to kiss you again, Belle,' he murmured against her neck, determined to make it a question, even though the hunger was crucifying him.

'Where?' she asked—in that puzzled, polite way she had that he was beginning to realise masked so much passion.

His lips quirked. How could she be so hot and yet so adorable?

'Anywhere you'll let me,' he replied.

Her eyes glazed with arousal, but her teeth dug into her lip, the panic resurfacing. Grasping her shoulders, he turned her to face him—before she could get out the no he suspected might be coming.

'How about we start with this mouth?' he said, lifting her lips to his.

She blinked, then nodded.

Thank the Lord.

* * *

Isabelle's breath guttered out as Travis's lips captured hers.

But unlike the kiss she had obsessed about for weeks, this kiss wasn't coaxing or careful, it was demanding and forceful. A groan she couldn't control reverberated through her as she opened her mouth to welcome him in. Vicious sensation centred in her sex as his tongue thrust deep.

The pleasure spread like wildfire as he wrapped his arms around her to bring her flush against him. She could feel the thrust of his erection against her belly. Hard and long, and more than a little overwhelming even through his shorts. She writhed against the thick ridge, suddenly desperate to relieve the aching pain emanating from her core.

His head rose suddenly, and he tore his mouth from hers.

'I'm sorry,' she mumbled.

His lips curved in a wry smile, which had her wariness resurfacing. Could he see what he did to her?

'What for?' he asked, his gravelly voice scraping the many sensitive parts he had exploited so easily.

Because I don't know how to do this.

The words reverberated in her mind, too revealing to be said aloud.

'I'm still not sure this is a good idea,' she muttered.

He nodded. But the demand on his face remained as he cradled her cheek and dragged his thumb across her lips.

'If you want to tell me where you like to be touched, we could see if I can change your mind,' he said, the purpose in his gaze as intoxicating as the renewed throbbing in her sex.

Again, she should say no—she had no idea where she liked to be touched.

But her control was already in tatters, the aching desire consuming her, and another nod became inevitable when he skimmed his thumb under her bare breast—and shocking sensation arrowed down to her core.

He turned her around to face the mirror again. 'How about we start there?' he said, nuzzling the skin under her earlobe as he took her wrists to gently release the arms she had shielding her breasts.

Her harsh intake of breath echoed around the room as he cupped the heavy orbs.

'Good?' he asked as he circled the throbbing peaks while kissing the pulse in her neck.

She groaned. 'Yes.'

He let out a raw chuckle, but continued to caress her, toying with the responsive peaks as she leaned against him, her legs becoming boneless.

'So where next, Belle?' he asked, the husky tone making her body quake anew.

Her eyes fluttered open, and she met his molten gaze in the glass. That he was letting her set the pace, dictate his moves, felt empowering somehow—and spurred the reckless excitement.

How could this be wrong? When it felt so right?

'Just… Anywhere…' she managed, her voice thick with the yearning she could no longer disguise.

'Good choice,' he said.

His hands left her breasts to wrap around her body, holding her against him, making her aware of his need as well as her own.

She gasped, the surge of pleasure so immense she could no longer resist it, or him.

Fireworks burst in the night sky outside to mark the end of their wedding day.

'We missed the fireworks,' she murmured, inanely.

His gaze roamed over her—the coloured lights reflected in his eyes. 'No, we didn't.'

He wasn't wrong, she realised, because the thunder and pop from outside were nothing compared to the fire sparking across her nerve-endings as he held her close while his hands stroked and caressed, her breasts, her waist, her hips...

Her chest heaved as she stared at their reflection—her so small and needy, him so tall and commanding. He lifted her arm, draped it over his neck. She clung onto him, her breasts thrust out, the air trapped in her lungs as anticipation fired through her. Long strong fingers traced across her ribs, circling her belly button and finally delving into her panties, to locate the swollen folds of her sex.

'You're so wet for me, Belle,' he growled, sending a fierce wave of validation and approval through her molten flesh.

She moaned, her body a mass of sensation, the guttural sound both plea and prayer as he skimmed over her centre at last—the bundle of nerves begging for his touch.

Her legs weakened, her knees trembling, her thighs tensing and releasing as he circled and delved, forcing her to focus on that one raw secret spot as the pleasure built, and twisted, and burned.

'Please... I...' She couldn't talk, couldn't really say what it was she wanted. She'd never felt so exposed or so needy before, her senses heightened beyond what she could bear.

'I've got you, Belle, just relax.'

She tried to do as he asked as the tension gripped her body.

Then he eased one thick finger—with aching slowness—into her. She bucked, shocked by the intrusion, which triggered a bolt of pleasure so immense her desperation increased.

Then his thumb touched the very heart of her. The violent pleasure centred and crested—fierce and raw and unstoppable—shooting her over the edge, the vicious coil releasing in a rush.

She cried out as he worked her through the staggering sensations. She clung to his neck, bucking against his hand, as she rode that unending, unendurable wave of bliss to her limits and beyond.

The waves of orgasm weakened at last. Her whole body shook as he finally released her from the decadent torture. The glittering afterglow gave way to brutal reality as he clasped her waist and murmured against her neck.

'Ready for round two?'

She opened her eyes to find him watching her intently, his gaze dark with yearning. The long column of flesh thrust against her back as his palm moved to cup her backside.

She lurched away from the possessive touch. 'I... We can't.'

'No?' The fog of desire cleared a little. 'Why not?' Her heart lurched in her chest as he bracketed her hips, the thick ridge cradled against her bottom. 'It's just sex.'

Except it's not just sex to me.

She turned, folding shaky arms back over her breasts—which were still tender from his ministrations.

Why had she let it go this far?

She wanted to believe theirs was nothing more than a strong physical connection—as he did—and perhaps the culmination of denying this aspect of her life for far too long. But her heart continued to do somersaults in her chest, and she knew she felt something for him, something she had never felt for another man, or she would never have let him dismantle her defences so thoroughly.

'I... I need to go to bed,' she said, frantic now, as well as scared. 'We have a long day tomorrow.'

One dark eyebrow hiked up his forehead. 'For real?'

'I'm sorry.' She eased past him, the fear rioting now, the feel of those strong fingers on her, inside her, still humming in her sex. 'I can't...'

She glanced down, aware of the thick erection straining

against the front of his shorts, the outline making the throbbing in her sex worse.

'I'm not on any birth control…' she lied, grasping at a way to extricate herself with some degree of dignity. And poise. And conceal from him how utterly he'd overwhelmed her.

'I've got condoms,' he offered.

'But I can't risk…' she began.

'It's okay, Belle, we can always take a rain check,' he said, the passion clearing from his eyes to be replaced by— well, nothing. She couldn't tell if he was angry with her or not. 'This isn't a transaction,' he murmured, his expression shuttered and unreadable.

Was he angry? Could he sense her distress?

'Thank you, for being so understanding,' she said, in a desperate attempt to distance herself again. But what else could she do? She'd let him see too much.

He'd given her something incredible, something she hadn't really believed existed until this moment. But beneath the woman he had awakened was that little girl who could be hurt far too easily—if she let herself want too much.

She needed time to rebuild her defences. And to close down the aching vulnerability in her heart, which he would never understand.

'Right,' he said, the slight edge in his voice making her feel ashamed once again of her cowardice.

She dashed from the bathroom and locked the connecting door.

It took her hours to finally fall asleep, though, her body still humming from his caresses—as she listened to him showering and imagined him naked and aroused.

By the time she finally fell into a fitful sleep, she had examined and discarded every possible outcome of her foolish decision to become intimate with her fake husband…

And every one of them was a disaster, starting with how

on earth she was going to survive ten nights in his home in Colorado with her dignity and her sense of self intact. Because he had a power over her now that wasn't equal, or equitable. And she had already committed much more to this relationship than she could possibly afford to lose.

CHAPTER TEN

'YOUR MAJESTY, LOOK this way! Can we see your smile? Are you looking forward to your first Christmas as a married woman?'

'Travis, what's it like to be a member of European royalty?'

'How is your first day of married life going, Your Majesty?'

Travis wrapped his arm around Isabelle's waist, tugging her closer, as the reporters and photographers fired questions, and the barrage of camera flashes blinded them both. They were supposed to be putting on a show here, for the world's media. A show he hadn't wanted any part of and wanted even less part of after the way last night had ended. Because touching her now—after watching her lose herself in his arms, then close herself off—was torture.

His frustration built, though, when she stiffened against him.

He tightened his hold on her. 'Relax,' he whispered in her ear as they stood together on the tarmac at the palace's private airfield, his company jet fuelled and ready to take them away from this circus.

Last night had knocked him sideways. He'd never experienced foreplay like it before. She'd been so vibrant and responsive to his touch, despite the weird innocence that clung to her.

For a moment, as she'd writhed and groaned, her body flushed with pleasure, her inhibitions gone, he'd felt as if he'd achieved something rare and special—which was sentimental crap, of course, but, even so, his ego had taken a hit when he'd heard the door lock click.

He'd had to turn the shower temperature down to frigid—and take himself in hand like a teenager, which had been humiliating. But it wasn't sexual frustration that had made it impossible for him to sleep afterwards.

He hadn't lied to her. As far as he was concerned, sex was never a transaction. It was always a woman's prerogative to say no. And he guessed the birth control thing was an issue—he certainly didn't want to add any more complications to this relationship when it was already complicated enough. But he'd seen the lie in her eyes when she'd offered up that excuse. And the panic and regret as soon as the afterglow had faded. Which had forced him to ask the question, why had she freaked out?

Because the hollow ache when she'd run out on him had reminded him of when he was a twelve-year-old kid, at his first junior snowboarding championship, and his old man had showed up with his 'real sons' and stood in the crowd to cheer for them, instead of Travis.

That would be the needy kid he'd buried a long time ago.

He didn't need anyone's praise or approval any more, especially not from the woman standing next to him—who wasn't even his real wife. So how had she made him feel like that dumb kid again?

'Travis, can you tell us why you two left the festivities so early? And missed the fireworks? Was that planned? Or was it a spontaneous decision?'

Travis zeroed in on the young female reporter at the front of the pack who had shouted out the intrusive question. And was grinning at him now with deliberate innuendo.

Isabelle stiffened, but of course she didn't respond. Her dignified silence, though, and the memory of exactly what they had been doing when those fireworks had gone off had the last of his patience with this crap snapping like a dry twig.

He'd been advised by the press secretary not to respond to the reporters—that they wouldn't expect answers to their questions as it was all part of the protocol that the Queen didn't react.

But no way was he letting that pass.

'Why do you think we left early?' he said. 'We're newly-weds. How about you take a wild guess…?'

He heard Isabelle gasp, just before the media horde exploded into a cacophony of sound—each shouted question cruder and more provocative than the last.

The palace press secretary looked as if he were going to have an aneurysm. The expressions on the faces of the members of Isabelle's court and the representatives of the privy council—who had been assembled to see them off—had gone varying shades of shocked and appalled. While the palace guards had to use their decorative rifles to restrain the surging tide of tabloid hacks sensing an exclusive.

Isabelle went deathly still beside him—her cheeks stained a vivid scarlet, her emerald eyes glassy with shock.

To hell with this.

He grasped her hand. 'We're out of here.'

She didn't object, didn't utter a sound, probably because she couldn't without making even more of a scene. But somehow her refusal to react only infuriated him more.

He didn't break stride as he marched across the tarmac with her hand gripped firmly in his, then led her up the steps into the waiting plane.

The steward closed the plane door behind them, shutting out the media circus. But as he led Belle into the jet's lounge, he could sense her disapproval, even as the regal mask—which had slipped spectacularly last night—remained firmly in place.

The volatile emotions hit critical mass and the hollow ache in his gut widened, just as it had on that day so long ago, when he'd aced every race, broken a ton of records taking stupid risks to impress a man who had looked right through him as if he didn't exist.

'Mr Lord, we're cleared for take-off whenever you're ready,' the pilot said, greeting them in the gangway.

'Great. We're ready now,' Travis replied. 'Let's get the hell out of here.'

The pilot nodded and headed to the cockpit.

'We'll strap ourselves in, Bill,' he said to the steward. 'Give us some privacy.'

'Absolutely, sir.' If the guy was surprised, he didn't show it. 'Just let me know if you want any refreshments once we reach our cruising altitude,' he finished before disappearing into the service pantry.

Travis walked through to the lounge, so on edge now he was surprised steam wasn't coming out of his ears. Isabelle had taken one of the leather armchairs and fastened her belt. Her face was still hot with embarrassment, but her expression remained impassive as she stared out of the window.

The tension tightened like a vice around his ribs.

He took the seat opposite her. The plane's engines rumbled to life, drowning out the furore outside.

He held his tongue as the jet taxied down the runway, waiting for her to give him hell for the crude comment, which was probably slapped all over the Internet already.

But Isabelle remained calm and unmoved, her hands folded in her lap, the only sign she even had a pulse the staggered rise and fall of her breasts beneath the tailored silk blouse—those would be the breasts he'd had in his hands the night before and discovered were supremely sensitive.

When the jet reached its cruising altitude—and the pilot informed them over the public address system of their eleven-hour flight time to Denver International—she still hadn't said a damn word. She hadn't even made eye contact.

Was she giving him the silent treatment?

To hell with that.

Leaning forward, he grasped her chin and directed her gaze to his.

'If you've got something to say to me, Belle, you best spit it out.'

She blinked, the mask of indifference collapsing to be replaced by something he liked even less... And recognised from the previous evening... Panic, and regret.

'I apologise. For last night. I should not have let things become so...intimate...' Isabelle murmured, both mortally embarrassed and out of her depth in the face of his anger—while also feeling like the worst kind of fraud. 'It was wrong to leave you unsatisfied.'

She'd sensed Travis's frustration, the impatience bristling under his skin, ever since she had met him in the chauffeur-driven car taking them both to the airstrip half an hour ago for the photo call before their flight. She had wanted to say something, *anything*, to defuse the tension and make amends for her selfishness, as she suspected it was not the done thing to enjoy a man's touch with the fervour she had enjoyed his, and then leave him visibly erect without offering him some relief.

But what could she say? When she knew not one thing about the etiquette of sexual relationships. So, she had remained silent.

She had paid for her cowardice though. Because having to stand so close to him during the photoshoot, while trying not to react to the heavy weight of his palm resting possessively on her waist, and the brush of his breath against her ear when he told her to relax—exactly as he had done the night before—had been excruciating.

He let go of her chin and cursed.

She flinched. Had she said the wrong thing? He didn't look pleased by her apology. If anything he looked even more frustrated. And appalled.

'Don't do that polite reserved crap with me, it drives me nuts. And don't apologise for last night. What the hell does that even mean?' He lifted his fingers to do sarcastic air quotes. '"It was wrong to leave you unsatisfied."'

She looked away from him again, her face on fire. 'It means I had an orgasm and you didn't,' she said, as calmly as she could while her hands were shaking. 'And I suspect that sexual frustration—and more specifically anger with my selfishness last night—is the reason you were unable to control your temper with that reporter,' she added, determined to acknowledge her part in this fiasco. 'Which is why I felt an apology was appropriate.'

He swore again, the word low with fury now. 'Exactly how much of a jackass do you think I am?'

'I don't know,' she snapped, her own patience starting to evaporate.

She was trying to do the right thing here. But she'd had a virtually sleepless night. And while she had no doubt at all she was partially responsible for this morning's outburst, there was a limit to how much blame she was prepared to take.

'Although so far you haven't surprised me,' she added, her voice clipped.

How was last night's fiasco and his difficult behaviour this morning all her fault? He was a grown man. And he was the one who had pushed to reset the terms of their agreement as soon as they had been alone together. Yes, she had been a willing participant in what had transpired—far too willing—but shouldn't he take some of the responsibility for this disaster, too?

He collapsed back into his chair and yelled another profanity at the ceiling—the anger making his chest flex under his shirt. The sight sent an inconvenient shot of awareness through her tired body—because the memory of exactly what all those muscles looked like, flexing in unison as he worked her into a frenzy, was now apparently tattooed on her frontal lobe.

Fabulous!

'Wow, you're really a piece of work, aren't you?' he said, his gaze fixed on her again, his dark eyes flinty with temper. 'How do you do it?'

'How do I do what?'

'Pull off the "ice queen" act like that.' He leant forward, resting tanned forearms on his knees. 'When we both know there's enough passion inside you to set fire to Alaska.'

'It's not an act,' she said. Disturbed by the way he was staring at her now, with the same intensity that had terrified her the night before, as if he could see past all her defences, all the emotions she had learned to control, to find the insecure, needy girl beneath.

He laughed, the sound raw and brittle. 'Yeah, it is. Don't forget I've seen you when you're aching for my touch. Smelt your need when you're clambering for release. And there's nothing cold about you then, is there?' He leant back, his gaze searing in its contempt. 'You know, it would be pretty funny that you think I'm good enough to pretend to marry, but not good enough to touch you—if it weren't so damn insulting.'

Shock reverberated through her at the accusations she didn't understand.

Superior? Not good enough?

Her own temper died, consumed by confusion and regret.

Clearly, she had insulted him, without intending to. The thought seemed incongruous—given the man's ego up to now had appeared stronger and more resilient than the White Ridge itself. But when he turned away, she noticed the muscle clenching in his jaw and the dark flags of colour on his cheeks—and it occurred to her she might not be the only one who had allowed themselves to get carried away last night.

Strangely, the thought calmed her rampaging pulse and her own feelings of inadequacy.

She hadn't meant to insult him, certainly did not believe herself to be superior to him. But the fact he had not been completely unmoved by their intimacy made her feel a little less insecure, a little less powerless.

She swallowed, struggling to contain the inexplicable spurt of exhilaration at the thought she was not the only one who had been overwhelmed.

But how could she convince him her decision to leave so abruptly had nothing to do with her opinion of him and everything to do with her own inexperience? Without creating an even bigger minefield for them to tiptoe through in the days ahead?

'You said it was just sex,' she said at last.

His head whipped round, skewering her with a look that could immolate lead. 'So what?'

But this time, she wasn't fooled by that furious glare.

'I assumed that to mean you were not emotionally engaged in the physical intimacy we shared last night. But how can that be so if I hurt your feelings by leaving you unsatisfied?'

Okay? What now?

Travis stared at the woman in front of him, totally speechless for the first time in his life. And not sure now whether to be insulted, or angry... Or simply stunned.

He wanted to hang onto his temper, but it was impossible in the face of that curious expression that seemed as confused as it was forthright.

Hell, not only did he not know what to feel, he didn't

even know what to think. Her careful analysis of last night both vaguely insulting and yet brutally honest at one and the same time.

One minute she'd been accusing him of being a class-A jerk who figured she owed him sex just because he'd given her an orgasm. And the next... Had she just accused him of being a drama queen as well as a jerk?

'I wasn't hurt,' he managed at last. 'That's just dumb. Believe me, I know how to handle rejection.' Even if he hadn't had to handle it in a long time, and certainly not in the bedroom before now... He had always respected boundaries when it came to sex—simply by never getting too invested in the outcome. Sex was fun, sex was recreational, it wasn't about emotional engagement for him and it never had been. Because that would make him a chump as well as a jerk.

But even as the denial echoed in his head, he was forced to admit no other woman had ever made him feel like he had as a kid again.

Surely that was just because she was a queen though, and their whole situation was more complicated than any relationship he'd ever had... And he hadn't even slept with her, yet.

'I see,' she said, in that infuriating way she had that made it sound as if she doubted he was being honest with her, or with himself.

'Listen, I don't get emotionally engaged when it comes to sex. Or relationships for that matter. And I never look for validation and approval from other people, because my old man taught me that was a mug's game when I was twelve years old,' he blurted out, determined to convince himself now, as well as her.

This relationship was no different from all the others he'd had over the years. Maybe their circumstances were a lot weirder. And her status had bothered him more than he'd thought—exposing an inferiority complex he hadn't even known he had until last night—plus the no-sex rule had added a challenge that he had found impossible to resist once their chemistry had become obvious… But that was it.

The sharp light in her eyes softened though, the curiosity turning to compassion.

'I thought you didn't know your father's identity,' she said, and he realised he'd said too much. *Way* too much. Because he'd just let slip a piece of information he'd worked hard to keep hidden. Not because he gave a damn what people thought of his origins, but because he'd never wanted to answer any questions about someone who meant nothing to him and had chosen not to be a part of his life. Plus, he hadn't wanted anyone looking at him the way she was looking at him right now—as if that bastard or his absence had had any impact on him.

Sure, not having a father had been tough at times when he was a kid, because his mom had been forced to work like a dog to keep them clothed and fed. But never having anything given to him on a silver platter had been a blessing in disguise, because it had made him that much more determined to win at all costs and on his own terms.

'I always knew who he was,' he said, because denying the truth now would just make it look as if he cared. 'My mom cleaned his place in Aspen for years.'

He shrugged, uncomfortable now, because she was still looking at him as if any of this mattered, when it never had, not to him anyhow.

'I think she had some dumb notion that if he knew about me, he'd want to be my dad. Because she was a romantic, who always believed the best in people, even him. And it was easier to kid herself he had loved her once—than face the reality that he'd taken advantage of a seventeen-year-old virgin who had a summer job cleaning his vacation home, while his wife and kids were out of town.'

He stared out of the window, the bitter taste in his mouth when he spoke about his old man annoying him. It was kind of lowering to realise that thinking about his mom's misguided attempts to rewrite the narrative of his parents' relationship could still make him mad.

'As far as he was concerned,' he added. 'I was a mistake he'd made that he didn't want to acknowledge. That upset her, but it was fine by me.'

'He sounds like a selfish and unpleasant man,' Isabelle said.

He let out a hollow laugh. 'Yeah, probably, I never met him,' he lied easily enough, because he'd given her too much information already.

She frowned. 'But if you never met him, how did he teach you about rejection when you were only twelve?'

For the love of Mike! Why hadn't he kept his mouth shut?

'It's a long story,' he growled.

'We have eleven hours,' she countered.

'It's a long *boring* story…'

Which is none of your business, he wanted to add. But didn't, because he was the dumbass who had made it her business and it sounded way too defensive.

'And I'm shattered,' he added, unclipping his belt.

'I understand,' she said. 'Royal duties are often more taxing than they look.'

'You're telling me,' he said, ignoring the prickle of unease that she was treating him with kid gloves now—as if he were some kind of hothead who couldn't keep it together under pressure.

But then he'd created that rod for his own back, by behaving like a jerk this morning—not just to the press, but also to her.

He'd accused her of judging him, when what he'd really been doing was judging himself—just as he had as a kid. No wonder he'd gotten all bent out of shape about nothing.

He thrust his fingers through his hair as he stood up, the pressure of the last twenty-four hours taking a toll.

He'd never been a guy to overthink anything, especially not his own emotions, but then he'd also never had to spend eight hours straight pretending to be in love with the whole world watching, while wearing a monkey suit and not being able to touch what he was already supposed to have.

Note to self: marriage in name only totally sucks when you have the hots for your fake wife.

He still didn't know why Isabelle had run off like that, why she hadn't wanted the quick stress fix that great sex could provide. Because one thing last night had proved was that she had the hots for him too.

But he had ten days in Colorado to figure out if there was a way they could make their chemistry work as a stress-relief valve without having it blow up in both their faces.

He'd also been pretty arrogant thinking the duties of monarchy were nothing. He could see that now. After less than twenty-four hours of living in the full glare of that spotlight he'd somehow managed to dredge up stuff from his childhood that he'd gotten over years ago.

He had to give her some credit for holding it together this morning when he hadn't. He was also pretty curious now about how she did that, while also being so artless and unworldly. Maybe it was just an act, but he wasn't as convinced about that any more.

'I'm gonna head to one of the bedrooms at the back and crash,' he said. Then, because she was still looking at him like a stick of dynamite that might explode at any second, the devil got the better of him again. 'If you want to finish what we started last night, you're welcome to join me.'

Her face flushed a deep shade of pink—and her eyebrows rose. 'I... I don't think so,' she sputtered.

He grinned at her reaction. Good to know he could still unsettle her—because she sure as hell unsettled him.

'Lady's choice, Your Majesty.' He gave her a mocking bow, then headed to the bedroom. Alone.

One thing was for sure, he needed to get some shut-eye if he was going to stop himself from behaving like a dumbass again.

But as he showered, the thought of *actually* finishing what they had started had a predictable effect, and it occurred to him he needed to find a way to handle this hunger, if he was going to get what he wanted out of this deal—without crippling himself in the process.

'I understand.'

Isabelle stared after Travis as he strolled to the back of the plane, his teasing offer of finishing what they had started only making her feel more insecure and confused... And hopelessly turned on.

Why on earth had she said she understood him, when she didn't understand the man at all? Admittedly, her knowledge of men and relationships was extremely limited, but Travis Lord was already turning out to be a great deal more complex than she had assumed.

The revelations about his father had shocked her, but also saddened her—the curt, clipped tone when he talked about that relationship, or rather the lack of it, so unlike the relaxed, confident, and frankly shallow man she had believed him to be.

Because she had seen the strength of feeling even as he had boasted about his lack of emotional engagement and heard the suppressed rage in his voice, even as he had pretended his father's rejection had meant nothing.

How could that be the case? Surely no one could be treated with such casual cruelty by their own flesh and blood and come out of it unscathed?

But what had moved her even more was the sense of connection.

After all, she had suffered a similar loss in her childhood too, when her parents had died so suddenly. At the time, the one thing that had helped her recover from that loss was the knowledge they had died together, and that they had loved her very much—even if they had been unable to show it in demonstrative ways.

How did you survive the loss of a parent, though, when their absence in your life had been a choice, not an accident? Had Travis survived it by persuading himself he couldn't be hurt by it, even though he clearly had been?

Whatever the answer, it was clear a fascinatingly complex and passionate man lay beneath the veneer of relaxed charm and devil-may-care confidence. A man she needed to get to know better.

Surely if she could understand him, it would enhance the time they spent together over the next year. It would also help to ease him into the role of consort, and help her better manage the charade they were forced to play, which was clearly going to be more difficult for both of them than either one of them had assumed.

That said, she also knew she needed to be careful. Because while Travis Lord presented an intriguing emotional puzzle, he also had an aura about him—a latent, potent, sexual energy—which she found disturbingly attractive.

How could she be sure she wouldn't freak out again, and make matters even more difficult between them? Or worse, give in to this chemistry only to become overwhelmed by feelings he had made it clear would not be reciprocated?

She yawned as the young steward popped his head around the lounge's doorway.

'Would you like me to serve lunch now, Your Majesty?' he asked. Then peered around the lounge area. 'Is Mr Lord in the restroom?'

Isabelle found her cheeks burning again. How did she explain Travis had repaired to his bedroom, without her? Would the young man think it odd? Given that they were newly-weds? And what if he had heard their argument? Of course, she had to trust Travis's staff, like her own, knew how to be discreet. But it would be necessary over the next ten days to learn how to create the illusion of intimacy for a wider audience—and contain any more emotional outbursts.

'Um… No,' she murmured. 'Thank you. I think we're good for now.'

She frowned. Having spent her whole life knowing exactly what to say at any given time or do in any given circumstance, she had no idea what was the done thing in an intimate relationship with a man, let alone a marriage.

Apparently, if she was going to teach Travis how to assume the responsibilities of royalty over the next ten days, they would have to teach each other how to look like a couple in love. Even though it was obvious he had no more aptitude for that than she did.

As she made her excuses to the steward and headed to the *other* bedroom at the back of the plane, it occurred to her the tangled web she was currently weaving might very well end up strangling her… Especially given that the fascinating man she'd chosen to weave it with had also proved to be impulsive, headstrong, dominating, far too hot and completely unpredictable.

Bother.

CHAPTER ELEVEN

ISABELLE'S BREATH CAUGHT when she glimpsed the huge steel and glass house as the helicopter flew over the forested gorge, before landing on a heliport on the far side of the ridge.

The vivid blue sky cast a clean, clear light over the Rocky Mountain range as far as the eye could see, spanning a staggering three thousand miles—south to New Mexico and north all the way to British Columbia. While the rock formations lacked the dramatic peaks and sharp descents of Androvia's younger Alpine range, there was something about the rugged, breathtaking terrain that made the land here seem wilder and more untamed.

Isabelle wrapped the thick down coat that she'd donned when they'd landed in Denver International around herself to climb down the helicopter's steps while Travis finished the flight checks with his co-pilot. She had hardly spoken with him since she'd woken on the jet to find him working on his laptop in the lounge, looking relaxed and far too handsome. Her grand plans to discuss all the things they should work on while they were in Colorado had hastily been put on hold as another bout of inappropriate yearning had assailed her.

Travis and the pilot began loading their luggage onto a two-seater quad bike parked next to the heliport once the chopper's blades had stopped.

How odd... Where are the house's staff?

'Hey, grab that bag, Belle,' Travis shouted at her.

She lifted the small suitcase that contained her cosmetics and toiletries. And joined him at the quad.

'Sling it in the back and hop in,' he said.

She felt the surge of affection at the casual way he spoke to her. Then felt foolish for her giddy reaction. Surely, he spoke to everyone in the same way? Exactly how sheltered was she?

She thanked the pilot, who had finished loading the bags—which appeared to be all hers apart from a large ruck-sack—and climbed into the quad.

'Thanks, Chad,' Travis said, slapping the pilot on the back. 'We'll see you on the first for the pick-up. I'll check in with Megan if we need anything, but otherwise have a great Christmas.'

Isabelle tensed. She'd conveniently forgotten about the up-coming festive season—thanks to the pressures of the wed-ding and the wedding night. She forced herself not to panic.

She had a plan to refocus their working relationship over the next ten days.

All she needed to do was find the right time to suggest it.

The pilot waved goodbye, promising not to lift off until they were at the house.

After jumping into the quad, Travis drove through a grove of aspens laden with snow. The track opened out onto the valley ridge. Isabelle's breathing clogged again as his moun-tain home appeared. The striking multi-level structure was much larger than she had expected, and as breathtaking as the stunning panoramic view across the Rockies.

He'd called the place a cabin, so she'd envisioned some-thing cosy and quaint made of wood. She certainly had not expected anything this modern—or this imposing. The steel and glass edifice was several storeys high and built into the ridge-line with terraces on two levels that ran the length of the house. A seventy-five-foot lap pool encased in glass hung over the cliff on the lower level. Steam rose from the water, which was open to the elements.

'You swim outdoors? At this time of year?' she asked.

He braked the quad in front of a four-car garage. 'Yeah, the water's heated to twenty degrees, so I don't freeze to death. Swimming is a good way to iron out the kinks after a day's boarding, or a workout in the gym here if the weather's not cooperating.' He slung his arm across the steering wheel, his gaze roaming over her—and sending her pulse into overdrive. 'I've always had a surplus of energy. I need to find ways to work it off during the day, or I'm ready to crawl out of my own skin by nightfall.'

'I... I see,' she stuttered.

He smiled, that slow sensual smile that had heat curling in her abdomen and made her feel as if she were about to crawl out of her own skin, too. Even though she had *never* had a problem with hyperactivity.

'Yeah, I guess you do now,' he murmured, the suggestive look making her sure he wasn't talking about swimming any more.

Apparently, their truce was over.

Before she could come up with a suitably non-confrontational response—and stop the heat from sinking any deeper into her sex—he had jumped out of the quad.

He slung his rucksack over a shoulder, then stacked a couple of her suitcases under his other arm. 'Grab what you can, and I'll come back for the rest.'

She lifted the biggest suitcase she could manage, not wanting to seem like a shirker, but wondering again where his staff were. Not that she minded carting her own luggage, but she was starting to become concerned about the silence... And that intense feeling of intimacy that had been so electrifying—and so problematic—the last time they'd been alone together.

'Open up.' He barked the command into the frosty air as they headed across the terrace. A glass panel slid open in the house's façade.

The electric door slid closed behind them as they entered the indoor space. The double-height living area was stunning, the glass walls giving them an unencumbered view of the frozen landscape, while the flames from a granite fireplace in the far wall threw a warm glow over the luxurious furnishings.

Isabelle spotted a strikingly modern kitchen on the other side of the living area—with bespoke wooden cabinetry and state-of-the-art appliances—but then she stopped dead. In the other corner of the living room was a ten-foot freshly cut fir tree, decorated with red silk ribbons, gold baubles and white fairy lights.

Emotion wrapped around her ribs, like a suffocating blanket, threatening to yank her back into the past, as the memories she had suppressed for so long, and so diligently, slammed into her and the scent of pine resin got trapped in her lungs.

'What's wrong?' The husky question from behind her—which was far too perceptive—made her jolt.

She blinked furiously, the twinkle of lights blurring, as she struggled to cut off the melancholy thoughts.

'Hey, are you crying?' he asked.

'No, of course not,' she said, but the denial sounded weak and unconvincing.

Biting into her cheek, she shoved the memories back into the box marked 'ancient history'. 'It's just… The tree is a surprise. I didn't think you would be the sort of person to have one,' she managed, struggling to cover her reaction.

He stared at her, for the longest time, and she had the

awful suspicion he could see through the lie. But then he glanced past her at the cause of her distress. 'I guess Megan, my housekeeper, had it put up,' he murmured. 'I can take it down if it bugs you.'

Yes, please.

She swallowed the pathetic reply.

Pull yourself together, Isabelle. It's just a tree, and a beautiful one.

There were Christmas trees all over Androvia at this time of year—even if she never had one in her private quarters. She was used to seeing them and immune to their charm. She was just stressed and jet-lagged and had not been prepared to see one here, that was all.

'No, don't take it down. I like it. It's very festive. And I wouldn't want to insult your staff,' she managed. 'After all their hard work.' She pushed the words past the blockage in her throat.

He was still watching her, with that searing intensity, which made her feel transparent. But then his eyebrow quirked. 'I wouldn't worry about that. They won't know.'

'But aren't they here?' Isabelle blurted out, the silence pressing down on her.

'Nope,' he said, but his gaze remained fixed on her face. 'I always give my employees paid vacation from December twentieth until after New Year.' He was looking at her now with that vague sense of judgment. 'So they can enjoy some quality time with their families, instead of having to wait on me.'

'Oh…' Her lungs deflated, while emotion swelled in her throat and the fireball of need sank into her abdomen.

'What's the deal, Belle?' he said, making no attempt to hide his mockery now. 'Not used to cooking for yourself?'

She wanted to be indignant, insulted even, that he considered her position had made her spoilt and entitled. But all she could do was muster a vague embarrassment—beneath the wave of anxiety now holding her lungs in a death grip.

After all, he was correct—she had never cooked more than the most basic meals for herself, and that had been several years ago in college. But far worse than the realisation he thought so little of her was the news that for the next ten days she was going to be entirely alone with him.

And she would have nothing to do or think about other than her inability to look after herself, and how much his attention still disturbed and excited her.

What if having to celebrate the festive season with him risked exposing the vulnerable little girl again, behind the façade of competence and composure?

Had her fake honeymoon—which was always likely to be a challenge—just morphed into a full-blown Christmas nightmare?

'Could you show me to my room?' she asked, trying to keep her tone firm and even.

'You don't want anything to eat?' he asked.

She stared back at him blankly. Was he going to demand she cook a meal now? To test her culinary skills?

'I'm really not hungry,' she said, which was true, because her stomach was currently tying itself into tight greasy knots at the thought of what the next ten days had in store for her.

He shrugged. Then pointed past her shoulder. 'Elevator is over there. Guest rooms are all on the top level. Take your pick.'

She grasped her suitcase handle and began to wheel the bag to the lift.

'I'll be out boarding tomorrow. So, help yourself to food,' he called out, forcing her to turn again. 'The chef will have left some meals in the freezer, which you can nuke in the microwave,' he added, with that note of judgment she was already starting to hate. 'Feel free to check out the house.

Pretty much everything is voice activated because I hate reading instructions.'

She nodded. From the rigid look on his face, she suspected he was regretting having to spend his Christmas alone with her now, too. But given he was the one who had insisted on putting them both in this untenable position, she had no sympathy for him—whatsoever.

She stored up the spurt of anger, hoping it would help fortify her for the days ahead.

'Thank you,' she said politely, because good manners had always been the shield she used to hide wayward emotions. And inappropriate urges.

A cynical knowing smile edged his lips.

And too late, she remembered her handy shield was about as useful as a thimble of water in an inferno when it came to not getting burned by her counterfeit husband.

'Relax, Belle. We agreed, this is a marriage without conjugal rights...' His gaze drifted down her figure, making her panic—and the curl of heat—flare alarmingly. 'But if you change your mind again, let me know. I'm always looking for an entertaining way to let off steam.'

'I won't,' she said, with a confidence she didn't feel but was determined to fake.

But as she turned her back on him again, the desire to hide until New Year from that mocking smile—and the hunger that refused to die—made her race towards the lift in another unseemly retreat.

CHAPTER TWELVE

Two days later

TRAVIS DUMPED THE heavy snowboard in the mud room. He tugged off his boots, and his outer wear, ignoring the throbbing pain in his leg.

Once he got down to his shorts and T-shirt to examine the swollen knee though, he swore under his breath.

No wonder it hurt like a bitch.

He'd pushed himself way too hard over the last two days. Boarding from dawn to dusk, then working out in the pool or the gym like a madman to take the edge off a lot more than just his excess energy.

He chugged two heavy-duty painkillers. Keeping out of his wife's way—since that crack when they'd arrived had made her blush like a nun—had seemed like a smart move. He didn't know what had possessed him to bring up their one night together again, even as a joke. Perhaps he wasn't over the rejection as much as he thought. Because each day, after he'd exercised himself into a coma so he could sleep peacefully, he'd still woken up hard and ready for her.

He walked—or rather limped—through the house, heading for the kitchen and the ice machine. The tree lights glittered on the granite flooring, reminding him of her weird reaction when she'd spotted the fir on that first night.

What had that been about? Because he'd seen devastation in her eyes.

His heartbeat slowed. Now he thought about it, her private apartments in the palace had not been decorated, despite Androvia being the Christmas capital of Europe. Did she have some phobia about the season?

He'd considered taking the tree down the next morning. But in the end had decided against the idea. It would be a major job getting the ten-footer out of the house. And he liked it there, because it reminded him of how far he'd come since those Christmases with him and his mom when they'd had to settle for the last scraggy tree on the lot on Christmas Eve.

He should have asked Isabelle what the issue was, but they'd been avoiding each other since that first night—with him boarding all day and only returning to the house at nightfall, by which time she had escaped to her rooms.

He didn't even know if she'd used any of the facilities. The only signs she was even still here were the meals that had been disappearing, and the empty containers that appeared washed and stacked neatly on the sideboard each evening.

But from the state of his knee, it looked as if he was going to be housebound until after Christmas now. His heartbeat kicked up a notch at the thought of bumping into his invisible house guest. He probably ought to have a conversation with her about their plans for tomorrow, because it was Christmas Eve already and it looked like they were going to be stuck together tomorrow.

Great.

What did royalty do on Christmas? He hoped she wasn't expecting him to do the catering.

He huffed out an annoyed breath. It had always been just him and his mom on Christmas Day until that final Christmas before she'd died, when he'd messed up. The guilt and grief still hit him on the day itself, so he wasn't in the mood to socialise.

Having to spend the day with Belle wasn't going to make him feel any less raw, especially as he knew his mom would have chewed him out for ever agreeing to get married for a business opportunity in the first place.

Not for the first time, he wondered what his mom would have made of Belle.

He pushed down the prickle of disappointment when he found the living room and kitchen empty. Having to deal with her would only be more awkward while dealing with his bum knee.

But as he limped across the living area in the dusky light, a splash from outside had him scanning the pool terrace.

His heart stopped as Isabelle rose from the pool, her blonde hair tied in a knot, wearing just a couple of swatches of lace. Soaking-wet see-through lace, which reminded him of the panties he'd had his hand inside three days ago.

She tugged on a thick dressing gown and grabbed a towel lying on one of the heated loungers. Starting to shiver, she slid her feet into a pair of oversized slippers and shuffled across the terrace as fast as she could.

'Open the door, please,' she requested of the house's integrated system with her typical politeness.

The glass panel slid across, and then back, as she shot into the indoor space. She hadn't spotted him standing by the tree, his hands braced on the back of one of the couches to take the weight off his leg.

He stood there like a dummy, or the worst kind of peeping Tom, and watched as she shook out her hair. The curls fell in disarray onto her shoulders. His stomach muscles tightened, the familiar heat plunging south, at the memory of releasing her hair from the tangle of pins. The feel of the silky tresses, the sound of her groan as he massaged her scalp and the phantom scent of flowers and her assailed his senses all over again. And the pain in his knee moved north.

She looked as glorious now as she had on their wedding night. Young and fresh and approachable, without the regal reserve she so often cloaked herself with.

As she began to dry her legs with the towel, her full breasts—the rigid nipples poking through her wet bra—played peek-a-boo with the open robe.

She shivered again, then let out a soft laugh. His heart skipped several beats. And the tension in his gut cinched tighter, because her expression was a captivating combination of excitement, exhilaration and mischief—like a kid let out early from school on the first snow day of the semester.

This wasn't the controlled, unapproachable monarch, this wasn't even the forthright woman who had skewered him with her logic on the journey here and made him feel like a hot-tempered jerk... This was the other Isabelle, who hid behind both of those. The bold, impulsive girl who loved to ski too fast, who had the throwing arm of a Major League baseball pitcher, who kissed with a passion that could blow his head off—and who had come apart in his arms three nights ago.

His need—and his fascination—made him forget not just the pain in his knee, but all the reasons why he didn't want her here.

The gruff chuckle came out before he could stop it. Her head rose, the towel slipping out of her hand as surprise crossed her features. But right there with it was the thrill of desire.

Yeah, she felt it, too. The livewire chemistry they'd been trying to ignore by avoiding each other.

'Travis,' she whispered, her expression wary as she gathered the robe, cutting off his view of all that delicious skin. 'You're back early.'

The fierce need charged through his veins as he watched her eyes darken with arousal.

He'd messed up. That night. They both had. But there had to be a way back from that. Because they had a week left, and he couldn't think of a better way to get them through a vacation period that they both seemed to have hang-ups about than feeding this incessant hunger.

'Yeah,' he said, the husky word scraping his throat. 'Great swimwear,' he added, loving the way her pale skin pinkened all the way to her hairline. 'But don't wear it for anyone but me.'

Isabelle stared at the man less than five feet away as hot yearning rushed over her chilled skin. He'd been gone yesterday morning at dawn and returned after dark—and as she'd roamed the house alone during the last two days, she had convinced herself his absence was for the best.

But as the ache in her breasts and the glorious heat in her sex pulsed, her heart turned over in her chest. Because she was happy to see him. Excited even.

'I didn't wear it for you,' she said, but the hoarse tone and the thrust of her swollen nipples against her damp bra called her a liar.

She had been bored and stressed without him here—overthinking every aspect of their interactions so far. And miserable at the thought of spending another Christmas alone.

Because something about being in his home, with that huge Christmas tree here, had made the bad memories all the more acute.

'Oh, yeah.' His gaze raked down her body, which suddenly felt naked despite the heavy robe.

It's just sex.

The words echoed again, from that night, when she'd been scared… But not of him, she could see that now. What she had always been scared of was herself. And how much he could make her feel.

But what was she so terrified of? That this could mean

more to her than it should? But why should it? When he had such a casual approach to physical intimacy? If it could be just sex for him, why couldn't it be for her?

Maybe he was right, maybe this would be a good way to make their relationship less stressful, not more so. There was no shame in sleeping with her own husband. And enjoying it. Their union was legal, even if not strictly speaking authentic.

'I didn't bring a swimsuit with me,' she explained, even as the riot of sensations was incinerating her self-control.

'Tsk-tsk,' he chastised her. 'Not very queenly of you to take a dip in your panties.'

She released her arms from around her waist, allowing the robe to fall open again, aware of his gaze gliding over her exposed skin.

She gathered every ounce of courage she had to flirt back. 'I thought you said you liked my swimwear.'

His gaze sharpened, even as the heat flared between them like a physical force, triggering an endorphin rush that felt as powerful as it was terrifying.

'Maybe take off the robe, Belle,' he mused. 'So I can review it properly.'

Exhilaration combined with panic as she peeled off the robe. It slid down her body to drop onto the warm stone flooring.

Her nipples were so hard they hurt, her breasts swollen and heavy, and the throbbing in her sex catastrophic.

'Come here,' he said, the rough command freeing her from the last of her inhibitions.

Stepping out of the slippers, she walked across the room barefoot. But as she reached him, he took his hands off the sofa, and stumbled.

'Damn it.' He bent to grip his leg.

'Travis, what's wrong?'

But as she came round the sofa, she could see the bruised, swollen flesh around his knee. And gasped.

He braced his hand back on the sofa. 'I just need some ice. It's nothing.'

It didn't look like nothing. But she stopped herself from saying as much because she could see the closed expression. Was he embarrassed at having shown a weakness in front of her?

'Let me get it.' All thoughts of seduction fled as she raced to the kitchen in her wet underwear.

By the time she had figured out how to work the refrigerator's ice machine and filled a freezer bag then wrapped it in a cloth, he had settled himself on the sofa and placed his leg on a leather footrest.

She perched next to him and placed the ice bag gently on the sore knee.

He flinched. 'Thanks,' he said, taking the bag and holding it on his knee.

'How did you do this?' she asked, horrified she had been thinking about sexual gratification while he must have been in agony. 'Did you fall? You should have told me you had injured yourself. I would never have—'

'It's okay, Belle,' he cut into the panic babble. 'I'm not gonna die from a swollen cruciate ligament… It's an old injury. The painkillers will kick in soon.'

So the swelling was a legacy of the accident that had destroyed his snowboarding career. Sympathy for him and the injury that had robbed him of so much engulfed her. But before she could offer him her condolences, he brushed the swollen peak pressing against the lace of her bra with his thumb.

She jolted, the dart of pleasure from the light touch immense.

'The sexual frustration, on the other hand…' he murmured, the erotic pull in his voice delving deep into her sex.

As he played with her, skimming his thumb under her breast, and making her breathing accelerate, a sensual smile spread across his face. 'Could definitely kill me.'

'I feel dreadful,' she said, confused now as well as embarrassed.

'What for?' he said. 'Distracting me?'

He shifted in his seat. And she noticed the impressive bulge in his shorts. He was wearing another pair of those stretchy boxers she remembered from their wedding night—which left absolutely nothing to the imagination.

'In fact, you're still doing a great job of distracting me.'

'I should put my robe back on,' she said, suddenly aware she was practically naked... And so was he. 'You're in no condition to pursue this now,' she said, attempting to be the sensible one.

But as she went to get off the couch, he snagged her wrist. 'Don't,' he murmured.

The smile had gone, the intensity in his expression bringing the riot of sensations back with a vengeance.

She shivered, but it had nothing to do with her wet underwear.

His thumb pressed the thundering pulse point on her wrist. Making her brutally aware of the one still throbbing in her sex.

'Fire higher,' he commanded. Warmth enveloped her as the banked flames in the firepit flared. Orange flickers reflected in the dark brown of his irises, turning them to a rich chocolate.

'I'm in the perfect condition to pursue this, Belle,' he said his voice hoarse with need now. 'I want to touch you.'

It didn't sound like a question. 'But what about your knee?' she asked. 'I don't want to take advantage of you.'

His eyebrows rose up his forehead, then he chuckled. 'I'd love you to take advantage of me,' he said, the fierce light in his eyes brooking no more arguments. 'But you need to know, stopping again might be a problem this time...'

'I... I understand,' she said. And for once she did.

This really didn't have to be a big deal. At all. She'd made too much of the sex part of the equation, because of her inexperience. More than anything she wanted to see this through now, if only to defuse this terrifying need.

'But just so you know,' he added. 'It's not my knee that hurts right now.'

'I'm glad,' she said.

His eyes flared, dazzling her, as his grin became more than a little feral. 'Me too,' he murmured.

Shifting, he slipped one fingertip under her bra strap, eased it off her shoulder. Then dealt with the other. 'You want to unhook it, Belle?' he asked. 'As much as I like the improvised swimwear, I'd prefer you out of it.'

She stood, her heart pressing into her throat. Clumsily, she released the hook and peeled off the wet lace. His gaze intensified and he let out an unsteady breath as the bra dropped to the floor.

'You're stunning,' he murmured.

Her confidence swelled, along with the heat in her abdomen.

She could do this. However inexperienced she was, she could make him ache, too. The thought was so empowering, her excitement soared.

He patted one muscular thigh. 'Sit on my lap.'

'But won't that hurt your leg?'

'Belle,' he said, his expression rueful. 'Believe me, you'll hurt me a lot more if you don't.'

She choked out a laugh. 'Okay, if you're sure.'

She stepped over him, careful not to jar his sore leg, and settled on top of him, aware of the thick ridge pressing against the molten spot in her panties.

He groaned as she found herself rubbing against it. 'Careful,' he said. 'Or this is going to be over too soon.'

'Oh… I'm sorry,' she said, trying to shift back. But he banded one strong arm around her hips, holding her in place.

'No, you don't,' he murmured, then pulled her closer, to capture one stiff peak between firm lips.

She gasped as he suckled her yearning flesh. The drawing sensation arrowed into her sex, and her back arched, instinctively offering him more. Offering him everything.

He lathed and sucked, playing with one peak and then the other, trapping the swollen flesh against the roof of his mouth, to increase the devastating suction. Until she was rocking against his hips, desperate for relief as the waves climbed higher. And the heat coiled tighter at her core.

His hands found her bottom, those sure fingers diving beneath her panties, until she was riding his lap. She clung to his shoulders, aware of the iron bar in his shorts, pressing against the perfect spot. Liquid heat exploded along her nerve-endings, making her cry out.

She threw her head back as the orgasm ripped through her, fast and furious and unstoppable.

The pleasure battered her until all that was left was the glittering sensation. And the mindless drop into afterglow.

She drifted down, her whole body quivering and humming.

'Damn but you're glorious when you come,' he groaned.

Her eyes opened, to find him watching her with a harsh possessive fury in his eyes that seared her soul.

He pressed his lips to hers in a sensual, provocative kiss.

'Good?' he asked, his large palm stroking her hip.

She nodded. 'Incredible… I've never…' She caught herself just in time, before she blurted out the awful truth. That no one had ever made her feel the way he did. But her heart lurched, thumping her ribs when he smiled lazily.

Just endorphins, Issy. Just sex…

'You've never what?' he asked.

'I never expected us to be so good together...' she lied, trying to sound as if he hadn't just blown her mind again—completely. And he wasn't the first man to ever make her want so much.

One dark eyebrow hiked up his forehead. 'I figured it was kind of obvious from our wedding night we had some serious chemistry...'

She shifted, suddenly uneasy at how much he saw. And how needy—and exposed—she felt.

She glanced down, aware of the thick erection—still rigid between her thighs.

'What do you want me to do...?' She paused, cleared her throat, the fierce longing—at the sight of him, so large and hard, for her—not helping her to appear nonchalant, and sophisticated... And not completely overwhelmed.

He let out a strained chuckle, and placed a kiss on her nose, the affectionate gesture not helping with the dryness in her throat, or the thunder of her pulse.

'I want to be inside you,' he murmured. 'But first I'm going to have to limp up to my bedroom and find the condoms.'

'You don't need them,' she blurted out. Then realised her mistake when his brow furrowed.

'How come?'

'I'm... I'm on the pill,' she offered, forced to come clean about the lie.

He tilted his head to one side, then lifted one hand to rub her reddened nipple. 'How long have you been on it? Are you sure we're protected?'

'I... Yes.' She jolted against that possessive caress, the last of her fear washed away on the wave of longing. 'I was prescribed contraceptives when I was seventeen, because my cycle was so erratic and the cramps could be crippling.' The words came out in a rush, the stream of too much information a way to stave off the nerves, and to prevent more questions.

'My cycle began to impede my schedule of engagements, so the mini pill was considered an effective way to manage my menstruation better and prevent the prospect of having to cancel anything at the last minute... I'm sorry I lied. I...'

'Shh. It's okay, Belle.' He brushed his thumb across her lips, the fierce need in his eyes—which hadn't faded—making the strange feeling of connection press against her ribs. 'I get it,' he added. 'You weren't ready on our wedding night. All I need to know is that you are now.'

She swallowed past the lump of emotion. It was a practical question about consent, nothing more. 'I... Yes, I am.'

He kissed her again, even as his palm landed on her bottom, and edged under her panties. 'Then we need to be wearing less clothing.'

'Oh, yes, of course.' She stood to take off her panties, embarrassed at her gaucheness but trying hard to keep the latest spurt of panic at bay.

But when she turned back to him, he had lost the T-shirt and eased down his shorts... Her heart bounced into her throat and became wedged between her thighs simultaneously.

Oh, my.

She let her gaze drift over his physique, attempting to gather her wits and slow her racing pulse as she took in the strong bulge of muscle and sinew, the toned, tanned flesh, the small scars and imperfections—which only added to the savage masculine beauty of his body. The name tattooed across his pec still fascinated her, as well as the sprinkle of hair that surrounded his nipples, then tapered into a line through washboard abs, which were even more magnificent now, gilded in firelight.

'You want to sit back on my lap?' he prompted.

Her gaze lifted to his amused expression. Fire scorched

her cheeks. Could he see, did he know, she had never done this before?

Just get on with it, then, Issy.

She forced a smile to her own lips.

'I'm just admiring the view first,' she managed. Then reached out to touch him.

He sucked in a breath, his stomach tensing. The long, thick erection thrust upwards, as if it had a life of its own. Had it got even bigger in the last few seconds?

'You may have to hurry up,' he muttered, his voice strained. 'Or I'm seriously gonna embarrass myself here.'

The pained announcement had her own embarrassment fading, to be replaced by the surge of power.

This isn't hard, Issy, stop overthinking this and go with your instincts.

Luckily, she had a lot of instincts where he was concerned.

She trailed her fingers through his abs—loving the tensile strength, the feel of his skin, soft and warm. She circled a small tattoo on his hip flexor, the badge of the world snowboarding logo somehow captivating her, then—biting into her lip—lifted her finger to touch the bulbous head of his erection.

It jerked towards her touch. She sucked in a breath as he groaned, and a bead of moisture appeared at the tip.

She circled the thick girth, captivated by the velvet softness of his skin, and the contrast with the steel beneath. Her breath clogged in her lungs as she rubbed her thumb across the head. His hips rose and she felt the answering pull in her sex.

What was it going to feel like, to have all that hardness, that length and girth, inside her? It had felt so good with just his finger, but suddenly the urge to feel all of him—as he took her for the first time—was fierce and intense.

She bit harder into her lip as her fingers surrounded him, then drew her fist up and down the thick length, aware of his breathing becoming heavier, and harsher, and more urgent.

But then he gripped her wrist. 'As much as I'm enjoying that, we need to get to the main event, Belle, before I explode.'

She nodded. And climbed over his lap again, the feeling of power and excitement strengthening her resolve. She sucked in a lungful of his scent—the delicious musk of cedarwood and salt. Going with her instincts, she leaned forward and placed her mouth on his.

He clasped the back of her head and took over, thrusting his tongue deep, even as he lifted her hips and positioned himself at her entrance. She flinched, the pressure at her core painful, but the slickness of her recent orgasm allowed him to slide deep in one thrust.

She groaned, impaled to the hilt.

He swore softly, breaking the kiss. 'You're so tight,' he said, the strain in his voice making her aware of how close to the edge he was too. 'Are you okay? I'm not hurting you?'

She pressed her face into his neck, her breaths coming out in ragged pants as she struggled to adjust to the pressure, to ease the pain, aware of him so thick inside her, the full, stretched feeling too much.

His fingers threaded into her hair, to pull her head back and force her to meet his gaze. 'Damn it, Belle, are you a virgin?'

She blinked, wanting to deny it, but he must have seen the truth before she could find the lie.

He let out a stream of curses and dropped his head back against the sofa.

'I… I'm sorry,' she managed, ashamed now, as well as sore. But when she tried to lift off him he clasped her hips to keep her in place.

'Don't… Don't move.'

'But I thought—' she began.

'You should have told me, Belle,' he interrupted her again,

the flicker of deep emotion stunning her into silence. 'But it's done now, and there's no undoing it.'

Was he angry with her? It was impossible to tell, and hard to concentrate on anything but the overwhelming feeling of having him inside her. Her sex throbbed, and burned, but when he shifted slightly, fierce pleasure pierced the tenderness.

'Tell me what you need,' he said, his voice rough with urgency now.

'Honestly, I don't know,' she replied, hideously exposed.

He swore again, but then he touched his forehead to hers. 'You're crucifying me here, Belle,' he whispered, the tone as raw as she felt.

She wanted to say something, anything. But it was all *too* much.

He cupped her cheek. 'Can you move?' he asked. 'Without hurting yourself more?'

'It doesn't hurt so much now,' she managed.

'That's good,' he said, the strain in his voice helping to ease her anxiety about his reaction. 'Why don't you take the lead, then?'

'How...? How do you mean?'

His eyes darkened, his focus on her—and only her—making her lungs seize.

Slowly he lifted her hips. Then eased her back down. The renewed jolt of pleasure rippled all the way to her toes.

'Good?' he asked.

'Yes... Good.'

'Then let's do that again. You decide how fast, how far you want to go. Whatever feels good, okay?'

'But what about you?'

He groaned. 'Don't worry about me. I'm just trying to hang on long enough to give you an orgasm before I lose it completely.'

He looked dazed, drained, and even though the vicious

need still pulsed inside her—desperate to be filled—the wave of accomplishment at seeing what she did to him was its own reward.

She eased off him again, then sank back to the hilt. He was still huge, still overwhelming inside her, but the ripples began to build and merge as her clumsy movements became more focussed, more sure.

He moved with her, surging up as she sank down. And gradually, the exquisite pain turned to brutal pleasure.

He reached down to where they joined, finding the heart of her. And the hard pulse of pleasure rose again, harder, faster, more furious, more desperate.

He worked the spot, even as he grew larger inside her— his grunts matching her sobs. The heady wave of sensation rose to slam into her at last. She tumbled over into the abyss, her cries of completion followed by his shout of climax.

She collapsed into his arms, spent now, and worn out.

He shifted against her as she listened to the strong steady beat against her ear—the afterglow like a drug.

Was it supposed to feel this intense? As if she had been changed for ever? How did anyone survive something this intimate without losing their sense of self?

'You good?' he asked, not for the first time. But his voice sounded distant, lacking the playfulness and then the fierce passion she had found so beguiling.

She lifted her head off his chest, shocked by the painful clutch of emotion making her ribs hurt. A chill swept through her at his shuttered expression.

He settled his hand on her back, but the touch felt impersonal somehow. 'You need to dismount,' he said. 'My leg's starting to ache.'

Brutal humiliation chased away the last of the golden glow.

She climbed off his lap, the tenderness in her sex nothing compared to the sore spot in her heart. She scooped up the robe, feeling awkward and unsure, and more naked than she ever had before.

How could she have been so naïve to believe that throwing herself at this man, having sex with him, would be a simple fix?

He had stood up and put his T-shirt and shorts back on by the time she had tugged on her panties under the robe. But as she went to pass him, to escape to her room, he grasped her wrist.

'Not so fast, Belle,' he said.

'I… I need to shower,' she replied, trying to tug her arm loose.

'Don't you think we ought to have a conversation first?' he asked, but as before it wasn't really a question.

'About what?' she said, but she already knew from the frown on his face.

'You know what about,' he said. 'Why didn't you tell me you were a virgin until I was inside you?'

She heard it then, the suspicion in his voice, alongside the frustration. She forced herself to push the guilt to one side—and that old familiar feeling of inadequacy that she had spent so much of her childhood conquering.

'I didn't think you would care,' she replied, even though it wasn't entirely the truth. She hadn't thought about his reaction because she'd believed she could hide her inexperience, that he wouldn't know, that he wouldn't find out. But why had she been so scared of him discovering the truth? What exactly was she so ashamed of?

'Seriously?' he said, the brittle cynicism cutting. 'You don't think I deserved to know, before I'd done something I couldn't undo?'

She heard it then, the note of accusation, as if she'd tricked him somehow.

Her own temper sparked, burning away some of the guilt and anxiety. Surely her sexual history was her own to divulge, as she chose. And what exactly was he accusing her of?

'If you didn't enjoy it,' she announced through gritted teeth, 'I apologise.'

Maybe she'd done something wrong. It wouldn't be the first time—given the disastrous way their wedding night had ended. But she refused to stand here and let him make her feel less than.

'You know damn well I enjoyed it,' he all but snarled. 'You practically blew my head off. That's not the point.'

The pulse of heat at his back-handed praise only upset and confused her more.

'Well, what *is* the point, then, Travis?' She threw the words back at him to cover the emptiness inside her, and the hum of arousal that made her feel like a fool.

'The point is, we were just supposed to be blowing off steam here, but now this… This…' He jerked his thumb back and forth between them, his gaze dark with a turmoil of emotions. 'This *thing* between us is a much bigger deal. And you know it.'

She stared at him.

'Why is it?' she asked, hopelessly confused now as well as upset. Why was this a big deal for him?

'Because I don't seduce virgins, okay? Because that would make me an even bigger bastard than the son of a—' The words cut off abruptly, his tanned cheeks darkening with the flush of temper—and emotion.

He swore under his breath. Then raked unsteady fingers through his hair. 'Forget it.'

Her own anger faded, the shocked, unhappy expression on his face making him seem suddenly vulnerable.

He let go of her wrist and walked away from her, the slight limp making her empathy for him rise up to choke her as she recalled the way he had spoken with such disgust about the father he insisted he had no feelings for.

The man who had taken advantage of his mother by seducing her as a seventeen-year-old virgin.

He stood, alone, looking out at the dark snowy night, his back ramrod-straight, his body rigid with tension. As he fought demons he had pretended not to care about a couple of days ago.

The urge to go to him, to help him conquer those demons, made her heart thunder against her ribs. But she stopped herself from giving in to that urge, however powerful.

The sex had already meant more than it should have—the emotional fall-out still churning inside her, too. And while a part of her wanted desperately to take that haunted, ashamed expression off his face, she knew she couldn't afford to make herself a part of his struggle. Especially as he had made it clear he didn't want her to.

So she simply said, 'I'm not seventeen, Travis. I'm twenty-two. And I understand this can never be more than just sex.'

He didn't respond, didn't turn around, his only reaction the way his back muscles tensed.

She turned and walked to the lift, without saying any more.

But as she washed the scent of him off her body in the guest room's power shower, the raw feeling remained. Her body felt sore, tender, and well used—but also more alive than it had ever felt before.

Worse somehow, though, was the painful regret—that she had hurt him somehow with her silence, without intending to—and that fierce yearning, to know him, to understand him and to nurture the strange connection between them, which she now knew had always been more than just physical for her.

It was a realisation that scared her to her core.

CHAPTER THIRTEEN

TRAVIS FLIPPED THE grilled cheese sandwich in the pan, then stiffened as he heard a throat clear nervously behind him.

He turned to find the woman he'd been thinking about all night standing in the living area, looking guarded—and hot—in a pair of tailored pants and a simple sweater. She'd tied her hair in a ponytail, her fresh skin devoid of make-up… Which only made her look more artless. And innocent.

Probably because she was, you chump.

The fierce possessiveness that had freaked him out the night before hit him all over again.

'Good morning,' she said, with her perfect manners, which he now knew were a cover for an emotional intelligence he lacked.

He cleared his own throat. 'Hi,' he murmured. 'And merry Christmas.'

'Yes, merry Christmas,' she replied with about as much enthusiasm as he felt, which wasn't much.

He swung back to the stove and pulled the grilled cheese off the heat. He was a master of no-stress mornings after. Because he'd had a lot of practice at striking the perfect balance between 'I've had fun' and 'I'm out of here now'.

But he'd screwed up so badly last night, this threatened to be the most awkward morning after in the history of the world ever.

He'd made an ass out of himself. He'd browbeaten Belle,

when the person he'd really been mad with was himself. For not reading all the signs that had been staring him in the face since he'd met her.

The tentative, curious way she'd kissed him that first time in her office... The eager passion of their stunt kiss in Sari-yelva—which hadn't felt like a stunt the minute he'd put his mouth on hers. The artless passion that had overwhelmed her on their wedding night, then the way she'd panicked and run out. Her vibrant, vivid but totally unstudied responses to him yesterday—which had blindsided them both.

He should have figured out he was the first guy to touch her—but he'd enjoyed her responses so damn much he'd chosen to ignore the signs to satisfy his own lust. So whose fault was it really that taking her virginity had turned this relationship into a much bigger deal than it was supposed to be, and turned him into as big a bastard as his old man?

'How is your knee?' she asked, the caution in her voice making him hate himself that much more.

'Good. How are you doing?' he asked. 'Not too sore?'

'Oh... No... It's... I'm fine,' she said, her cheeks lighting up like the Christmas tree behind her as the awkward quotient hit a hundred. 'You were very careful.'

'Not as careful as I should have been,' he murmured. 'And I behaved like a jackass afterwards,' he continued, trying to get the knots in his gut to untangle.

He could see he'd surprised her, even as she tried to cover her shock.

'Which is why I've got a peace offering for you this morning,' he continued, sliding the grilled cheese sandwiches onto the plates he'd laid out on the breakfast bar. 'Take a load off and dig in.'

He took one of the stools on his side of the kitchen island and pushed her plate and cutlery across to her side.

She hesitated, clearly unsure of his mood. He knew how

she felt. He wasn't super sure of his mood either. He'd never felt this awkward or exposed before. But then he'd never been a woman's first lover either.

'It's okay, Belle. I promise I won't bite you,' he said as he grabbed his fork and started chunking up his sandwich. 'Not unless you ask me to,' he added, trying to lighten the mood.

She blushed—because of course she did—but relief crossed her features.

And he wanted to kick himself some more, for trying to make her feel bad when he was the one who hadn't been able to get his reaction to her virginity into perspective.

He wasn't even sure what had made him feel so raw. Clearly, he had more hang-ups about his old man than he'd ever realised. Plus, Christmas Day had always made him feel kind of crap about himself after the way he'd treated his mom that last Christmas. But even so, his knee-jerk freak-out—and the weird surge of emotion that he was pretty sure had helped trigger it—didn't make a whole lot of sense.

'I...' She paused again. 'Thank you,' she said graciously. Then she climbed onto the stool opposite him. Relief gushed through him. Maybe this didn't have to be that big a deal after all. If he could just get last night into perspective again. She'd said it was just sex. And that was what they both wanted. Wasn't it?

'I appreciate it,' she added, then lifted her knife and fork and sliced off a corner of the sandwich. She tucked the bite-sized piece into her mouth—and licked the sheen of melted butter off her bottom lip. The inevitable bolt of lust shot straight into his groin.

He set about demolishing his own sandwich while ignoring it.

He finished way ahead of her and poured himself a cup of black coffee. 'You want some?' he asked, lifting the pot.

She nodded. He poured her a cup then pushed the cream

and sugar her way and watched her add a generous helping of both to the coffee. She took a hefty sip, before tucking back into her sandwich. Making him wonder if her throat was as dry as his.

Probably.

'Thank you,' she said for about the tenth time between bites. 'This is absolutely delicious. What do you call it?'

His lips quirked, the question as cute as it was surprising. 'You're pretty sheltered, aren't you?' he said. Then felt like a jerk when she stiffened.

'Yes, I suppose I am,' she said with her typical honesty.

'Hey...' He reached across to place his hand over the fingers she had clenched tight on her fork. 'I didn't mean that as a criticism. Or an insult. Just an observation. Okay?'

She nodded, and her fingers relaxed. Resisting the urge to stroke the soft skin, he shoved his hand into the pocket of his sweatpants.

'It's grilled cheese on rye,' he said while she polished off the last of the sandwich. 'My mom taught me how to cook them when I was around seven. It was one of our favourites. I'd make them for both of us on Christmas morning and we'd eat them in our PJs. It was our favourite Christmas tradition—right up there with grabbing the last tree on the lot next to our trailer park and decorating it on Christmas Eve.' He paused, realising he was the one babbling now. 'So it felt appropriate today, that's all...' He trailed off, feeling kind of dumb. Why was he rambling on about his mom and their Christmas traditions? Especially as he hadn't even been there to cook the grilled cheese sandwiches she loved for her on her last Christmas because he'd been too busy being a selfish bastard to read the signs then, too.

'That sounds like so much fun,' Belle murmured, the understanding in her eyes something he knew he didn't deserve. 'You must miss her terribly, especially at Christmas, then.'

'Yeah.' He shrugged, uncomfortable with her sympathy. After all, she'd lost both her parents long before he'd lost his mom.

'Did you have a lot of Christmas traditions?' she asked, the warmth in her gaze turning her green eyes to a rich emerald.

'I guess. Doesn't everyone?' he said.

'Yes, I... I suppose they do,' she said, but the curiosity in her eyes died as her gaze slipped away from his—to land on the tree across the room.

Reaching across the bar, he covered her hand again.

Her head turned back to his.

'What's the issue with the tree?' he asked, aware of the unhappiness swirling in the emerald green even as she tried to mask it.

She drew her hand out from under his. 'Nothing.'

He propped his elbows on the bar and studied her face.

'You do know you're a crummy liar, right?' he countered, and her face went an interesting shade of pink. 'Is Christmas when you lost your folks?' he probed, wanting to know what had put that wistful look in her eyes.

Which was a novel experience for him—normally he wouldn't be interested in figuring out what made a woman tick.

But Belle had always been different. She fascinated him on so many different levels. Not just the livewire chemistry they shared, or that captivating innocence—his OTT reaction to which he was still trying to figure out—but also all her contrasts: the shyness behind the competence, the innocence beneath the reserve, and all those tantalising glimpses of the reckless girl, the vulnerable woman behind the mask of the confident queen.

'No, they died in a helicopter crash right before my ninth birthday in July,' she said.

'That must have been really tough,' he said, his chest tightening at her carefully guarded expression. He knew what that felt like, trying to hold it together, so no one could see you bleed.

'Yes, the country went into deep mourning. It was a dreadful day for Androvia,' she said, her voice still carefully devoid of emotion. 'They were both such exemplary monarchs—always so focussed on their duty to the throne. I'm not sure the country and its citizens have ever really recovered from the loss.'

He frowned. 'I meant, it must have been tough for you. You were just a little kid. And you'd lost both your parents.'

Her brows rose slightly, almost as if she were surprised at the question. 'Yes, but...' She paused. 'Of course, I missed them terribly,' she said, but her voice sounded hollow, almost as if she was trying to persuade herself. 'But ultimately, I was glad they died together, as they loved each other very much.'

Huh?

It was Travis's turn to frown. Wasn't that sentiment way too mature for a kid of eight? But he could see from the brave acceptance in her gaze she had come to terms with her loss a long time ago. Then again...

'So, what's the deal with the tree, then?' he asked. Even curiouser now. Surely it had to be something to do with her childhood, because he'd sensed her lack of sentimentality about the season right from the start.

'It's nothing,' she said. But then she shrugged and stared down at her plate, to toy with the last bite of her grilled cheese. 'It's silly, really.'

And then he knew it wasn't nothing—because she wasn't meeting his eye, and he knew that was the tactic she used when she couldn't hide her emotions behind the shield of manners.

'Is it nothing, or is it silly? Because it can't be both,' he asked gently, curious now not just about the woman, but also the little girl. Had she covered her grief then too, behind a shield of polite conformity? And duty.

The thought made him sad for her. And angry.

Shouldn't every kid be allowed to act out, especially at a time like that? She would have been thrust into the public eye even more after her parents' death. The pressure to be perfect would have been a massive burden. Had they ever even given her a chance to grieve? And how could she not have buckled under the strain?

Her gaze met his at last. 'Honestly, it's very silly and also quite self-indulgent. I'm embarrassed to talk about it.'

'Try me,' he said, beginning to wonder if she had always thought her feelings, her needs, were less important than her duty to the Androvian throne.

Because it was certainly starting to look that way.

Why else would she have suggested marrying a total stranger? When she'd never even had a proper relationship before now. Never even dated.

Did she have any idea how damn vulnerable she was? Especially to a guy like him.

A man who had spent his whole life taking what he wanted, when he wanted it, without a thought to how it might impact anyone else. Not even his own mom. While she'd subjugated her own desires to assume the burden of a whole country's expectations when she was only eight. He'd always been proud of how single-minded he was, how he'd always kept his eyes on the prize, his take-no-prisoners approach to everything from his business to his love life. But his drive and ambition were starting to look kind of selfish now, compared with her loyalty and dedication to her subjects and her country and her parents' legacy.

She gave an impatient huff. 'Okay, but you must promise you won't laugh, or think less of me,' she said.

'Yeah, that's not gonna happen,' he said. But when she sent him a sceptical look, he crossed his little finger over his heart and kissed the tip. 'Pinkie swear.'

Her gaze strayed back to the decorated tree across the room. 'Seeing Christmas trees, all lit up like that...' She gave a wistful sigh. 'They're so festive and bright, but they make me feel so lonely. Which is ridiculous, of course.'

Why was it ridiculous? 'Do you know the reason why they make you feel that way?'

'Yes,' she said without hesitation. 'The reason is even sillier actually. And also very selfish... I used to get terribly upset when I was a child that my parents couldn't be with me on Christmas Day.'

'That's not dumb at all,' he said, vehemently defending feelings she seemed unable to defend herself. 'Of course you missed them. I still miss my mom on Christmas Day and she's been gone for over a decade.'

She turned to him, her cheeks reddening. 'You misunderstand. This was before they died. Christmas was very important to them as a couple. They loved each other very much and they got so little time to spend together, because they had such busy schedules. My father explained to me the three days over Christmas were very precious—and the only time they could spend together just the two of them—which was why they left me at the palace with the staff on Christmas Eve. But I always cried anyway. He would get annoyed with me, making such an unnecessary scene. And now that's one of the few memories I have left of him—which is awful really.'

'You're not serious?' he murmured, his voice tight with

shock—and anger for that kid who had been gaslighted by her own dad. 'Who the hell leaves their only kid home alone at Christmas, so he can go off on a three-day booty call with his wife?'

Her eyebrows launched up her forehead, her cheeks darkening, but at least he'd shocked the guilt right out of her eyes.

'You don't understand,' she said, the misplaced loyalty making him hate her father even more. 'That's not how it was at all.'

'The hell it isn't,' he said. Because he understood just fine. Not only had her old man left that dumb instruction in his will that had forced her to marry, but he hadn't even stuck around for Christmas when she was a kid, and he'd taken her mom off with him. Leaving his daughter with nobody but people who were paid to be there. 'Your father sounds like an even bigger jerk than mine, and that's saying something.'

'But you're wrong,' she said, although she didn't sound quite as sure any more. 'Obviously, he loved me very much,' she added. 'And after their death Mel and her mother came into my life and that helped immeasurably. We became such good friends, even though we are quite different. Of course, they couldn't spend Christmas with me either,' she added, in that matter-of-fact tone that didn't dim the sadness in her eyes. 'Because it was the only time Mel's mother could take her to visit their family in London. Maybe that is also why Christmas still makes me feel lonely, which is doubly selfish of me.'

'That's garbage, Belle,' he said, getting more annoyed by the second. 'Maybe Mel and her mom couldn't stay with you. But your father could have, and so could your mom. What you're describing isn't love, it's neglect. If you love someone, you spend time with them—you make memories that matter with them. My mom worked three jobs, but she never missed a single competition I was in. And we always spent Christmas Day together. Just the two of us.'

The anger twisted in his gut, becoming sour and bitter as it turned inward. And he recalled his mom's email to him that last Christmas—every word of which he still remembered with crystal clarity.

Travis, honey, will you be able to make it back for the twenty-fifth? I'd love to see you if you can. But don't sweat it if you can't. I've put the enormous spruce you sent me and all the presents in pride of place in my new lounge. I intend to decorate the tree tomorrow, now I'm finally over the chemo. Knock 'em dead on the half-pipe, that title is already yours.

Love Mom x

The courage and selflessness in that email still sickened him.

Who was he to judge her old man, or his own, when he was just as much of a selfish jerk?

'Except her last Christmas,' he blurted out, not sure why he was confessing to her.

But when he saw the misguided sympathy cloud her eyes again, he knew why.

Isabelle's selflessness—her willingness to blame herself for something that had never been her fault—put his own selfishness into context. Plus, it was way past time he confronted the crappy way he'd behaved back then—to the only woman who had ever made the mistake of loving him.

'She must have known the cancer was terminal,' he said, the guilt twisting in his gut, the hideous fear and panic after that initial diagnosis still there after all these years. 'But I was way too focussed on winning some dumb competition to notice what was right in front of my eyes. I didn't ask about her prognosis, because I was scared to hear the answer. So, I stayed in France over that whole Christmas, convincing myself I needed the extra time in training to work on my jumps. But the real reason was that I didn't want to go home and watch her struggle. I didn't want to have to confront the truth. It was cowardly and mean. And I still regret it. Which is why I'm not much fun to be around at Christmas either.'

Instead of seeing what he was trying to tell her—about what selfishness really looked like—Isabelle's eyes darkened even more, with a compassion he had no right to.

She reached out and clasped the hand he had resting on the bar. 'But, Travis, you were just a boy. And she was so important to you. Of course you were terrified,' she said, the empathy in her voice rich with emotion.

He tugged his hand free to cup her cheek, feeling her tiny shiver of awareness. And wished, if only for a moment, he could be a better man. A man worthy of a woman like her.

Not the queen, but the woman beneath. Her loyalty to the people she loved could never be shaken, even when they didn't deserve it. She was much stronger than he had ever been.

'Don't feel sorry for me, Belle,' he said. 'I don't deserve it.'

She opened her mouth to protest, but he slid his thumb across her bottom lip to stop her. And felt her delicious shudder.

'The point is, if your folks had *really* loved you, if they had deserved you, they wouldn't have abandoned you like that,' he said. 'They would have stuck around to be with you. Especially at Christmas.'

Just as he should have stuck around for his mom.

'That they didn't is on them. Not you,' he finished.

The glitter of tears in her eyes crucified him a little more, especially when she eased out an unsteady breath and nodded. 'I guess… Yes, perhaps they really shouldn't have been quite so willing to leave me like that,' she said. The sadness was still there, but somehow the hopelessness was gone.

He was glad.

'Ya think?' he murmured, and she smiled, the bright sweet smile that lit up her whole face.

'Come on,' he said, walking round the breakfast bar to grab her arm, suddenly determined to make this Christmas the best she'd ever had—which wasn't going to be much of a challenge, by the sound of it. After all, it was the least he could do after the crummy way he'd treated her, too.

'I can't go nuts today thanks to my bum knee,' he said. And as much as he would love to, they couldn't lose themselves in sex either, because she was probably still a little sore. Although he saw no reason not to make the most of this chemistry now they had come to an agreement about what this meant and what it didn't. 'But how about I teach you how to snowboard so we can both get through today without any more drama? I've got some spare kit you can use.'

Her eyes gleamed, the sparkle of excitement as captivating as it was refreshing. 'Actually, I think I would like that very much,' she said.

His own excitement soared. But as he dragged her into the mud room, to get them both tooled up, he could almost feel his mom looking down on them both and hear her voice— her tone loving, and supportive, but also well aware of all his flaws.

About damn time you stopped moping around, Travis. I swear, what are Christmases for but to have fun? You've wasted far too many of them since I've been gone.

As they messed about in the snow for the rest of the day, the guilt that had crippled him at Christmas for so long let go its hold on him. Because they ended up creating new memories, full of laughter, while they wrestled together in the snow, and he taught her the basics of boarding while trying to prevent them both from falling on their asses.

But that night, while they stripped off in front of the fire—and he watched her give herself over to the explosive passion they shared—the emotion he still didn't understand, that surge of protectiveness and possessiveness, blindsided him all over again.

And scared the heck out of him. Again.

CHAPTER FOURTEEN

One week later

'HOLD ON, BELLE, don't go over yet. I want you with me this time...'

Travis's harsh demand brushed against Isabelle's ear as his strong arms held her upright, and his driving thrusts impaled her.

'I can't... It's too much.' She panted, clinging to his shoulders, and tried to prevent the wall of pleasure from barrelling towards her at breakneck speed.

'Yes, you can,' he demanded, still thrusting heavily inside her, working all the places he had discovered over the past week that would trigger her release.

Her back thudded softly against the stone of the power shower. She threw her head back, stared up through the room's glass ceiling, and the sprinkle of snow in the night sky, and tried to focus on holding back, holding on. But the coil drew tighter as the heavy thrusts became faster and more frantic.

Her skin sparkled and glowed, still alive from the steam room, and the cold plunge before they had ended up in the shower... And things had heated up even more.

But she couldn't focus on anything but the power of him, stretching her, pushing her, remaking her, caressing that spot inside her that ached for him, always.

Her sex tightened and pulsed, clamping down on his as the unstoppable pleasure crested, bright, beautiful and never-ending, bursting through her body.

She sobbed as the brutal release overwhelmed her.

'Yes!' he shouted out, climaxing too, as they flew over together.

The storm of sensation sent her tumbling into the abyss she had become addicted to in the last week and the only thing tethering her to the earth was him.

'Water off.' He barked out the command.

She flinched, as she released the still firm erection with difficulty.

'You good?' he murmured, as he so often did, while holding her.

Her heart swelled in her chest as she nodded, but she kept her eyes closed, the emotions still swirling inside her—incandescent joy followed by crippling fear.

A reaction she knew she needed to contain—if she didn't want to lose even more of herself.

Just sex, just endorphins, no biggie.

She tightened her arms around his neck, too wobbly and needy to stand as he carried her out of the shower. She buried her head against his shoulder, waiting to regain her equilibrium, and the sense of self she always seemed to lose in his arms. But as she breathed in the delicious scent of cedar and soap and he held her so securely, so tenderly, her heart grew so big it began to push against her throat.

He put her on her feet beside the vanity to grab them both a towel.

She stumbled and he grasped her arm. 'You okay?'

'Yes, of course.' She braced her knees and wrapped a warm towel around her aching body, still too tender. And exposed.

He hooked a towel around his waist as she crossed to the

door, needing the safety and security of her own bedroom—the bedroom she'd abandoned a week ago. But before she could make her escape, he grasped her arm.

'Hey, where are you off to so fast?' he asked, calmly.

Too calmly, while her heartbeat continued to rabbit in her chest. And scour her throat.

How could he be so collected, so casual, she wondered, when she was always in bits after they made love? And how could their physical connection have become even more intense—for her at least—when she had been trying to wean herself off the endorphin fix for days?

'I should sleep in my own room tonight,' she said, taking the coward's way out, even as the pain in her chest refused to subside. 'We have a long day ahead of us tomorrow and I need to pack.' The thought of which suddenly seemed overwhelming, too.

'Don't go,' he said, tugging her around, his rough palm warm on her cheek. 'It's our last night here before we have to return to the circus,' he murmured, with the sting of bitterness that had begun to disturb her, too.

They'd spoken a few times over the past week about the duties he would need to perform as her consort once they returned to Androvia. But there had been so little time for the practical—in between their hastily prepared meals, the days spent out on the slopes messing about in the snow like carefree children, and the increasingly intense bouts of lovemaking.

She understood his reluctance, of course, because she had been guilty of avoiding those conversations, too—to indulge in all the ways he could make her feel so good.

The sex had been a revelation for her. She had never imagined she would find it so energising and exhausting and yet also so utterly addictive. Every time he looked at her now with that hooded gaze, the desire in his eyes unmistakable, she could feel her body softening as it prepared itself for him…

But as the riot of sensations rippled over her skin again, her body no longer felt like her own.

Why couldn't she resist him, or the things he could do to her? Or control the increasingly confusing emotions making her ache for so much more than just sex?

Ever since their conversation on Christmas Day, when he had given her an insight into his close relationship with his mother—and made her realise she had never been to blame for her distant relationship with her own parents—the insatiable need to know more about him had grown and grown. Until she had become desperate to know everything.

But when she'd probed, however gently, in the days since, he'd studiously resisted any more personal conversations—making her feel alone even as she lay in his arms, listening to his heart thud against her ear, steeped in afterglow.

Somehow, he had rediscovered that needy little girl, and reawakened the foolish yearning for the closeness her parents had always denied her. But she couldn't risk threatening their friendship—and the working relationship they would need to establish going forward—so she needed to start resurrecting her boundaries.

'I thought I'd sling a couple of steaks on the grill and we could watch a movie in the cinema suite tonight. Your pick. And celebrate the New Year together…'

His smile was warm and so inviting, but the distance remained in his eyes, which she had noticed more and more over the last few days, every time they made love…

The distance she should be establishing, too.

Why then did she still feel the vicious dart of disappointment and regret at the thought of saying no to him now? And the dull ache of sadness—because she couldn't help reading far too much into the casual suggestion.

Is this what love feels like?

The question that had been lurking in her subconscious for days popped out without warning.

Surely, she could not be so foolish? So naïve? This was just the endorphin overload talking too, it had to be.

'I'm really not hungry,' she managed, backing away from him. 'And I think it's probably best we sleep apart from now on. Plus, I need to contact Mel and thank her,' she began to babble, the familiar anxiety rising up to tangle with her panic as she headed to the door. 'I had to ask her to host tonight's New Year's Eve ball with Rene, who is not one of her favourite people.'

Rene and she always hosted the Saltzaland New Year's Eve event together, in a symbolic celebration of the close union between their two countries. Mel never attended because she usually took the opportunity to spend some vacation time away from Androvia over Christmas and New Year —either in London with her mother who was now retired, or elsewhere. It was just one of the many favours Isabelle had been forced to ask of the people close to her, the palace staff and her privy council, to accommodate this honeymoon.

The honeymoon that now felt far too real.

Guilt pushed at her throat—because she hadn't thought of Mel, or Rene or even of Androvia since Christmas Day, jettisoning all her responsibilities far too easily too.

A call to Mel—to get a debriefing on the event which would be finished now given the time difference and catch up with her closest friend—would surely help to ground her again. Get this past week back in perspective. And prepare her for a return to her real life.

She couldn't be in love with Travis Lord. She was just tired and struggling to cope with a host of new emotions in the past week that were way outside her realm of experience. Travis had mentioned how sheltered she was, and in many ways he was right. Her life had always been studiously planned and managed. She simply wasn't accustomed to having to deal with anyone this exclusively on a daily basis, for this length of time, with no schedule or other distractions to focus on—while also discovering she had an insatiable sex drive.

She had to start getting these volatile yearnings under control—and build a working relationship with her fake husband for *after* their honeymoon that wouldn't distract her from her priorities.

She'd binged on the strong sexual connection they shared, they both had, but how could she continue to be a slave to her newly discovered libido without losing sight of what their marriage was supposed to achieve? Her role as Queen had always been exceptionally demanding, and now she was legally able to take full control of her inheritance, it would only become more so.

But as she tried to make a speedy exit, Travis strode across the room behind her and slapped his palm on the door, slamming it shut.

'Wait up, Belle,' he murmured, his breath hot against her nape, the easy manner gone.

She turned in his arms, to find him leaning over her, his hand still braced on the door above her head, the dark frown on his face wary and intense.

She breathed in a lungful of his scent and turned away from the sight of his bare chest glistening with moisture from their shower—and the tattoo of his mother's name, which she had discovered he had had etched on his skin a few days after her death.

He's a man who feels so much, but not for you.

She swallowed down the pathetic thought—which reminded her of the child who had once begged her parents to stay, and watched them leave regardless.

Surely this reaction was exactly why she needed to get a grip.

'What did you mean by us sleeping apart from now on?' he asked, his tone strained. He grasped her chin and raised her face to his. 'Explain.'

She tugged her chin free, hideously aware of her body clenching and releasing at his nearness, even though he had given her several orgasms not five minutes ago. And the tremble of vulnerability, the wayward emotions she couldn't control.

'I think it is probably best we don't continue our sexual relationship when we return to Androvia...' She forced the words out past the aching pain in her throat and the deep feeling of loss in her chest. 'It will only complicate the working relationship we need to establish.'

His eyes flashed with something searing. But before she could gauge his reaction, he had dropped his arm and stepped back, his gaze becoming flat and emotionless.

'Yeah... I guess you're right.' His gaze roamed over her body, which felt naked now even under the thick towel. 'Too much sex is kind of distracting.'

Her heart shattered, the brittle tone, the assessing gaze as insulting as they were hurtful. And suddenly she was that little girl again... Rejected and alone.

She gave a stiff nod, blinking furiously—as she struggled to shore up the turmoil of emotions.

This was what she had wanted from him. To stop the yearning, to stop believing in the vain hope that more could be possible between them. He had simply told her what she already knew. Why on earth was she so devastated?

'I'm glad you understand,' she managed at last, before she shot out of the door.

But as she returned to her own room, and lay shivering, curled up under the covers, she couldn't seem to reconcile her duty to her throne with the empty space that had always been inside her, and had only ever been filled in his arms, but was now emptier than ever.

CHAPTER FIFTEEN

'WHAT DO YOU mean you haven't heard from her, either?' Isabelle demanded as the anxiety that had been clawing at her throat for over twenty-four hours started to restrict her breathing.

The last day had been nothing short of horrendous. Returning to Androvia had been hard enough, the responsibility of monarchy weighing her down as soon as she stepped off Lord Culture's private jet on the White Palace airstrip, to be greeted by her staff and several members of the Ruling Council, all with new problems to solve, or duties to fulfil.

But it had been so much harder to leave Colorado—and the woman she had become in Travis's home—behind.

The days there had merged into one long escape from reality, which made her life now in Androvia seem like so much more of a burden than before. But far worse, she had plunged down the rabbit hole of believing she and Travis might have been able to build something more out of their relationship. Because she couldn't look at him now without the yearning coming back, not just the physical desire to be held, to enjoy the pleasure he could give her, but more than that.

How could she have allowed herself to become so reliant on his companionship, too?

They had generally avoided any thorny topics about their pasts—or their emotions—after Christmas Day, but even so, simply talking to him about the resort project, his business, the intricacies of her role in Androvia, which he had begun to show an interest in as the days wore on, had allowed her to share at least some of the burden for the first time in her life.

And she hadn't even realised how much that had meant to her until she had thrown it away in her panic, on their last night in Colorado.

But as she glared at Arne now, she had to believe she had made the right decision to end their intimate relationship. She couldn't rely on Travis, couldn't lean on him, couldn't risk confusing the endorphin rush of sex with the development of a real relationship. Because that would mean a commitment from him that he had made it clear he was not willing to give—from the way he had so easily accepted the end of their intimate relationship.

In the days since, he hadn't made any attempt to change her mind. As they'd left the house and travelled back to Europe on his jet, their conversations had been stilted and far too polite—which was ironic given how much his lack of boundaries had once unnerved her.

She had missed the casual touches—and his irreverent relaxed way of speaking to her most of all. Even more than the physical intimacy. But she had forced herself not to reach out to him simply because she felt lonely again.

But she had been unable to sleep again last night, knowing he was in the room on the other side of the bathroom. It had been a titanic effort not to knock on his door and beg him to make love to her again. Just one more time.

She needed her friend Mel. She had to offload about all this. Because bottling it all up was only exhausting her more. But she hadn't been able to get in touch with her PA since she had left on her not-so-fake honeymoon with Travis. Mel always took a Christmas and New Year break—if not to see her mother, then to some sunny clime where she could get away from the winter—and Isabelle had always respected her privacy. But it was beyond odd that if Mel had chosen to take leave after the ball, she hadn't told anyone where she was going. Not even Arne, who was in charge of the palace personnel and their schedules.

'Her phone has not been answered since the New Year Ball, Your Majesty. And she has not sent word about her whereabouts, but Prince Rene's security detail said he relieved them of their duties in the early hours of New Year's Day and has not reappeared either. So we suspect the two incidences are most likely linked,' Arne finished.

Isabelle's heart sped up. 'What are you trying to say?' she managed, her already agitated stomach starting to churn. Why was Arne behaving as if this were all perfectly normal?

'Ms Taylor and Prince Rene were photographed leaving the ball together, Your Majesty. He dismissed his security detail it is believed to escort Ms Taylor back to Androvia alone.' Arne cleared his throat, a dull red staining his cheeks, confusing Isabelle even more. 'But when they didn't return to Androvia it was assumed they...' He trailed off.

'For goodness' sake, Arne, please just say whatever it is.'

He coughed. 'They decided to have an assignation together.'

Disbelief came first, swiftly followed by a new wave of anxiety.

'As you know, Prince Rene has a tendency to...' Arne continued in that strained tone '...disregard his schedule when he is in the mood for...female companionship.'

'That's not possible,' Isabelle cut into Arne's painful explanation. 'Mel would never go off with Rene.' Because she hated him.

For the first time, fear gripped her throat.

'Are you telling me no one has seen either one of them since they left the ball three days ago?' she demanded.

'Well, not specifically,' Arne announced. 'But I have been assured by Prince Rene's private secretary it is not at all unusual for the Prince to be unavailable on occasion.'

Isabelle simply stared. She'd known Rene was troubled, and that he struggled with his role, but she hadn't realised he went AWOL on a regular basis.

'I don't care if it's not unusual for him,' she said, knowing that while Rene might be extremely unreliable, Mel certainly was not. 'It's utterly unprecedented for Mel to disappear without a word. We need to contact the police,' she said, her fear rising. Mel simply would not do something so irresponsible as to go off like this, especially with a man she could barely say two words to without starting an argument. 'And start a search for them both.'

Arne's eyebrows rose. 'But, Your Majesty, that will create unnecessary press speculation. And be an embarrassment for the Saltzaland monarchy.'

'I don't care if it's an embarrassment,' she shouted, forced to raise her voice. Why wasn't Arne listening to her?

'Hey, Belle, what's all the yelling about?'

Isabelle turned to see Travis leaning against the door frame of her office. Relief flooded through her at the sight of him—so tall and indomitable—and the wild rush of pleasure followed... He had called her Belle. Her heart bounced into her throat. Stupid to think she had missed that silly nickname so much, too. But before she could find the words to explain to him why she was so anxious, Arne bowed deeply and began speaking in that patronising tone again.

'Your Highness,' Arne said, addressing Travis. 'The Queen is concerned about the whereabouts of her personal assistant, Ms Taylor, but I have assured her there is nothing to worry about.'

'Arne, I think I should be the judge of that...' she began, becoming increasingly annoyed with her courtier. He had always had issues with female authority, but she had never had her direct requests countermanded before.

As Travis pushed away from the door and walked towards them both, the flood of yearning only increased the emotional turmoil inside her.

What was happening to her? Why was she so happy to see him? *Was* she overreacting? As Arne suggested? She didn't think so—her concern about Mel was totally justified. But somehow the sight of Travis was playing havoc with her composure, as well as her convictions. Especially when he reached her and she got a lungful of that familiar scent. The yearning surged, but right alongside it was the foolish feeling of hope that had been crucifying her for days now.

'I want you to contact the police, Arne,' she said to her chief courtier again. 'There is no need to contact the media as yet. But we may need to arrange a press conference if the two of them cannot be found,' she said, determined to ignore her overwhelming reaction to Travis's nearness to focus on the problem at hand.

'But, Your Majesty—' the courtier began again.

'Arne, do what she tells you,' Travis interjected, the commanding tone brooking no argument.

To Isabelle's relief Arne bowed again, finally having got the message. 'Yes, Your Highness,' he said to Travis, before leaving the room.

But as the office door closed behind the courtier, and she found herself alone with the man who was not supposed to be her real husband, the relief twisted inside her, becoming hard and jagged. Why did she feel so weak and needy all of a sudden? She shouldn't rely on Travis's support. Any more than she should be grateful Arne had listened to him and not her—when she was his queen, and Travis wasn't even a real consort.

'Okay, so what's the problem? And why do you feel you

need to involve the police?' he asked. But she could see the shuttered look in his eyes that had made her feel so alone in the past few days.

'Mel has gone missing,' she said, retreating behind her desk, her feelings far too close to the surface. 'She and Rene haven't been seen since they left the New Year's Eve Ball, which I forced her to go to in my stead,' she added, the guilt washing over her.

Travis propped his hip against the desk and crossed his legs at the ankle, the casual stance displaying a confidence she had never felt around him.

Why was this so easy for him? When it was so hard for her?

'So why isn't Arne concerned?' he asked.

She sat down, and stared out of the window onto the gorge, determined not to feel intimidated by his relaxed demeanour. Or to second-guess her reaction again.

The snow had been falling since New Year's Day, blanketing the country and making travel increasingly difficult. What if Rene and Mel had somehow got lost in the whiteout? It was a five-hour drive through the high country to the White Palace from Gaultiere Castle in Saltzaland. And they would have been driving at night. But when Travis continued to wait for her answer, she was forced to admit the other explanation.

'Because Arne—and apparently everyone else on my staff and Rene's—thinks that Mel has suddenly lost her senses and gone off on an...' she lifted her hands to do air quotes '...an "assignation" with a man she has never liked.'

Travis let out a gruff chuckle that stabbed at the heart of all Isabelle's insecurities. It angered her that Arne hadn't taken her seriously, but it hurt to see him do it too.

'The Playboy Prince strikes again, huh?' he murmured.

She stood to slap her hands on the desk. 'Don't you dare

laugh, or make light of this,' she said, allowing her temper to seal up the empty space, at least a little bit, which was always there now when she was near him.

'Cool it, Your Majesty.' He lifted his hands and levered himself off the desk, the mocking gesture belied by the hard glitter in his eyes. 'I'm just offering an opinion.'

'I don't want your opinion,' she said, determined to finally stand up for herself. 'And don't call me Your Majesty when you have no respect for my office whatsoever.'

The hard glitter darkened, the flash of emotion behind the mask of casual charm somehow vindicating. Until he spoke.

'That would be the office you use as a shield, so you don't have to feel any real emotions, is it?' He ground the words out, his anger as shocking as the chasm opening up in the pit of her stomach at the contempt in his eyes. 'You're damn right I don't have any respect for it. But hey, your friend's booty call is not my problem. I only came to tell you I'm heading back to Colorado for a couple of weeks.'

He turned to leave.

'But you can't leave.' She dashed around the desk to grasp his arm. 'I need you here.'

The chasm expanded when he glanced down at his arm, where her fingers gripped the cool fabric of his suit jacket.

She wished she could grab the words back when his gaze met hers. And what she saw there threw her back to her childhood, when she had begged her father to stay, to care for her, and he had looked at her the same way—with pity and impatience—as if she were an inconvenience to be managed, a burden to be handled.

'Aren't you forgetting something, Belle?' he murmured. 'This isn't a real marriage.'

She released her grip on his arm, even as the yearning in her heart sank into the chasm too. Along with the last of her strength and resilience.

As he walked away, without a backward glance, fear and sadness shattered her heart and made her feel like that broken child all over again. Wanting—and hoping for—something she could never have.

'Take me to the airport in Androlov,' Travis demanded, slinging his bag into the back of the cab.

'Your Highness?' The driver seemed stunned as he climbed in.

'The name's Travis Lord,' he snarled. It had taken over two hours to get packed and arrange a flight out of Androvia—because his company jet had returned to the States—and he needed to leave now, before he lost any more of his cool. 'There's a hundred-buck tip in it if you can get me there in under an hour.'

He'd lost his temper with Belle, something he'd promised himself he wouldn't do. Ever since she'd turned to him in Colorado and told him—in that carefully polite tone—that she really didn't think they should share a bed any longer. And made him feel like nothing.

He got that he'd overreacted. Theirs could never be more than a sexual relationship—they'd agreed to that, hadn't they? But he'd thought they'd eventually become friends during their time together in Colorado. Every time she'd turned to him with need in her eyes, every time she'd trusted him to hold her safely while he'd taught her some moves on the snowboard, every time he'd watched her go over and he'd held her afterwards... It had started to feel like—more.

He still wanted her, sure, but he could get over that. What he couldn't handle though was the feeling of being used.

So, when she'd told him he didn't respect her, he'd let her have it. With both barrels. But he refused to feel guilty about it.

The cab pulled through the gates of the palace, but had

to stop on the verge to let through a couple of trucks with a US news channel's logo on.

He glanced over his shoulder as the cab headed out of the royal compound. Then leaned forward to tap on the glass.

The driver slid open the divider. 'Yes, Your... Mr Lord,' the man said, correcting himself.

'What's with the news trucks?'

'They have been arriving for the last hour. Her Majesty is giving a press conference in ten minutes,' the man replied, sending Travis a puzzled look. Probably because he was supposed to know what was going on in his wife's life. That would be the wife he'd just walked out on in a storm of hurt feelings.

'I need you here.'

The plea echoed in his skull—as it had been doing for the past couple hours while he'd been slinging stuff into his bag and rearranging his schedule commitments to make his getaway to Colorado—but this time he couldn't seem to convince himself she'd been playing him.

He'd seen the panic in her eyes, felt the tremble of her fingers holding onto his suit—and he'd decided it was all an act. Just like all the other moments when he'd sensed the volatile emotion under the polite indifference.

He couldn't pose as her loving husband any longer. Not until he could stop wanting her, all the damn time. Not until he could get over his obsession with her—which had grown to impossible proportions since their marriage. Not just the constant need to touch her, and caress her, and make love to her... But worse than that, the desire to listen to her voice— so precise, so determined, so honest and forthright—talking about everything from palace business to the crummy way her old man had treated her as a kid—and see the emotions swirling in her eyes. The emotions he had kidded himself she had hidden from everyone but him.

But uncertainty rolled around in his chest, along with the great big boulder that had been lodged there ever since their heart-to-heart on Christmas Day.

He glanced at his watch. Then grabbed his phone out of his pocket, to switch on the local news app. Within seconds, the newsfeed was interrupted for a 'special report' from the White Palace.

The conference had been set up in one of the palace's many staterooms, the same room he had walked through close to three months ago now.

Isabelle appeared in front of the desk, and the camera flashes went off instantly.

He enlarged the picture, to gauge her expression. She looked demure, controlled, reserved as always. But behind the façade of composure, he could see the cracks. The smudges under her eyes, which he had spotted during their argument but chosen to ignore. The slight tremble in her fingers as she read from a prepared statement.

The words didn't really compute. Something about the disappearance of her assistant, Mel, and the Playboy Prince—the police's concern that not a trace of them had been found.

Guilt made his throat ache, her distress clear to him now. Why the hell had he let his temper stop him from seeing what was so damn obvious?

Maybe because he hadn't had the guts to confront his own feelings, about her.

After the local police chief added his information about the investigation, the palace's press secretary opened the floor to questions. There were a couple about Prince Rene—seemed this wasn't the first time the guy had disappeared without warning—but then the reporters from the international press broke ranks.

'Where is your new husband, Your Majesty?' one of them

asked. 'Is it correct that he has left you to deal with this situation alone while returning to Colorado?'

Anger burned in Travis's gut. How the hell did they know about that already? He'd only made the decision to go a couple of hours ago.

But before he could figure it out, the camera closed in on Belle's face—and what he saw had nausea rising up to replace the fury he wanted to feel, with her, with himself, with the whole damn situation.

That same sick sense of guilt that had crippled him as a kid of nineteen—when he hadn't stood by his mom. Because he'd been so damn terrified of admitting he might need her too.

'He had important business to attend to,' she offered.

But colour rose in her cheeks, and she blinked furiously, to compose herself, the reserve slipping to reveal the vulnerable, devastated girl beneath.

He could feel her struggle to remain aloof, to remain a queen, but he could see the shield crumbling before his eyes and something broke open inside his chest.

It's not a damn act, Travis, you dumbass.

She looked so scared in that moment. And he understood finally that it was Mel's disappearance that was freaking her out. Hadn't she told him how much the woman's friendship had meant to her as a kid? She had to be terrified.

But he had refused to see her distress, hadn't acknowledged it, not least because of the little flicker of jealousy at the mention of Rene. But it wasn't Rene she cared about, it was Mel... And it wasn't Rene who she needed with her now, it was him.

Dropping the phone, he leant forward and rapped on the glass. 'Take me back to the palace,' he demanded, his heart rising into his throat. 'And if you can get me back there before this damn presser ends, I'll double the tip.'

CHAPTER SIXTEEN

'ARE YOU HAPPY for Mr Lord to prioritise his business over the needs of Androvia and the monarchy?'

'Why would he leave you in a time of crisis?'

'Is your marriage already in trouble, Your Majesty?'

Isabelle stood dumbly, unable to speak, while the questions—intrusive, cutting, painful—were fired at her from all angles.

Everything had moved swiftly once the police had been informed of the disappearance—and had ascertained after triangulating Rene and Mel's phone signals that both mobiles had been dead for since New Year's Day. A press conference had been called to ask for information, and Isabelle had insisted she participate.

In many ways, she had welcomed the activity, not just because she was becoming increasingly anxious about Mel and Rene's whereabouts, but because she did not want to have to process Travis's absence, or his parting words.

She was processing it now though. The chasm in her stomach filled with the crushing weight of culpability and regret.

She had brought this on herself by believing she could circumvent the terms of her father's will. Was this why her father had insisted she needed a husband? Because he had seen the weakness inside her, even as a little girl? Had he known then that she would never be loved for herself?

The press secretary stepped in, to try and deflect the questions back onto the subject at hand, but the media—particularly the world media, who had no respect for Androvia's monarchy or its traditions—had scented red meat.

And still she stood—tongue-tied, unable to defend herself or her marriage. How could she, when they were correct, her marriage was a hopeless fraud? And why did it hurt so much to know that, when that was always what it was supposed to be?

Then a commotion began at the back of the room, and suddenly striding towards her was Travis. In jeans and a T-shirt, he looked like the man she had known in Colorado. The man she had fallen hopelessly in love with within the space of one week—like the worst kind of romantic fool.

He came back.

She couldn't see the camera flashes any more, couldn't even hear the questions—being shouted at him now as well as her. He strode towards the podium, the crowd parting. Jumping onto the raised platform, he slung his arm around her waist. The heavy weight of it seemed to pull her out of the nightmare and into something even more fraught, even more painful.

He can't have come back for me. He doesn't love me.

'Okay, quieten the hell down,' he shouted to the reporters, his deep voice cutting through the furore like a knife. The room fell silent.

'Our marriage is great. I'm here to support my wife.' His arm tightened on her, tugging her against his side in a show of strength, of love, which only made the pain worse. Because she wanted so much to believe it. But she knew it wasn't true. 'Now maybe stop focussing on dumb gossip and concentrate instead on helping the Queen to find two people who matter to her.'

He turned to her and pressed a kiss to her cheek—making the room explode again—before whispering in her ear for only her to hear. 'Let's get the hell out of here.'

She followed him off the podium, the press secretary and the police chief fielding the questions as Travis led her up the staircase at the back of the stateroom, to her library.

But once they were inside the room, away from the media hordes, she gathered what was left of her courage and her strength and pulled her hand out of his.

She walked into the middle of the room, the scent of lemon polish suffocating her.

She turned to find him watching her, with the intensity she had once found so exciting. But it only made the chasm inside her feel more real. And more empty.

'Why are you here? Why did you come back?' she asked, her voice surprisingly firm, given that she was breaking apart inside, because she knew he could only have returned to fulfil the terms of their agreement.

'Haven't you figured it out yet, Belle?' he asked, softly.

She shook her head.

He walked towards her. 'I've done something real dumb,' he murmured, his voice low. 'I've fallen in love with my fake wife.'

He placed his rough palm on her cheek. She reared away from him, even as the fierce yearning gripped her all over again.

'Please don't touch me,' she managed, but her voice broke on the words, shaming her even more. 'And please don't lie to me.'

She might be needy, desperate, delusional, but she refused to let him see her break. Or she would have nothing left when he walked away again.

'I'm not lying, not this time,' he said, his voice implacable, the gaze coasting over her full of admiration and something else… Something fierce and…

She yanked herself back for the second time. But it was so much harder this time.

'All I need to know is do you feel the same way?' he asked.

'Please don't ask me that,' she begged, hating the neediness in her voice. 'It isn't fair.'

The tears rolled down her cheeks, the tears she had promised herself she wouldn't shed. She scrubbed them away with impatient fists.

He stepped forward again and grasped her shoulders to tug her against his chest. That sure solid chest, the steady beat of his heart something she had come to trust.

'Damn it, Belle, I'm sorry. I was a coward.' He wrapped his arms around her. Strong and unyielding, but it wasn't enough to control the fear. 'I knew what was happening between us. It was always more than just sex. But I didn't want to acknowledge it, because it would mean admitting I needed you. And I haven't admitted needing anyone since I was a kid.'

She lurched out of his arms again. The accusation sharp in her voice to hold the traitorous tears at bay. 'I—I don't believe you... You left me, like they did, when I asked you to stay.'

The words spewed out on a wave of vulnerability, leaving her feeling more exposed. But when he grasped her upper arms, and pulled her back towards him, this time she couldn't resist the urge to be held. To matter.

'I know, baby...' He pressed his cheek to her hair. 'Like I said, I was a coward. But if you can forgive me, we can build something better. I swear.'

The bubble of hope pressed against her ribs, but the fear of rejection only made it more painful, more terrifying. 'You have to tell me why.'

He lifted his head, his expression tortured, yet sincere. 'Why what?' he said, but she suspected he knew what she was asking.

'Why did you find it so hard to admit there was more between us?' she forced herself to ask, demanding more from
him despite the terrible uncertainty that still remained between them. 'Why did you walk away when you knew I
needed you to stay?' She sighed, finally asking the question
she had asked once before, and he had refused to answer.
'What happened to that boy, Travis, to make him so sure he
didn't need anyone?'

He swore softly, then let her go. She felt the loss immediately. But the hope expanded in her chest when he crossed
to the library's tall, mullioned window. And stared out into
her kingdom. The kingdom she wanted so desperately to
share with him.

'Does it have anything to do with your father?' she asked.

He swung round. 'How do you know that?'

'Because I know exactly what it feels like to never be
enough,' she said simply.

He stared at her for the longest time, then he turned back
to the view of the gorge. But when he began to speak, she
could hear the insecurity in his voice, which he had always
refused to share, until now.

'When I was twelve, he came to one of my events. For
some dumb reason, I thought he was there for me.' He
hitched a shoulder, the movement stiff and jerky and so
unlike him. 'And I was overjoyed. I knew I could win—I
was the favourite.' He dropped his head, his back so rigid
she could feel him remembering the pain of that rejection,
and her heart hurt, too. 'I figured if I could ace the field,
he'd finally want me. I killed myself that day, took a ton of
dumb risks. But what I didn't know was that a couple of the
other competitors were his real sons, the kids he was really
there to support.'

He shook his head. 'I climbed onto the podium to take
the gold, so proud of myself and what I'd achieved and sure

he had to be too. In that moment, I had all these wild fantasies, that he would come up to me, that he would offer to be my dad, that he would apologise for never being there for me…' He cursed under his breath.

'My mom was there and she spotted him, too. She saw how devastated I was when he looked at me like I was nothing, as he left with his "real" sons,' he added, lifting his hands to do air quotes. 'It gutted me, that he still didn't want me. But it crushed her, too—which was worse somehow, because she had always been there for me and he never had.' He turned back towards her. 'Ever since then, I made sure never to open myself to that kind of rejection again. It was just me and my mom and we were fine. And when she was gone, it was just me. And that was the way I liked it…'

He headed towards her. His gaze roamed over her face, and made her feel truly seen—not just the competent queen, but the strong woman beneath, and the vulnerable, terrified girl too—as he always had.

'Until you came along and blew that I'm-the-only-person-I-need crap to smithereens.'

She gripped his hands, held on tight. 'I'm sorry,' she said. 'Sorry he was so unworthy of you. You deserved a much better father than that.'

'Yeah,' he said. 'We both did… But don't tell me you're sorry, Belle, just tell me I haven't spilt my guts for no reason.'

She felt the smile crack her face—at the forthright way he spoke to her—and the smile reached into her chest to wrap around her heart. They had a long way to go yet. She had never loved anyone before, never needed them the way she needed him. And never trusted that they could love her back with the same fervour.

But the hope felt worth the pain now. And the obstacles ahead of her, ahead of them, didn't feel so scary any more, if they could face them together.

'You didn't,' she said. The tear that edged down her cheek, though, didn't hurt any more. 'I want to make this work, to build something better, something that could last. You mean so much to me, too. I need you with me, Travis,' she said, the hope in her heart obliterating what was left of the fear.

'Thank God,' he murmured, then covered her mouth in a furious kiss, which showed her not just how much he wanted her, but how much he needed her, too.

She kissed him back, with the same fury. The same fervour. But as her mind drifted towards pleasure, her heart continued to thunder against her ribs.

She drew back, forced to confront the whole truth.

'I want to make this a real marriage, more than anything in the world,' she said. 'To make us a real family. But how do you feel about being Androvia's consort for ever?' she asked.

She loved him beyond reason, but her life was not her own in many ways. And he would be taking on a commitment far greater than simply loving her, if he were to join his life to hers, fully.

She held her breath, scared to hear his answer.

But he only grinned, and cupped her cheek in his rough palm, his expression unguarded, and so full of love she thought she might burst from the sheer wonder of it all.

'I love you, Belle,' he said. 'Your fierceness and your compassion and your determination to see the best in everyone and I especially love that reckless, artless, passionate girl you keep hidden from everyone but me.' He wrapped his arms around her, to hold her close, and pressed his lips to her hair. 'But I also love your loyalty, and your steadfastness,' he murmured. 'And your selfless dedication to this country.' He pulled back, his expression intense, but still full of that charming irreverence she loved.

'I'd like to make it my country, too,' he added. 'But be warned, I'm never going to be great at dealing with the press, or sitting for hours on end listening to boring speeches, or handling all the other protocol and security stuff that goes with your job.' He planted a fierce kiss on her lips, rueful amusement shining in his eyes when he spoke again. 'But if you can handle how crap I am at being a consort, I can sure as hell handle living in a palace and having my wife being the Androvian queen.'

She beamed back at him, so moved by his declaration, she felt as if her heart were going to explode out of her chest now with sheer joy.

She knew, too, he would be a much better consort than he believed, bringing his own special brand of authenticity and approachability to the role, which she already adored and she knew her subjects would adore, too.

'Understood,' she said solemnly. 'I love you, too, Travis.'

He tugged her back into his arms, his gruff chuckle reverberating in her heart.

But then he slayed her all over again.

'Before we get to grips with any of that, though,' he said, his tone sobering, 'we need to find the rest of your family for you, first.'

'Yes,' she whispered, banding her arms around him and blinking back tears again at the realisation he already understood exactly how important Mel was to her. And how anxious she was about her disappearance. But as he held her, and she listened to the sure steady beats of his heart, she somehow knew they would find a way through this, together.

And whatever it took, he would help her to bring Mel home.

A home that meant so much more to her now, because he was in it, too.

* * * * *

GREEK'S ENEMY BRIDE

CAITLIN CREWS

MILLS & BOON

For Flo and sweet Nancy

CHAPTER ONE

IT WAS A resoundingly foul day for a wedding.

Not even the splendor of the internationally acclaimed, widely beloved wonder that was the historic Andromeda Hotel, standing proud on one of the loveliest cliffs in the Cyclades, could maintain its trademark resplendence in such a relentless downpour. It was as if the heavens above were as appalled by these particular nuptials as the participants.

Standing beside the great windows overlooking the churning sea in her wedding dress, an understated affair that she had sourced from her closet in an elegant, pearlescent dove gray—because black was too obvious— Jolie Girard felt quietly and personally vindicated.

It looked the way she felt.

But pointed gale sent from the gods as a metaphor or no, this wedding was happening. There was no doubt about that. There was no escaping it, and they'd both tried. They had more than tried.

They had both exhausted every possible legal angle. They had insulted each other in every possible way, then started all over again, and then moved on to insults that had likely left scars that only time would show. The intense arguments after the will had been read had gone on for so long that it was a shock it hadn't been noted by the ever-hovering paparazzi who had been clustered outside the hotel after the funeral.

There was nothing for it, sadly.

Jolie Girard, widow of the infamous and ancient tycoon Spyros Adrianakis—who had taken his Cretan grandfather's stately mansion on a less-traveled-to Greek island that his father had made it into a hotel and turned it into a destination that, these days, attracted only the most exclusive and glamorous clientele—was marrying the devil himself.

That being her arrogant and unpleasant stepson, Apostolis Adrianakis, who was also individually famous the world over—mostly for his excesses and colorful romantic entanglements.

Colorful was a euphemism. It was more of a swamp, in Jolie's opinion.

I will take care of you, Spyros had promised her in his last days. *Never fear, Jolie* mou, *I will see to it you are taken care of for the rest of your life.*

She should have known better than to believe him. She *did* know better.

If men could be trusted, after all, the span of her whole life would be different.

It was so dark and gloomy outside that she could see her reflection in the glass, though it was fully morning by now. She adjusted the expression on her face, because the battle was already lost. There was no point giving the irritating Apostolis, her groom, the satisfaction of imagining that she was coming to this wedding diminished in some way.

She would do the diminishing if there was any about,

thank you. Just as she would do the allotted time—five eternal years of matrimonial prison—and on the other end of this nightmare, she would be free.

Jolie would finally be free. Her cousin Mathilde would also be free, because that was the bargain she'd made. And she could go off and do...whatever it was she wanted.

Maybe she would know what that was by then.

She felt a prickling down the length of her spine and then, a moment later, saw a shadow pull itself into the form of a man in the doorway behind her, like some kind of fairy-tale monster.

He was not a monster, she told herself stoutly. He only wished he was.

The truth about Apostolis Adrianakis was that he was no more and no less than a man.

Jolie intended to remind him of that, should he be tempted to believe his own press and consider himself something more akin to a deity. Or anything supernatural at all.

She turned to face him because he might not be a monster, but that didn't mean she fancied having him at her back. Might as well bare her neck and belly while she was at it—

But the visual that accompanied that thought landed... wrong.

Because she was looking directly at him as she envisioned *baring* any part of herself and *looking at him* had always been deeply problematic.

Much as she might wish otherwise, another unfortunate truth about Apostolis Adrianakis was that he was darkly gorgeous, impossibly beguiling despite his many obvious personality flaws, and almost hypnotically magnetic. Even to someone like her, who was no fan of his. It was no wonder that the better part of the earth's population followed him around with stars in their eyes.

Jolie did not believe in gods, Greek or otherwise, but it was impossible not to look at Apostolis and wonder if maybe, just maybe, they were still wandering the earth. If they had taken to islands like this one and now lurked in villages rife with celebrities and holidaymakers in the summer, whispering their own legends and myths from every charming alley. If they were made of flashing dark eyes in a shockingly beautiful face crafted to wedge itself between the ribs of anyone who dared glance his way.

Perhaps, she thought sharply, she ought to have been grateful that he came by his arrogance naturally. It was better than the alternative. She could not imagine what a chore it would be to deal with a man who imagined himself as indisputably magnificent—visually, anyway—as Apostolis, yet wasn't.

This version was trying enough.

Her erstwhile groom had decided to express himself in his choice of apparel as well, she saw. He wore the expected suit, but it looked almost as if he'd slept in it—or, knowing Apostolis, had slept with someone else on top of it. Or several someone elses.

Jolie told herself she would not care in the least if he had.

"Kaliméra," Apostolis murmured in that rough-edged drawl of his that made a meal of both his accent and the simple *good morning.* "What a perfectly hideous day to marry my wicked stepmother. A luckier man has never walked this earth, I am certain."

"The joy is all mine," she replied with a polite smile

that she knew he would take as a thrown gauntlet. The flash in his dark eyes assured her he did. "Nothing could bring me more happiness than forced proximity with a man who is the human equivalent of landfill. Felicitations all around."

Apostolis laughed at that as he slouched into the room, every step liquid and low, as if he did not so much walk as *glide*. The rumpled effect was not helpful. It made her think about *how* his thick, dark hair had come to look like that, as if greedy fingers had tugged at it and run their way through it. It made her wonder if he had misbuttoned his shirt deliberately or in a hurry, or if someone else had done it for him.

Obviously she would die before she asked him. Before she gave him the slightest reason to imagine she cared when she did not.

They had come to a resigned *détente* after it was clear that no victories could be won in their situation, not even Pyrrhic ones. It was an uneasy truce at best, no good faith treaties in sight, because neither one of them wanted any part of this. Left to their own devices, they would have maintained the chilly, exquisitely *precise* courtesy that had characterized their relationship since Jolie had married Spyros through the old man's funeral and the reading of his will, then never spoken to each other or interacted again.

Apostolis had not been able to forgive his father for marrying her, a girl the same age as his sister, Dioni. A girl who his father had, in fact, met at the finishing school where Dioni and Jolie had been classmates graduating together.

And he had not been able to excuse Jolie for not accepting his unsolicited advice on the topic of the forty-year age gap between her and his father. His arguments had been, boringly, that the only reasons a girl would accept an old goat like Spyros were either because she was a victim...or a gold digger.

It had been obvious what he thought *she* was.

Or maybe, she'd told her newly minted stepson the night before her wedding back then, who was ten years older than her himself, *I just like a power dynamic.*

That was the one and only personal conversation they'd had in the seven years she'd been married to Spyros.

She had not even tried to forgive him. Jolie preferred not to think of Apostolis Adrianakis and his much-lauded cheekbones at all.

And now she was marrying him.

Jolie had no idea what she could possibly have done to deserve this fate. First her aunt and uncle's behavior, which had led to all of this, but now *this*. She suspected it involved whole previous lifetimes of wickedness, at the very least, and she only wished she could remember them. That sounded like a lot more fun.

Apostolis came to a stop beside her, looking at her only briefly before he turned his attention to the gale outside. And she turned with him, instinctually, and regretted it immediately. It seemed too pat, somehow. Too coordinated, as if she was trying to mirror him.

Or maybe it was simply that she had gone out of her way to never, ever stand this close to him before.

She wished she hadn't broken that unstated boundary that had always been between them now. Or perhaps he had broken it, but either way, it did her no favors. This close to him, she was regretfully aware of him in ways she would have liked to never, ever have comprehended. Jolie knew he was tall, of course. And that he could look lean and elegant or broodingly fit, depending on his mood or the photograph in question or even what he chose to wear. And even that he, regretfully, radiated a certain kind of charisma that she liked to tell herself was repellent.

But it was easier to convince herself of that when he was across a room, aiming nothing but freezing, pointed courtesy in her direction.

Next to him, she found that her head barely cleared his shoulder and she was not a tiny woman. Today she was wearing only moderate heels, but she was instantly aware in the way taller women were that even if she been wearing her highest stilettos he would still tower over her.

She told herself that made her feel angry.

But it didn't.

What Jolie felt was fragile. And deeply, deeply feminine in a way that probably would have shocked her if she'd allowed herself to think more about it.

But she couldn't, because he also smelled good.

Jolie could have gone the whole rest of her life without the unfortunate knowledge that Apostolis Adrianakis *smelled good*. Not too much. It was nothing overbearing. Just a hint of something not cloying enough to be cologne. A whisper of scent, something that made her think of cloves stuck in oranges, the kind of Christmas decorations she pretended she couldn't remember, from a childhood that she worked hard to forget.

Because softness had never been an option. It had been a mirage like everything else, and thinking about it did her more harm than good.

Meanwhile, she was discovering that Apostolis was also warm. It was like he was a radiator, emanating heat from where he stood—

Or maybe he is simply standing there, she lectured herself. *And here you are reacting like this.*

"Appropriate weather," he drawled from beside her. "At least we have that going for us."

She stopped thinking about *scent* and *heat* and *height,* for God's sake. "The metaphors write themselves."

When their gazes tangled together, she thought he seemed equally horrified that they had stumbled upon a moment of accord here. That was so profoundly...not them.

"I had my legal team doing an eleventh-hour rustle through all of those nasty little clauses," Apostolis said, almost idly, looking back out toward the rain and the sea that looked so gray and uninviting today. "But it all seems iron tight, as ever."

Jolie did not bother to ask him why it was that a man of such epic and widely annotated uselessness required a legal team, allowing herself only a careless shrug. "I admire your commitment to imagining, even now, that there's some way out of this."

"I don't know what my father's relationship was with you, Jolie," Apostolis said with a certain silken, lethal note in his voice. He looked at her and it was somehow more silken. More lethal. *Disastrous,* something in her cried out, but there were too many disasters to count. And he was not finished. "I cannot account for the fact that he thought to leave me his leftovers. It will never make sense to me."

He had called her far worse things than *leftovers* in

the weeks since Spyros had died. That was practically a compliment in comparison. Apostolis let his mouth curve, as if remembering with great fondness all of the names he'd come up with, and she could see that his eyes looked darker than before despite that gleam like gold in them. She knew that it was malice.

She could feel it all over her.

And she did not like the sensation. "I'm not sure why your father would think that you, who have showed no interest in anything aside from your own hedonistic pleasure in at least the past ten years, would somehow wake up the morning after his will was read with the burning desire to become a hotelier." She let her smile widen. And sharpen. "Might as well take a match and set the entirety of the hotel on fire, if you ask me."

"Yet he did not ask you." Apostolis's voice was lower than usual. Jolie was tempted to imagine that she was getting to him, but she doubted it. "Just as he did not ask me how I might feel about taking on the burden of his trophy wife. Alas, here we are anyway."

With exaggerated courtesy, he turned and extended her his elbow. "The wedding party, such as it is, is waiting. The priest is in place. You are welcome to stay in here, wishing it all away, but that will not change a thing. It will only delay it and not, as I think you know, for long."

"Oh, I'm ready," Jolie assured him, with the sort of merry laugh she used at cocktail parties. "Between the two of us, I think I'm far more prepared to deal with this sentence. I mean marriage. What is five years, after all? *I'll* still be young when we divorce."

She could admit to herself that there was a certain level of exhilaration here. They'd spent so much time these last weeks shooting at each other, looking for the right weapons to use. And it felt like a victory when she happened upon one, like now.

His eyes narrowed, and she wished she knew what it was that had actually gotten to him. Was it the fact that she would be a mere thirty-two when this farce was done? Or was it their own age differential that got to him? She had only just turned twenty-seven. She wondered if that counted as the sort of outrageous age gap he'd been so concerned with when his father had married her.

Then again, she supposed they had years to find and name each and every one of these weapons, then learn how to aim them more effectively—and directly at each other.

Mutually assured destruction. All wrapped in a lovely marital bow.

She linked her arm with his because they were both out of options, and pretended she didn't feel a single thing when she did. None of that prickling awareness. None of that unacceptable heat that made her not only too focused on him, but on herself.

On the way each breath she took made her breasts brush against the bodice of her dress. Making her feel as if she was wearing something daring when she was not.

She had learned long ago that there was no need to gild the lily, as it were. People made assumptions about her by simple dint of her presence at her husband's side. The more understated she dressed and behaved, the more fevered their imagination about what must go on behind closed doors.

And she had profited from those fevers, hadn't she?

Or her aunt and uncle had. And did. And would continue to for the foreseeable future—

But she cut herself off there.

Was she disappointed that Spyros had not simply rewarded her for her part in their marriage outright? She was. More disappointed than she would ever let on, because there was no safe space for her to confide in. Though she doubted that Apostolis had any idea that she and Dioni, his sister, were close—Apostolis being the sort who made declarations and assumed that everyone leaped to obey him, without ever checking up to see if that was the case—Jolie knew better than to test that relationship.

She suspected that the other girl was able to maintain their friendship because they had tacitly agreed, long ago, not to discuss Jolie's relationship with Spyros. At all.

It had been her little secret while he was alive. It would remain her secret.

And, apparently, he had decided she would have five more years to keep up the act.

Apostolis led her from the great room, taking her through the grand old house that would be theirs, now, to maintain and run together. An enterprise that she thought almost certainly doomed to failure. So, today, she tried not to think about it.

She took in the graceful accents of the lovely old place that she had loved at first sight. Legend had it that Spyros's grandfather had built the place for the love of a young island girl he'd met and married here. Right here in this house that rose up on its cliff, an elegant presence on this end of the island. The only thing, or so the story went, that rivaled the beauty of the girl he took to wife—and made it possible for him to live apart from his beloved Crete.

It was Spyros's father who had turned the Andromeda from a family home into a hotel. Despite claims that he did so out of a desire to share the house's bounty with the public, it was well known—if rarely openly discussed—that it had far more to do with his debts than any interest in sharing the family house with outsiders.

Spyros was the one with real vision. He was the one who had spent the first part of his life turning the Andromeda into what it was today. A boutique luxury hotel that catered to exclusivity above all else. It was not advertised anywhere, save word of mouth.

What matters are not so much the words, but the mouths that form them, Spyros had liked to say.

And in his case, the mouths that spoke praise of this place were some of the most glamorous around, with lives wildly coveted and usually extensively covered in aspirational media. Too bad he had enjoyed appearances rather more than any admin work. The hotel had been in some difficulties when he'd married Jolie.

But it had been booked solid two years running now, and almost at full capacity the year before that. With repeat customers and a waiting list that grew by the day.

Spyros claimed that the hotel ran on the *myth* of itself. He therefore insisted that Jolie *act* as if all she did was waft about, catching the perfect light and making other men jealous of what they could never touch. Her *grubby little figures,* as he called her bookkeeping and actual administration of managerial duties, were always to be kept a secret.

Far better the guests should think the hotel ran itself.

Jolie agreed. Myths and legends were far more appealing than ledgers and vendors and besides, managing the hotel was the one thing Spyros let her do without supervision or much commentary.

It had been her escape. She should have known that Spyros would exact a price for that, too.

Today, their wedding was being squeezed into a morning when their current high-profile celebrity guest and his entourage had gotten stuck on another island, thanks to the storm. They had been waiting for a window just like this.

And by *waiting* Jolie meant *hoping fervently for a windowless season.*

Because here at the Hotel Andromeda, the goal was the near invisibility of not just Jolie's true role, but of all the staff. Their guests preferred to operate under the impression that it was magic at work. Intuitive, effortless magic.

A wedding between non-guests would ruin that illusion.

Jolie fixed her face into something smooth and impenetrable as Apostolis walked with her into the little room they used to serve breakfast over the sea, sometimes the odd high tea, and so on.

Waiting there, looking equal parts concerned and anxious, were their witnesses. The sum total of their wedding party and guests. Dioni, who looked as scattered as ever, her dark hair falling down from the twist she'd attempted to secure it in, and, as ever, her dress not quite in place. It had used to drive their headmistress batty. She could oversee Dioni's wardrobe and dressing herself, and yet within two breaths, Dioni would somehow have the perfect ensemble looking…unkempt. Hems frayed at the merest contact with her. Straps never stayed put. She always looked *ever so slightly* bedraggled, as if elegance was a gene and it had passed her by entirely.

It was the first moment all morning that Jolie felt emotional, and she had to fight to keep that to herself. There was no place for emotion here, not even for her only friend.

But the cure for stray feelings was to look to the other side of the room, where the man who was somehow Apostolis's dearest friend in all the world stood. There were a number of things Jolie found impossible about Alceu Vaccaro. The most glaring was the fact that he had any friends at all, but especially Apostolis. Alceu was a stern, brooding, unforgiving sort of man from Sicily, with a grim mouth and an iron gaze that she was fairly certain would make every tropical flower in Greece wilt at once if he wished it.

It was hard for her to imagine a man like that giving an international playboy and professional wastrel like Apostolis the time of day.

Much less showing up for him at this tragic mockery of a wedding.

But here they all were.

Jolie felt a bit as if she was retreating to some higher plane, where she could look down on these proceedings from afar, as Apostolis shook hands with his supposed *friend*. And had to allow that it seemed more than possible that they really were friends then, because the grim Sicilian actually smiled. Slightly.

Then Apostolis was taking her arm again and they were standing in front of the priest, who looked unduly jolly, given the circumstances.

Beside her, Dioni held a bouquet of flowers, because of course she did. She offered them to Jolie.

"Keep them," Jolie murmured. "The ceremony feels flowerless to me."

Dioni sighed. "I can't imagine a flowerless wedding," she said softly. "What's the point?"

That was another thing Jolie had always adored about her friend. She was the product of all of this wealth and outrageous consequence, rubbing elbows with some of the most extravagant people to grace the planet, and yet somehow the core of her was still so innocent. Her father had called her *matia mou,* his eyes. And he'd meant it, as far as that went for a man like Spyros.

Jolie had understood that Dioni would not have the sort of life she'd had. Dioni would be allowed to choose the life she would live. Dioni could even marry for love, if she wished.

Dioni did not have the family Jolie did, Jolie reminded herself. She was mercifully free of the kinds of pressures that Jolie had been navigating for years now. If she had to, she thought then with a certain ferocity, she would do whatever she could to keep it that way.

The same way she kept her cousin safe, she would do it for Dioni, too. If she needed to.

Though she supposed that would not be necessary. Apostolis could be a monster, it was true, but not where his little sister was concerned.

The priest cleared his throat.

Jolie took one last look at Apostolis, soaking in this last moment of blessed widowhood before he became her husband.

He looked back, that gleaming gold thing in his gaze, but his expression unusually serious.

For a moment, it was as if she could read his mind.

For a long, electric moment, it was almost as if they were united in this bizarre enterprise after all, and her heart leaped inside her chest—

"Stepmother?" he said, with a soft ferocity. "If you would be so kind?"

No, she told herself harshly. *There is no unity here. There is only and ever war. You will do well to remember that.*

And then, with remarkable swiftness and no interruption, Jolie relinquished her role as Apostolis's hated stepmother, and became his much-loathed wife instead.

CHAPTER TWO

THE NIGHT BEFORE his travesty of a wedding took place, Apostolis Adrianakis dreamed that he dug up his own father's grave, when he knew full well—while awake— that his father had been cremated and his urn placed in the family crypt. Still, he found himself out on an unfamiliar cliff beneath a strange moon, digging in the dirt with his hands. Once he reached the coffin, the old man had been hale and hardy.

And laughing.

Why are you doing this to me? Apostolis had demanded, with the temper he had deliberately never showed his father when he'd been alive. *This is how a father treats his only son?*

You are welcome, my boy, Spyros had replied.

And kept on laughing.

Now it was done, and if the old man was still laughing from the Great Beyond, the good news was that Apostolis could not hear him.

The terms of his father's will had been a stunning blow, to put it mildly, and he could not say that he had covered himself in anything approaching glory.

In order to lay claim to the Hotel Andromeda and the estate, the lawyer had droned out, as if he was parceling out the tchotchkes instead of ruining lives, *my only son, Apostolis, and my widow, Jolie, must act as follows: marry within three weeks of this reading, run the hotel together as a seemingly happily married couple for five complete calendar years, which will entail cohabitation with no gaps of more than two weeks at a time, with no more than one such gap every quarter.*

He had been certain both he and that woman, his father's hateful wife, would *implode* with the same fury when the lawyer stopped and looked at them, as if expecting the same. But they had not. It had not been pleasant, and he could not look back upon those first few moments without mortification, but it had also not escalated to anything but a few words he supposed they'd both kept to themselves for good reason during her marriage to his father.

He despised himself for counting that as a victory.

But then again, he had never met a woman, or any other person alive, who gnawed through his carefully erected barriers and boundaries to stick her claws in deep the way his stepmother did. And always had. Without even seeming to try.

Yet despite all that, they had cleared the first objectionable hurdle. Now what remained was the grim march through the next five years, chained together in infamy. The heir to one of the great Greek fortunes…and one of the most notorious women in Europe, a subject of furious speculation and gossip since she'd married his father, a man at least forty years her senior.

And more, they were to *seem happy.*

Oh, joyous day, Apostolis thought darkly.

Neither he nor Jolie had indicated the slightest interest in any kind of reception, given how little there was to celebrate in this disaster. But his sister, forever too sunny and hopeful for her own good, ignored their rather loudly stated wishes in that respect. The moment the wedding was done, she clapped her hands together and announced that she had a surprise for them all. And sure enough, out came a wedding breakfast that Dioni clearly expected them all to partake in as if this was a regular wedding between lovebirds.

He had thought his friend Alceu, more of a brother, really, might explode.

But no one said *no* to Dioni. Not even the usually unmovable and eternally brusque Alceu, and so here they sat. *Breakfasting.* Together.

Dioni chattered on about nothing and everything, though it was difficult to tell if she was nervous or just Dioni. Alceu stared stonily back at her in aggrieved silence. And Apostolis and his brand-new *wife* fairly hummed with indignation and malice.

Or perhaps that was just him.

"You must make a toast," Dioni told his friend when the meal that no one had really touched seem to be drawing to its inevitable and painful finish. In that the food was finally going cold. "I have it on great authority that sometimes the best man, or the *koumbaros* since we are Greek—"

"I will pass on that honor," said Alceu at once.

Icily.

"But as it turns out, I would love to make a speech," Apostolis found himself saying. Beside him, he didn't so much *see* Jolie stiffen. But he felt it. And truly, nothing could have pleased him more. "I can't tell you how it felt to discover that my birthright is not only no longer mine, but is to be shared with a woman whose notoriety exceeds my own to such an extreme degree."

He didn't stand. Instead he lounged back in his chair, lifting his glass in the direction of his blushing forced bride, who was not actually blushing. She looked the way she always did, to his endless frustration. Angelic and untouched, when she was obviously neither. As if she floated high above all the messes she'd helped make and could not possibly be called to account for any of them.

Maddening woman.

"Seven years ago, we sat around a similar table, grasping for felicitations and platitudes, while congratulating my darling wife on her first marriage. Is it a May/December romance when it encompasses four decades? Or is that more of a January/December?" He smiled as if he was enjoying himself. And discovered that, in fact, he was. "I should be flattered that my erstwhile stepmother even considered lowering her standards, and her minimum age gap requirements, to a mere *single* decade."

"I didn't lower my standards at all," Jolie said with a limpid sort of serenity that seemed to scratch all over his body, like fingernails. "It has nothing at all to do with my standards. It has to do with honoring my late husband's will."

"I think it has to do with greed," Apostolis corrected her with a lazy smile that he doubted reached his eyes. "I suppose that it is possible that you fell head over heels in love with a man who just happens to be so many years your senior and also, coincidentally I am sure, unimaginably wealthy to boot. I am told that lightning strikes where it will, though I confess I have been thus far unenlightened. But I will confess, Jolie, that I have always imagined that your motives are far more...prosaic."

His sister was staring at him with wide and distressed eyes. "So far, Apostolis, this is not a very good toast."

But he was only warming to the topic, and there was a kick to it, like particularly good spirits. "I must salute you, my lovely stepmother and wife, for managing to fall in love so *practically.*"

If he expected this to shame her, and he could admit that he did, he was destined for disappointment. Jolie reached for her own glass and sipped from it as if she needed a bit of the bubbly stuff to ward off the press of ennui. "Perhaps your sister never told you that our head-mistress used to tell us, with great sincerity—and especially when we were all pining away for the grubby sort of boyfriends we imagined we wanted at the time—that an elegant woman always keeps in mind that it is just as easy to fall in love with a rich man as a poor one, and only one of those choices leads to a life of grace and comfort."

"It's true," Dioni agreed, with a nod. "She did say that. Quite a lot, actually. Though I always wondered why she hadn't gone off and married herself a wealthy man, then, if it was all the same and by her telling, such men were just littering the earth like overripe fruit."

Beside her, Alceu aimed an incredulous and frigid look at Dioni. *"Overripe fruit?"* he repeated in tones of censorious amazement.

But Dioni was not even remotely cowed. She didn't look as if she recognized that she should be.

"Like rotting stone fruit," she said merrily, in a conversational aside to Alceu as if she truly believed he wanted to continue that tangent. "Strewn about the dirt of Europe, by her telling."

Apostolis carried on before his oldest and best friend stroked out. He aimed his glass and his smile at Jolie once again. "When I first heard the terms of the will I wanted to burn the entire hotel to the ground." That got the murmurs of shock he wanted, though only from his sister. But at least she was no longer ranting on about fermenting fruit. He continued. "To save it, somehow, from the unsavory claws of a woman whose ambition must clearly outreach my own in every possible way, since she managed to end up with half of my inheritance."

Jolie, the picture of angelic serenity, let out a tinkling laugh that sounded more like bells than any human should. "In fairness, my dear stepson and husband, if you're speaking of your ambition that is a very low bar."

Apostolis laughed. Dioni stared at her plate as if it had just occurred to her that forcing them all together like this was not the best idea she'd ever had. Alceu, meanwhile, looked as if he was seriously contemplating hurling himself out the window and off the side of the cliff, for which Apostolis would certainly not blame him.

But none of that made him want to stop. He was enjoying this too much. He was finally saying all the things he'd wanted to say for weeks. For years. Forever. He'd always held back, beyond the odd, inevitable comment here and there. Even at the reading of the will he'd kept himself from a deep dive into *all* of the things he'd kept to himself over the years, because he'd still had hope that he could contest the damned thing. He was not about to squander this opportunity. They could *seem happy* tomorrow. "I have to ask myself what exactly I did that he should force the two of us to marry. That he should make the ownership of this hotel, and therefore the bulk of his estate, contingent on you and I making it through five miserable years together. Acting the part, of course, as the myth demands. I cannot imagine it, but I assume that I will soon be the recipient of the sort of tricks that lead a man to make such rash decisions. I'm expecting nothing short of Cirque du Soleil."

His sister, bless her, looked confused. His friend politely averted his gaze.

His wife smiled in that way she had that looked polite enough if a person didn't know her, but felt like razors. And if a person did know her even a little bit, well then. It was easy to see the shine of the blade.

"What is the saying?" she asked in a musing sort of tone. "Ah, yes, it goes something like, *not my circus, not my monkeys,* I think."

"But do you not see?" Apostolis made a grand gesture with his wineglass, encompassing the two of them. "This *is* the circus, Jolie. And you and I are nothing but monkeys who must dance, for five long years, as my father has a revenge I did not know he wished to take upon me from beyond the grave."

"I think he thought he was being kind," Dioni offered.

But neither Apostolis nor Jolie looked over at her.

Because Jolie, Apostolis was perhaps too delighted to see, was not holding on to her calm, angelic demeanor quite so tightly as before. "What astonishes me is that you imagine this is something *I* lobbied for," Jolie said with a different sort of laugh. Less bells, more mayhem. "After seven years of marriage, I expected a settlement commensurate with the time and effort I put in. I did not expect there to be further hoops to jump through. I certainly did not expect that I would be forced to indulge in a charity case, with a man of low character, far lower morals, and a reputation so dire that it would make the average howling alley cat seem like a cloistered monk."

"Are we discussing morals?" Apostolis asked, with true delight moving through him, like that lightning striking him after all. "Do you dare?"

"As I believe I made clear to you seven years ago and every year since in one way or another, it's not your business. It wasn't then, it wasn't at any point along the way, it isn't now." Jolie, he discovered in that moment, got colder when she was angry. Her temper was like a blast of ice but, perversely, he felt warm. And warmer by the second. "And it will never be your business, because it has nothing to do with you."

"Except behold." Another grand, sweeping gesture between them, because he could see it annoyed her. "His will made it my business and now you are also my business as well as my stepmother *and* wife, for my sins."

Jolie made a disdainful noise. "I categorically reject the idea that your sins, voluminous and colorful as they undoubtedly are, should be rewarded. Not even your father, who had an alarming soft spot for your antics, would consider those antics worthy of anything but a sigh and a trip through his own memories of sordid seasons past." She eyed him as if he had woken up this morning something less than his usually resplendent and tempting self when he knew very well he had not. "Upon reflection, all I can think is that your father was so certain that you were not up to the job of handling his estate and the Andromeda that he realized you needed training wheels, if you will.

A guiding hand. And since he knew that no one in their right mind would take on such a job, he made certain that I had no other choice but to guide you as best I can."

Apostolis laughed at that, and kept laughing, though it was more a flash of that fury that had been a fire inside him since the will was read than anything approaching amusement. That she dared to harp on and on as if *he* was a failure of a man. As if *his* sins were so terrible when she could not possibly know the truth about him *or* Spyros and *her* hands were not exactly clean either.

Though the fact his own father had chosen to believe the stories about him was, he was forced to acknowledge, something he had never done enough to combat.

The truth was never as salacious as it appeared. But he had always assumed his father knew that.

That he had not, that it was possible he really had thought Apostolis required *training wheels,* as she did so revoltingly put it, was like a knife in his rib cage.

He blamed her for that, too.

It was turning into a rather long and epic list.

"Everyone knows what is happening here," Apostolis told her, letting his laughter trail off and his eyes blaze right at her, like his fire could melt all her ice. "It's a tale as old as time. A young, avaricious girl seeks an older man to give her a life of comfort and ease. There is only one payment for that, as I think you know. Beauty will always be traded in whatever market that can afford it. No doubt you've spent the last seven years convincing my poor, deluded father that he somehow owed you more than what he'd already given. His name. This life you do not deserve." He made a meal out of a sigh. "Though I do not know why you bothered. No one will ever forget who you really are. No one ever does. A greedy, social climbing trollop who fancies herself a trophy when she is nothing but a sordid little gold digger."

"Do you know what I've noticed?" his bride and nemesis asked, in a deceptively light tone. Apostolis was dimly aware that she was leaning closer to him and that he was leaning closer to her, too. He didn't know when she'd moved, or when he had, only that they were now nearly as close as they had been at that makeshift altar. He could see every furious icicle in her gaze. "Truly wealthy and powerful men take great pleasure in the things that wealth and influence bring them. One of those things being the attention of beautiful women of any social strata."

One of her perfectly shaped brows rose in challenge. "Truly confident men of real authority are never worried about gold digging. Why would they be? They *like* lavishing the women in their lives with the fruits of their labors. And the joy it brings them. For she is the prettiest diamond he could find and oh, does he love polishing her while she gets the chance to truly shine. And do you know who is worried about the apparent scourge of gold diggers traipsing about the planet, looking for unsuspecting marks?"

She nodded sagely, as if he had answered her. "That's right. Tiny little men. With precious little power or authority, who know, deep down, that they'll never measure up."

That she considered him a member of the latter category was obvious.

And for a moment, it was as if Apostolis...*whited out*.

It was as if everything simply...flatlined.

Except not, because he was fully and totally aware of Jolie.

Jolie, that impossible woman, who he had expected would grow brittle to match the void within as the years passed, but she hadn't. He'd expected that gaunt, bird of prey look that so many women in her position adopted as they fought the ravages of time that would eventually get them replaced, but not Jolie.

If anything, she was more beautiful than she'd been on that first wedding day, seven years ago. When she'd stood in a white dress right here in the Andromeda, but that day the sun had been shining and the sea had been so blue it hurt.

And there Jolie had been with her hair the color of the sun, and her eyes a match for the Mediterranean all around her, and only Apostolis seemed to see the truth of who she was.

The sheer avarice in her smile. The calculation in her gaze. The way that she had treated his father as if she was his nurse, not his wife.

I don't expect you to be friends with her, his father had told him with a laugh. *In fact I would prefer you keep your distance, dog that you are. But I do expect you to be polite.*

Apostolis had been certain that *she* could not manage to stay polite. Women like that never could. He had expected her to do what women in her position always did, having secured the older man—as his father had suggested. No doubt they both assumed that the flirtations would start with any younger man who happened by. The coded invitations. The clear and obvious signs that she would be more than willing for some extracurricular with him behind his father's back.

He had spent his father's wedding reception coldly laying out how it would go in his head. How he would expose her and be rid of her.

But those invitations had never come.

To his astonishment, this conceited, manipulative woman had treated him as if *he* was beneath *her*. A charity case she engaged in purely for his father's benefit.

A trial, at best.

For seven years. Without even the slightest deviation.

In fact, it had seemed as if her opinion of him—low to begin with—had only gone lower as time went on.

Even today she was under the impression that *she* was the one doing *him* a favor.

It was an outrage of epic proportions.

Sheer indignation thundered in his veins—and not only because of her temerity.

When he thought about the way he had worked, all of his life, to maintain a relationship with his father, he wanted to...break something. And he knew that while Jolie was an ignominy at best, she was not to blame for the fact that the old man had always loved his work and his women far more than his family.

That he had preferred to bask in the reflected glory of the guests who came and stayed in this hotel, because it gave him some kind of mystique. There were the articles about him, the tycoon who was on a first-name basis with the most powerful and beloved people alive.

The Andromeda is the glittering scene, such articles would claim, *and in the charming epicenter of all that glamour and elegance stands one man. Spyros Adriana-kis, the curator of it all.*

Curating that scene had always been more interesting to Spyros than his son. Or his long-suffering wife. Or the baby girl that had not saved his parents' marriage but had instead taken his mother's life and relegated Dioni to her older brother's care. Because he could not trust his sister with the nannies who Spyros had treated like a pool of lovers. All of them auditioning for time in his bed, not the care and maintenance of poor Dioni.

All of this, Apostolis had done his best to forgive. Forgiveness that he was well aware he had never quite achieved.

So he had gotten his father's attention any way he could.

But he was not about to tell this woman, his stepmother *and* wife and *enemy,* such things. He couldn't think of anyone he would trust less with such delicate truths about who he was or what he was about or what this family really was when there was no one about but them.

He studied the enemy in question.

Jolie looked delicate, but she wasn't. He had made a study of her all these years and he knew that the way she presented herself was a lie. The effortlessly willowy form, to easily inhabit this glittering world his father had created, made her look more like one of the grand film stars who flocked to this place, or the high society darlings, than they did themselves.

The greatest lie of all was that she never looked as icy as she truly was. She *looked* like a pure, long shot of a perfect Mediterranean day. All of that golden hair. Those impossible blue eyes. That perfect, symmetrical face, classical cheekbones and the kind of sensual mouth that set pulses to skyrocketing all around.

He knew exactly why his father had chosen her. Aside from the obvious, she was precisely the sort of hostess the Andromeda's extraordinarily particular clientele expected. Demanded, even.

And one thing Apostolis had always known about his father was that as much as Spyros indulged his baser impulses, he never left a mess when it came to the myth of his business. Jolie really was the perfect Lady of the Andromeda, as he had heard her called.

It only made him dislike *his wife* all the more.

Then again, the fact that she'd been forced to marry him could work in his favor. Aside from everything else, it meant that he had ample opportunity to plot and enact the perfect revenge.

His father might not be able to pay for what he'd done, but she could.

And would, Apostolis vowed then, with something like iron in his gut.

Again and again.

"Cat got your tongue?" asked the maddening woman in question, with a certain glee in her voice and all over her lovely face, likely not just because she'd insulted him, but because he'd let her see the insult had found its target.

It was more expression than he'd seen on her face in some time, and he took a dark sort of pleasure in that. Even as he realized with some surprise that while he'd been sorting through the fury and the rage and the fire in him, Alceu and his sister had slipped away, leaving only Apostolis and Jolie in the breakfast room.

How had he failed to notice that?

"It is lucky for you that I am such a small man," he told her then, and stood. Cataloging, as he did, the way her expression changed, and surely not only because he was, in fact, a large man no matter what she thought of him. It told him all manner of interesting things that he filed away for another time. "Or I might be tempted to return the favor."

Jolie's mouth curved in that way it did, that made him think only of sharp blades, polished to shine. And slice. "I wish you would. I can't wait to hear what a rich fantasy life you've been entertaining yourself with all these years."

But revenge was a long game. If the aim was to win.

And he intended to do just that.

Apostolis shook his head. "There will be time enough for that. Five long years."

She stayed where she was, seated with a certain insouciance at the table yet turned in her chair with one arm thrown almost languidly across its back. Yet he found he did not believe her attempt to appear bored by this.

Or him.

"One thousand, eight hundred, and twenty-five days, give or take," she agreed in a quiet voice that was in no way *soft*. "But who's counting?"

And it was a more solemn moment, then, between them. They were looking at each other, for a start. Usually, Apostolis knew, he avoided direct eye contact with this woman like the plague. It was too dangerous—

He wasn't sure he cared to think about why that was.

Apostolis extended his hand, slowly, and did very little to curb the glittering, sharp dislike—that was the only word for it, he was sure—curling through him and no doubt visible on his face.

She wore a very similar expression, ice to his fire.

But she rose.

"Come, my darling wife," Apostolis said in his darkest and most sardonic voice. "And let's start counting the days until we are free of each other."

Jolie smiled again, sharper still. But still she put her hand in his. And hers was smooth, but warm, and he did not wish to acknowledge how he could feel the contact inside him—everywhere—like another thread of that same...*dislike.*

"Until we see, you and I," she said, the blade of that smile honed to a deadly gleam, "who is the most damned."

CHAPTER THREE

THE FUNNY THING about the world ending was that it kept right on going as if her pain didn't matter at all. Her world had ended before, of course. Jolie should have been used to the fact that her pain didn't matter to anyone but herself, and certainly couldn't keep the sun from rising, the tides from turning, or the days from passing as they would.

Her grandparents' deaths had been the first, hardest series of blows. They had raised her after she'd lost her parents when she was two. She often felt profoundly guilty that she couldn't really remember that. She suspected that what she called her memories were actually stories her grandparents had told her about her parents and the pictures they had used to supplement the tales they'd told—of a couple so good it only made sense that they'd been *too* good for the world.

Her grandparents had been Jolie's world. And then, in the course of a bewildering few years, everything had changed.

She had been thirteen when her grandmother died. She and her grandfather had mourned together until he had decided that regular school was not enough for his only grandchild, and so had sent her off to finishing school when she was barely seventeen. So that she, like her grandmother before her, could learn how to be a woman of consequence.

I thought finishing schools turned girls into women who married consequence rather than becoming it themselves, she had complained.

Her grandfather had laughed, his kind eyes crinkling in the corners. *Perhaps. But married to whom, pray? One thing this particular school will do,* mon rayon de soleil, *is teach you how to* think.

He had maintained that the school would be the making of her until she had gone to take her place there. And within a few months he had succumbed to pneumonia and was gone, too.

That would have been quite enough change. But her grandfather had possessed what he liked to call *a bit of a buffer against the world's trials.* What it was, in fact, was a small fortune. When he died he left the whole of it to Jolie.

But because she was only seventeen, there were strings attached.

And those strings were her aunt and uncle. The court had appointed them trustees. They had oozed sincerity and warmth, despite the fact that her aunt—her mother's sister—had been estranged from the family for as long as Jolie could remember.

Jolie had believed they were who they said they were. Concerned relatives who wanted only to help their poor niece after a loss so devastating it must surely smooth over any past troubles.

She had not been so naïve since.

Jolie realized with a start that she'd been more or less

sleepwalking through the hotel, thinking about all the various *ends of the world* she'd lived through thus far. She blinked, shaking her head as she looked around, hoping that none of the staff—or more importantly, Apostolis—had seen her in such a distracted state.

Today was a changeover day, a week since her doomed wedding. Their last famous guest had left the day before, and as the Hotel Andromeda did not enforce checkout times on the clientele they treated like family, the guest in question and his expansive selection of acolytes had not chosen to leave until so late last night it was actually this morning.

This was why they always did their best to put a day of padding in between. There was no telling when a guest would ignore their checkout day altogether and have to be gently and politely—but never directly—encouraged to move on before the next guest arrived.

They had the whole day today, which was less time than it seemed after a tornado of fame and money went through the place. Their handpicked, miracle-working staff was already deep into the process of turning the entire old house inside out and upside down so that when the next set of guests arrived it would be as if the hotel had been waiting for them since their last visit. This time it was a family that would stay for a month, and liked the Andromeda to feel as if it was their home.

With occasional effortlessly glamorous drinks with the owner, of course. Since Spyros's death, the guests had liked to get together in the evenings and reminisce about the old man. Jolie only hoped that she could manage to keep her cool, as expected, now that she would not be reminiscing with the guests on her own.

This was not easy because Apostolis was not easy. A funny thing to say about a man who made such a point of acting lazy whenever possible, but it was true. She had imagined they might simply go about their business and ignore each other as much as possible, but he was always poking at her. Always seething in her direction, right there under the surface where, apparently, only she could see it.

He really is the most gloriously charming man alive, isn't he? one of the former guest's acolytes had sighed at Jolie only a few days ago, her eyes dancing with stars and focused on Apostolis. *I don't know how you can* bear *being around him all the time.*

This after Apostolis had managed to quietly insult her in a variety of ways throughout the evening, but apparently at a frequency only she could hear.

It is a great trial, she had replied. Truthfully. Though she'd had to smile enigmatically while she said it to make it seem as if she meant the opposite.

There was something so unfair about it, she thought now. That despite their mutual loathing—or perhaps because of it—she and Apostolis were the only ones who could see each other clearly.

She had been doing a walk-through of all the floral arrangements before she'd been sidetracked into unpleasant memories, one of her managerial tasks that she liked best. She had built a relationship these past seven years with all the florists in the village and used each of them all in a rotation, depending on the guest in question. The Andromeda liked to present each guest with a floral theme, a *flowerscape*, as Jolie and Dioni liked to call it.

Spyros had praised her for her attention to such things,

and his only compliments were always about the business. Like the scent profiles she curated, a comprehensive collection of scents that worked with each other, never against, and only completed the floral arrangements. It was not as simple as one might think.

Jolie carried on moving through the old mansion, in and out of the rooms that could all be locked up into separate suites but were left open and welcoming today, anticipating that the family group would wish to move freely. The rooms were large and graceful, and let in the light. Since that storm that had soaked her wedding right through, the best wedding gift she'd received, the island had returned to form. Everything was gold and blue, with bright flowers bursting into vibrant color everywhere. Inside the hotel, the palette was more understated, allowing the unmistakable beauty of the landscape and the sea to shine.

She loved this place. This grand and glorious old hotel. It had been one of the unexpected gifts of this path she'd been forced to take.

After checking out all the arrangements on this floor, she wandered into the library to assess the flowers that stood on the table directly beneath the vaulted skylight, one of Spyros's additions to the house. The flowers were appropriately theatrical, but she found herself drifting over to the shelves stuffed with books, never artificially arranged.

It had been the first room she'd found herself gravitating to when Spyros had brought her here. She supposed that it reminded her of her grandfather's study in the chateau outside Lausanne with its view of Lake Geneva and the Alps, filled with books, dear old rugs, and funny little items of art and interest that her grandparents had collected from all over the world.

The chateau, too, was gone now. What had been meant to be her birthright had been sold right out from under her.

Jolie had been almost done with finishing school before she understood what was happening. She had never cared much about her grandfather's will, or the fortune she had hardly been able to comprehend was to be hers. Because she hadn't had to worry about it, she understood now. And by the time she realized that she was no longer protected, it was too late.

The pain of that never quite left her.

She sank down in one of the comfortable seats in the Hotel Andromeda library and blew out a breath, remembering that terrible day when she'd finally fully understood the truth of things. She'd been nineteen and she'd thought that she was misunderstanding something, that was all. She had tried to use one of the cards her grandfather had always designated for her use, only to have it declined. That had sent her on what should not have been an arduous journey to locate her aunt and uncle, who were not living where they'd told her they were.

Jolie had tracked them down at the chateau. The chateau that did not resemble the home she had left that fall because they'd stripped it clean. And were in the process of selling it off, piece by piece.

I... I don't understand, Jolie had managed to say, close to tears as she stood in the entry hall, looking around at bare walls and empty rooms beyond in shock.

I deserve it, after the way they treated me, her aunt

had said, an ugly triumph making her face twist. *And I've taken it.*

And you're welcome to do something about it, if you like, her uncle had chimed in with an unpleasant laugh. *But by the time you do, it will all be gone.*

Their daughter Mathilde had been sitting on the steps behind them, her eyes wide. And Jolie had seen that same frightened awareness in her cousin that she knew must be written all over her. It had made her heart lurch inside her chest.

But... But that's not right, Jolie had sputtered.

Because back then, she'd still imagined that something like honor, or truth, or *what was right* mattered to anyone.

The truth was, her aunt and uncle had taught her a series of very valuable lessons.

At first, Jolie had felt helpless. They had sacked her home, pillaged her future, and taken everything that had meant anything to her. Oh, she knew that they thought she was upset about the money. But she'd never had any comprehension of that. Of what it meant.

What they had thrown away were her memories.

All those pictures. All those objects, softened by all the fingers she'd loved that had touched them. Paintings that were not just art to her, but windows into the marvelous stories of their travels.

All of it, gone.

But what is to become of me? she had asked them.

Her aunt had laughed and laughed.

Her uncle had snarled. *That school of yours should set you up just fine to marry one of the rich men always hovering about. That's what Mathilde will do when it's her time, and she won't be breathing in your rarefied air, will she?*

Again, the cousins had gazed at each other, each entirely too clear about what he must mean. Though, looking back, Jolie knew that she—at the least—had truly had no idea.

Some of us have to make do, her aunt had said with another unpleasant laugh. *You will find out, little* mademoiselle. *Soon enough, I should think.*

Sitting in an armchair in the library of the very rich man she'd gone ahead and married, Jolie found herself feeling something like rueful.

Because, of course, she had not wanted to marry anyone. She had vowed that she would do no such thing.

But over the course of her last year at school, her stark financial situation had been made clear to her. Her grandfather had paid her tuition in advance, but she was otherwise penniless. She had confessed everything to the headmistress one cold winter's day, and the older woman had listened with sympathy.

And then had fixed Jolie with a gimlet eye. *I am not saying that your horrid relatives are right, in any regard,* she had said. *But the fact remains that while this institution has been happily responsible for the education of many strong and powerful women in their own right, from politicians to activists to philanthropists of all kinds, its original purpose was to do all of those things but in the form—*

Of a wife, Jolie had said hollowly.

Not just any wife, the headmistress had replied, a stern sort of glint in her gaze. *This institution does not create trophies. It assures triumphs.*

What she did not ask, but what had hung there between them anyway, was, *Do you have any better ideas?*

And so, when her classmate's very old father had paid her close attention that spring, she'd accepted it. She had returned it, cautiously. And had gotten far more than financial security out of the bargain.

She had become instantly famous, everywhere, the moment her name was linked to *the* Spyros Adrianakis. Having not heard from her aunt and uncle in a couple of years by then, they had found a way to get in touch with her again once they heard the news. Perhaps unsurprisingly—though it made Jolie sad and bitter in turn—they had already run through the fortune they'd stolen.

Yet by that time, married to Spyros and living at the hotel in the company of so many different kinds of powerful people, Jolie was a far cry from the naïve girl they had taken advantage of years before.

The only reason she hadn't cut them off without a second thought was Mathilde. Who was, by that point, all of thirteen. And deserved her parents as little as Jolie had.

She was afraid she knew exactly what kind of things they might do with a pretty girl like Mathilde.

How could she live with herself if she let them? When she could do something to stop them? She couldn't. She just *couldn't.*

So she'd done the only thing she could. She'd struck a bargain.

And she'd been paying for it ever since.

Still, it was good to remind herself that she hadn't simply *ended up* here, she told herself now, gazing at the bookshelves before her that fairly *ached* with all the books they held. Even this marriage she found herself in now was a choice she'd made. Because, after all, a lack of *good* choices wasn't the same thing as a lack of choices.

You survived this far, she reminded herself. *You'll survive a little longer.*

Maybe then, when all the surviving was done, maybe she would give *living* a try.

But first there were flower arrangements and incoming guests. Bookkeeping and bills. Myths to embody and legends to keep afloat. Yet just as she was preparing to get back to her to-do list, something changed.

There was a disturbance in the air. And it seemed to be connected directly to her nervous system, or perhaps it was simply in her bones.

It was a winnowing. A tightening. A sudden shift.

Jolie was completely unsurprised to look up and find Apostolis there in the door to the library.

"Working hard I see," he said with his usual censure. When they were alone, he didn't bother to dress it up in a charming, playboyish smile. And she could have disabused him of the notion that she was lazy. That all she did here was lounge about, avoiding work. But that might indicate that she cared what he thought of her.

She couldn't have that.

Jolie went even more languid in the chair. She made her hand wave a work of artful ennui. "I am the trophy wife, remember? Why should I work?"

She had the distinct pleasure of watching those distractingly sensual lips of his firm, then press into a tight line. Maybe one day she would find herself adult enough—mature enough—to keep from feeling joy when she jabbed at this man. One day she would find her way to blessed indifference.

But that was not today.

"I am not my father," he told her, with that seething note in his dark voice.

He drew closer and everything in her urged her to stand up, to face off with him. To do what she could to at least stand tall before him—which was not tall enough, but certainly put her more the level of his face than she was now.

But she didn't.

Jolie lounged in that chair, giving every impression that she was exactly the sort of spoiled little party girl he thought she was.

"Is this an identity crisis?" she asked as he stalked closer. "If so, my suggestion for you is to seek therapy. Daddy issues can be so pernicious."

He didn't respond to that directly, but she did enjoy the slight flare of his nostrils, and the way the muscles in his jaw clenched tight. It was the little things.

"I understand that you might think that nothing will be expected of you. I imagine that's how your life has gone up to this point. But I have no intention of carrying you along like dead weight. You will work—"

"Or what?" she asked mildly. "For one thing, we're stuck with each other and no one put you in charge. For another, what exactly do you know about the business of running the Hotel Andromeda, Apostolis?"

"Anything my father could do, I'm quite certain I can do better."

She made herself laugh, though that hard look he had trained on her made it more difficult than it should have been. "And again I say…daddy issues."

"It is nothing to do with *daddy issues*." And the way he said those words made her think that the very taste of them in his mouth was sour. She liked that, too. "It is a simple fact that he was an old man. His attention to detail has slipped, to put it mildly." He shook his head at her, doing nothing at all to hide his distaste. "As his wife, I would expect you to have noticed that."

This time she laughed to cover her own surprise. "You'd be surprised the sorts of things I know about the men I've married."

She made that sound airy, as if she was just talking rubbish to annoy him. Inside, however, she was more than a little shaken.

Because in the past, she would have asserted with total confidence that Apostolis did not know a single thing about his father. His visits, spaced out as they were, were always all about him. There was no possible way he could know the first thing about Spyros as a man. Or the challenges the old man had faced in his waning years.

And she wondered if she would have felt this surge of something like loyalty to his father if she had been married to anyone but him. If it was actual loyalty to Spyros she felt—when she had never felt any such thing before—or a simple, possibly childish desire not to give Apostolis *anything*.

Not even the things she knew about his father that he didn't.

"I am sure that you are a great talent and know many, many fascinating things," Apostolis said then, his meaning clear as he swept a gaze over the length of her body. "None of them, I think, useful in the running of a hotel."

"Because you are the expert, is that it?"

Jolie regarded him steadily, because she'd found that it made him uncomfortable when she did so and today was no different. She could see the way he lowered his chin. The way his jaw tightened even further, almost certainly risking his famous smile.

And then, a far more telltale sign, he crossed his arms.

That felt like a win, so she smiled. "I think you'll find, Apostolis, that spending many a debaucherous evening in whatever hotel crosses your drunken path is not *quite* the same thing as running one. And even if it was, the kind of hotels that cater to your sort of character are very different from the Andromeda."

"I'll thank you to remember that the Andromeda is my birthright, not yours."

"Birthrights are funny things," she said, and there was, regrettably, more emotion in her voice than she might have wished in his presence. She hoped he would think it was temper. "They seem like rocks, do they not? Slabs of immovable granite that one can stand upon. Until they're gone."

His gaze was a wildfire. "Is that a threat?"

It hadn't been. It had been a bit of foolishness and wistfulness, nothing more—but then her breath caught because he moved forward. And before she could do anything at all, he was leaning over, bracing himself with a hand on each arm of her chair.

Caging her in.

He wasn't touching her. She knew he wasn't touching her—

And yet her body exploded into a riot of sensation, as if he was.

She felt hemmed in on all sides, as if she was trapped in his closed fist, but there was something far worse than that—and it was that she felt *precious* there.

As if that fist closed around her was protecting her, not confining her at all.

And it didn't help that the way he was leaning over her meant he'd put his face entirely too close to hers.

So that she was forced, entirely against her will, to remember in excruciating detail that final moment of their wedding ceremony.

You may kiss the bride, the priest had intoned.

She and Apostolis had stared each other down, with varying looks of horror and distaste.

But she was no coward, so she had stepped forward and tipped her head back, daring him. And he had accepted that dare at once, moving in and sliding a hand around to the small of her back, which had been...unpleasant.

Wildly, riotously unpleasant, she had assured herself.

And then—never closing his eyes, which she knew because she never closed hers—they had glared at each other while their lips brushed.

Jolie had instantly repressed that moment, until now.

Because now he was much too close, *again*. With that archangel's face of his and that look of burning distaste—for that was surely what it was—in his too-hot gaze.

She remembered the glare, the brush of their lips.

And the immediate, almost terrifying brush fire that had soared through her in its wake.

Here, in this chair in the library where she doubted she would find peace again, she could feel the lick of those same flames.

"Why are you worried about threats?" she had the presence of mind to ask him. "Do you feel threatened, husband?"

"The nature of a threat is mutable. Is it a promise? A suggestion?"

She lifted her chin, feeling defiant and not entirely understanding why. "I did not realize you were such a philosopher."

"And I thought you were an expert on your many husbands," he retorted in that sardonic tone of his. Almost chiding her. "But then again, you clearly enjoyed a certain...intimacy with my father that you and I do not share."

Something about that prickled in her, some mix of indignation and shame and not a little bit of temper, besides.

"Are you talking about sex?" She laughed into the breath of space between them. "And here I was beginning to think that the modern-day whore of Babylon himself had come over all missish. What would all your favorite tabloids say if they knew?"

"I suppose it would take one whore to know another," he replied, too easily. Too smoothly.

Because it took her one whole breath and half of another to understand that what he had really done was slide a knife in deep between her ribs.

The pain of it was so intense and so surprising, because it was so unfair, that she felt her eyes go bright.

"Don't think that I don't understand where all of this animosity is coming from," she told him, using whatever blades she had to hand, and hurling them as hard as she could. "It must be so confusing for you to finally meet a woman immune to what I think I've heard called your *charm*."

"Immunity would look like indifference, my darling

wife," he said, so softly. Too softly. "And you are many things in my presence, but indifferent? I think not."

"By that metric, I suspect you must be half in love with me," she said, lightly enough, yet sharp enough, to leave scars.

But before scars, there was blood, and they both knew she'd drawn his.

It seemed to shimmer there, in the air between them.

"Should we test that?" he asked, a scant breath that took the shape of words.

Even if she'd understood what he was asking, she would not have backed down from the challenge. Any challenge.

But she didn't understand.

When he leaned in even closer, then set his mouth to hers, she was wholly unprepared. And there was nothing for it but to burn.

She had never confused Apostolis with his father. For a host of reasons, none of which she intended to share with him, now or ever.

But if she had, this would have scorched any stray wisp of a memory of Spyros from her brain.

His hands stayed on the arms of the chair. The only place they touched at all was at the mouth. The lips. The tongues.

But that was more than enough.

Because he did not simply brush his lips over hers and call it a kiss.

That there was any resemblance between that first kiss and this *incineration*, that they should both share the same name, was almost laughable.

Because what he did was lick his way into her mouth,

flooding her with the most intense sensation she had ever felt. Then, as if that would not have knocked her on her bottom had she not already been sitting, he angled his jaw.

He made it all...hotter. Deeper. And decidedly worse. So much worse.

Distractingly, outrageously, irresistibly worse.

And this kiss that was so much more than a kiss went on and on.

It was a feast—a banquet of sensation—and she found herself responding against her will. There was nothing she could do but follow that fire, chasing that sensation any way she could.

Until it was as if their tongues were engaged in the same sweet, slick dance. As if they were both trying to burn each other alive, but this was not a flame that either one of them could control.

Nor should you want to, something in her whispered.

It was too bright, too bold. It grew too big, too fast.

And maybe she already knew that he would leave her in cinders.

Jolie pulled away and she felt a kind of triumph that she could. But it was a close call. And she only realized, then, that it hadn't occurred to her to keep her eyes open in protest the way she had before.

Something that was obvious to her because now, she could see him.

She could see the look on his face, intent and too hot to look at directly, though she did.

And let it sear straight through her.

Jolie decided she had only one play here. Only one chance to win this battle despite losing herself—and clearly losing her head—with this kiss she should never have allowed.

She'd know better now. She'd be more careful.

He had weapons she hadn't dared imagine, but now she would.

First, though, she had to win. Or more accurately— he had to lose.

So she sat forward and slid her hand over his jaw, the better to smile at him as if she meant it.

"Tell me, husband," she said quietly. Almost sweetly, her gaze steady on his. "Does that feel like threat enough to you now?"

And it was worth it to watch his face shutter, instantly. To watch him straighten and move back as if she had kicked him in the gut.

It was worth it to smile in the face of the look of pure loathing he threw her way, and keep smiling as he wheeled around and strode from the room.

And only then, only when she was alone, did Jolie cover her face with her shaking hands and do the best she could to keep from falling apart.

CHAPTER FOUR

THAT HE WAS a cursed man living a cursed life became, over the next weeks, a foregone conclusion even if it was not a surprise. Apostolis had spent the bulk of his life sorting out his own personal tragedies and attempting to come to terms with them.

Why should his marriage be any different?

"The scandal of your wedding has saturated the culture to such an extent that it has even reached me," his friend Alceu told him on one of their calls one day.

"I have always been a scandal," Apostolis said idly. "Why shouldn't I compound it now? Maybe I'll keep going. At what point does a scandal become too much scandal?"

"When there is any hint of scandal at all," Alceu said in his usual repressive tones. "I suspect, my friend, that there is no hope for the man who made his stepmother his wife."

"But was there ever any hope for me?" Apostolis asked in the same musing sort of way.

He could hear his friend's sigh. "I have never had any."

And yet, somehow, the conversation left him in a more hopeful frame of mind than he'd been in before.

He moved to the window of the hotel's executive offices, such as they were, that were located on the bottom floor of the carriage house that had sat beside the Andromeda for almost as long as the hotel itself. Longer, according to some accounts. The grounds of the hotel lounged about along the cliff top and in addition to the mansion itself, there were a number of outbuildings. Maintenance sheds, garages, stables, and so on. There was also the carriage house, which was not only the offices but also his own quarters since he'd been about ten. And the back house, as it was called even though it was technically to the side of the hotel, where he had lived as a small boy, his sister still lived, and his father had lived with Jolie.

Apostolis found that as time went on, he grew less and less sanguine about the fact that Jolie had been his father's wife first.

He found it harder and harder to accept that reality.

Yet he could still taste her in his mouth. She had invaded his sleep.

This was a new development.

He loathed it.

In his dreams, that scene in the library did not end where it had that day. In his dreams he lifted her up into his arms and took her down onto the library floor. He stripped her of those clothes she wore—all that casual, offhanded elegance, no match for the real Jolie there beneath the things she wore.

In his dreams, he tasted every centimeter of her flesh and drank deep between her thighs until he had her moaning and writhing in his grip.

And his dreams never stopped there, either.

Every night, his dreams presented him with another way to slake this wildfire in him. Every night, he found that there was no balance to his imagination and no brakes besides. Not when it came to her.

As if, all along, he had not so much hated her for all the appropriate reasons, but desired her—

But no. He could not accept it.

And it made interacting with her in the light of day a challenge.

She would stand before him throwing all her usual barbs and all he would think about was how deep inside of her he'd been in last night's deliriously hot dream. How she had arched her back and pressed her breast to his mouth. How she tossed back her head in abandon when she rode him hard and deep.

Are you listening to me? she had asked a bit sharply this morning.

But he'd studied the way her gaze widened as he looked at her.

And he'd wondered if she'd had an idea what he was thinking about without him having to say a word.

Of course I wasn't listening, he had told her, after a fraught moment or two passed. *I never listen when you're insulting me. Which means, my darling wife, it's as if we live in this lovely spot in perfect silence. Nothing but the waves and the wind.*

He had been proud of that.

She had looked rather more incandescent, though she had walked away before he could see if she might truly lose her cool at last.

Apostolis was enjoying imagining how else that moment might have ended when he heard a knock at the office door. He turned, aware that something in him leaped a bit at the notion it might be his wife.

But he tempered that reaction almost as soon as he had it. Because, for one thing, Jolie rarely knocked on any door at the Andromeda, since she was half owner of the hotel. As she liked to remind him daily. And for another, that was not the reaction he should have been having where she was concerned.

And besides, it was Dioni. He smiled at his sister with genuine warmth. "You don't have to knock, Dioni *mou*. This is your house as well as mine."

Dioni inched into the room and he felt the same swell of affection and bafflement that he always did at the sight of his sister. Their mother had been exquisite. A woman of such impeccable taste and glorious style that, to this day, he had never met a person who'd known her who didn't mention those things immediately.

And yet this was her daughter. His sister, the jewel of the house of Adrianakis, who scurried about like some kind of woodland animal.

"Well, that's a lovely thing to say but it's not really my house, is it?" If someone else had said something like that, it would have been a complaint. But this was Dioni. He had never heard her complain. Because a complaint was part and parcel of some kind of darkness, and as far as he was aware, she had never known even the faintest shadow. "It's your house. And Jolie's house. Father did not leave me anything."

"He left you me," he corrected her, surprised when perhaps he should not have been. "And I will see to it, as he did, that you will never want for a thing."

His sister made her way further into the office and sat in the chair before his desk. And he looked at her, struck by the notion that he hadn't really looked at her closely in some time. Not since the wedding, which was weeks ago now. She looked…

Different, he thought. It took him a moment to realize why. Her hair wasn't falling down all around her. He could see no stains or tears in her clothing.

He frowned. "Are you all right?"

He could have sworn that she flinched then, though she hid it in the next moment. But then again, this was his sister who had never hidden anything from him. He was certain that he must have been mistaken.

She frowned at him. "Why would I be different? What do you mean?"

Apostolis had always thought that his role as her brother was not to mention her appearance, which he knew everyone else harped on. Or worse, tried to *help her*, which she always suffered with good grace only to turn up disheveled just the same.

He had always found it charming.

"Only you can tell you're different or not, little mouse," he said, and again, she did something out of the ordinary. It was as if she bristled, but then caught herself.

"I finally decided what I want to do with my life," she said. And he thought she sounded unlike herself, but he was not going to tell her that. "I've decided that I'm going to pack up and move to America."

"America?" He didn't laugh. He could sense she wouldn't like it. "America is a large place, Dioni. Have you picked a specific *part* of the country?"

"I will." She frowned at him again, and more deeply this time. "What I need you to do is be okay with it when I go."

And maybe he was a worse brother than he'd ever

imagined, because he didn't think about anything at all in that moment except having the privacy to handle Jolie the way he wanted. At last.

Because he thought he finally knew how. It came to him in a blinding flash the moment he understood that he'd been wanting this privacy all along. He and Jolie had settled into their marriage, such as it was, by playing their roles in public—but continuing to live in their separate quarters. This arrangement had not seemed to worry his sister at all, or cause her to question their marriage in any way. *Seeming happiness* could involve separate beds, as far as the innocent Dioni knew.

Yet *happy* was not how Apostolis would describe himself. Or his marriage.

He'd been dreaming this solution all along. It might be inconvenient to find he desired his stepmother in this way, and he chose not to question why it felt more like a long overdue *recognition* than some new bolt from the blue, but he could use it. He *would* use it. Because he finally had the weapon he needed to win this war decisively.

But here and now, he had to force himself to concentrate.

"First of all, you can go wherever you like, for as long as you like, and do whatever takes your fancy." The Dioni he knew would have smiled brightly at that and started chattering on merrily about the great many projects that were already lighting up her mind. But today, his sister only looked back at him, but with that steady frown in place. He was tempted to think she was making him the slightest bit uneasy, but of course she wasn't. This was *Dioni*. And he did not get *uneasy*. "If you wish to go to America, there is no need for mystery. I have properties in New York, Miami, and Los Angeles. And, of course, Hawaii."

That got a reaction from his sister. She blinked. "You do?"

"Don't tell anyone," he told her, with a grin. "It would ruin my image. The world prefers to consider me the grand waste of space our father did. And perhaps I am. But either way, I also have a robust real estate portfolio."

He smiled blandly as his sister came close to gaping at him and wondered how she would react if she knew how he actually spent his time, or that Alceu was his partner in those far more low-profile activities. "Remember, Dioni. It's a secret."

"I think I'd like to go to New York City," she said after a moment, then turned her frown toward the windows. "I don't want any more beaches. I want concrete canyons and furious impatience wherever I turn."

Somehow Apostolis thought that she would find the brownstone he owned in Manhattan's West Village neighborhood, complete with its own garden, a little less *impatient* than the rest of the city. But she could discover that for herself. "Are you sure?" he asked. When she nodded, he carried on. "Then only say the word, and we will have—"

"I am ready for a change," his sister said, cutting him off. "Now."

Her asserting anything so strongly was so unusual that he actually gazed back at her in something approximating shock.

"All right then. You can leave tonight if you like."

"Wonderful," Dioni replied, but even then she didn't sound like her normally cheerful self. There was something brittle about her. He didn't like it.

But if she didn't want to tell him, he didn't see how he could force her. And in any case, he knew from his own experience across many brooding years that while the geographic cure never quite lived up to its name, sometimes, a Band-Aid in place of an *actual cure* could do the trick just the same.

His sister deserved to find these things out for herself.

Everything happened swiftly, then. He called to have the plane readied. She went off to oversee the packing of her things—or perhaps, for all he knew, she was already packed.

And that evening, only a few hours after Dioni had come to speak to him in the office, Apostolis and Jolie stood out on the tarmac on the other side of the island—together—and said their goodbyes.

"I will miss you," he told his sister fiercely when she hugged him.

"Really do miss me, then," she replied, but she was smiling. "Don't get weird and spy on me."

"I would never dream of it," he lied, and made a mental note to pare back the security detail he'd planned to keep in her vicinity.

He watched as Dioni hugged Jolie and thought it seemed longer and harder for someone merely taking off on a new adventure. Particularly when she was late to that game. Many people did such things when they were younger, with their gap years and their regrettable twenties.

But he was a terrible brother, clearly, because the only thing he could truly concentrate on was the fact there was the hotel and its guests waiting for them—but other than that, only and him and Jolie on the property. Staff quarters were further down from the cliff, giving them a bit of a break from the hotel when they weren't on duty.

Members of the family had no breaks. And now his wife had nowhere to hide.

And maybe the anticipation of that was humming in him a little too brightly, because Jolie looked at him in askance when he started the sleek Range Rover and aimed it at the coastal road that hugged the coastline, then meandered along the length of the island to the Andromeda.

Especially when he drove a bit too fast.

"I have never known Dioni to be so..." Jolie began.

"Independent?" he offered. "Secretive? Strange?"

"Solitary," Jolie replied.

Perhaps a little repressively.

But he found that whatever else he might object to in this woman, her friendship with his sister was something that could only win his approval. Especially when Jolie possessed precisely that sort of effortless elegance that his sister lacked so profoundly.

Others had been cruel. He had realized in his time here that Jolie, no matter her many other faults, was never anything but kind to Dioni.

It was tempting to imagine there were whole other parts of her he could not see—

But he cast that worrying thought aside.

She was sitting in the passenger seat, so there was only so far away from him she could be based on the dimensions of the vehicle. Yet Jolie, somehow, managed to make it seem as if she'd put an extra ice floe or two between them.

He took satisfaction, tremendous satisfaction, in knowing that that was something she was not going to be able to do for much longer.

Not with any success.

"Change is good," he said, thinking of the various ways he knew to melt ice. "There were whole years of my life where change was the only constant. It's time Dioni discovered who she is and who she wants to be, away from the shadow of all this."

"And do you think you managed to do it?" came Jolie's silky, too serene tone, though her gaze was trained out the window. "Do you think you successfully removed yourself from any pesky shadows or do you worry that all you've done is run about to no avail, only to end up where you started?"

Normally he would have shot right back. But there were all those dreams in the night. Every night. There were all the ways he'd already had her when he had barely touched her. There was that kiss and the repercussions of that, and the way it echoed through him, even now. As if it was simply a part of him.

That wasn't anything new. What was new was that he knew that everything between them was about to change.

And, perhaps, the fact that beneath her icy exterior, she cared for the sister he had always protected to the best of his ability.

It allowed him to answer with more candor than he might have otherwise. "I never considered myself to be in my father's shadow. Quite the opposite. He would have had to be present in my life in some meaningful way for me to consider myself overshadowed by him."

"Some would say that his legend alone does that work," Jolie murmured.

"His legend has never meant much to me. I have read about it in magazines, like anyone else. In fawning articles that carry on about the secret lifestyles of famous men and the places they like to habit, like the Andromeda. I'm fully aware of the mystique. Of the hotel *and* the man." Apostolis shrugged. "But for me it was my childhood home. A mother who tried to please her husband, and then died. And a father who was always too busy chasing women—before and after he was widower—and courting the attention of celebrities to pay any attention at all to any of us. I like my family's legacy. I want to continue it, as my mother would have wanted. The hotel and its legend is important to me. My father's personal legend I could do without."

He felt her turn to look at him then, and he congratulated himself, because surely allowing her to imagine him vulnerable was the greatest weapon he'd employed yet.

But he found himself glancing over just the same, to gauge the particular color of her Mediterranean blue eyes.

"I was orphaned when I was two," she told him after a long curve in the road brought them past one of the villages, white-walled and blue-shuttered. "I never really knew my parents, so I can't say that I mourned them, specifically. But I have to imagine that having parents and yet not having them must in some ways be harder than not having them at all. I never wondered if our relationship could improve. I never tortured myself with fantasies about the way that things could be different between us. And when I imagine them, it's the fantasy versions of them my grandparents created for me, as bedtime stories. I never got to know their flaws and foibles. I never had to measure myself against them and see where they came up lacking, or I did." She let out a long, low breath. "So I don't envy you, Apostolis. Whether you call it a shadow or not, it must be a weight all the same."

He had pulled up to the hotel and now he navigated the car to a stop in front of the carriage house. When he did, he looked over at her and could not tell if the weight he felt inside him was that shadow she'd spoke of, or if it was that unexpected mix of compassion and grief that she'd shared with him.

Apostolis was in knots, but Jolie wasn't even looking at him. She looked almost supernaturally composed, her head angled away from him, her gaze out toward the sea.

But he had the strangest urge to reach over and trace the line of her jaw, because it looked sharper than usual, as if she'd set it against the same memories she'd just shared with him.

He stopped himself right there. Whatever game she was playing here, whatever battle tactic this was, he would be a fool to fall for it.

She turned to look at him then, and suddenly he could feel shadows everywhere, as if they were both soaked in them. Or maybe it was the ghosts of what could have been. Of what might have been.

If he had met her somewhere other than on his father's arm, years ago.

He had never felt anything like it, that sudden pang of loss. And never so keenly, the ache of it so intense it made his bones hurt.

And though he couldn't read anything on her face, he somehow thought that what he saw there was a thread of true vulnerability. Or something more akin to openness.

Whatever it was, it had no place between them.

This *hurt* had no place in this war.

And she must have told herself the same thing, he thought, because she was the one who spoke first. She was the one who broke this odd moment in half.

"We will have to hurry," she said, in a brisk sort of voice, as if they hadn't been talking about *shadows* only moments before.

"Hurry?" he repeated, feeling...off-kilter.

It was not a sensation he enjoyed. And he would consider it one more mark against her, he decided. One more offense she would need to answer for, in the most delectable way possible.

"It is almost time for cocktails on the terrace, which most guests demand," she told him, that edge in her voice back as if it had never been gone. "This is the sort of thing that the proprietor of the Andromeda must never forget, Apostolis. It is one among many tiny little details that must be welded to your bones, as much a part of you as breath. Our last guest and his entourage preferred their own company, but that is unusual. Normally, not only must you follow the schedule every day in and day out, you must make certain that our guests feel as if there is no schedule at all. As if it is merely spontaneous, the joy we find in their presence, and so we celebrate it with a bottle of something lovely beneath the stars of an evening."

He wasn't sure what moved in him then. Was it a dark thread of laughter? Or was he more inclined to...shout?

"I don't know why I am always so astonished that every last part of you is a work of theater," he found himself saying, his voice low and urgent in a way that might have alarmed him, but it was better than shouting. And he was too busy trying to work out that look on her face. Why couldn't he categorize it?

"I can tell that you mean that to be an insult." Jolie rolled her eyes as if to say, *and a weak one at that.* "But I'm not insulted. On the contrary, you could not have complimented me more if you tried. Your father made it clear that he wanted me to inhabit the role of the iconic hostess here. Unknowable, yet everyone's confidante, and so on. I'm glad to know I've done that."

She didn't wait to see his reaction to that, the way any other woman he'd ever known would have. And always had. Instead, she opened up her door and climbed out of the Range Rover as if she'd finished with this conversation.

Or perhaps with him altogether.

That wasn't the reason he found himself following suit, and quickly, he assured himself. He was simply exiting the vehicle.

And he found her again in the middle of the drive, the sea at her back, the olive trees on the hill, and standing there above them, the Andromeda. Keeping a silent, watchful eye on everything, as always.

Only a fool would complicate the situation by touching her, but Apostolis did it anyway. He took her wrist in his hand and found himself staring down at that point of contact. It took him too long to lift his eyes to hers again, and when he did he found her regarding him.

Again with a look he could not name in her gaze.

"Careful," she said, almost too quietly. "Just because you can't see anyone doesn't mean we're not in public. That's one of the first things your father taught me."

"I suppose I'm delighted to hear that he was able to

impart his version of wisdom to someone," Apostolis gritted out.

Something not quite a smile moved over her face. "Says the man who claims there's no shadow over his life, when he is little more than an eclipsed moon trying too hard to act the part of the sun."

It felt like a knife to the gut.

He told himself it was comforting, somehow. A return to form.

"I thought I'd lost you somewhere on the coastal road," he said, not breaking eye contact. "Unexpected vulnerability? A perfectly civil conversation, no less? I hardly knew you at all."

She pulled her hand from his grasp, both of them aware that he could have held onto her if he'd wanted to. And he took an atavistic pleasure in the way her own hand went to cover the place he'd touched her, as if she needed to soothe the sensation.

Or hold it close.

"Dioni is a good friend of mine," she told him with that quiet dignity that he knew was meant to make him feel small. He told himself it didn't work. "I'm going to miss her. She has…always been here. As long as I've been here, anyway. It will feel empty without her."

"It won't for long," he told her then, deciding in that instant that telling her now actually made it harder on her. He wasn't pulling a punch, he was making sure it landed harder. That it reverberated more fully.

He certainly wasn't attempting to make her *feel better*.

A faint frown sketched itself between her brows. "I can only imagine what that's supposed to mean."

"No need to imagine, my dear and darling wife," he

drawled, enjoying the thick weight of that satisfaction deep within him. "It's not a secret. I've had all your things moved into the carriage house. Isn't it wonderful? We will finally live together as man and wife."

And then he left her there, sputtering on the drive, and went to play the role of *iconic host* himself.

Because she might have won some points, reminding him that his role here had more to do with the longevity of the hotel and less to do with his childhood here. And that much of that longevity relied upon the kind of legend he built in the wake of his father's.

He hoped he was man enough to take good advice when he heard it, no matter the source, because he'd always prided himself on that before.

Because he was here to make sure that the legend his mother had given her life to could sustain itself despite Spyros. That it could carry on, long after Spyros was entirely forgotten—the most fitting end to the story of his narcissistic father he could imagine.

And later tonight, after committing himself to a role he'd once vowed he would never take—*Because I want more than to run a* hotel *like a servant*, he had sneered at his father, when he'd imagined such words could hurt Spyros's feelings, back when he was young and assumed his father had any—he intended to win a decisive battle in this war with his wife.

Once and for all.

CHAPTER FIVE

ON THE OFF chance that he had merely said that *man and wife* nonsense for the pleasure of alarming her—and how she hated to admit he'd succeeded—Jolie took the fifteen or so minutes she had left before evening drinks usually began to go and see for herself.

Surely even Apostolis would not be *that* peremptory.

But he'd been telling the truth. The back house where she'd lived and worked for seven years now looked like… any other part of the hotel. Quietly welcoming and richly appointed to best suit the island and the Andromeda's reputation for elegance, but stripped of anything personal.

Her heart hit against her ribs so hard it was a wonder a bone didn't crack from the impact.

With a sense of mounting horror—because surely that was what all the warring sensations inside her were, that weight in her belly and a tingle that was much too close to a kind of shiver radiating out from it—she left the back house and went over to the carriage house instead, walking in briskly the way she always did.

She had always thought of this house as a temple to all the things that were wrong with his family, and Apostolis specifically. There was the office that she now shared with Apostolis, that Apostolis had claimed with a huge, black desk years ago. It took up the lion's share of the space in the office and was a particularly odd choice for a man who...had not worked here until his father had passed.

Then again, he seemed to think she was only there to play on the internet, as if she didn't have a mobile.

Though she would have died before commenting on it.

But the house announced itself in the entry hall. It started with the row of black-and-white photographs that lined the walls, framed to better proclaim their self-importance, as each and every one had been taken by a world-famous photographer who had been a guest here. Spyros had liked to say that he'd traded the bill for their stays for the photographs, but Jolie didn't have to be familiar with the hotel's books to know that was untrue.

Spyros loved a good story, but he loved money more.

Her heart was performing cartwheels inside her chest now that she'd made her way inside. She told herself—rather sternly—not to react to the place as if it, too, was waging a battle against her.

"It's just a house," she told herself crossly.

That was true. It was a house. That worked well enough when she was here to deal with hotel business. But it was *his* house. And tonight she was here because he'd moved *her* into this house.

With him.

Instead of heading down the hall to the office, she turned the other direction instead, and hated it.

The ground floor was lovely, having long ago been opened up to let in the light, and was now a flowing, open space that included a kitchen, a dining area, and a living room with doors that led out to the carriage house's private patio. She walked through all the white and blue and vivid accents, aware of the sea watching her from outside the windows and the excruciatingly modern art on the walls that always seemed to sit in judgment of her.

"Three splashes of paint on a canvas cannot *judge* anyone," she muttered as she passed a particularly snobbish painting on her way to the open, winding stair that rose up from the ground floor to the open gallery that ran above it.

Jolie ran up the steps, her feet tapping out a staccato that was still too slow to match her pulse. Upstairs, there were low-slung leather couches and views of the ocean, and sculpture pieces in recessed alcoves.

But she was here to check the bedrooms for her things, so that was what she did. Jolie's heart was still clattering about, but she was starting to feel almost…giggly. That was new and shocking enough to make her stop short.

Then she remembered the sort of silly games she and the other girls had got up to at school, sneaking about the place after curfew for the sheer joy of…not being where they were supposed to be.

It felt like breaking the rules to be up on this floor, and it must have always felt that way, because she'd never come up here before.

"Focus," she ordered herself, marching down the hall that led off the gallery and opening up doors as she went.

One room was clearly a guest room, and given Apostolis's lack of guests, Jolie doubted it had been used in years. The next room looked as if it could be converted into guest quarters if necessary, though it was currently doing duty as another sort of library, with books stacked neatly on every surface, which made her feel…odd.

Was Apostolis a reader? Or was this overflow from the Andromeda's library? She didn't know which answer she wanted more. She didn't know which one would make her feel better. Or worse.

Maybe she didn't know how she wanted to feel about any of this.

Take Dioni, who had gotten strange over the past few weeks. Jolie had wondered if it was a reaction to her friend marrying her brother. If Dioni hadn't minded when Jolie was married to her *father*, but Apostolis, who Dioni had always looked up to, was something else no matter that she'd initially celebrated it. Because Dioni hadn't felt that Jolie marrying Spyros was really anything but a bit of a personal tragedy for her friend, but great news for *her,* because she got to have her best friend around all the time.

But Dioni was not a liar, and she had nothing but positive things to say about Jolie's marriage.

Maybe, she had whispered fiercely on the tarmac, *my brother and you will find what you need in each other.*

And she had sounded so hopeful. Jolie hadn't had the heart to tell her that Apostolis had never been even remotely heroic—not to Jolie.

That was something he saved for his sister.

In the car ride back, she'd had to face the fact that Dioni, for the first time in as long as Jolie had known her, was keeping secrets. Like why she suddenly wanted to move halfway across the planet, alone, when she'd never indicated the slightest interest in such adventurousness before.

She should have been proud. She had always told her friend that she needed to go out there and *claim her life.*

Jolie should have specified that she hadn't meant that

Dioni should do that while leaving *her* behind, neck-deep in another round of her *choices*.

She was going to miss her best friend terribly.

She already did.

It made her tell the blasted man things she shouldn't. He made her forget herself, and that was unforgivable.

She blew out a breath, there in the hall. Calm was what was needed, not more storming about lighting fires. After all, she'd already done seven years in this lovely prison. What were five more? There was no need for more fire, thank you.

Jolie chanted that to herself as she opened the larger door at the end of the hall and all her breath deserted her in a rush.

Because this was clearly the master bedroom. *His* bedroom.

She drifted in, feeling jumpy. As if she expected to trip an alarm, when that was silly. She knew where all the security measures were in this house and all the other buildings on hotel property.

But her gaze was drawn immediately to the bedside tables, where some member of staff had carefully stacked the things she'd had on a similar table in her room in the other house. Just so.

It made tears prick at the backs of her eyes, and a lump fill her throat.

It was *not good,* she told herself.

She whirled around, seeing a succession of spaces that were clearly meant to mimic the flow below. But she found her way into a massive dressing room, where she saw all of her clothes. Just *hanging* there, suggesting an intimacy with all of *his* clothes.

As if their clothes were more married than they were.

Jolie had to put her hand out to the nearest wall to steady herself. From the surge of *fury* that swept over her. Because this was clearly a moment of *temper,* she assured herself, as her body...*reacted.*

And then kept reacting.

She dashed a hand over her eyes. Did he truly believe that he could simply...move her things in and that would be that? That he could simply *decide* that it was time to commence a relationship that involved *sharing a bed* when they'd never agreed to anything of the kind?

When they'd never discussed it at all?

Jolie refused.

And she was certain that that rushing sensation in her body and the way it all pulled down low into her belly— almost uncomfortably hot, like *fury* or *flu*—was confirmation that he was out of his mind.

But she made herself take a long, steadying breath. She pushed away from the wall and went into the attached bathroom suite, so she could check her face and make sure she looked nothing but effortless.

Because he wasn't the only one who could play mind games.

After a quick stop at the hotel's front desk, she drifted out onto the terrace where the family that had been staying with them for weeks now was already gathered. The adults were enjoying their drinks and talking in low, happy voices as they looked out at the sea far below, waiting for another one of the predictably spectacular Mediterranean sunsets.

She found Apostolis at once, and all of that chaos and riot inside of her seem to spiral into a kind of sharp focus.

So sharp it almost hurt.

Jolie smiled, murmuring greetings to the guests as she passed, and then went directly to her husband to slip her arm through his and even hug it a little, as if they were close like that. She knew exactly how to make it seem as if they possessed a deeply physical connection, and so she did that, too. All it took was tilting her head up to look at him and smiling a bit dreamily as he looked down at her, his dark gaze burning hot.

And deeply wary.

Good, she thought.

"I'm so sorry I'm late," she said in a voice calculated to *accidentally* reach everyone. Then she offered the guests a faintly sheepish smile, as if surprised they'd heard her. "My only excuse is that I am a newlywed again. I never expected such a thing to happen."

It was like she'd changed the temperature with a flip of a switch, because suddenly everyone was all smiles. And open in a way they hadn't been, not quite, since they'd arrived. There had been too much speculation, too many whispers, too many raised brows.

But this new spirit of openness went on all evening.

Perhaps because of this, the family invited their hosts to have dinner with them. They all sat around the great table beneath the pergola, basking in the soft evening breeze, with its hint of salt and flowers in the air.

"We did wonder," said the matriarch, sitting next to Jolie and even pressing her shoulder against hers. "There has been a great deal of talk about the changes here, as I'm sure you can imagine."

"It's been a time of transition," Jolie said with a nod.

"It's hard not to talk about that, I suppose, when it involves a place that means so much to all of us."

"Spyros was a dear old man who everyone knows you loved well," said the older woman, and Jolie knew that her *everyone* encompassed more people than simply the family members she gathered here each year to celebrate her birthday. "We all thought so. But you are a young woman with her whole life ahead of her. And what is it they say? *The heart wants what it wants*." She smiled then, as if dispensing her good favor. "I think that a brand-new love story is exactly what the Andromeda needs."

Jolie reached over and put her hand on the old woman's hand. "I can't tell you what it means to me that you understand," she told her softly. "I know how it must look from the outside, but…"

She trailed off helplessly, and it was true that she meant to do that. To sound so helpless in the face of the *Apostolis* of it all. But it was also true that her heart had not calmed down at all. And she was beginning to suspect that neither fury nor flu had anything to do with the situation inside of her.

A situation that was not getting better the longer she sat here, playing a woman *madly and recklessly in love.*

"Anyone who looks at the two of you can see the chemistry between you," said her guest, with a bit too much confidence for Jolie's peace of mind—but she reminded herself that she wanted that. That it was a commentary on the act she was putting on and no more. No one knew what was happening inside of her. No one—including herself, if she was honest. "Just as anyone who saw you and Spyros could tell that what you had was real, not what they liked to hint in the papers. Don't you worry, child. Real love *always* wins over the gossips."

Jolie murmured her thanks. And when she lifted her hand from the woman's and shifted her gaze across the table, Apostolis was gazing straight at her.

Very much as if *he* knew exactly what was happening inside her. All of that heat and weight and helpless wonder, God help her.

She found it *hurt* to tug her gaze away from his.

It was a long evening, filled with wine, conversation, laughter, and reminiscing. Sometimes she lost herself in moments like these and pretended she really was the mysterious and yet approachable hostess they thought she was, elegant and endearing in turn. Sometimes she forgot that these were roles that she played, not versions of her *actual self.* If she squinted, she could almost imagine that what the canny old woman had said about her was true. That she and Spyros had really had that kind of affection between them. Or that she and Apostolis had fallen head over heels in love.

That she'd really fallen into that kind of charmed life, here in one of the most beautiful places on earth.

And because there was an audience, because there was always an audience, she made sure that was exactly what it looked like.

At the end of the evening, when everything had been cleared away, she and Apostolis waved good-night to the guests. Then they walked back across the drive and she took the act one step further, threading her fingers through his and she turned back to wave over her shoulder once more.

His fingers closed over hers, tight. As if he had no intention of letting her go. And she could feel the tension in him. That humming awareness that she knew was in her, too, though she doubted it was for the same reason.

Hers involved the side of righteousness, after all.

She let herself droop almost languidly into him as they crossed the drive, enjoying the way he tensed the whole of his big, hard body at the contact. Then they went into the carriage house like they were exiting a stage.

Jolie went first. Apostolis followed. It was a perfect rendition of *careful*.

But once inside, she turned to him and laughed.

Right there in the hall, in front of all the artsy photographs of happy moments that she doubted had ever been as happy as they seemed, she made sure that her laugh was almost too brittle to bear.

"What do you think of that performance?" she asked him, in a completely different voice than the soft, cultured, dreamy one she'd been using all night. "Did you like it? Do you think that I'll win an award now that the curtain's gone down?"

And it felt like a blast of sheer triumph when all he could do was stare at her. Jolie took a deep breath that felt as if it was shuddering all the way through her, but she told herself that was just another part of this victory. That Apostolis actually looked stunned.

So stunned that he couldn't even mask his reaction.

She laughed again. "Did you really think that you could just…move me into your bed? Without discussion? What planet do you live on?"

"I live on the planet where when I kiss you we both go up in flames," he shot back. Clearly no longer quite so stunned. And his eyes were on fire. "And unlike you, I'm not afraid to play in that fire. Can you say the same?"

She shook her head slowly, feeling a great wash of rage move over her. What else could it be, so hot and flushed and *furious?*

"I'm not afraid of anything involving you," she told him, very deliberately. "My worst nightmare involving you has already come true."

"Prove it," he invited her, something more than a simple flame in his gaze.

"I don't have to prove it. All I have to do is pretend I'm sleeping with you and it achieves everything I need it to do. Why would I actually *do* it? What's in it for me?"

"I think you know that it's the last battlefield, Jolie."

"And I suppose you think that you have all the weapons necessary for victory?" She made a new opera out of the roll of her eyes, and the bored shake of her head. "How naïve you are. You forget, I think, that this is a marriage, not one of your tawdry affairs. We have no choice but to stay together for forty-four weeks of each and every one of the next five years. If you blow something up you might have to live in the rubble, Apostolis. You and I both know that you're not built to handle that."

It was his turn to laugh at something that wasn't funny at all. "You speak with great authority for a person who doesn't know anything of importance about me."

Jolie lifted a languid shoulder and tracked the way his gaze followed the movement. "The only thing I need to know about you is that you've never stuck anything out. On the other hand, I was married to your father for years. And contrary to what our guests seem to think, it was not exactly a trip through the tulips. It was work." But she didn't want to get into that, so she kept going, especially when she saw the query in his gaze. "What do you know about that kind of work? I mean real work. The gritty intimacy involved in having not only to live with the decisions you make, but to marinate in the consequences of those decisions day after day, year after year."

"Has it happened?" he asked, she realized somewhat dimly that he had moved closer, then, because her back was suddenly against the wall. And the only thing she could see was him. "Have we finally arrived at the moment where you admit that your reasons for marrying my father were mercenary, that he was a monster, and that you were miserable?"

"I envy you," Jolie told him softly. "What a gift it is that you could reach your advanced age and still believe things could be so black and white. I'm afraid that privilege was taken from me quite early. And I have nothing to complain about in my life. I have been well provided for, with only a short period of anxiety about such things. On the other end of the next five years, I will be able to do as I please. I'm not sure that I would change any of it if I could."

Jolie had never said that out loud before. She wasn't sure she had even thought it. Because that was the trouble with regret, wasn't it? With peering back through time, imagining that the things that haunted her could be taken away somehow… If they were, then it meant everything else would also change. She could have ignored Spyros when he'd turned his eye toward her, but where would she be now if she had?

She didn't have to imagine what Mathilde's fate would

have been if she'd turned him down. The possibilities were etched on the inside of her eyelids.

"You're such a liar," Apostolis said then, in a voice that was nearly crooning. Nearly soft, like a lover's. "Everything about you is a lie. What I can't decide is if you believe the lies you tell or if you are entirely callous, spitting them out one after the next like every other falsehearted grifter who ever lived."

That might have hurt, coming from someone else. And she felt a phantom pain in the vicinity of her chest anyway. She told herself she was imagining what that would feel like if he'd mattered to her at all.

"That sounds a lot like projecting," she said, lightly. Easily. As if she had never been hurt by a thing in all her days here, and certainly not by *him*. "Once again, I think you'd be an excellent candidate for therapy. And no need to worry. It would only take… Oh, I don't know. Twenty years or so to untangle all these things in you that have become so rotted and terrible." She reached out and patted him on the arm, her smile fairly dripping with false sweetness. "Trust the process, Apostolis. You can do it."

He laughed again, then, and there was something about it. The way it rolled through her, and him, too. She could see it. Or she could feel it, maybe, something shimmering and starkly dangerous, winding around the pair of them and filling up the hall.

Filling up the whole house.

That was when Jolie realized that, possibly for the first time, they were truly all alone.

Not in a moving vehicle. Not in a place where staff might appear at any moment, because they never came here without an invitation and an appointment.

Dioni was flying across the Atlantic even now.

That meant it was just the two of them and this wild, chaotic war of theirs. She could hear the beat of those war drums, a deep *insistence* within her. She could feel the march of booted feet, up and down her spine.

"There are only so many ways this can end." And there was still that dangerous laughter all over his face. It made his eyes gleam in that way they did sometimes, that bittersweet gold. "We could kill each other. For obvious reasons, I would prefer to avoid that. One of us could kill the other. For legal reasons, I can't support that either. But if we continue like this, constantly upping the ante, constantly trying to outwit the other, it's going to be one of those two endings. I hope you know that."

"Spoken as someone who, once again, can only imagine things in the short term." Jolie leaned back against the wall and crossed her arms. Then tilted up her chin, hoping she looked as insouciant as she wished she felt. "And more than that, only thinks with one part of his anatomy. None of this is a surprise to me, you understand. But I think you're going to have to learn that not everything can be solved in the way you think it ought to be, just because *you* lack imagination."

"What amazes me is that you think that headlines are facts, Jolie, when I would think you'd know better, personally. And I suppose it would be easier for you if I really did only think with one part of my anatomy. But your tragedy is that, deep down, you know I'm right."

He moved forward then, just a little. Just enough to make her brace herself—

But she shouldn't have.

Because doing so gave away too much. She knew it instantly.

His smile confirmed it. "You might have had my father wrapped around your finger. You might have been the one who used sex as a weapon in that relationship. But in this one?"

This time he leaned even closer, bracing himself with one palm on the wall beside her head. She thought for a terrible, thrilling moment that he might actually put his mouth on hers once more—

But he didn't. He put his mouth to her ear instead.

"This time the best you can hope for is mutually assured destruction," he whispered, and she suspected he knew the way the sound and *feel* of those words curled through her like smoke and warning. "And I have to tell you, my darling stepmother and wife, I think that *my* destruction is highly unlikely."

Words crowded into her mouth as if fighting to get out, but Jolie did not allow herself a retort. She angled herself back, only slightly. Partly because the wall was at her back, but more importantly, because he was *right there*, still bracing himself against the wall.

Still leaning over her.

She found his gaze, bittersweet and gleaming, and held it.

Then, so slowly it was almost like *thinking* about moving instead of moving, she reached out. She trailed her fingers over his face, noting that when he took a swift and surprised breath, it was as if she could feel it inside her, too.

And that wasn't all she could feel. Touching him felt remarkably like touching herself. She could feel the trail of sensation. She could feel the way it moved in her, a slow, languorous heat.

Jolie moved her hand from his face to touch the side of his neck, and his collarbone, sneaking her fingers beneath the open collar of his shirt to test the rich warmth of his skin. There was a hint of the hair that she already knew dusted his chest and went all the way down to below his navel. A thing she wished she hadn't known, if she was honest. But she had seen him once, years before, coming out of the sea with water cascading all over his toned body and making him gleam in the Greek sun.

Gleam even more than he usually did, that was.

In this moment, she could admit that she had held that image close all this time. But then, she felt about images of him the same way she felt about sugar. Of course she liked the taste of it. Who wouldn't?

Maybe it was time she admitted that *hatred* was the thing she hid behind when it came to this man, because there was *this* underneath.

Maybe it had been there all along.

She had never felt anything like it before, and she had been marrying his father when she'd met him, so how could she have called it what it was?

But acknowledging that uncomfortable truth didn't change anything. If she allowed herself to indulge, just like sugar, she paid for it for too long after to make the indulgence worthwhile.

Down and down she went, moving her hand outside of his shirt again so she could lazily trace the line of the buttons that held it together, all the way down to that hard-ridged abdomen that she'd just been remembering.

And then, her eyes still fixed to his, she moved lower

still, and traced a pattern over that hard, proud ridge that already pushed against his trousers.

It grew even more when she settled her hand against it. He was hard. So very, very hard. And she could feel that hardness seemed to rebound through her, as if he was already deep inside of her body.

Jolie had never wanted him more than she did in this moment—but she wanted to win this battle more.

She angled herself closer, tipping her head up as if asking for a kiss. And she drank in the way his eyes went dark and greedy.

"Look at you," she whispered, huskily, pressing her hand against the length of him. "You look a little bit... destroyed, Apostolis. There are worse things than death after all, are there not? Like losing."

And then she ducked under his arm and headed for the stairs, moving across the flow of rooms and up the circular steps before she even dared look over her shoulder. Her heart was pounding too hard for her to hear anything. The heat of the hardest part of him was a brand across her palm.

And she was not sure if he was right there on her heels, or still down below.

But when she looked, he stood at the bottom of the stairs. He looked up at her, a tortured expression she had never seen before on his face. And she couldn't enjoy it the way she should have, because she worried she wore the same expression herself.

More, his chest was moving as if he'd run a marathon to get from the wall to the first stair.

And she felt that, too, like a touch.

"If I were you," he told her, his voice a dark ribbon

through the dark of the house, with only the stars outside to bear witness to this, "I would run. While you can."

To her shame, there was a part of her that wanted to do just that, and run—but straight to him, so she could see where this fire went. So she could see if they would truly turn each other to ash after all—

But that was too close to surrender.

So she ran to the room that she'd chosen for herself, the guest room she'd made sure the staff had come and arranged for her while she'd been playing hostess games—taking all of her things out of *his* bedroom as if she'd never been there in the first place—and locked the door behind her.

Though as she lay there on the bed she'd made, wide awake and staring at the ceiling for far too long, she had to ask herself—had she really been locking *him* out?

Or herself in?

CHAPTER SIX

THE WAR WAS now begun in earnest, making it clear only minor skirmishes had happened before. All antes were upped. Survival was the only goal, and it was no foregone conclusion.

Apostolis had never felt so alive.

He told himself it was the thrill of his impending victory coming in hot, whether *she* thought that he would win or not.

He knew that he would.

Or in any case, that was what he told himself as the season rolled on. As one set of guests left and another arrived. As he was involved with handling the daily issues that cropped up at the hotel that he had only observed before from the distance his father insisted upon.

And was forced to face an unpalatable truth.

Jolie was not simply a trophy, as he'd thought. Or perhaps as he'd hoped.

She was an integral part of the hotel's operation.

In all the ways that mattered, she *was* the proprietor, and given the way the staff deferred to her in all things, clearly had been.

Perhaps since her marriage to his father.

It was entirely possible that was one of the reasons Spyros had married her, when he had never bothered to marry the other women he'd taken as lovers over the years.

He was forced to view the woman—his stepmother, his wife, his co-proprietor—in an entirely new light and he found himself longing for the dark.

Because the fact that Jolie was both good at the guest-facing parts of her job—the consummate hostess, a study in effortless and yet engaging mystery—as well as all the things that happened behind the scenes…annoyed him. It would have been easier if she'd been a disaster, or as useless as he'd expected—but then, if she had been, the hotel would have been in dire straits and that wouldn't have been any kind of victory.

Apostolis found himself torn between wanting to do nothing but come to a kind of reckoning with Jolie—and trying to understand his own relationship to the hotel that had stood as a cornerstone of his family for so long.

He talked often with Alceu, for a variety of reasons but also because his friend lived in what was more or less a fortress—though it was more delicately termed a *castle*—on the island of Sicily.

"You know what it is to care for a house that is more than a house, and that is considered more important than the family that lives in it," he said one day.

"It is called a legacy," Alceu replied in his usual arid tones. "A word I believe you are familiar with. And legacies require care and maintenance. Sometimes this is inconvenient. Very seldomly does it involve the attentions of supermodels or paparazzi, which I know is a significant lifestyle change for you."

"Thank you," Apostolis replied, perhaps more stiffly than he might have wished. "I am aware."

What he *wanted* to say was something like *Et tu, Brute?*

Though he knew that wasn't fair. Alceu had always been the more serious of the two of them. Or, perhaps, what he really meant was that Alceu had always known that his legacy was secured—and more, that said legacy would be his to steward.

He had not had to perform for his father's attention the way Apostolis had.

It was something Apostolis found seemed to weigh on him more and more, especially when his relationship with the co-owner of his hotel was fraught with all the other battles they were waging.

He found her in the office one morning, going through paperwork that he was certain he'd mentioned he had intended to get to himself.

Once he accepted that until now, she had been doing it in front of him and he had willfully ignored the possibility that she was actually...working.

It filled him with something he knew too well was not temper. Temper was easy. This lingered in his gut. It was too thick.

"Do you do this deliberately?" he asked her as he took in what she was working on, there in the large office suite in its own wing of the carriage house. "Do you ignore what you are told because it makes you feel better to think you're doing this all by yourself?"

"This might come as a great shock to you," Jolie replied to him in that sharply serene manner of hers, complete with that smile that might as well have been a dagger, "but I do not spend a great deal of time thinking about you at all."

He stopped at the desk where she was sitting, and leaned back against it so she had no choice but to lift her gaze to him. "Liar."

Jolie sat back in her chair, and he thought that while she might have looked languid from a distance—he was closer than that. That meant he could see the awareness in her gaze. He could see the faint hint of color in her cheeks.

No matter what she said, she was not unaffected.

And that, in turn, affected him.

Tremendously.

But he knew better than to show his hand again so soon. That night when she'd teased him and left him standing there in the hall, wild with frustrated need, haunted him.

In more ways than one.

Back when he'd believed she was a useless bit of fluff he could simply maneuver around as he pleased.

"What is it that you want from this interaction, Apostolis?" she asked, and there was a hint of impatience in her voice—perhaps more than a hint—but he could see the truth in her gaze. There was a heat there that had nothing to do with *impatience*. He could read that, clear as day. "I walked into the office this morning, these things weren't done, and so I'm doing them. That's all it is. Not everything is a plot against you." She shook her head as if she'd never heard of something so silly. "Why do you think that it is?"

Apostolis thought about the conversation that he'd had with Alceu. And he also thought about strategy. He told himself it had nothing to do with the fact that she wasn't looking at him as if he was a science experiment when she asked the question.

Not at the moment, anyway. She looked as if she was genuinely interested.

"Have you not heard?" he asked lightly. "My father was always disappointed in my business acumen. I feel certain he would have mentioned it. He and I spoke of very little else on the rare occasions we spoke."

"Your father liked cocktail parties," she replied in the same tone. "He left the business to me. And that was a fairly overwhelming task, most days, so I did not spend a lot of time worrying about anyone else's *business acumen*."

He frowned at that. "What are you saying? He can't possibly have let you run the whole of the hotel business all on your—"

But he cut himself off, because why was he astonished to hear such a thing? He was well-versed in his father's hypocrisy. He had lived it.

"Your father had a business manager many years ago to do all of this. Firing him was one of the first things I did when I arrived." Her smile sharpened as she looked up at him, as if defying him to argue once again that none of this could be true. That he still doubted what he had seen unfold in all parts of the hotel, before his very eyes, since their marriage. "And if you're wondering if anyone took a young woman like me seriously at first, the answer is no. Of course they didn't. But it didn't matter. Your father wanted to continue on as he had always done. He liked to be the life of the party, but he didn't like to *plan* the party. And as it turns out, my education made me a perfect fit for party planner extraordinaire."

They both seemed to realize they were actually *talking* to each other for a change at the same time. It clearly shook her as much as it did him.

Jolie stood. Apostolis straightened from the desk.

For a moment, maybe two, they frowned at each other as if there was a *trick*, here. As if one of them had *done something* to force this unheard-of moment of accord.

"And here I thought your marriage to my father was blissful in every regard," he heard himself say, but it wasn't as scathing as he'd meant it to be.

Surely he'd *meant* it to be.

"It had its ups and downs." Jolie's chin rose just slightly as she said it. Just enough to hint at defiance without entirely committing to it. "You seem overly interested in my previous relationship. If I were you, I'd worry a little bit more about this one."

"But I have heard your relationship with my father described as *affectionate,*" he reminded her, with, perhaps a little too much sardonic inflection in his voice, if such a thing existed. "Surely this cannot all have been a mirage."

Her eyes flashed and he expected her to strike back at him—but instead, she shook her head. A bit as if she despaired of him. Or was exhausted by him.

Not the reaction most women had to his presence, he could admit.

"You think that everything is about greed," she said in her quiet way that still managed to land hard. "That tells me that the only thing you think about is greediness—maybe other people's, maybe your own. Meanwhile, there are other reasons in this world to do things that others might find unpalatable. That you might find hard to bear yourself. I'm happy for you, Apostolis, that you've never had to make such choices."

This was as close to an admission that things had not been wonderful with his father as she'd ever given him.

"Tell me," he said, suddenly seized with an urgency that he did not understand. "Just once, tell me the truth. Why did you marry him?"

Something exquisitely sad moved over Jolie's face at that, and as if she knew it, or sensed it, she looked away. Out the window toward another bright and sunny Mediterranean day unfolding spectacularly before them. The sunlight outside fell on her face and he was struck once more by the fact that this woman was truly flawless.

That even bright, direct light did not *reveal* her. It only enhanced her beauty.

"I made a practical decision," she told him, as if this topic made her tired. "And I would make the same decision again." She looked back at him then, but the expression on her face had changed. It was more opaque now. There was no trace of any *sadness*. "I had no idea you were such a romantic, Apostolis. I confess, I'm shocked."

"The chasm between mercenary and romantic is almost as vast and wide as your capacity for lying," he said, but almost…conversationally. As if they were having a friendly chat. *Almost*. "What I wonder is if you're lying to yourself as well as everyone else."

Her eyes narrowed slightly, but that was the only reaction she saw on her face. Her lovely, flawless face, like a work of art.

"Mercenary is such an interesting word," she murmured.

She crossed her arms in that neat way she had that made it look like an elegant way to hold them, not a gesture stemming from any kind of anger or negative feeling. Everything with her was that kind of performance, he knew. Everything about her was calculated.

He wasn't sure what the matter was with him that he should find that something to admire.

"Is it really all that interesting?" he asked. "Or does it describe a set of behaviors—for the sake of argument, let's say *your* behaviors—perfectly?"

She let her mouth curve into something gracious. She did not unfold her arms. "For the sake of argument, let us take the son of a very wealthy man. A case study, if you will. A son who had the very best of everything, always. An upbringing of well-documented ease, waited upon hand and foot by servants, and then sent off to some of the finest schools in the world."

She lifted a hand and he realized that he was frowning. Possibly even scowling. "This is not to say that there were not stumbling blocks," she allowed. "Or periods of grief and disappointment. It is a life, after all. But let's say that time goes on for our wealthy man's son. Some people would be forced to find employment. Others might decide that they need employment. Not for money, in the case of our heir to everything, but because every person needs some form of industry to feel fulfilled as a human." She shook her head, almost fondly. "But not our golden son. He prefers instead to live off the proceeds of his various trust funds. He wafts about, making a case for gluttony and self-indulgence, year after year after year. Because, of course, there is no point in him chaining himself to some other profession when his true profession awaits. Like any little princeling, his entire life involves marking time, waiting for his father to die. Only then can he assume control of the whole family fortune, not merely his little sliver of it. Only then can he truly *do something* with his life, such as it is, and assuming he knows how to go about it after all that laziness."

Again, that curve of her lips. "But you have the audacity to call *me* mercenary."

The urge to simply strike back at her was so intense that Apostolis was shocked it didn't take him from his feet.

Instead, he thought of her hand, tracing its way down the length of his torso. He thought of the way she had gripped his sex, just enough to make him imagine the kind of things that they could do to each other—and in more detail than he already had by that point.

He had thought of little else since.

And it was growing harder and harder to convince himself that these thoughts had a basis in anything but the most intense desire he had ever known.

Then again, Apostolis acknowledged that sometimes, choosing the less obvious weapon was the better strategic choice. It couldn't all be rocket launchers and carpet bombs.

"I shouldn't be surprised that you are so imaginative," he drawled, choosing not to focus on *desire*. "It almost hurts me to tell you that I'm afraid you've got it all wrong. I've never touched any of the money held in trust for me. And not, I can admit, by my own choice. Not at first."

He was questioning the wisdom of this line of conversation, so he turned away from her, going over to look out of the window himself. The Andromeda rose, stately and reserved, as if some kind of counterweight to all of that impossible Mediterranean sunshine that streamed all around it so recklessly.

While in the distance, always, glinted the deep blue of the sea.

And as always, these things soothed him. No matter how many ghosts there might have been hanging about. No matter how many memories and regrets seemed to sink into his skin, simply by his being here again.

"Old Spyros felt that my attitude was lacking," he said, staring out at the sea but seeing only those ghosts and regrets. Those memories he'd never been able to shake. "Or perhaps, that week, he didn't like my tone. It's so hard to remember. But at some point, not long after I left university, he decided that cutting me off would be the making of me."

He looked back over his shoulder to find her watching him, and decided that it would do him no good to attempt to categorize the expression she wore her face just then. It would haunt him enough as it was, with that ferocious way she was listening to him. As if it took the whole of her body.

"The irony, you understand, is that Spyros himself never worked a day in his life," he continued. "He was committed to behaving atrociously right up until my grandfather died. Entirely to be done with him, some claim. But by the time I had the temerity to enjoy myself, too, he fancied himself quite the man of business. No son of *his,* etcetera. So there I was. The princeling you imagine, but tragically with no access to the funds that could keep me in the lifestyle I preferred."

"He cut you off?" She was frowning now herself. "That's not the way he told it."

"As such a fan of great fictions yourself, I would have thought you would understand by now that there were few more dedicated storytellers than my father. Particularly when it came to his own behavior." He turned to face her fully then, leaning back against the windowsill and watching the sunlight dance all over her, lighting her up. "I could have come back here and spent the past years loafing about the islands, making myself disreputable beyond any reasonable doubt. Instead, my friend Alceu, no stranger to familial disputes himself, suggested that rather than waste our twenties in the manner of so many of our peers, we might go about making our own money. So that whatever happened in the future, we would never have to depend on handouts ever again."

He was shocking her, and he liked it, though it did make him wonder what exactly his father had told her.

Not because he cared what Spyros had said about anything. That realization surprised him, because it came with another, even more shocking one. It was because he cared what *she* thought.

That this was a clear indication that he was, perhaps, not as in control of this particular skirmish as he might wish was obvious. But there was no stopping now. "Alceu is formidable. Always. I am...charming. Together, we make a rather devastating team. No one ever sees us coming."

"What is it you do?" she asked.

And something shifted inside of him, down deep. Because he'd expected her to laugh at the idea, he realized, the way his father had when he'd even hinted that he and Alceu were handling themselves, thank you.

But it was more than that. He would have sworn on any stack of holy books offered to him that this was the very first time Jolie had ever asked him a completely honest question, without any edge to it.

He wanted to savor it. Instead, he shrugged. "We buy

things," he told her. "And we saw that sometimes the things we bought required…refurbishment. So we took it upon ourselves to provide it. When we're done, we sell them on."

That was more or less true.

"Are you talking about…antiques? Or something more like a corporation?"

"Alceu is particularly well attuned to locating the wounded," Apostolis said after a moment's consideration. "It is as if he can sniff them out. Whether it is an estate, a hotel, a corporation, it doesn't matter. If it has a weakness, Alceu will know it. Often before the entity in question does. In the beginning, we were concerned with selling ourselves to these entities, to prove what we could do. Now we simply offer something too good to be refused."

Her blue eyes glinted. "And this is what you do. You swan about bullying people and making money off of misery."

"Never that," he said, instantly. "We fix broken things, Jolie. We paste them back together and make them better than new. And when we leave, we leave the things we've fixed happier than when we found them." He laughed when he saw her skeptical expression. "You do not have to believe me. I cannot say that I care if you do or not."

That was…not as true as he wanted it to be, so he pushed on. "But I can tell you that Alceu informed me some years ago that if he did not know me personally, he would have put the Andromeda on our list." This was the sticky bit, and he was almost unwilling to do it. He reminded himself that this was a strategy, that was all. It was an admission that he had been forced to make to himself once he'd realized the truth. And then, today, the *extent* of that truth. "Before you, that is."

He heard her sharp, indrawn breath. He saw the way she stiffened. "I don't know what you mean."

"You do." He waved a hand over the desk where she'd been sitting. "My father cared only about the party, as you said. This is not under dispute. But seven years ago, there was suddenly a steady hand on the wheel. And now the hotel is no longer bleeding out its resources in every possible direction. I know exactly who is responsible for that."

"Your father gave me free rein with the office work," she said, though she looked guarded. "I assume that might be one of the reasons he left me part of the hotel. He clearly knew that you didn't need his money."

"But you did need the money," he said, softly. He had anticipated playing this particular card later, but something told him it was better to do it now. "Did he tell you to take a salary?"

"He insisted upon it."

"It is not very difficult to track money, if you know where to look," Apostolis said softly. Very softly, and he saw her spine straighten. That was what happened when secrets were exposed. "What I have noticed is that every time money goes into your account, you take ninety percent of it and send it back out again." He watched her closely. "Why?"

And for a moment, she looked…panicked.

It was the only word that fit, and he wasn't sure that he quite believed it. Jolie Girard Adrianakis…*panicked?* He couldn't imagine what that meant. It was certainly not the response of the hardened mercenary he'd expected. Or that of the Andromeda's proprietor and personal savior.

If he had been under the impression that she was somehow larcenous, which he hadn't been, he might have expected to see a hint of panic—but not like this. Apostolis
had intended to simply note that there were no more secrets between them. That he knew every move she made.

And, yes, he had wanted very much to watch her reaction to that reality.

Now she looked as if he'd gone over and punched her
in the stomach.

Looking *caught* was different from this, whatever *this*
was.

He almost moved toward her, but held himself back—
and it was harder to do than it should have been.

"What does it matter what I do with money I've
earned?" she asked, but her usual fire was gone. If anything, she sounded shaky.

"You should consider trusting your husband," he replied.

"But I don't." And her chin tipped up, as if she was
remembering herself in her defiance. "I don't trust my
husband. I didn't trust my first husband and I trust my
second husband even less."

"As someone who knew Spyros well, I find that difficult to believe."

"Spyros was always exactly who he said he was," Jolie
told him with a laugh. Though it sounded strained. "For
better or worse, what you saw was what you got. The
same can't be said about you."

He did not give in to the urge to interrogate her on
that—though he realized that she wanted him to. She
wanted him to lose the thread of this conversation, so
that they got back to talking about him instead of her.

"You do not send this money to the same place every time," he said, to make sure she knew he wasn't bluffing. That he really did know. "But you send it all the same, like clockwork." He considered her. "Who are you paying off? Who knows the truth about you, what is that truth, and why would you pay so much to keep it hidden?"

He could see that he taken a wrong turn, because her shoulders inched down from her ears. "Everyone deserves their own secrets, Apostolis. Even me."

He shook his head. "You do understand that I'm going to find out these answers on my own, I hope. And I'll tell you right now, Jolie, that it can only go better for you if I hear them from you first."

But he'd lost her. There was no hint of panic anywhere on her now. On the contrary, she looked almost lazy and amused, instead.

"Well then," she said, as patronizingly as possible, "I certainly hope I wrap up all of my nefarious doings before that occurs. Though what do you think will happen either way? We still have to be married to each other the next five years. Or have you forgotten?"

"I cannot imagine that I will ever forget," he shot back.

"Did you think the exchange of confidences would make *me* confide in *you?*" she asked, as if astonished. "You did, didn't you? You thought you would lead me, all unknowing, into some or other moment of vulnerability." She sighed at that. "Haven't you learned yet? I'm better at this game than you are."

"I'm glad you think so," he replied, and he was. "Because all that means to me is that you're not ready for what's coming. Given we both already know you're not clever enough to keep all your trespasses hidden."

And to his surprise, then, and something else—something like the light that was dancing all over her like it was specifically attracted to her—Jolie tossed back her head and laughed.

It wasn't a soft laugh. It was sharp and pointed and he was certain he could feel its talons, deep inside him.

"You've caught me," she said after a little too long with all that laughing. "I'm an idiot. Aren't you smart, Apostolis, to work that out so quickly."

She couldn't have been more sarcastic if she tried.

And maybe that was why he found himself closing the space between them.

The only thing he could think about was giving her back that laugh, with interest. All he could think about was restitution, especially when her blue eyes took on that challenging gleam that he'd last seen when her hand was on his sex—

And he didn't know what might have happened if the door to the office didn't open then.

If one of the staff members didn't stand there, looking apologetic. "I'm so sorry to interrupt," the woman said, looking back and forth between the two of them in a mix of alarm and speculation. "But the guests are asking for a host?"

"Allow me," murmured Jolie. It was only as she stepped around him that he realized how close to her that he had been standing. How much his hands actually twitched with the desire to get them on her, and all over her.

She glanced back at him when she reached the door as if she expected Apostolis might lunge after her. As if he was that far gone.

Then again…wasn't he?

Moving her into the carriage house had been a tactical error. He was certain that she disturbed the very air that he breathed, simply by existing in the same space. Sometimes he thought he could find traces of her scent…everywhere.

In rooms she wasn't in. When he woke in the night, his heart pounding thanks to one more distractingly detailed dream about the two of them wrapped together, rolling over and over each other in his bed.

Literally anywhere and everywhere, she made her presence known.

Maybe she could see these things stamped all over his face. Because once again, her lips curved and her blue eyes gleamed. And then she shut the door behind her.

Quietly, as if to indicate that *she* was unbothered by this *thing* between them.

But she left him with a puzzle to solve, above and beyond the maddening fact that he wanted this woman who seemed determined to keep him at a distance.

It wasn't that she didn't want him. He knew better than that. And that wasn't his ego talking, though he was fully aware that he possessed one of remarkable size.

He didn't have to put his hands on her to know a truth as stark as the one they'd both tasted when he'd kissed her. The same one he'd showed her the night she'd run her hand down his body.

Apostolis wasn't sure when he'd accepted that he was not only attracted to her, but that he always had been. It had been its own slow simmer. And it was difficult not to torture himself with wondering if she'd known exactly how he ached for her since the very beginning of her marriage to his father. If his father had known it. If it was that bleedingly obvious to everyone else alive.

But that didn't matter.

He crossed back over to the window and this time, he braced his hands on either side of the glass.

What mattered was that it was only a matter of time before he had her.

He understood that. And he couldn't know if Jolie had accepted that inevitability yet, but he had. There was a certain peace in that, because there was no need to push for something that was inevitable. There was no need to worry himself over something that was as unavoidable as day following night.

It was only a matter of time.

But that being so, finding out what secrets she was keeping became more important than ever.

He went over to his laptop, taking his chair at the obnoxiously huge desk that took over the room, a monument he'd placed here to annoy his father when he was not around to do it himself.

But he wasn't thinking about Spyros. He was determined that this time, he would know the answers to the questions he asked her before he asked them. The better to plan how and when to ask them at all.

Because there was no better way to break someone down than to peel them open.

And when it came to the frustrating enigma that was Jolie, his wife in almost no way but legally, he had to believe it was the most important weapon of all.

CHAPTER SEVEN

IT WAS LOWERING indeed to realize that if it weren't for Mathilde, she would have run.

Locked away in her little room some few evenings later—and still not sure if she was locking him out or herself in—Jolie found herself grappling with that deeply unflattering and unpalatable truth.

"Then again," she muttered aloud, glaring out her window toward the Andromeda, "if it weren't for Mathilde, I could have moved to any city in Europe and found myself some kind of job after I graduated."

Sometimes she dreamed about the life she might have had if she'd gone that route—but it was something she'd discussed at length with the headmistress over the course of her last year at the school. She'd gone around and around about her prospects.

Until the day the older woman had looked at her, once again with entirely too much knowledge in her gaze.

Listen to me, she had said. *I believe that all women should be as independent as possible, but there is a fine line between independent-minded and foolish. Right now you are penniless.*

She had said that with the precision of a knife thrust in deep.

It would be different if you had something to fall back on while you looked for an appropriate situation somewhere, but you don't. The rest of these girls, with their trusts and their funds and their wealthy families...

She had shaken her head, her gaze kind—but certain.

They have more options than you do, I am afraid. It's not that I think you can't find a decent life for yourself, Jolie. I just worry that you don't have enough time.

I'm hardly over the hill just yet, Jolie had protested.

I'm not talking about your prospects. The headmistress had shaken her head. *I'm talking about poverty. Everyone thinks that there is a huge gap between the rich and the poor, but the truth is that there is not as far to fall as most imagine. For most people, it's a very thin line. And the reality, my dear, is that you're already living on borrowed time. Your grandfather paid your tuition in full years ago, but you have nothing extra. You have no savings. How would you establish yourself somewhere in order to begin even looking for the kind of job you want? If you managed to secure a job, how would you afford a flat? Food? Transport?*

The headmistress had waved around at the castle-like building where she kept her office.

I worry that when you meet the real world, it will flatten you.

*I've already survived—*Jolie had started to argue.

But the headmistress had laid both her hands flat on the top of her desk. *I am not an heiress, Jolie. I grew up working-class. I had to scrape and worry over every bill, every day, when I was your age. And I had* significantly more resources than you have right now. *Do you understand what I'm telling you?*

The headmistress hadn't come out and said that she should think hard and fast about whether she wanted to find herself in the position of having to sell herself on a street corner to pay her rent. When she could instead make a bargain with a rich man who would keep her comfortable in most of the ways that mattered.

It was easy enough to tell which was the better option when it was offered to her.

And maybe the fact that she'd understood that there were worse things out there than a controlling old man and all his many demands had made it easier to inhabit her role as Spyros's scandalous younger wife. She had not found him *surprising*. He had not done a single thing she would call *unexpected* in the whole time she'd known him.

Except, she supposed, dying. She had expected him to live forever, if only to spite his son.

It was that son who was the problem.

It was Apostolis who had surprised her—floored her, completely, and not only because he wasn't the wastrel that she imagined. She had checked on that, of course. She certainly hadn't *taken his word for it*. But then, it hadn't taken much digging to find that everything he'd told her was true. She was forced to acknowledge that it had been Spyros who had asserted that Apostolis was a waste of space and she'd believed him, when the evidence was easily accessible all along. And worse, he and his forbidding friend were not the soulless corporate raiders she'd imagined, but rather, *saviors*.

That was what the people they saved called them. That was how the companies and hotels and sometimes families they'd helped thought of them.

That had been upsetting enough.

But he also knew about the money she sent to her revolting aunt and uncle. Monthly.

Jolie couldn't risk that. She couldn't risk him knowing what she was doing because she was certain that if he did, he would somehow disrupt her payment plan—and then what would she do?

It had been made clear to her years before that even the slightest hiccup would be interpreted as a green light to go right ahead and use their daughter's greatest asset to enrich themselves as best they could.

And somehow, she very much doubted that her loathsome aunt and uncle would find a way to marry Mathilde off to a rich man the way Jolie had managed to do. She suspected it might be significantly more unsavory than that—possibly even those street corners that had haunted her all these years.

Even the thought of Mathilde at risk like that made her furious.

But she was running out of ways to control what was happening here. She knew that. She could feel the noose of all that awareness and fury between them tightening by the day.

"Too bad," she told herself sternly. "You don't get to mope about in your feelings."

Because it was already evening, and she had her duties to attend to, like it or not. She blew out a breath and got to her feet, then set about getting dressed for the night ahead. More drinks, more laughter. More confidences and effortless hostessing, whether she felt effortless or not.

And still more game playing, where her husband was concerned, which was...dangerous.

Because only Jolie knew, down deep in a place that she did not like to examine in the light of day, that sometimes, while she was playing this role for their guests, she pretended that it wasn't a role after all. She pretended that it was real, what she and Apostolis supposedly had together.

That they were lovestruck newlyweds, hardly able to bear *not* touching each other. All those lingering looks. Hands that found their way together and were difficult to part.

She pretended far too much, too often, and she very much feared that one of these days she was going to forget to disengage herself on the walk back to the carriage house. That she was going to forget to put her mask back into place when they were alone.

Worse still, there was a part of her that *wanted* that day to come. Even though she knew that was nothing short of madness.

Because every time she thought about surrendering to Apostolis Adrianakis in any regard, something deep inside of her sounded out a low, wild sort of tone. It seemed to reverberate all through her body, taking her over until all she could do was shake.

Deep inside where no one saw it, but she could feel it.

Some days she felt nothing else.

And yet she knew that if she surrendered to him, she would never be the same.

Jolie padded down the circular stair, the shoes she wore barely a whisper over her feet so that she was entirely too aware of the *feel* of the steps beneath her feet. And as she walked through the open house toward the door, she was aware of everything else, too. The way the simple dress she'd decided to throw on seemed to caress her as she moved. The way the cool breeze from outside rushed in through the open glass doors to whisper its way over her skin. Even the necklace around her neck seemed to press against her the way his hand might flatten against the wall beside her head—

She rolled her eyes at her own fancy, something close enough to amused at her inability to keep her attention where it belonged. Or at least, away from the places where she knew better than to let it go.

Outside it was another magical Mediterranean evening. As she walked across the drive and the yard, it was so easy to let the beauty of this place wash away all the rest of it. It was so easy to pretend that these moments would be the bulk of the five years looming ahead of her, and not...the other moments. The more difficult ones.

She could hear the sounds of the guests before she rounded the corner of the hotel, and it felt natural for her lips to immediately curve into the specific shape she used for her public-facing duties. When she was doing her best to be enigmatic and alluring, the consummate hostess, beloved and yet a perfect, blank canvas for the guests to fill in as they pleased.

For a moment, right there at the corner of the building, she stopped. And she stood there, just beyond the terrace where she could see everyone there beneath the pergola wrapped in vines and twinkling lights, but no one could see her. Not unless they were looking for her specifically.

Their guests at present were a very famous singer and his expansive entourage of friends, backup singers, and longtime band members, some of whom stayed in the nearest village and went back and forth from there as they pleased. It meant that the terrace was filled with sparkling conversation, spontaneous bursts of music, and the sort of laid-back luxury that could only be achieved with a tremendous amount of money. Many of the faces she recognized, and not because she'd seen them here before. But because everyone had seen them, everywhere.

Yet her gaze skipped past all those famous visages and found him.

Apostolis, looking right back at her as if she was standing in a beaming spotlight instead of the shadows of the evening.

As if it was only the two of them out here tonight. As if the only thing between them was the sultry Greek air.

And even across the brightly clad, sophisticated group of cocktail partiers, Jolie could feel the weight of the way he looked at her. It was as if he trailed his fingers all over the surface of her skin from afar and she had no choice but to hum in reaction.

As if it was that or *combust* where she stood, eaten alive by all that sensation.

She felt certain he knew it, though there was only that faint curve in the corner of his mouth to make that clear. It occurred to her that she knew how to read him by now. And more, that the fact she could suggested a measure of intimacy with him that she wanted, badly, to deny.

But she couldn't.

And instead of walking onto the terrace to take up her duties, Jolie watched Apostolis instead—impressed despite herself that he was far better at this job than his father had ever been. At least during her tenure at the Andromeda.

She imagined the old man would turn over in his grave at the very thought. But that didn't make it any less true. Spyros had been overly impressed with his own legend. Toward the end of his life, he had believed that part of what the guests were paying for when they came here was *his* notoriety. *His* own considerable star power. The hotelier himself.

Apostolis did not sit as Spyros had done in his favorite corner of the terrace, holding court. He did not set himself apart from the guests, as if *he* was the guest of honor.

All the things that had made him such a tabloid staple, he put to good use here, with the guests. He made them laugh. He leaned closer as they poured out their confidences to him. More than one set of guests had already left convinced that they had become *best friends* with the next generation of Adrianakis men.

Yet he called her the actress.

Part of her ached at that, because surely, since they were both so surprisingly good at this, they should have been able to band together. To work *with* each other, not *against* each other. Surely there had to be some way to make themselves a team instead of dire enemies, forever and ever, amen.

But even as she thought that, she felt something bitter twist her lips.

Who was she kidding? She was the too-young woman who had married his father. She should count herself lucky that he was able to maintain the level of civility he already did. Maybe she would have to learn how to be thankful for that.

And besides, she had duties to perform. She couldn't keep hiding out here, not when there was so much at stake. Not when she knew that he would take anything she did and make it negative.

So Jolie welded her smile into place and did what she did best. For years now.

She made herself *indispensable*.

The sun took its time sinking all the way down to the horizon. It stretched out as it went, shooting glorious hues as far as it could reach. Oranges. Pinks. Deep tendrils of violet.

When it was dark at last, the singer was prevailed upon to gift a few songs to the assembly. Everyone gathered around, listening as he played. The first two songs were contemplative. Almost mournful, like quiet elegies into the night as it settled around them.

And once again, Jolie found herself drawn to Apostolis's gaze—only to find that that he was closer now.

He smiled at the person beside him as if they had bonded, soul to soul, and then made his way over to Jolie.

Because, she reminded herself sternly, that was what a married couple *would* do. That was what people were truly intimate did. They went out of their way to be close to each other even when that closeness had nothing to do with sex.

Hadn't she watched her grandparents model this behavior for years?

Jolie thought that it must have been the music that was making her think about her grandparents now. About grief and loss, and how it was woven so tightly into every moment that came after that, perhaps, it became its own complicated tapestry. Made up of joy and despair, because that was what made a life. Without them, what would living be but boring?

Maybe that was why, when she felt that blast of heat beside her that she knew by now was Apostolis, come to stand next to her, she risked tipping back her head to look at him directly.

He was already gazing back down at her. And beneath all the lights that were strung about the pergola, there was no pretending she couldn't see all the different shades of deep, rich, brown and black his eyes were. That bittersweet gleam with something magical shot through it all, as if he was made of the same gold that they'd all watched dance over the waves tonight. A part of the sun's last breath before it surrendered to the night.

The crowd jostled slightly then and she found herself pressed up against the length of Apostolis's body—in a way that *truly* married people would not mind in the least.

She made herself smile. She made herself laugh a little, as if this was the time of her life, because she needed people to believe it was. That was one of her most important duties.

So she did her best. When he wrapped an arm around her shoulders. When he tucked her up against him so that she was straddling the side of his body. When she was stood there like that, one hand on the front of his chest and the other at his side.

And the fact that they were touching like this in public, paradoxically, seemed to her like the most intimate they had ever been.

Maybe it was because the touching wasn't the point.

They weren't locked up in that carriage house, slugging it out in yet another round of their endless battle. This was the sort of offhanded intimacy that long-term couples accepted as their due. This was the kind of familiarity that simply happened over time and togetherness.

This was as if they actually were the story they pretended they were for the guests.

And when the music changed and the singer began to sing something silkier and more suggestive, it was as if the melody...simply swept them away.

Everyone began to dance. All around them, people paired up into couples, and then everything was that sway, that silk, that sultry little song. How could she resist?

Jolie didn't.

And it was something perilous and precious indeed to be in Apostolis's arms, then. To have this music to move them, but to be aware of very little else but that look on his face, the heat in his gaze, and the way they fit together so perfectly.

She was not exactly surprised to discover that he was an excellent dancer. She supposed that both of them had been trained for that, one way or another. What surprised her was that it didn't feel in the least bit awkward.

What it felt like, she almost didn't dare think to herself, was that if they could just stop talking—stop sniping, stop looking for weaknesses—they might actually be perfect for each other.

There and then, because *perfect* was too scary to contemplate with a man sworn to destroy her, she decided instead to stop worrying where all this would lead.

It was one night. It was one song.

It was just a dance, that was all.

And though it wasn't a total surrender, she still felt as if that was what she did, here. She surrendered to the music.

She surrendered to the sparkling lights up above her and the stars beyond. She surrendered to the lure of the grand hotel and the sultry invitation of the singer's music.

She surrendered to the press of the crowd around her and the current of joy and excitement that ran through every one of them, at the same time, when the other singers joined in and brought out their own kind of percussion—on tables, with their hands, whatever worked.

And all the while, she and this man who had already claimed more of her than she'd intended to give away, danced and danced and danced.

It was much later, after a leisurely meal, too many drinks, and several more wild, unpredicted dances around the terrace that even the staff joined in, that Jolie finally left the main hotel building to head for the carriage house.

And she wasn't alone.

Apostolis was with her, his arm slung over her shoulder as it had been far too much this night. She could feel the weight of him, pressing into her, making her walk at a different pace. Making her feel as if she was a part of all his heat and lean muscle.

They didn't speak. The night was too hushed all around them. The stars were too close.

He led them over to the door and opened it, then walked her inside without untangling his body from hers.

And then there was that moment. The moment that grew harder and more unwieldy every night. The moment where they had to decide if they would drop their act…or not.

If they would perhaps…let it linger. If there would be a hushed, drawn-out moment—

Usually one of them broke it by starting up the usual hostilities.

But tonight, it didn't seem to work that way. He didn't turn the lights on. She didn't pull away.

They stood there in the shadows of the hall and somehow he had turned her so that she was facing him. They were standing almost as if, at any moment, they might break into a new kind of dance. One that didn't need any music. One that would simply be…theirs.

They were *so close* now. And they had danced so much tonight that she felt she knew him in a whole different way. Her breath began to *hurt* as it moved in and out of her body and she was fairly certain that the pulse she felt inside her skin was his. As if hers matched his completely, making a kind of beat all their own now, too.

"Jolie…" he began.

Normally that would be the start of something. A spark that would quickly flare, and then they could both gain some distance with harsh words, with accusations, with this *thing* between them.

This architecture she was beginning to think was a whole lot of scaffolding disguised to hide a terrible truth. A fragile, impossible swelling of something that was nothing like *hate* at all.

Or even anything as relatively simple as attraction.

It felt a lot more like hope.

And that was why, before he could puncture it, she said something she'd vowed she never would. Certainly not to him. Because she preferred to let him think whatever he liked. Because that said far more about him than it ever could about her.

"My marriage with your father wasn't what you think," she told him.

His breath escaped him in a rush, as if to suggest she might as well have kneed him in the gut. Or lower still.

"This is the conversation you wish to have? Right now?"

She knew she couldn't let him throw gasoline on the kindling she could hear in his voice. Because once he did, when would they feel like this again?

When she thought about it that way, five years felt like an eternity.

"I thought it would be what you imagined it was," she said.

They still hadn't turned the lights on, and that was a help. It encouraged her. She could feel how taut he was as he waited for her to go on. She understood without him having to say a word that she was running out of time. That there was only so much space he would give to whatever stories she wanted to tell him before he moved them back to familiar footing.

"You already know that I met him at your sister's and my graduation," Jolie said. "There were events before-hand, and all that week he paid particular attention to me. So I paid particular attention back. And yes, I had no money. None. My situation was dire and I knew it, but your sister had already invited me to spend the summer here. And I had already accepted, thinking that on an island like this, surely I could find something—or, yes, *someone*—who might be a good prospect for the kind of life I wanted."

"A life of ease and comfort, with your every whim

catered to?" he asked, but very sardonically, because of course he thought he already knew the answer.

"The headmistress had made my situation very clear to me." Jolie found his face in the shadows. "When I said I had no money, I don't mean I had only a little. All I had was the kindness of friends, and you and I both know that people find it very easy to be generous to those who don't appear to need it. And somewhat less easy to be equally generous to those who do need it, especially if their need is obvious. I was grateful for your sister, but I was nervous about what came next. I already knew that it would be difficult to spend a life like that, drifting from friend to friend and then, perhaps, to the questionable kindness of strangers."

"Because a job was out of the question, of course."

"It wasn't out of the question at all," she retorted. "That was actually what I was hoping I could find here."

He shifted against the wall, leaning back and crossing his arms as he regarded her in that narrow, dark way of his. She still couldn't understand why he, out of all the people in the world, could make her *shake* with the need to prove to him that his opinion of her was wrong. "I assume that the moment you arrived here, you raced down into each and every village and put yourself about, shaking the olive trees for employment."

"That would not be effortless, would it?" She said it softly, and though he didn't reply, she could tell he understood what she was getting at. "That was the trouble, of course. I was afraid that if your sister saw how desperate I truly was, she would ask me to leave. I decided to wait for opportunities and then take them where I could. In the meantime, I spent a lot of time with your father."

"I bet you did."

Jolie sighed. "Did it occur to me that he might want to *marry* me? Absolutely not. I assumed that he might be interested in an affair." She sighed, remembering. "He had showed no interest in marrying any of the other women he was linked to over the years. It never occurred to me that he might wish to marry *me*."

"So you thought you could get what you wanted if you just rolled around with him a bit," Apostolis summarized. Witheringly. "Give the old man a little sugar and see if he paid for the pleasure."

She was already regretting the urge that had led to this. "Your sister is actually the one who played matchmaker. Dioni thought it would be fun if she got to keep a friend here with her, which wouldn't happen if I was just another affair. They all tend to storm off, sooner or later. So one night she laughed quite loudly while your father was telling me some story, leaned in close, and said, *Father, really. If you're going to captivate my friend's attention every time you see her, why not marry her yourself?*"

Apostolis looked as if he wanted to claim she was lying about Dioni, too.

"I don't know if that was the first time he considered it," Jolie told him. "But I do know that he changed his approach after that. He asked me to marry him that August. And I accepted."

"Of course you accepted. It would be foolish to turn away a meal ticket."

"But this meal ticket is not quite the one you think it was," she made herself tell him, because she'd started this, hadn't she? And there was no point telling only half the story. "After he proposed, and once he understood that I was prepared to accept, he didn't sweep me off for some romantic evening. He sat me down and had a long talk with me about what he wanted. What he demanded of me, and would expect of a wife."

Apostolis's bittersweet gaze flared. "I'm certain he did exactly that, and I'm equally certain that I would rather not hear of it in any detail."

"It's not as lurid as the things I read about you in widely circulated newspapers," she tossed back at him, with more heat than she wanted to show him. She tried to compose herself. "First and foremost, he regretted to inform me that—to his great regret—*that* part of his anatomy was not in service."

Apostolis made a strangled sort of sound. "I… That's not better."

"What he wanted was a daydream. A fantasy. A beautiful young woman on his arm, who could convince the world by her very presence that he was still the man that he liked to see when he looked in the mirror. A pretty girl who could charm his guests, laugh at his jokes, and make him feel like a king for whatever time he had left. He told me he doubted very much that he would make it ten years. I assumed that meant he would last at least fifteen and more probably, twenty." Jolie squared her shoulders. "The only thing he required from me was my assurance that I would never let anyone know the truth. That ours was not the intense, wildly sexual connection he wanted them to think it was. The connection you seem to be sure it was. The connection I think I wanted to pretend it was, too, because that was better than the truth. Better than a *transaction*."

"And…" Apostolis's voice was so soft. But she shivered, because she could hear the menace in it. "Do you expect me to believe that the two of you were simply... *playing charades* for seven years? That my father, who made a point of pushing what he liked to call his *earthiness* on anyone who strayed near, was involved in this... chaste bit of dinner theater? You must think I am the most gullible fool who ever drew breath."

"He was more my boss than my husband." Jolie told him this quietly. "He was not entirely unkind. But both of us knew who was in control. Of everything. Every night he would critique my performance and to be honest with you, I don't think he was very much interested in sex by then. Earthy or otherwise. Not when total control of another person was so much more exciting to have."

That control had even extended to Mathilde, not that she wished to so much as whisper to Apostolis that her cousin existed. But Spyros had been very clear that Jolie was to exist out of time and only for him. He liked that she was an orphan, just as he liked that she was penniless. No family. No connections aside from his own daughter.

He wanted her entirely focused on and dependent upon him.

That she sent money to Mathilde was of no matter to him—but woe betide Jolie if she ever reminded him that her cousin existed. Or that she spent even one moment in his presence thinking of her.

Across from her, Apostolis muttered something dark and very Greek that she found she was perfectly happy not to understand.

"If you think about it, Apostolis," she said in the same low voice, "I'm sure you'll realize that what I'm telling you is the truth. He liked to manipulate people. He liked to watch everyone around him dance to his tune. It didn't matter if it was a happy thing or a sad thing or if they hated it. He just wanted to see what he could make other people do. So it wasn't charades, it was a puppet show. Does that make it better?"

Apostolis ran a hand over his face. Then he let out a dark black laugh that filled the hall, and worse still, filled her as well.

Then he pushed off the wall and came toward her—all of one step, then another.

Her throat seemed to clench tight at that, because he was as close as he could get. Because he was *right here*, and not one part of her body cared how dark the expression on his face was.

What she wanted, more than anything, was to pretend that this was a part of the dancing they'd been doing all night—

Especially when he slid an arm around her waist and hauled her even closer, so she sprawled into his chest and had to prop herself against that hard, muscled wall when all she really wanted was to melt into all his heat and strength.

"Jolie," he murmured. Then he said her name a few times, as if he was chanting it, like some kind of prayer, a breath away from her lips. "I don't believe a word you say."

She jolted, as if he'd tossed her off the cliff and into the sea far below. "But—"

"Not one single word," he said, his voice a rough thread of sound.

And then he closed what distance was left and licked his way to her mouth.

Making everything within her, everything she was, nothing but fire and desire.

It was a punch of need so bright and so hot that it threatened to take her down.

So wild that she was tempted to forget that he could hear the truth from her own lips and doubt it—

He kissed her, then kissed her again, as if he didn't mean to stop.

And she understood that despite everything, she didn't want him to.

Apostolis pressed her back against the wall and held her wrists beside her head, and Jolie arched up against him, exulting in this. In every bit of heat and dark need and wild temptation. As if only when this man held her still did she feel most free.

His mouth moved on her, consuming her, and she knew that she should fight him. That she should push him away and gather up her weapons, point them in his direction and start firing them, one after the next.

She knew that she should handle this the way she'd handled everything since she'd married Spyros. He had called it her *maddening dignity*. He had never come close to piercing it in all their years together.

He had never gotten past her walls.

She had let him play his puppeteer games and had smiled through it all. And never, not ever, had she let him see that he got to her. Jolie couldn't tell if he'd loved her for that or hated her for it, toward the end.

But she didn't know if she had it in her to keep that up. Not with Apostolis.

Not with the man who kissed her like this, as if devouring her whole. The man who could say, straight to

her face, that she was a liar and he didn't believe her—
then kiss her as if he couldn't bear the thought of another
breath without the taste of her in his mouth.

This was the one game she didn't know how to play.

So she kissed him back.

And she told herself it wasn't *hope* that swelled in her,
but that fascination that—if she was scrupulously honest—she'd always felt toward him. From the very start,
there had been something about the way Apostolis disliked her. The way he'd made sure she knew it.

This dynamic between them had always excited her.

She could admit that tonight.

And she had five years of this ahead of her. She had
told him the truth, he didn't believe it, and now there
was this.

She kissed him back, their tongues started their own
war, and this time she knew that there was no winning.
That either way, win or lose or draw, it was the same
thing—and maybe it needed to end up naked. Maybe it
had always needed to go straight to bed.

Maybe this was seven years overdue.

So when he swept her up into his arms and carried her
up the stairs, then down the hall to his bedroom—where
she had refused to set foot—she let him.

Because if she couldn't have *hope*, she might as well
have *him*.

In whatever way she could manage.

CHAPTER EIGHT

HE DIDN'T BELIEVE a word she said.

But this last, best battlefield did not require words. Words had done their worst. Now there was only the enduring truth of this connection he was certain neither one of them wished to feel.

The time for wishes was past, too.

He spread her out on his bed, aware of a great, glowing thing inside of him—as if the fact of her presence alone set alight something in him he wasn't sure he could identify. It made sense, he assured himself. Once he had reluctantly accepted that there was no way out of this marriage, he had always assumed that this moment would come. Sooner or later.

Now it was here.

Apostolis could taste her in his mouth. And her kiss had been a revelation, again.

And now he had to wrestle with that great glow within, the greedy demands of his sex, and the simple fact that he had wanted her almost *too* long.

They all crowded together inside of him, as if jostling for position.

If he was someone else, Apostolis thought, he might well have found himself paralyzed now that this moment had arrived.

But he felt as if he'd spent his whole life getting ready for this. For her.

Jolie pushed herself up onto her elbows, shaking back that golden hair that he thought about far more often than he should. He did not let himself think too much about the things she'd told him, and not only because he didn't believe her.

But because the very last thing he wished to think about just now was his father.

Or anyone else, for any reason.

Something that might have alarmed him under different circumstances.

"Are you having second thoughts?" she asked, back to that arch, mocking voice of hers that he found still set him on fire. As if he needed more encouragement to let the flames in him reach high. "Or is it…" She smiled, benevolently, which between them was akin to a sword strike. "It's all right. It happens to everyone from time to time, or so I hear. Despite their best intentions, they just can't manage to make the equipment work."

"I think," he said as he crawled onto the bed and sprawled himself out beside her, at last, "that I'm finished with all of this *talking,* Jolie."

Before she could argue about that—because he knew that she would argue about that—he set his mouth to hers once more.

And this time it seemed impossible that anything, even the end of the world itself, would stop them.

Apostolis would see to it personally.

He kissed her again and again, taking note of when she kissed him back even more fiercely. Of how and when her lips clung to his. Or how and when she became more urgent, more demanding, pressing her body into his until he let her push him over to his back so he could hold her above him, feeling her body all over his, and this time, not while dancing on a terrace packed full of people.

This dance was far more intimate. And only his.

Her hands moved over him the way they had once before. But this time he could also feel the press of her soft breasts as she unbuttoned his shirt, tracking her way down the length of his chest until she could shove aside the sides of his linen shirt and bury her face between.

She made a low noise of pleasure, as if she'd been waiting to do that for a very long time.

He stopped her when she got to his trousers, hauling her up again then sitting up as he set her astride him. So he could help himself to the hem of the gown she wore and peel it up and then off her body, revealing her to him at last.

It was different than the times he'd seen her by the pool or sunning herself on a boat, in even the skimpiest bikini.

It was different because he was touching her this time. And she was spread open before him like an exquisite feast.

Best of all, the hardest part of him was pressed into the V of her thighs, and he got to watch the way the feel of him against her softest parts made her sigh.

Her eyes when they found his were so blue it hurt.

But this was the kind of pain Apostolis enjoyed.

Indulging the first of a series of near-ungovernable urges, he sank his hands deep into her hair. And allowed himself, for a moment, to catalog nothing.

To *feel,* first and foremost.

Because her hair was a warm silk, flowing over his

hands. And when he curled his fingers, her head angled back, giving him access to the fine line of her throat. He skated his lips over her jaw, then found the throb of her pulse.

And he wasn't sure which one of them groaned as she moved her hips against him, but the pleasure that shot through him was almost too intense to bear. Apostolis was certain it was the same for her.

Keeping one hand buried in all that hair, he used his other hand to smooth its way to the jut of her breasts, reaching between them to snap open the fastener to her bra. He tossed it aside and then, at last, helped himself to the plump curves he had only imagined before. He used his thumb to gently abrade one nipple while he set his mouth to the other. And he made sounds of appreciation as she melted against him, arching her back the way he'd imagined she would—to press her breasts into his mouth, his hand.

To stoke the fire that burned white-hot in both of them.

She was rocking herself against him, making greedy little noises in the back of her throat with every tug on each of her proud nipples. And Apostolis felt the exact moment that she stiffened—

Then cried out as she began to shake against him.

Losing herself so completely that he actually questioned, for a too-long moment—if he could keep himself under control.

And he still had his trousers on.

He held her as she shook, whispering nonsense words in Greek as he kissed his way back up the length of her body, and combed his fingers through her hair again. He moved it back from that flawless face of hers, marveling at her beauty the way he always did.

But tonight he admired her fire even more.

And when she opened her eyes to look at him again, her eyes were a shade of blue so brilliant he should have been blinded.

Apostolis thought he felt a kind of scar begin to form, deep inside him.

He kissed her again, slowly. Deeply.

Taking his time, and mindful of that scar and her fire, he began to pour all the intensity and tension inside of him into her mouth. He rolled her over while he did it, so he could set himself to the sweet task of stripping the panties she wore from her body, a filmy little bit of lace that he tossed aside.

This time, when he made his way down her body, he gave her gorgeous breasts only the most cursory attention before he traveled on. He enjoyed the indentation of her waist before her hips flared out again. He took a detour to the shallow delight that was her navel.

And then, at last, making his way down between her legs, he found that she was even prettier than he'd expected she would be, lush and ready.

She was shaking, though it was not the same kind of *shaking apart* as before, more's the pity.

"Apostolis—"

But something was growling in him as he shifted her legs wide open so he could wedge his shoulders in between her thighs. He let her legs dangle there over his back, and then he bent down, slid his hands over the sweet, soft curves of her bottom, and wasted no time licking his way deep into her. As if he was trying to eat her alive.

Maybe he was.

Because there were no words, there was only this.

The sweet truth of who she was. The salt of her, the tart delight.

The way she lifted herself to meet his mouth. The way her shaking changed again to something more rhythmic, a sultry circle of her hips. When he glanced up, she looked like a goddess. Her arms were thrown back over her head, her back was arched up, and her lips were parted as if she couldn't quite take in the glory of what was happening.

Neither could he.

Apostolis built this fire carefully and thoroughly.

And when he was ready, he threw a little gas on it, using his teeth against her most sensitive center, and she screamed.

Jolie bucked against him as she shook on and on and on.

He rolled from the bed, stripping his clothes from his body and more than a little surprised to find that his own hands betrayed the slightest bit of unsteadiness. As if he was as affected as she was.

As if, something in him whispered, *you're not in control of this at all.*

But there was no time to worry about things like that, not when she was naked and still quivering on his bed.

And this time, when he crawled onto the bed beside her, he tucked her beneath him. He propped himself up on his elbows, settled between her legs, and finally pressed the hardest part of him into all that sweet softness that he could still taste on his lips.

That he imagined he would always taste, always yearn for, always dream of—like the ghost of her was forming all around him as they breathed like this, together.

Her eyes were dreamy and lost. And he watched as awareness took her over, as her body shifted and flushed as she felt all that heat and thickness that waited there for her.

What he hoped she did not understand was that he was holding on to his control by the slimmest of threads.

Her breath shuddered out of her. She slid her hands up to hold on to his neck.

And Apostolis expected her to say something cutting now. To bring this back to the ground he knew well.

Jolie didn't say a word. It was all blue eyes and that same expectant wildfire that burned in him, too.

And so, feeling less *triumphant* than he expected to and something far more like *reverent,* he thrust deep into his wife. His stepmother.

His, something in him asserted.

But she sucked in a harsh breath. And he felt the way her body flinched beneath him.

Apostolis froze.

Her eyes were closed, squeezed tight, and he waited without moving even an inch, aware of every single place she was clenched too tight.

"Breathe," he told her quietly. Intently. "I apologize. I didn't realize it had been so long for you."

Slowly, carefully, he felt her settle beneath him. Only when she released the nails she'd dug into the back of his neck did he even understand that she'd pierced him in the first place.

But it wasn't until she opened up her eyes that he relaxed, just slightly.

"Jolie," he began, but stopped dead.

Because the way she was looking at him…

Her eyes were wide, and too bright with what he could

not pretend he didn't know were unshed tears. And she said not one word.

Still, he understood.

Her tightness. Her tenseness. One small breath when anyone else might have screamed, and no matter that she'd found her pleasure twice already.

He couldn't believe it.

He didn't *want* to believe it.

"You are a virgin," he said, a flat statement of fact.

She closed her eyes for another moment, giving him entirely too much time to wonder how anyone's eyelashes could be so long, so thick. When she opened them again, the brightness that had been so ripe with tears was gone.

But there was still a softness there that hadn't been there before.

A vulnerability he had not known she possessed.

That scar she'd left in him began to throb, as if it was lengthening, and cutting him deep.

He pulled back, slowly, and then thrust in again, so gentle it almost undid him. But he was focused on her. He watched her pull in a breath, then sigh it out a little.

And he felt the rest of her quiver.

Slightly, but it was there.

"I am told the pain is fleeting," he said. "We will make sure that it is."

"Are we a *we* now?" she asked softly, in a thick voice that sounded nothing like the Jolie he knew. "How lucky that there is physical proof that I'm exactly who I told you I was. No need for you to believe me in any act of faith. No need for you to concern yourself with the reasons why you might be predisposed to distrust me. You can just—"

"Quiet," he whispered. "You do not have to take every opportunity to fight me, Jolie. Especially not now."

And when she looked as if she might continue arguing, he kissed her.

It was different from before. It was…seeking.

Penitent, perhaps.

He kissed her over and over while holding himself perfectly still, so that when there was movement again, it was hers.

And he felt something far too close to relief in every slow, incremental movement she made against him. Moving her hips this way, then that. Lifting herself up, then lowering her hips once more.

Slowly, carefully, he let her learn him. He let her find her way back to pleasure.

He let her work herself into a new fire of her own making until she was frowning, not quite complaining, but digging her fingernails into him as if that could make him move with her.

When he did, when he finally took over and set a deep, hard rhythm, she came apart almost instantly.

Still he held himself back, keeping that same, steady, maddeningly slow pace. She flew apart again and then she was back, and wilder. Her eyes too wide and much too blue.

And she knew, now, how to meet his thrusts. How to prolong the drag, then strike sparks with the pump.

She was a marvel, and she was his.

Only and ever his.

And it was that thought, he was certain, that had him breaking from his rhythm. That let his hips find their own intensity as he threw her over the cliff once more.

Only then, at last, did he allow himself to follow.

Only then did he lose himself completely.

It was much later, well into the dark of the night, when she finally stirred beside him again. They had still not turned on a single light in the house and so it was only the moon, rising high outside the windows, that illuminated his bed.

And the way she looked at him was something like shy.

Once again, too many words and too many weapons crowded into him, making him feel tangled up with it all, but he ignored it.

He picked her up, enjoying the silk slide of her skin against his. In the bathroom, he still didn't turn on any lights. He took her into his expansive shower and set her on the bench. He set the water pressure and the heat, and then he took his place on the bench, too, so that she was seated between his widespread legs, leaning back against his chest.

Then he took his time washing her. Taking care with her body. Worshiping her in an entirely different way.

And when he found traces of her virgin's blood upon her thighs, he washed it away, murmuring words of regret as he did it.

But in Greek, which he wasn't sure she entirely understood.

He risked a glance at her, leaning back against his chest with her face tipped up toward him, and found the glint of those clever blue eyes of hers.

"No need to parade the sheets through the village, then," she murmured. "Lucky me. Or do I mean lucky you?"

A phalanx of retorts lined up inside him, but he tamped them back down. "I would think that you would be pleased that you possessed, this whole time, the means to prove yourself. What I do not understand is why you did not use it sooner."

"Because I shouldn't have to prove myself to you," she said, but quietly. "Or anyone."

"You would prefer that I continue to think the worst of you?"

"Apostolis." She breathed out his name in a way that made him think she liked to taste it as much as he liked hers. Her gaze laughed at him, though she did not smile. "I already know the truth. That doesn't change. So what does it matter what you think of me?"

He felt that glowing thing inside of him swell once more. And he didn't like the way her question made him feel, so he shifted, letting her head fall back on his shoulder so he could kiss her once more.

But she laughed as she pushed him away, and surprised him by turning around so she could straddle him on the bench.

"Maybe you should ask yourself why it is that nature did not provide men with a similar, handy little lie detector test. Is it that men are more trustworthy? Or less, rendering everything they say moot before they say it?"

"I am not the liar here."

"While I am sure you will find a way to make sure that I still am," she replied. "Now that I cannot use my innocence to shame you."

But then, to his surprise, she reached down between them and busied herself with stroking the length of him.

Already at attention, he grew harder, thicker at her touch, and then had to grip the edge of his seat as she rocked up on her knees and guided him into her heat once more.

And then she took them both on a wild, glorious ride that had them both shouting out their pleasure as the hot water pounded down all around them in the dark of his shower.

It was much later when he found himself wide awake, staring at the moonlight that fell across his room and caught at all her blond hair as she lay there, tucked up beneath his arm.

As if she had always been meant to fit just like that.

Apostolis found he was having trouble breathing. There was a tight band across his chest and it had nothing to do with the arm she'd thrown over him.

Jolie had been a virgin. She had been a *virgin,* and that meant so many things that he was almost reluctant to look at.

The band around him pulled tighter and tighter.

It got no looser as the night wore on.

He held her as she slept and found himself going over every single interaction they had ever had, looking for clues that this was possible. How had he missed it? How had he misread her so completely?

By the time the sun rose over another perfect blue-and-gold day, he had moved over to the window. He heard her stir in the bed behind him and turned, rubbing a hand over his chest to make sure that the last of that band that had clamped so tight all night had finally loosened its hold on him.

He was relieved to find that it had. Because he had discovered the solution.

Jolie sat up, pushing all that hair back from her face. That wild blue gaze of hers settled on him warily.

He watched her, aware of a kind of spiraling fury that

rose in him, because she was still so damned *beautiful*. She still looked like a dream, every dream he'd had. A bit of tousled elegance in his bed after such a long night.

It was entirely possible that this woman was going to be the death of him.

But if that was true, he had every intention of taking her with him.

And he had five years to work on the perfect exit strategy.

That wariness in her gaze intensified when all he did was stare at her.

But if he expected her to let the tears he'd seen in her gaze the night before take her over again, he was mistaken. He'd expected her to cringe away, but she sat up instead.

Until she was very much giving the impression that he was the one currying her favor here.

He expected her to say something. Anything. Instead, she waited. And did not pull the sheet up over herself, but simply sat there, the glory of her lovely body on display.

He suspected she knew that very well.

Perhaps he was not the only one who woke determined to find new weapons.

"I was up all night castigating myself," he told her.

"Were you?" She tilted her head slightly to one side as she considered him. "You seem to have come through it well enough."

"I could not imagine how it was that I could have thought you so wicked when all this time, you were as pure as the driven snow in every respect."

Perhaps wisely, she did not respond.

"But then," he said softly and with intent, "after I sifted through what I know to be true and all the many stories you've told me over time, I remembered."

"That your father was a monster and he made everyone in his orbit miserable?" she asked lightly. "Isn't that what you said to me once?"

"That is a foregone conclusion." He moved closer to the bed so he could stand above her. Or maybe he just liked it when she had to tip her head back like that to look at him. Maybe there was something in him that took entirely too much joy in how defiantly she looked at him, even now. "But that does not explain the *money,* does it."

He had the satisfaction of watching a kind of electric shock go through her at that.

At last, he thought with great satisfaction, they were back on familiar ground.

"Nothing to say?" he taunted her in a low voice. "No explanation?" He shook his head as if her response made him sad, when it was the opposite. "I suppose I will have to hunt these answers down myself."

Jolie surged up, coming onto her knees, and she was flushed once again. With temper, he supposed, though he liked that much better than the unbearable notion that he had *hurt* her.

She pointed a finger directly into his face and she did not waver as she made an entirely anatomically impossible suggestion of what he could do with his anatomy.

In her clearest, coldest, most outrageously *serene* voice.

"Tempting," Apostolis murmured, and then he hauled her up and into his arms. "When this is so much easier. No yoga positions required."

And then he bore her back down onto the bed and threw them right back into the heat of their battle.

CHAPTER NINE

EVERYTHING CHANGED.

Again.

This time, the world ending and yet beginning again felt to Jolie as if she was trapped inside some kind of dream. Long, golden days, impossibly blue skies, and these hot, impossible nights that seemed to last whole lifetimes.

She had thought she understood sex. What it was, anyway. And she'd imagined how it would feel.

What she discovered was that while she understood the *performance* of it, the *suggestion* of it, she knew nothing about the *reality* of sex. Because real sexual intimacy was almost shocking in its intensity. It created vulnerability. Impossible need. It was raw, unpredictable, and had far-reaching ramifications that she wasn't certain she'd even fully discovered yet.

She felt as if she could feel them, rumbling along beneath her like new fault lines she'd never understood were there before, lurking. Waiting for the opportunity to shake apart everything she thought she was. Everything she *wanted* to be.

On the one hand, life at the Andromeda went on the way it always had.

Jolie performed her typical duties. She was the same

smiling, endlessly accommodating hostess, going out of her way to appear to do very little while making certain that everything was in its place. That all the details were *just so*. Out of sight of the guests, she and Apostolis would sit down together in the office and talk about numbers, accounts both payable and receivable, staff and vendor issues, and all the rest of the things that fell to both of them to handle now.

Whenever they were in public—or anywhere that they could not be completely certain of their privacy—they would play their happy, newlywed games for the benefit of their guests and the hotel's enduring legacy.

Only now, when they went back to the carriage house, they imploded.

It was like fireworks.

They rarely made it three steps into the house before they were tearing off each other's clothes. Before they were climbing on each other, licking and biting and digging their fingers into each other's flesh, as if they weren't quite certain if they wanted to feast on each other or simply ride out the sensation.

It was always impossibly perfect, the glory and raw intensity of the things they did to each other.

She learned that despite what she'd imagined all this time thanks to images she'd seen or things she'd read, she actually loved kneeling down before him. She loved taking him in her mouth, and listening to the noises that she could make him let out.

As if she was not the only one who could be torn into pieces in this fire of theirs.

She found that she loved the taste of him, the salt of his skin, the richness that was all man and entirely Apostolis.

There was nothing she did not allow him. There in the dark of the carriage house, it was as if the pair of them were made of nothing but flesh and need.

And if it was harder, every morning, to pull herself together and back into one piece again, she supposed she should have expected that. For surely there could not be such exquisite pleasure, and so much of it, without a price.

"It's called hate sex," he told her one night as he moved deep inside her body from behind, his hands gripping her hips as he plunged again and again. "And just think, my darling wife—we have years of this ahead of us."

The very idea had made her shatter into pieces, there and then.

Afterward, she lay awake in the bed they now shared, tangled up in him in more ways than one. And she wondered how it was possible to survive like this. If she would make it—because it seemed impossible to her that these were the kind of storms that anyone could actually live through.

But then again, she had to. She had no choice. There was someone else to consider beyond these wild passions and besides, she had already come so far. There could be no going back.

Yet as time went on, funnily enough, it wasn't the long, explosive nights that she feared might break her.

It was the performance of a very different relationship than the once they actually had that they put on, night after night.

It was the way he gazed at her across the table filled with their guests. It was the way he put his arm on the back of her chair and let his thumb gently stroke the bare flesh of her shoulder.

It was the way they danced, now and again, as if the whole of the starry sky above them was nothing next to the flame that moved between them.

She found herself making up stories about the two different lives they led, all wrapped up and tangled into this one.

Maybe he was as astonished by it as she was. Maybe he had not expected this kind of connection either.

She told herself that it was more than likely that they were both as shocked by this as she was. That they were both humbled and exalted and made new, one day at a time.

But she didn't dare ask him, no matter what she told herself.

"I keep expecting to hear that the Andromeda has been reduced to rubble," Dioni said on one of their infrequent phone calls. "Or that you've both incinerated each other into a crisp or something equally dramatic, and there's nothing but a crater left behind."

Her friend didn't sound like herself. And Jolie didn't want to ask, because surely Dioni would tell her if she wanted to. She had to pick her way through these fraught and strained conversations, but that was better than not talking to Dioni at all.

"The Andromeda still stands," she said, with a laugh. "You have my word."

"That's a good thing," her friend turned stepdaughter turned sister-in-law said, and there was the sound of something clanging in the background. Like a cafetière being stirred too roughly with a metal spoon. "Are you happy?"

Jolie longed to tell Dioni the truth. Or some part of the

truth. She wanted nothing more than to unburden herself, to open up and lay out for her friend every single thing that had happened since she'd left the island.

But she couldn't.

Because Dioni looked up to Apostolis. He was, in many ways, her own, personal god. He was the one who had taken care of her when she was small. He was the one she'd run to. Dioni had told Jolie all of this long before Jolie had ever met him.

And, of course, she had never actually met the Apostolis Dioni knew. That was a gift he gave only to his sister.

The Apostolis Jolie knew had always been little more than a wildfire.

How could Jolie possibly tell Dioni, who thought her brother nothing short of a hero, that he was—in fact—simply a man?

A maddening, glorious, impossible man.

How could she explain to her innocent friend what it was like between them without tarnishing him in Dioni's eyes?

Jolie found she couldn't do it.

It was far better for Dioni to imagine that Jolie and Apostolis had sorted things out in the wake of their contentious wedding, and were now...reasonably content.

"I am no expert on happiness," she told her friend now. "But every day dawns no matter what went on the day before, and that feels like a gift. The sun rises and when it sets again, I have very little to complain about."

Dioni laughed from all the way across two seas. "What an ode to joy. You should open up a business in inspirational talks. Perhaps a line of greeting cards?"

"Are *you* happy?" Jolie asked her in return.

She heard Dioni pulling in a breath. "I am an Adrianakis," she said after a moment. "Happiness is in our blood. Ask anyone who's ever visited the Andromeda. Happiness is a requirement of residence."

And Jolie sat on the window seat in the room she now shared with Apostolis for some time after they both rang off, frowning out at the place where the blue sky met a deeper blue sea.

Because neither one of them had answered the question, had they?

Still, she resolved to take it as a challenge. What she'd said to Dioni was true enough, or not a lie, anyway. She had nothing to complain about. She had decided to sleep with her husband. She had allowed it this time when he'd had the staff move her things back into this bedroom. She did not see it as a concession, but a *choice.*

That being so, why shouldn't she be happy about it?

Whether it was *hate sex* or not, the sex that she and Apostolis were having was extraordinary. She might not know the difference, but she had never heard stories that came close to the things they made each other feel. Every time they finished, he looked at her in the same wild astonishment. Sometimes he murmured revealing things into her ear.

You will be the death of me, he liked to say. *I do not think we will survive this.*

How can you be real? he had asked last night.

In Greek, which she still pretended not to understand.

Not because she wanted to deceive him—though she didn't much mind if she did, to be clear. Not where language was concerned. But because she had discovered long ago that if she affected a charming inability to only mangle Greek, people found that delightful. It made them think she was silly. A little bit foolish. It allowed all of the guests, and even the villagers, to feel more comfortable around her.

Jolie knew that many women felt that they should not have to minimize themselves for any reason whatsoever. But she was far more sanguine. She liked any weapon she could find.

And as the days rolled on, one into the next with only the odd bit of weather to distinguish between them, the things he whispered grew more intense.

This is untenable. You are impossible.

Every night they seemed to reach a new and different kind of intensity. They did not necessarily speak to each other. They did not *discuss* the fire they danced in and through.

But Jolie often thought that the way they looked at each other left scars behind.

She could feel them forming all over her, both when they were in private and when they were playing their besotted roles of the newly wedded couple for the guests.

Sometimes he would take her hand and brush a kiss over her knuckles, and everything inside of her would go still, then quiver into goose bumps.

And she would feel it inside her, carving its way into her like every touch was a blade. It marked her just the same.

Those were the sorts of night when the people around the table would talk about their relationship in such disarming, magical phrases that she found herself believing the things they said. Even when she knew better. Even when she knew the truth.

"My wife is a beautiful woman," Apostolis told a group of riveted guests one night. "This goes without saying. But she was married to my father for many years and my appreciation of her beauty was akin to that I have for the hotel itself." He waved a hand at the Andromeda, bearing her graceful witness all around them. "And we take pleasure in that, Jolie and I." The look he gave her was so warm. So bright with love and passion that it made reality seem to slip for her, or perhaps the trouble was, she wished it would slip and then stay. "Because if we had ever seen each other truly before, we could not trust each other now. We would always wonder."

"There is nothing more important than trust," one of the guest sighed happily.

"Sometimes," Apostolis said quietly, "the most marvelous things are hiding in plain sight."

Jolie had always prided herself on the armor she'd learned to wear over the years. But it was her heart that was betraying her now. The poor heart she'd thought was too broken to function after her grandfather died was still there, it seemed.

And it wasn't tough enough for whatever game this was.

Despite her best efforts, it kept on *hoping*.

She found herself sitting on the terrace of the Andromeda, night after night, laughing with this or that collection of shining, resplendent people who loved to come here and gleam out into the Mediterranean. Every night was another bit of brightness, making her feel lit up as if the stars themselves had found their way inside her—even though she knew that they would turn those stars inside out later.

Every sweet moment, every loving gesture, every hint that there were all these beautiful emotions between them had a price.

And Apostolis was a master at exacting those prices, each and every night.

She would forget, all the same. Or she would wrap it all up in the same big bow. Or her foolish heart would beat too hard, because all she could think, more and more with each passing day, was...*what if?*

What if they really could love each other the way they pretended they did?

What if the truth of them was somewhere between the romantic stories they told the enraptured guests about a couple who was not quite them and what he called *hate sex,* which she had never found *hateful* at all?

What if all his talk of *trust* was an olive branch? She, after all, had been the one married to his father. Maybe it was up to her to extend one herself.

Once she started thinking that way, it was the only thing she could think, as if every shuddering beat of her hopeless heart was forcing her to hold nothing else in her head.

It might have scared her if it didn't feel so good.

"You seem distracted today," he said one morning as they waited for the staff to gather for the usual new guest rundown. He eyed her with a certain knowing heat. "Perhaps it is because you screamed yourself hoarse last night, poor thing."

He did not sound the least bit apologetic.

Jolie could feel her cheeks flush as the memories of last night's intensity swept through her, though by now she should have been free of any maidenly blushes. The way he took her apart was so comprehensive that it was a wonder she had any modesty left in her at all.

Then again, it was possible that the way she flushed had nothing to do with shame and everything to do with anticipation. Because every night was only a day away.

Her heart thumped at her, urging her on. "I was just thinking…" she began.

But all her years of necessary and prudent self-preservation kicked in then, hard.

It was as effective as a hand over her mouth. Her pulse sped up. Her whole body tensed.

Was she really ready to risk everything? On a man who had risked nothing at all?

"I prefer it when you are incapable of thought, my darling wife," Apostolis murmured in that dark way that never failed to shower her in sparks, and she wasn't sure if she was grateful or despairing when the staff began to assemble to help create the service profile that would help their new guests imagine that the Andromeda anticipated and exceeded their every need and fancy.

But the urge to tell him things she shouldn't didn't go anywhere.

What she couldn't decide was whether she wanted to tell him for the right reasons. Did she truly believe that she could trust him? Or was she trying to get ahead of the other shoe that she knew he was holding in reserve, so that he could drop it on her when she least expected it?

After all, he was the one who'd brought up the money she paid her aunt and uncle that first night they'd slept together. He hadn't brought it up again since. She would have been very grateful indeed if she'd thought that he'd forgotten it.

She tried to remind herself that he hadn't. That *of course* he hadn't. And more, he had never given her the slightest reason to imagine he might let anything go.

But her heart kept *thumping* at her all the same.

That night Apostolis got caught up talking to one of the guests as the night was drawing to a close, so Jolie walked over to the carriage house on her own. As that hadn't happened in a while, she indulged herself. She tipped her head back to let the stars shine all over her. She breathed in the sea air. The she let herself into the hall, switched on the lights, and found herself examining the photographs once more. The wall that was a march of time and lives, or whatever it was that such captured moments were so many years and lives later. Unknowable without context. Changeable according to memory or the stories told about them.

She looked at each of them, wondering what was performance and what was real, and carried on down the hall until one caught at her.

It was a picture of Apostolis down on the beach at the foot of the cliff where the hotel stood, holding tight to the hand of a little girl. Dioni.

He could not have been more than twelve in the picture. Dioni was still a toddler. He was looking down at her with so much obvious affection that it never failed to make Jolie's treacherous heart beat a little faster. Years ago, when she'd first seen it, she'd assumed her reaction was because she'd always wanted the kind of older brother Dioni said that Apostolis was to her.

She'd always wanted *someone*. Anyone.

Instead, she supposed, she'd found a way to be that person for Mathilde. As best she could from so far away.

But this picture hit her differently, now. She had heard a great deal about Apostolis before she ever met him. He had been one of Dioni's favorite topics of conversation in school. Years before she'd met Spyros, Jolie had heard all about this big brother of Dioni's who was her champion in all things—notably unlike her disinterested father.

Apostolis is my hero, Dioni had said, time and again.

When she heard the door to the carriage house open behind her she turned and tried to look at him as if he was *that* Apostolis.

Not the bane of her existence.

Not her enemy.

Not the man she'd married despite the fact he had always been both of those things to her. The man who treated her like someone incalculably precious to him in public and told her he hated her in private, all the while making certain that they were more intimate with each other than she'd had any idea two people *could* be.

Those were all contradictions.

But then, what in life was not? All she had, all anyone ever had, was faith—however misguided—that if they picked one of the many paths available before them, they would be heading in the right direction.

Her heart was a catapult against her ribs.

"I want to talk to you," she said, as he started toward her.

He didn't stop moving, though she thought that the expression on his face grew…more forbidding, perhaps.

Jolie took one last look at that picture of Dioni and him on the beach. Then she moved ahead of him, flicking on every light she passed, perhaps because she wished to signal to him that this was different from their normal late-evening activities.

She moved through the flowing spaces, one into the next in a tumble of bright colors, and found her way to one of the comfortable chairs. And was aware as she sat down that she was choosing it precisely because it did not invite him to sit down with her.

Jolie had no doubt whatsoever that he was receiving all of these messages loud and clear. She could see it in the slight narrowing of his dark, brooding eyes.

"I don't know what you imagine we could have to talk about," he said.

She watched as he prowled around the room, fixing himself a drink at the bar, though he didn't taste it. He only rattled the ice cubes around in his glass tumbler and then lifted a brow in her direction. She shook her head, declining the offer of a drink for herself.

As if she needed to make herself feel even more precarious than she already did, after all the lovely wine she'd sipped at dinner.

"You can't imagine anything at all we might discuss?" she asked, almost idly. Almost in the way she asked questions of all their guests. "How curious. I can think of a number of subjects without even trying."

"I thought we agreed that time is behind us." He roamed closer, then sat in the chair opposite her. Only he sprawled out in such a way that he seemed to take up the entire flowing ground floor that easily. "We have different weapons now. Different battles entirely."

"This has nothing to do with your war," Jolie said, feeling something like exhausted, suddenly. That had to be why emotion seemed to be poking at the back of her eyes. Moving all through her and making her chest feel tight. She pressed her palm against her heart as of that might keep it from beating so hard.

He stared at that hand a long while. Then lifted his brooding gaze to her face. "Nothing that occurs between us is about anything else."

Jolie sighed. "Then you can view this as another attack, if you wish. I've decided to try a radical approach, Apostolis." And it wasn't that her self-preservation instincts had deserted her. She could feel them, kicking at her, as hard as ever. It was that on the other side of that were the things that he whispered to her in the dark. All those gruff, Greek words he thought she couldn't understand. And it was all these bright, golden nights of *maybes*. All these intoxicating *what ifs*. "After all, one of us has to be brave."

He swirled his drink around in its glass. "You think that bravery is involved in these games we play?"

"I think that bravery is required to make certain that we are not playing games any longer," she said quietly. "Aren't you tired of them? I know I am. So I've decided to tell you where that money goes."

She didn't know what she expected. For him to go still, perhaps. To take on that watchful look he sometimes did.

But instead, he seemed to go...*incandescent* instead.

It wasn't that he moved. It wasn't that he roared up out of his chair, like some kind of Roman candle.

But she watched him implode all the same.

"Have you now."

It was all he said, but Jolie could almost taste the bitterness. It seemed a decent match for the color of his gaze as he stared her down.

And it wasn't brave if she quailed at the first hurdle, was it? She forced herself to go on. "A few years after I married your father, the relatives who helped themselves to the estate that my grandfather left me got in touch. They were looking for a handout, naturally. Philosophically, I will say that I find it interesting that the people who steal things can never seem to hold onto them. It's almost as if they know that it was never theirs to begin with."

"Philosophically," he replied in a low, dark tone of voice, "that is a remarkably interesting position for you, of all people, to take."

Jolie chose not to take the bait.

"I wanted very much to encourage them to go to hell," she told him. "But I couldn't. I don't care what happens to the pair of them. When I look back, it isn't even the money that upsets me. It's the fact that they destroyed all the memories I had of my parents. And my grandparents."

She thought of the pictures in the hall. Moments that could change for her depending on who she was when she looked at them again. Moments that could have different meanings over time. That was what her aunt and uncle had stolen from her—that ongoing conversation with still images. That ongoing communion with those stories over time.

But Apostolis's gaze was getting darker by the moment so she kept going. "They sold it all or they threw it out, and the only thing that's left of the people I loved the most in this world is me." She shook her head. "That's the part I find unforgivable."

"You forgive theft, however." His tone was scathing. "What a fascinating morality."

"It's not that I forgive it. It's that, in the fullness of time, what haunts me about that situation isn't what I had to do to survive it, but what I must grieve because of their carelessness. Their greed. There is a distinction."

"If you say so."

But if anything, he looked…thunderous.

"The trouble is that they have a daughter," she said, and she could feel everything inside her revolt. As if her own body would fight her to keep this in, but she was resolved. "Her name is Mathilde. I've only met her once in person, but we have kept in contact ever since." She blew out a breath, because this was more difficult than she'd anticipated and she had expected it to be an uphill climb. "She texts me. That's how I know she's okay. Our deal has always been simple. I pay them off. And they… treat her well."

"You doubt this."

"I think they wouldn't know how to treat a piece of garbage well," Jolie said, more sharply than she'd meant to. "Much less a girl. But I have insisted that they educate her as I was educated. I have insisted that they do not treat her the way they treated me. Or worse." She searched his face, wanting to implore him, but somehow sensing that he would not be open to it. "Do you understand? I had to keep her safe. That's what I've been doing. And I need to continue to do it for the next few years, until I am free and can help her myself. In person."

And for an eternity, or possibly more, they only sat there like this.

His gaze on hers like a hammer.

"So let me make certain that I'm understanding this story," he said at the dawn of what must have been the tenth eternity. "It is richly detailed, and yet, somehow, it is missing some critical information."

Her chest hurt. "I don't think that it is."

"You met this girl once, but she has somehow become the center of your life."

Jolie eyed him. "Not everyone is like you, Apostolis. Some of us do not treat every interaction like a transaction, with prices to be paid at a time of your choosing. It's hard to imagine, I know."

"This is the daughter of two villains, according to your telling, yet you have somehow assumed responsibility for her. In a way that many parents do not assume responsibility for their own children."

"It's called empathy," she said quietly. Because it was that or shout. Or scream. Or worst of all, sob. "I can't say that I expect you to know the feeling, but I would have thought that you'd heard of it."

"But why?" He asked the question too softly. It made a kind of warning shoot along her spine. "There are so many lost girls in the world. Why this one?"

"Why...?" That warning shot through her again, but she had started down this path. She had to keep going. She had to see it to the end—and she wasn't sure why she felt that so keenly. As if this was a *do or die* situation. "I suppose she reminds me a little bit too much of me."

"Now it makes sense. Narcissism, I can believe."

Jolie shot to her feet, surprised to find that she was shaking. "You don't have to believe anything that I say. I don't know what possessed me to imagine that you might. But Mathilde is all there is, Apostolis. She's the last secret I'm holding onto." When he only stared back at her in that same way, she shook her head. "Now you know everything. And look at you, you're even angrier than before."

"I'm not angry. I just don't believe you."

And it cost her more than she wanted to admit to keep her voice calm. "It's almost as if you're afraid that if you did believe me, this whole fantasy world that you've built up will come crumbling down."

"Do I live in a fantasy world?" Apostolis laughed, and it was not a pleasant sound. "I rather thought that it was a prison."

She wanted to shout at him. She wanted more than that—what she'd really like, she thought then, was to take one of his priceless sculptures and throw it at his head.

But that would be another act of war.

And she was so tired of fighting.

So instead, she rose. Jolie found her feet and felt steadier when his gaze changed into something more like...arrested. As if he was no more sure of his power here than she was, no matter what he might claim. She crossed the space between them, moving over to his chair so she could sink down on her knees before him.

And she was glad that she had spent some time in this position, because if she hadn't, she might not have realized that it was not a surrender. She was not laying herself out before him in submission. Not when both of them knew how she could take her power here, rendering him little more than clay in her hands.

Not to mention what she could do with her mouth.

Part of the power, she understood now, was in the act of the surrender itself—not to him, but to what she believed was more important, here in this moment.

Not just Mathilde. She would always want to save her

cousin, and she *would* make certain she did, but this wasn't only about her.

It was about *maybe*. It was about *what if.*

It was about the versions of them she glimpsed when they were too busy taking care of their guests to snipe at each other.

It was about the stories she wanted them to tell, years later, about these moments.

She knelt there before him and she reached over to take his hand between hers. It was the hand that wore a wider version of the simple band that she wore on hers. The evidence that they really were married. That it really had happened. That this wasn't all some fever dream of sex and laughter, golden nights and desperate, needy dawns.

There was so much tension in him. And all of that wild and unconquerable heat.

Jolie looked up at him, holding his gaze as surely as she held his hand. "I'm telling you everything because I want things to be different. I don't want there to be secrets between us. I want to try, you and me, to make something real out of this, Apostolis."

He stared at her, looking almost…frozen. But that was better than openly mocking. Or scathing.

So she pushed on. "What if we could start over? Without your father. Without battles and wars, weapons and forced marches and trenches neither one of us wants to be in. What if we could just…be ourselves? Not the people your father made, but whoever we want to be, you and me?"

His laugh was a thread of bitterness. "What an imagination you have."

"I have always known how you care for your sister," she said, with a sour hint of desperation in her mouth.

"And even if I hadn't known it, even before we met, I now know that what you do is care for people. You've made it a business. You save people from disaster, Apostolis. And you came back home to save this hotel, too." She thought of all those photographs, lined up just so. "You care so much about these things that matter to you—your childhood home, your sister, the kind of good you do in the world. What if—" and she hated herself for the way her voice shook, or maybe she only wished she could hate the vulnerability that poured through her "—what if you let yourself care about us, too?"

And for a moment, all of those words seemed to dance there between them like their own kind of golden light, even though it was dark outside. It took Jolie a long moment to realize that it was one of the lights she'd switched on herself, flooding the pair of them where they sat.

That was when he leaned forward, flipping his hand so that he was the one holding her fast.

"The only time you tell the truth, my darling wife and favorite stepmother," and his voice was hoarse and so dark it made her shiver, "is when you come."

Something in her jolted in shock, as if her very bones were breaking.

Or maybe that was simply her heart.

"Apostolis. Please—"

"There are worse things than death, Jolie," he told her in that same dark voice. "Remember? Like losing. I hope you enjoy it."

And when his mouth came crashing down on hers, Jolie knew everything was lost.

But her deep tragedy was that she kissed him back.

CHAPTER TEN

APOSTOLIS FLEW TO Paris the next day, though he couldn't escape the feeling that he had not so much settled the issue between him and Jolie as postponed it.

They had exploded into their usual passion, but maybe that had been a mistake. It had all been…too much. Too real.

Or maybe it was his own weakness that so disgusted him.

Because he *wanted* to believe her. He wanted to believe it when she said those things about who they could be, about the kind of marriage they could have—

But he had given up on bedtime stories like that long ago.

And he had known the truth about Jolie from the first. He would be a weak man indeed if a pretty face changed his mind. He would be no better than his father.

He landed in Paris in a foul mood that the rain did not improve.

He met Alceu in one of the properties he kept in Paris, a town house a short walk from the Musée d'Orsay, and found his friend a curious reflection of his own odd frame of mind.

"You seem agitated," he told Alceu after they concluded the business that they'd ostensibly met to discuss.

"I am never agitated," his friend replied at once, making it clear enough to Apostolis that he was not quite himself. "You are the one who has the steam coming out of his ear. Is that not the phrase?"

As if Alceu did not know the damned phrase, fluent as he was in every language he encountered. But he did like to pretend otherwise for his own entertainment, and who was Apostolis to stand between his friend and his fun?

"What I cannot abide," Apostolis said instead, "is a liar who cannot determine that the time has come to stop spinning her stories."

But he regretted saying it instantly, because something in him...balked.

Rationally, it didn't make any sense. This was his oldest friend in the world. When he'd had no one, when his father had disowned him and made it clear that he was not permitted to come home, Alceu had been like a brother to him. Like more than a brother. They had forged their way through the world together. They had always, always stood tall at one another's backs.

He had always considered Alceu closer to him than his actual family.

All the same, something in him considered it the deepest kind of betrayal that he'd said even something so opaque about Jolie.

He understood in that moment that if she unburdened herself in a similar way to a friend of hers—or worse, his sister—even if she kept what she said as devoid of details, he would feel it like a knife in the gut.

And he could not say that he cared much for the way

that realization made him feel, now that it was too late. Now that he'd said the thing he shouldn't have said. Maybe he'd needed to say such a thing to understand that things really had changed between him and Jolie, despite his protestations.

But she is *a liar,* a voice in him insisted.

Because the alternative was untenable.

Perhaps it was lucky that his friend seemed entirely preoccupied with the view of Paris outside his windows. A view that Alceu had seen before. Too many times to count.

"You seem unduly interested in the city tonight," Apostolis pointed out. "You must have developed a love for Paris that I did not think you possessed."

His friend did not turn back to face him. "I live at the top of a mountain. My nearest neighbors are trees. Sometimes it amazes me that so many people live like this. And on purpose."

Somehow, Apostolis didn't think that was it, though he knew better than to push. Alceu was less flexible than the mountain he lived on. "My sister said something similar." He laughed, remembering his last call with Dioni, who had managed to sound even more flighty and *Dioni* on what had sounded like the busiest street in Manhattan than before. "Did I not tell you that she has taken himself off to New York City, of all places, for the duration."

"I beg your pardon?"

Apostolis thought that Alceu seemed…even stiffer and more forbidding than usual, then. "I too was amazed that the little mouse would take herself off to the big city. I thought perhaps, one day, she might spend some

time in Athens, I suppose, as many do. But New York?"
He shrugged. "Yet as she tells it, it is as if she has never
known home until now."

Alceu let out a laugh, then, and the sound made Apostolis frown. It was too bitter. It was…

But he never finished that thought, because Alceu
turned around and was looking directly at him again,
and his eyes were dark. And his voice was terse when
he spoke. "As far as liars go, at a certain point it is better
to choose to believe a lie if it leads to peace."

Apostolis blinked at that most unexpected statement
from a man he would never have described as *peaceful*
but Alceu was already moving, heading for the door as
if responding to an alarm only he could hear.

"I beg your pardon, but I must go," Alceu bit off in
that frozen way of his. "I forgot that there are some calls
I must make."

And he shut the door behind him when he went in a
manner that Apostolis thought boded ill for whoever it
was he needed to call.

But he did not brood any further over his friend's behavior—or the odd thing he'd said about *peace*—once
he'd gone. He moved over to the window himself and
looked out at the scene that had so captivated Alceu. Paris
at night, gleaming in the rain.

Yet he didn't see it. All he could think about was Jolie.

Jolie kneeling before him, whispering, *what if.*

And Jolie after that moment, spread out before him
like one more decadent feast, giving all of herself to him.
And murmuring things she should not while he took her,
as if all of this was a different kind of story than the one
he'd been telling himself all along—

But he could not accept it.

He would not.

The next day, he made a few calls. And as Alceu was nowhere to be found, he took leave of Paris and set off for Switzerland instead.

The last payment sent from Jolie's bank account had been to an address in Geneva, only two days before. It was time, he concluded, to find out the *real* truth. Then, perhaps, he would treat his darling wife to a few *what ifs* of his own design.

It was a short flight, and the closer he got, the more he felt that deep, dark, boiling fury inside of him.

He was certain that whatever he was about to find he would not like.

If she had not been a virgin, he would have assumed that she was supporting a lover. He could hear her as if she was sitting beside him on his plane, making arch comments about the power of her *built-in lie detector*.

Something about that seemed to shift inside him uneasily.

But he could not believe the things she had said to him. He could not believe she was simply an innocent, caught up in Spyros's game.

And then, the way she told it, in his.

He could not believe those things because if he did, he realized as his plan set down in Geneva, he would have to accept that he had not distanced himself from the old man the way he'd been so certain he had.

It should have been impossible that anyone could compare him to his father.

That it was not—

That thought was so horrifying that he found himself

clenching his own jaw so tight that it was a wonder he didn't crack a tooth or two.

He had a car waiting for him and he stalked off the plane and into the backseat, letting the driver worry about getting him where he needed to go. Though that allowed him perhaps too much time to sit and consider the problem that was Jolie.

Apostolis didn't want to think about her. He didn't want to think about the seven years she had carried the hotel on her own slender shoulders. He did not want to think about the reading of his father's will. Or that stormy wedding that they had both surrendered to with such ill grace that their only two guests had removed themselves to get away from the vitriol between them.

He did not want to think of the years that stretched ahead of them still when it already seemed as if a lifetime had passed since his father had died and his vindictive intentions had been made clear.

There was only Jolie, for five whole years, if he wanted to claim his own birthright.

Then he thought about that birthright, too. And wondered why it hadn't occurred to him that it was an act of aggression on his father's part to have left nothing at all to Dioni.

Then again, argued a voice inside of him that sounded suspiciously sharp, like Jolie's, *it's likely not* you *that he expected would take care of her. It's her friend. Her stepmother. Your wife. Spyros trusted her more than you, so does your own sister.*

In the back of the car, sliding along through the streets of Geneva, the lake gleaming at him and far-off mountain ranges standing proud. But he didn't see any of that.

Apostolis felt his own chest vibrating and realized that he was actually *growling*.

Out loud.

He stopped at once.

Jolie wanted him to trust her. His own father had never trusted him, but then Apostolis had known better than to trust him. And he could not remember how or when that had started. It seemed to him that it had always been that way, since long before he had gained enough perspective on the world to make such a decision.

It felt like a simple gut feeling, and one he'd had his whole life.

Spyros was untrustworthy. Everything he did had deep, sharp talons attached and he never seemed to care who got cut. It was easy, even as a child, to make sure to keep away from that type of person.

He looked down at his hands, stretching them out as if looking for the blades attached to his own fingers that he was sure, suddenly, he could feel.

And then, perhaps inevitably, he thought of his mother.

Apostolis so rarely allowed himself that kind of nostalgia. When he thought of her, it was always from back when he was very small. When she had been a voice, soft and loving and instantly able to soothe him. He could remember the way she smelled like summer and that sometimes, when he passed the flowers that Jolie took such pride in arranging about the hotel, there were certain varieties that stopped him in his tracks.

Though he would never have admitted it.

Apostolis had never blamed his sister for his mother's death, though he wondered, now, if his father had. Because it would be just like Spyros to nurse a grudge for nearly thirty years, act as if he felt nothing but tender feelings for Dioni, and then wait for his will to do the real talking for him.

This, he assured himself, was why he insisted on uncovering Jolie's lies.

They both needed to know where they truly stood, always. So that there could be no pretending.

So that what happened to him once already could not occur again. He would not be, again, the recipient of a terse voice message from Spyros shortly before he'd finished university, letting him know that he was on his own. And was not welcome to return home until he could afford to get there himself.

I cannot imagine that this will surprise you, Spyros had said slyly. *You know how irresponsible you are, do you not?*

But he had known that it was a surprise. He had planned it that way.

If he was on his own, Apostolis preferred to know it from the start. There was a reason that the only person he had ever trusted on this earth was Alceu, because they had proven themselves to each other. Time and time again.

What was that saying? *Trust, but verify.*

That was all this was, he assured himself, as the car pulled up in front of a block of flats in a neighborhood nowhere near the beautiful views that Geneva was famous for. He frowned down at the address in his hand, but told the driver to wait as he climbed out.

Then he strode to the door of the building, and wondered how, precisely, he planned to go about this—

But he didn't have to figure that out, because the door

opened as he stood there. A couple came out, bickering in low, bitter tones.

He caught the door and brushed past them without a second glance. Then, inside, he followed the stairs up three flights until he found the flat number that he had written down.

There was that band tied around his chest once more, and much tighter than before. There was something drumming in him, and he didn't like it.

Did he really want to knock on this door and have his questions answered?

For a moment he wavered, thinking of those golden nights out on the terrace, awash in starlight and wine. The flush of music and something that felt like magic.

You know what that magic is, a voice in him whispered. *It's only that you don't want to admit it.*

He thought of Jolie climbing over him in the bed they shared, moving over him like more of that same perfect light, as if every time she touched him was an act of hope.

But here, in a downtrodden building in a questionable neighborhood in a city he had never particularly cared for, he shook that off.

This wasn't about hope. It was about truth.

He stomped forward and pounded on the door in question. He waited. And heard faint sound from inside, so he pounded again. Harder this time.

And he was ready when he heard the latch. He was ready when the door swung open. He would handle this, whatever it was, and if she thought that this would end their war, she would find he had been keeping the tanks and missiles at bay—

But then the door opened, just a sliver, and he stopped.

Everything in him *stopped*.

Because a girl stood there, looking back at him through the latched opening. He estimated that she was in her late teens or early twenties, and he recognized her immediately.

It was the eyes, far too blue for any land this far north. It was the hair, chopped short around her face, but still, a shade of sunshine he knew too well.

"If you're here for debt collection," the girl said, in a voice that sounded controlled enough, though he could see a bit of anxiousness in her expression, "I'm afraid that my parents have just left—"

Apostolis felt an earthquake rip through him, mercilessly. A fundamental, seismic shift. He had to reach out to steady himself on the doorjamb, and the girl's eyes widened.

"Don't be afraid," he managed to get out. "I won't hurt you. I am not here for *debt*."

And he had no idea how he would go about paying his. How he would ever manage to make up for the things he'd said.

The things he'd done, so convinced that Jolie was a villain.

"It's only that you look ill," the girl whispered. "You've gone pale. Are you going to be sick?"

"That," he gritted out, though he was surprised he could even speak through the upheaval inside of him, "would be an upgrade."

And he had to wait until the racket inside of him stilled. Not entirely. Just enough that he could feel the destruction and function anyway.

"I think I passed your parents on the way in," he said

when he could speak without thinking it might knock him over. "Do you expect them back soon?"

She swallowed, but didn't answer—and he understood immediately.

"I'm sorry," he said at once. "I'm doing this all wrong. I am Apostolis Adrianakis. I am your cousin's husband, Mathilde. Jolie is my wife." And that he had claimed her like that, with no mocking aside, made everything in him shake anew. But he kept his eyes on Mathilde. The girl Jolie had given so much of herself for. How could he do any less? "It is time for you to be free."

Then he held out his hand and waited for Jolie's cousin to take it.

As if, once she did, it might redeem him.

CHAPTER ELEVEN

JOLIE WAS MAKING her way back up from one of the villages, her arms full of flowers, when she saw Apostolis's plane fly in overhead.

She told herself—sternly—that there was absolutely no call for the leap of hope in her chest. He had made himself abundantly clear when he'd left. He hadn't even told her where he'd gone.

It was the height of foolishness to think that whatever he'd done when he was away—for two interminable nights, during which she'd slept a combined five minutes, so impossible was it to sleep without him—might have changed his thinking in any way.

But she didn't feel the least bit tired now. And she couldn't deny that there was a spring in her step as she made her way back up the winding steps, cut into the hillside, that the locals took from the nearest village to the Andromeda.

She ordered herself to slow down. To take care with the flowers she was carrying to make an extra arrangement that she'd decided to put in the bedroom of one of their guests, a young girl who reminded her of Mathilde.

And herself, she supposed.

Both of them, maybe, if none of the things that had happened to them had been permitted to occur.

Maybe she wanted to celebrate that in another wide-eyed girl before her own life gave her reasons to stop smiling.

She got back to the hotel where there were questions to answer, small fires to extinguish, and then the flowers to arrange in the kitchen and send up to the girl's room.

Jolie wished that she could have lost herself in all of those things, instead of listening for that Range Rover on the drive. Or looking around every time a door opened, thinking it would be him.

She supposed that this was only to be expected. Some kind of Stockholm syndrome—or maybe it was the sex that was addictive. Never in her life had she felt more like a junkie than the last two nights without.

Or maybe she was simply *used to him* by now. She'd had time to think about that, these last couple of nights, lying all alone in that bed that seemed entirely too large and empty without him.

She couldn't sleep when he was gone, and that had shocked her. She kept waking up, reaching for him, and he wasn't there.

And there were two ways that she could think about that. One, that she was deeply pathetic to allow herself to have these kinds of feelings for someone who was more often cruel to her than not.

But the other way of looking at it was that they had been fighting their way toward each other all this time. And maybe, just maybe, she just needed to fight a little longer.

For how could she know how delusional she was until he returned?

When she was finished with her tasks, she let herself out the side door of the hotel and started for the carriage house, her pulse skyrocketing because she saw the Range Rover parked there in front.

He was home. He really was *here.*

And now she would have to decide which part of her poor heart was right, after all.

Jolie couldn't seem to stop her feet from moving and that was terrible, because right then, she thought she would give anything to stop time. To keep *not knowing,* because what if he gave her an answer that she couldn't live with?

What would she do then?

She hardly recognized herself as she raced across the drive, heedless for once of how it might look to anyone who might be watching. She was practically transfigured with desperation and something too sharp to truly be hope as she wrenched open the door and all but fell into the hall.

Into all those black-and-white photographs, all those frozen moments. All those possibilities of joy and life and light that she'd always felt was out of her reach.

As if she was stuck on the other side of a glass frame forever, always looking in, never a part of it.

That was not the story she wanted any longer. Not from Apostolis.

Not now that she'd started listening to her heart again, for the first time in a decade.

Jolie walked deeper into the house, already fairly certain that she knew the answer, because he wasn't there to greet her. He wasn't there at all, and her stomach twisted. Everything inside her urged her to turn and run. To hide somewhere, so she could still pretend that this might go the way she wanted it to go.

But she didn't.

And she was halfway across the grand, flowing space when she heard a noise and looked up—

To see him coming down the winding stair.

"Apostolis," she began, because she couldn't seem to keep his name inside of her, and there were so many other things that she wanted to say before he started in—

"We will talk, you and I," he told her in a low voice. "But there is something that I think you must do first."

"I don't want to do anything else, I just want to say—"

But he didn't come toward her. He stopped at the bottom of the stair and he didn't even cut her off with an impatient slash of his hand, or even his mouth on hers. All he did was lift a finger and point toward the gallery.

Jolie felt frozen solid, but she followed the line his finger suggested, looking up.

And then she stopped breathing, because there against the wall of art and sculpture stood a slim blonde figure.

"Mathilde," she whispered.

"Is it true?" her cousin asked her, her voice barely above a whisper, though it seemed to reverberate within Jolie like a shout. "Is it really true that I can simply come to you now, and live with you, and be free of them forever? He says that I can do this. That he has made it happen." Mathilde's face crumpled. "Oh, Jolie, tell me it's true."

And all Jolie could do was throw a shocked and overjoyed look Apostolis's way—because she was already moving, racing up those stairs, winding herself around and around until she burst out at the gallery level and took her cousin in her arms.

In a hug that she hoped would go on forever.

They made a good start.

And it was a long while later that she left Mathilde in the guest room that she had once tried to claim as her own, surrounded by the things that Apostolis had brought here with her.

Mathilde had told her an impossible story of Apostolis appearing at her door and ordering her to pack her things, which she had done with alacrity, because she'd recognized him. She'd seen the photographs and the commentary in the papers.

None of which I believed, of course, she assured Jolie, who did not know how to tell her younger cousin that she had not given a single thought to the gossips in ages. *They only make money on scandalous innuendo. I know you better than that.*

You do, she had agreed, beckoning her to continue.

She did. Even more improbably, Apostolis had stood between Mathilde and her parents when they'd returned and had made it abundantly clear to them that they were not only cut off from Jolie's money, but that it would be in their best interest to disappear entirely. Because, according to Apostolis, fleets of attorneys were already preparing to make sure that the rest of their lives were even more of a misery than they could expect if left to their own devices.

And more, that Jolie was off-limits. Mathilde's eyes had been so wide that they almost took over her face as she related each and every word that had been spoken.

And then he told them that I was off-limits, too, she had said. With reverence. *He said, 'If I were you, I would go away and stay gone.'*

Neither Mathilde nor Jolie could imagine that they would follow this advice, but one thing was certain—that particular reign of terror was over. At least for them.

Because Mathilde's parents would have to go through Apostolis now.

And that changed everything.

A long while later, Jolie left her cousin to settle in—and, she hoped, sleep off all the excitement and the travel and dream about the possibility that this long nightmare was truly over now. She went out into the hall, her pulse kicking into high gear.

It was time to find him.

It's finally time, she thought as she let herself into the master bedroom, but he wasn't there. She had to stop and breathe a little before she started hyperventilating.

Or sobbing.

When she thought she could keep herself together, she picked her way downstairs again, expecting that she would find him in the office. But he wasn't there either.

There was a kind of panic growing within her as she made her way outside and across the drive to the hotel. But when she checked into the kitchens and offices where the staff congregated, there were the usual tasks and issues to handle, but no one mentioned Apostolis—which meant that he wasn't already there, handling things.

Had he left again? Jolie couldn't believe that.

When she went outside again, she stopped in the yard. The ocean breeze picked up the length of her hair and played with it. There were guests down by the pool, so she smiled and waved.

But she didn't see Apostolis there with them, so she went the other way. She walked up to the edge of the cliff, where there were benches placed for taking in the sea. And that was where she saw him at last.

He was down below, standing alone in the rocky cove down at sea level where that picture of him and Dioni had been taken a lifetime ago.

Jolie started toward the stairs that had been carved into the side of the cliff to lead the family and now the guests down to the water, but by the time she reached them she was running. She hurtled her way down them as if every moment apart from him was torture—

Because it is, she thought, feeling almost feverish.

And then she was on the beach herself, running toward him.

It was reckless. She knew that.

But the truth was that she didn't care how they'd left things. She wasn't sure it would have mattered *before* she'd seen who he'd come home with. Now it couldn't.

All that mattered was that he'd brought her Mathilde.

Jolie didn't care why or how he'd done it, only that he had.

So when he turned, looking back over his shoulder just before she reached him, she didn't think.

She launched herself toward him with every confidence that he would catch her.

With *faith*.

With trust, because sometimes thinking about things made it more complicated than it was.

Jumping in the air wasn't complicated. It was a yes or no question.

And he answered it.

He caught her. And he held her tight in his arms for a moment, there against his chest.

And he looked as if it hurt him when he set her back down on the ground.

"*Apostolis.*" She breathed his name like a prayer. A prayer he had also answered. "How can I thank you enough? Thank you. *Thank you.* Thank—"

"Stop," he urged her, though it was in a different sort of voice than the one he'd used that last night, so bitter and dark, when she'd knelt before him and believed that all was lost.

Herself most of all.

"Apostolis," she tried again. "Please, you must—"

"I flew across Europe to prove you're a liar," he told her in that low, bittersweet voice. His gaze was so dark it made a lump grow in her throat. "Yet all I found was the truth, exactly as you'd told it to me. And the whole way back, while your cousin backed up all you told me and shared a good deal you did not, all I could think of was what you've been through. What you had gone to such trouble to save her from." He shook his head. "What my father must have done to you, all of these years. I have no doubt that he was imaginative. And vile. He always is."

She held on to him as if the sea might sneak in if she wasn't careful and steal him away.

"Your father is dead," she told him, her gaze on his. "There's no need to keep digging up his grave."

He made as if to put space between them at that, but she held on. And she could see that familiar light of battle in his gaze, but for the first time, it occurred to her that his first fight, always, was with himself.

As hers was with herself, too.

Because neither one of them had wanted this, and yet here they were, drawn together yet again.

"I don't want to dig up any graves, but I don't know how to begin to apologize to you," Apostolis told her, his voice almost too low to hear over the surf. But then, she thought she would be able to hear him anywhere. He was already etched into her skin. Her bones. Maybe it had always been a kind of arrogant foolishness to pretend otherwise. "I don't even know where to start. I can think of nothing else—but it has finally occurred to me what has to be done."

She frowned at him, still gripping the inside of his arms. "You can't divorce me. You can't even leave me effectively. It's right there, in the will."

His mouth curved, just slightly. And her treacherous heart, which should have been left in tiny little pieces too small to ever come together again, blossomed into a brand-new kind of hope.

"I owe you a reckoning," he said quietly. "Because I am the liar here, not you."

She found herself whispering his name.

"Seven years ago I did not give you marital advice, such as it was, out of the goodness of my heart," he told her as if he was making a confession before a court. "I took one look at you and told myself that I disliked you on sight. But I didn't."

"I was there, Apostolis. You did."

He shook his head, and there was gold in his gaze again. "My darling wife. My favorite stepmother." He ran a hand over her hair as if he marveled at the feel of it, just as she gloried in his touch. "I felt something at first sight, but it was not *dislike*. And it was not allowed. I believe that in that moment I decided that you must be evil if I could fall like that, and therefore a liar by definition. I excused myself, of course."

She thought of running down the steps to the beach. Of tossing herself so heedlessly into his arms. There were a thousand things she could have said, but all of them were ways to fight—because she thought she had to fight to protect the soft parts of her she kept inside.

But she'd already told him what she wished for. What did she have to keep safe now that she'd already exposed herself?

"I excuse you now," she said softly.

"You shouldn't," he returned, sounding almost outraged at the idea. "There are so many more lies. I told myself I hated you when, in fact, you are the only woman I have ever wanted enough to make me weak. To make me behave like this. This monster who has more in common with his father than I ever imagined possible. If I am honest, Jolie, I am disgusted with myself."

"This is why we have to stop these wars," she said, her eyes stinging with the effort of keeping her tears at bay. "Because all they do is tear us apart. Just imagine—"

"I have imagined very little else," he told her, hoarsely. "But I will tell you now, I don't deserve it. I will never deserve it. When I think of the things that you deserve, none of them involve me. The son of the man who treated you this way. The man who, all on his own, in some ways treated you worse."

But Jolie shook her head, moving even closer to him.

"Arguing with you has always been like a dance. I don't want to lose the spark of it." She shook her head, not sure she believed that she'd said that out loud...but then she realized that it was true. There were years that she had lived for his few visits and the opportunity to fence a few words and fake smiles with this man. After the will was read, after their wedding, she would be lying if she claimed there wasn't a part of her that was thrilled they got to poke at each other the way they did. And she could have moved herself right back to the back house. She hadn't. Because she'd wanted the excitement of waiting to see what he'd say next. Or what she'd say back. "All I want is for it to be different. To be about us, not about him. Do you think that's possible?"

He was shaking his head, as if she was causing him pain. "What I don't know is why you would want it to be possible. Why you would want any of this at all."

"Because," Jolie said quietly, as if it was a secret between her and him and the sea, "whenever I think of love, I think of you. Not because we found that, you and me. But because I want it from you. Because I want the *what ifs,* and the *maybes,* and all those nights we pretended to be real. I want to see where that goes. I want all those possibilities, Apostolis. I know you think that's losing the war, but I think—"

He whispered her name, like some kind of incantation.

"Nothing is worse than losing you," he told her. "Not even death. I would lose a thousand wars, every day, as long as I had this. As long as I have you."

He leaned in and kissed her. And it was sweet and light—until she kissed him deeper. More urgently.

Because sweet and light was not who they were.

She wanted him. All of him.

"I'm so sorry," he said against her mouth, between tasting her and teasing her, and making her feel like she was home at last. "I don't know the first thing about loving anyone, but I promise you, whatever I have in me, it's yours."

"I know even less," she told him, wrapping herself around him. "So we will have to do it together, you and me."

"My darling wife," he said, "my only stepmother, *asteri mou*, I am yours."

"And I am only and ever yours," she replied.

The next time they kissed, right there on that beach, was the beginning.

The end of the war.

And the beginning of *forever*.

CHAPTER TWELVE

THEY PRIDED THEMSELVES on falling a little more in love every day.

They worked on it.

They did not keep score—though Apostolis took some time before he forgave himself.

Jolie was quicker.

But then, she had a secret weapon.

When things did not seem to be going in the right direction, all she needed to do was smile in that sharp, barbed way that never failed to get his attention.

"Are you certain you wish to smile at me like that?" he would ask, dangerously.

"You sound like a small man making big noises," she said once in response—

And then laughed and laughed when he swept her up and tossed her, fully dressed, into the pool.

Then spent a good deal longer kissing her dry in the privacy of their bedroom.

Because they liked a spark. They would never run out of their fire.

She wouldn't know them if they did.

Mathilde settled into life at the Andromeda beautifully. At first she didn't want to leave Jolie's side. The two of them spent hours and hours together, first comparing notes. Then building new memories.

And it was no more than a couple of years later that Mathilde came to them and said that she thought it was time she tried a bit of independence—and she knew just the place.

Because by then they all knew about Dioni's adventures in New York.

"I cannot quite get my head around choosing a concrete city when there is all this," Apostolis confessed one evening.

The sunset was settling in, spectacularly. The guests had drifted out from the terrace to gather at the cliffside, the better to truly take it in.

"Everyone must find their own path, my love," Jolie told him.

He looked down at her, that smile on his face that was only hers. "As long as your path always leads to me, *latria mou.*"

Jolie let him pull her into his side as the sun put on its nightly show. Later, there would be dancing. It was that kind of night. Later still, they would walk back across the drive and laugh as they found each other in the dark hall.

They had no secrets left. He knew she understood Greek. She knew every last detail of his dealings with Alceu and the soft heart he kept hidden so deep inside of him.

There was only one thing that she was hiding from him, but it was new.

And she resolved she would tell him. Tonight.

Later, when they were both naked and breathing too hard, she turned so she could prop herself up on his chest and look deep into his fathomless eyes. And so both of them could bathe in all the moonlight pouring in the windows.

"I have something to tell you," she said. Solemnly.

Apostolis smiled. "I was wondering when you would get around to it."

She felt her smile bubble up from the deepest place inside of her. "Of course you know."

"My darling wife," he said, kissing her in between each word, "my favorite stepmother, *fos tis psihis mou,* I love you. I know everything about you. It is my religion."

And then, together, they shifted so they could both smooth their hands over her only very slightly rounded belly.

"This baby will be born a month after our five years is up," she told him, old ghosts dancing around them but not getting close.

There was too much fire between them for that.

"Good," he said, pulling her mouth back to his. "Now you will be stuck with me forever."

But he was laughing while he said it, and she was laughing, too, because they knew the only truth that mattered.

Forever, for them, was only the beginning. This baby would only be their first.

And their legacy would be love and it would stand the test of time, until long after the Andromeda was nothing but rubble.

That was the story Jolie liked best.

So together, day after day, they made it come true.

* * * * *

MILLS & BOON®

Coming next month

ENEMY'S GAME OF REVENGE
Maya Blake

Jittery excitement licked through Willow's veins as she watched Jario stride to the edge of the swim deck. Like her, he'd changed into swimming gear.

She tried not to openly stare at the chiselled body on display, especially those powerful thighs that flexed and gleamed bronze in the sunlight.

She sternly reminded herself why she was doing this.

He'd finally given her the smallest green light, to get the answers she wanted. Yes, she'd jumped through hoops to get here but so what?

'Ready?'

Her head jerked up to the speaking glance that said he'd seen her ogling him. Face flaming, she shifted her gaze to his muscled shoulder and nodded briskly. 'Bring it.'

A lip twitch compelled her eyes to his well-defined mouth, and her stomach clenched as lust unfurled low in her belly. God, what was wrong with her? How could she find him—yet another man bent on playing mind and *literal* games with her, and the one attempting to destroy what was left of her family—so compellingly attractive?

Continue reading

ENEMY'S GAME OF REVENGE
Maya Blake

Available next month
millsandboon.co.uk

COMING SOON!

We really hope you enjoyed reading this book.
If you're looking for more romance
be sure to head to the shops when
new books are available on

Thursday 16th January

To see which titles are coming soon, please visit
millsandboon.co.uk/nextmonth

MILLS & BOON

LET'S TALK

Romance

For exclusive extracts, competitions
and special offers, find us online:

f MillsandBoon

X @MillsandBoon

O @MillsandBoonUK

d @MillsandBoonUK

Get in touch on 01413 063 232

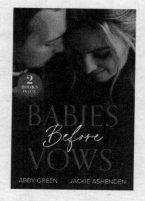
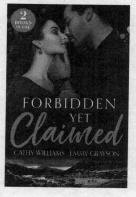

afterglow BOOKS

Afterglow Books is a trend-led, trope-filled list of books with diverse, authentic and relatable characters, a wide array of voices and representations, plus real world trials and tribulations. Featuring all the tropes you could possibly want (think small-town settings, fake relationships, grumpy vs sunshine, enemies to lovers) and all with a generous dose of spice in every story.

♪ @millsandboonuk

⊙ @millsandboonuk

afterglowbooks.co.uk

#AfterglowBooks

For all the latest book news, exclusive content and giveaways scan the QR code below to sign up to the Afterglow newsletter:

SCAN ME

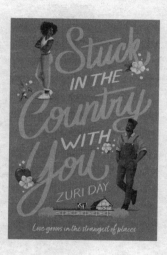
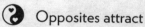
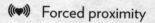
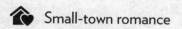

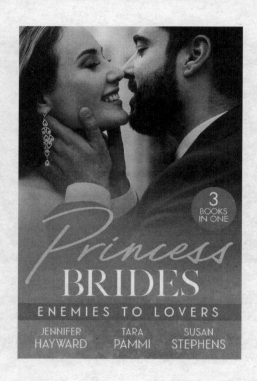